THE

WOMAN
LEFT
BEHIND

A MISTED PINES NOVEL

NEW YORK TIMES BESTSELLING AUTHOR

KRISTEN
ASHLEY

THE WOMAN LEFT BEHIND

A Misted Pines Novel

Book 4

KRISTEN ASHLEY

ROCK CHICK

PRESS

ABOUT THE AUTHOR

Tennessee native Rick Rothermel grew up in Huntsville, Alabama and lived in Southern California after a decade split between Alaska and Oregon. He was a columnist and freelance contributor for automotive magazines for twenty years and worked in the TV and movie production industry, specializing in automotive subjects. Classic TV and literature of the detective genre are hobbies that led to the creation of the C STREET MYSTERY series.

For Susan
My wee Starla's second momma

I'm so lucky you came into my life.
Thank you for taking care of her when we had her.
And thank you for being all that is you.

Prologue

GUT

Harry

S *hitty police work was one of the ugliest stains on society.*
   This was the thought Sheriff Harry Moran had as he sat in his ergonomic chair behind his desk at the sheriff's department.

He was staring at the two files in front of him trying to ignore the email that was up on the monitor of his computer.

Those files were two of fifteen stacked on his desk.

Each of those files had one thing in common: the shoddy, lazy or corrupt investigation overseen by Fret County's last sheriff, Leland Dern.

Dern was the man who came before Harry.

Which meant Harry was the man who had to clean up Dern's mess.

Due to recent circumstances—the latest being a double murder that wasn't properly investigated and an innocent man served prison time—a full and exhaustive, time-consuming and resource-heavy audit of every investigation under Dern's tenure had been done.

There were shambolic cases they'd had no choice but to file away. The police work hadn't been up to Harry's expectations of his department, but there was nothing that pointed to an injustice being done.

Now, he and his team had to go back over those fifteen cases and hope what Harry expected—Dern playing favorites, taking bribes, looking the other way or preferring to go hunting rather than working—wouldn't land them in lawsuits.

He was starting with these two.

He glanced at his monitor and felt his neck muscles tighten, which meant he again looked to the files and refocused.

They were the two cases that intrigued Harry the most, because the woman who had connections with both lived a block away from his department, only a five-minute walk from where he sat right there at his desk.

Lillian Rainier.

He'd lived in the town of Misted Pines his entire life, and because of his job, he knew or knew of a great many people in all of Fret County, and he'd never heard of her.

But Dern suspected, and investigated, her parents of a robbery sixteen years ago.

The investigation stalled, because Sonny and Avery Rainier had disappeared. And then, the case had simply died. Nothing else had been done. Not an interview, not a single follow-up of a lead.

A year later, Lillian married Willie Zowkower, a man Harry *did* know well.

Willie was a low-level gentleman dealer and a high-level charming asshole who currently had three outstanding arrest warrants in Fret County.

Recently, Willie had also disappeared.

And Lillian hadn't reported her parents, or her husband, missing.

Harry's gut was telling him something was up with Lillian Rainier.

And what was on Harry's computer monitor was telling him whatever that was, it was something bad.

So, no. His gut wasn't telling him anything. It was practically screaming at him to get off his ass, walk to her house and have a word.

Since Harry wasn't lazy, and he thought of law enforcement not as a job but as a calling, he got off his ass in order to walk to her house and have a word.

IT WOULD BE a good bet Harry had passed Lillian Rainier's house thousands of times in his life, and he never noticed it.

Standing outside it now, he wondered why.

A small cracker box painted a pale yellow with white trim, sporting a green roof and a shocking-red door, there were profuse plantings of bronze, butterscotch and yellow button mums in appealing but mismatched terracotta pots dotted up the front steps and all over porch. An attractive fall wreath of leaves, berries and pinecones was on the door. A white picket fence rounded the property, and he could see the numerous rose bushes that likely ornamented that fence in the summer had been cut back in preparation for winter.

There were two Adirondack chairs on the porch. They were painted white and had yellow, brown and green plaid lumbar pillows upstanding against the back of the seats, a wooden table with a lantern resting on top between them.

No kitschy SWEATER WEATHER! Or HAPPY FALL Y'ALL or FALL IN LOVE! signs marred the neat, well-kept property.

As he opened the gate on the fence and stepped foot on her front walk, that feeling in Harry's gut intensified.

Something was up.

Something was about to happen.

Something big.

He walked up the steps to that bright-red door.

He knocked.

He stood in his uniform and looked through the box of six square-paned windows at the top of the door, when he sensed movement inside.

And then there she was.

She opened the door.

The instant she did, the moment his eyes caught hers, Harry's chest caved in, and his stomach curled up.

Yeah.

Something was about to happen.

Something big.

And he wasn't ready for it.

ONE

Fresh-Cut Flowers

Lillian

I stared up and into the chocolate brown eyes of Sheriff Harry Moran, my heart in my throat, even though, when he'd made the announcement at the town council meeting that they were auditing Leland Dern's files, I knew this day would come.

I had answers to his questions.

I doubted he had any answers to mine.

But what was rendering me speechless, to the point I could feel gooseflesh raising on my arms, was that, from afar, he was an intensely handsome man.

Up close, he was taller than I expected, his shoulders were broader, his jaw was sharper, his cheekbones higher, his dark brown hair more lustrous, and after whatever was going to happen with him being on my doorstep happened, I might construct a shrine so I could worship his thick, long, curling eyelashes.

"Lillian Rainier?" he asked.

I had to clear my throat because…because…

He was just that beautiful.

But now I had his voice, which was deep and imposing. An authoritative cop voice. A man's-man voice.

Further, it was saying my name, deep, imposing and authoritative. And the sound of it wrapped around something that was only mine made me have a highly inappropriate response.

"Yes," I forced myself to answer.

"I have a few questions…"

He hesitated, but I could fill in the blanks.

He filled them in for me.

"About your parents. And about Willie Zowkower."

Willie?

That was a surprise, even when it wasn't.

"What's Willie done now?" I asked.

"Can I come in?"

Sheriff Harry Moran…in my house?

Every available woman (and some unavailable ones) from the age of eighteen (probably younger) to eighty (probably older) wanted Harry Moran in their house.

"Ms. Rainier?"

I jolted at his prompt, then I felt my cheeks heat because I was pretty sure I'd been staring at his mouth (I forgot to mention he had great lips, deliciously ridged, the bottom one full, the top one perfectly formed).

I shuffled out of the way, keeping a hold on the door and sweeping my arm out in front of me as an added invitation.

He came in.

I tried not to mentally inventory my living room in an effort to decipher how a man I did not know would react to it.

This was hard, because it was perfect. I'd worked my butt off to make it so.

I just wondered what Sheriff Moran would think of it at the same time I wondered why I cared so much (and I did, I cared *a lot*).

I didn't have a ton of space to work with, but in my humble opinion, I'd done a great job.

I closed the door behind Sheriff Moran and watched with unfathomable anxiety as he scanned the room.

Cream sectional, not huge, but it fit great in the space and was ultra comfortable. Cream and brown checked curtains. White walls. Exposed wood beams on the ceiling. Wooden chests instead of tables so I had extra storage. An inspired (again, my humble opinion) array of toss pillows. Heavy-bottomed ceramic lamps sprinkling surfaces.

This, along with the rest of the house, was accomplished through hours of trolling Target and World Market with splurges at places like West Elm and CB2. Not to mention, even more hours of painting, sanding, laying tile and all the rest.

I considered my house—and my garden—my finest achievements.

And as I stood there, stressed out waiting for a reaction, like Handsome Harry Moran would turn and give me a thumbs up for my endeavors, I realized he was having a reaction.

His entire long, muscled frame had grown tight.

"Sheriff?" I called.

He jerked to face me, and full disclosure, over the years, I (and every available woman in Fret County, be they eighteen or eighty) had paid a lot of attention to our local official. We'd grieved for him when he'd lost his wife way too soon. We'd championed him when he'd gone head-to-head with Leland Dern. And we'd commiserated with him when all hell broke loose in Misted Pines (more than once), and all of that—serial killers (times two!) and deranged, homicidal fans—had fallen into his lap.

And in that copious attention, I'd never seen him move awkwardly. He was a man who had command of his body, knew what it could do, and put it to use regularly.

Something about that movement was both alarming and endearing.

"You have a nice place," he said.

If feelings could bloom a flower, at his comment, my space would be covered with roses.

I smiled at him. "Thanks."

His eyes dropped to my smile.

My stomach dropped to my feet.

He lifted his gaze swiftly, and I pulled myself together.

"Would you like to sit down?" I asked. "And can I get you something to drink? I have coffee. Also tea. Some Crystal Light, the cherry pomegranate one. Fresca. I think I have a few La Croix, but I don't know the flavors. Then I have boba. Green apple. It's yummy."

Oh, my lord.

Did I just run down every non-alcoholic beverage in my house and call boba yummy?

His (yes, delightfully thick and arched) dark brows stitched together. "Boba?"

"It's tea. Bubble tea. From Taiwan. I mean, I don't think the kind I have is from Taiwan, per se. But it originated in Taiwan. I think. It has tapioca pearls in it. That's the bubble part. It sounds weird, but trust me, it's super good."

Dang it.

I was blathering again.

At least I didn't repeat the word yummy.

"Tapioca in tea?"

He looked revolted, and since that was definitely endearing, it made me smile, which made his gaze fall to my lips again. This time my stomach warmed and other places south clenched, but he quickly jerked his attention back up to my eyes.

"I know, it sounds strange." I shrugged. "There's a lot in this world that's strange to us, until we give it a go. Like anything else, once we try it, sometimes it's awesome, sometimes, not so much. Trust me, boba is awesome."

"I'll have coffee."

With that, he looked beyond me to my kitchen.

I'd had a wall taken down, but if I wanted my house to remain standing, there were some supports I had to work around even if the great room I was after would never be all that great because of the strictures of space.

However, I was noticing another reaction from Sheriff Moran. As he stared at my kitchen, he seemed to have frozen again, though his expression had changed.

I didn't know him, I couldn't be sure, but I could swear it looked like…

Longing.

Startled, I turned to take in my kitchen.

For the full front room, I'd gone heavy with the cottage-y, cozy farmhouse vibe.

The kitchen had wood cabinets. A Belfast sink. The beams on the ceiling continued from the living room. I'd had another window cut in on the side of the house so there was lots of light. The back edges of the counters were lined with pots growing fresh herbs. Crocks and glass jars and canisters abounded (we could just say I wasn't a minimalist—and fresh herbs made whatever you cooked taste a whole lot better).

And there was a beautiful French pottery pitcher resting dead center on the farm table that sat in the middle of the kitchen space. The pitcher was filled with the fresh-cut autumn flowers I'd picked up on my way back from getting my morning coffee at Aromacobana. Dahlias and goldenrod and hare's tail with some fountain grass (Jenna at Mistery Flowers and Gifts was an artiste, said me).

I swung back to the sheriff, who still seemed in the thralls of that odd stupor.

"Are you okay?"

At my question, he visibly pulled himself out of whatever trance he was in and cleared his throat. That was a very masculine sound too.

Man, I had it bad for Sheriff Moran. I knew this in a way, since it didn't escape me the many times I saw him in passing, I had a crush on him (and it didn't escape me because that crush was *huge*). But having him right there in my house was showing me just how bad I had it.

"Fine," he answered.

I bustled to the coffee maker.

"How do you take it?" I asked, opening the top of the Nespresso to drop a pod into it.

"Isn't that coffee expensive?" he asked in return.

I glanced over my shoulder at him on another shrug. "I allow myself a few splurges."

Like the Nespresso. And a walk to Aromacobana nearly every day. And fresh-cut flowers.

Seeing me in my environment, you wouldn't know I didn't have a lot. I'd learned to make it stretch. But everything around me, all that was me, had been the result of sixteen years of hard work, sacrifice, and penny-pinching.

I was good now. Comfortable, not rolling in it.

But it had been one very long row to hoe.

"Right," he grunted, giving me the impression he approved of me allowing myself a few splurges, just as long as they were a few, as in, within my means, at the same time he really hated the fact he approved of that.

Yes, I read all of that in a one-syllable grunt.

I just didn't know what to make of it.

"Just a little bit of cream," he belatedly answered my question.

I nodded and grabbed a mug, then went to the fridge to get some cream.

I'd dolloped "just a little bit of cream" in his mug, and when the Nespresso started chugging, I turned back to him.

He was standing by my farmhouse table, contemplating Jenna's flowers.

"I got those from Jenna's," I told him.

His head pitched up like he was surprised anyone was there and his regard returned to me.

"At Mistery Flowers and Gifts," I went on.

"They're pretty," he replied, again begrudgingly, like he didn't want to admit it.

"She has an incredible garden and greenhouse. Most of her flowers come from her own grows," I informed him.

"Mm," he hummed, provoking another improper physical reaction from me.

I was thinking that I shouldn't be talking about Jenna and her greenhouse, considering he'd agreed to a cup of coffee, which meant he expected to be here for a while on whatever business he had (and yeah, I was in deep denial about part of that business, then again, I had a ton of practice putting myself in that space).

I also suspected he was a busy guy and didn't have a lot of time to chat about flowers with a strange woman.

So I decided to help him get on with it.

"You mentioned Willie?"

After I voiced this question, I watched with some fascination as his entire being morphed from whatever he was experiencing in my house, back to something it was easy to read was far more comfortable to him.

Law enforcement officer.

"Your husband has several warrants out for his arrest."

I nearly rolled my eyes because this did not surprise me about Willie.

However, more pertinently, I had to share, "Willie isn't my husband."

He blinked.

"We married when I was twenty. When I was twenty and three-quarters, I kicked him out."

The sheriff's brows shot up. "But you didn't divorce him?"

"I tried. And then I tried. And I tried again. He dodged, and then he dodged and, of course, dodged again. Eventually, he disappeared altogether. I finally got one *in absentia* about a month ago after fifteen years of dealing with that mess."

"He disappeared, but you didn't report him missing?"

I heard the Nespresso stop, so I turned to it, stirred his cream, rested the spoon on the little spoon holder by the machine and walked the coffee to him.

It appeared he took great pains not to touch my fingers when he relieved me of the mug.

That kind of hurt, but I powered through it, mostly because it shouldn't. I was nothing to him but an open case I hoped I could help him close (for more than one reason), and the idiot who married a felonious moron.

"I said he disappeared," I reiterated after he took a sip of the coffee (and I was pleased to register his expression of enjoyment on that first sip, but I buried how pleased I felt because again, it wasn't mine to feel). "I didn't say he went missing. Willie isn't missing."

That got the sheriff's full attention. "You know where he is?"

I nodded. "He's in Vancouver. He's on his third wife, regardless of the fact he never legally divorced his first one. He was here last Christmas, and I think he's been back since. I can't know, because he avoids me like the plague, something I don't get since he's already moved on, illegally, but I suspect he keeps his visits home on the down-low because he has arrest warrants. Though I thought it was to avoid me. I also suspect he's living up in Canada for the same reasons."

"That makes sense," he muttered.

"Obviously, his family doesn't invite me to his welcome back parties, but I have friends who keep an eye out for him, due to all that divorce stuff. If I hear he's back, I can tell you, if you like."

"Yes, Ms. Rainier, I'd like that."

"You can call me Lillian," I offered.

His beautiful chocolate eyes locked with mine.

"Lillian," he murmured.

My skin tingled.

I powered through that as well.

"I don't hear much," I warned him. "The Zowkowers also weren't helpful in my bid for divorce."

"That family closes ranks."

"Tell me about it," I mumbled.

That's when those beautiful chocolate eyes hardened. "Have they been inappropriate with you?"

"If you mean evasive, unhelpful, doing everything they can to make sure Willie isn't found or papers go unserved, all to keep me tied to a man who has since married two other women, all for reasons I cannot begin to unravel, yes. They've definitely been inappropriate. If you mean something else, like being threatening or hostile, no."

"It's likely they think, if you knew where he was, you'd turn him in."

I smiled at him. "That's why you're the sheriff and I'm not. You unraveled it in a second. Though, I didn't know about the arrest warrants."

He took another sip of coffee.

Moving on.

I emotionally steadied myself.

Because I could mentally avoid it like a pro, considering I'd been doing that for over a decade and a half.

But the time was nigh.

And I knew this was going to be the hard part.

Strike that.

The *excruciating* part.

"You wanted to talk about my parents?"

He studied me over the rim of his mug (that was just plain sexy, God, did I have it *bad*) before he lowered it, took a beat, then in a voice that was still deep and gorgeous, but now I didn't like it, he suggested, "Maybe we should sit down."

I felt my heart squeeze as I stared at him, but I didn't move a muscle.

"Please," he said softly, his voice even more gorgeous, and more terrible, "come sit down, Lillian."

I didn't want to.

I really didn't want to.

But I led the way to my living room.

And we sat down.

TWO

Denial

Lillian

I sat on the short end of the sectional, and Sheriff Moran sat in the middle of the long end.

He took another sip of his coffee before he set it down on a coaster in the large tray I had on the cream square ottoman with navy pinstripes, which did double duty as a place to rest my feet and the coffee table where I set my drinks.

"That coffee is really good," he said quietly.

Oh God, he was totally setting me up for bad news.

I knew it, but for sixteen years, I refused to believe it.

"Probably makes it worth the money," he went on, still going softly.

"And they recycle the pods," I replied in a monotone, forgetting in this day and age any mention of climate change and doing things to alleviate it to a stranger put your chances at fifty-fifty that person would get up in arms about it. "Unlike the other pods, which are really bad for the environment."

"Gotta admit, I prefer our lakes and firs like they are, not consumed by fire or ravaged by drought," he said.

I liked his remark, a whole bunch, but I didn't like the look on his face a whole bunch more.

He started it. "I've had occasion, Lillian, to audit Sheriff Dern's files."

"I know. You mentioned it at a town council meeting."

His eyes sparked with surprise, and I had no idea what that was about. I also didn't have it in me right then to try to analyze it.

"One of those files was the Dietrich robbery," he told me.

I knew this was about the Dietrichs.

And that total dickhead, Dern.

As I had to direct all my attention to shoring up my defenses, I said nothing.

"Do you know the Dietrichs?" he asked.

"My dad worked for them," I said through stiff lips.

"Do you remember hearing about the robbery?"

Oh, I remembered all right.

I nodded.

"First, I want to say that the statute of limitations expired on that crime years ago, Lillian."

I didn't care.

Okay, sure, there was a possibility—a *slim* one—my dad committed that robbery.

Robbery was bad, I knew it. Totally bad.

That said, our illustrious sheriff was making things worse for my parents well before the robbery occurred.

I just never believed (*ever*) my parents had one thing to do with that robbery. What happened after, I knew they thought they didn't have any other choice.

But right then, that wasn't important.

"The information in that file gave me some concerns," he admitted.

"What concerns are those?" I asked.

"Your parents were suspects."

I closed my eyes.

Sheriff Moran kept talking. "I can't be certain, but it seems the jump to them as suspects was…*suspect*."

I opened my eyes, feeling something outside dread for the first time since he asked me to sit down. This being shock.

"Sorry?" I queried.

"Neither of your parents had a record. They were both well-liked in the community. I wasn't a police officer then, but in looking at the file, I vaguely remember a good deal of anger in town that Dern was investigating them."

"My mom had an in-home daycare. She charged peanuts," I whispered. "She loved kids. She hated how much daycare cost. One of the reasons they only had me was because they couldn't afford more kids. So she took in a few kids for folks who had to work, but could in no way afford anyone kind and loving and responsible to look after their children. And Dad could do anything. Plumbing, electrical work, he was great with computers, had a green thumb. I think he was handyman to half of Misted Pines."

"Right," Sheriff Moran said softly.

"He didn't charge an arm and a leg either," I went on. "They weren't…" I tried to find a way to describe all that was them and came up with, "Like that. They had each other. Me. This house. This amazing place where we live. They were both outdoorsy, active people. They didn't need any more."

"Okay," he murmured.

"Sheriff Dern, he…he was close to the Dietrichs," I said like I was admitting something, when it was not me who had something unscrupulous to admit.

"I'm aware," he replied.

"And he had a…well, a…*thing* for my mom. Dad was…is a pretty laidback guy. But that upset him."

"Is?" He jumped on that. "Do you know where your parents are?"

I shook my head trying really hard to keep the emotions blazing under the surface from erupting. "That Dietrich thing came up. Dern was being,"—I shook my head again—"it was a little scary." Make that a lot scary. "And they, um…took off."

"Have you heard from them since?"

I very much did not want my eyes to fill with tears.

But my eyes filled with tears.

"No," I said so quietly, even I could barely hear it.

Something warm and kind hit his gaze, even as he asked, "So they left sixteen years ago, and you haven't heard from them since?"

Left unsaid, *And you didn't tell anyone about it? Like law enforcement?*

I straightened my shoulders, took a deep breath, and pulled myself together.

"Okay, I think I need to explain something," I announced.

Sheriff Moran reached for his coffee cup, sat back in my sofa and encouraged, "Please do," before he took another sip.

"Well..."

How did I even begin?

"First they were..." I couldn't stop the small, sad smile that hit my mouth.

I was also descending into memories, the happy kind, so I didn't notice Harry Moran's attention dropping to it or the way his long frame stiffened when it did.

"They were really in love," I said softly. "Like, I've never seen anyone that in love." I looked at him, but I didn't really see him as I shared, "They'd move the furniture in the living room just so they could dance. And they'd *dance*. It might be ballroom. Or disco. Or slow dancing. They'd go for it, whatever mood they were in. They'd sit out on the porch, just talking, but they'd be holding hands. I was, um...a little kid, then a teenager, and erm...we can just say the walls are thin in this house, and I couldn't help but hear...*certain things*...and hear them...*a lot.*"

"Right," he said hurriedly to get me past that.

"At the time, that being the time the Dietrich thing was happening, I just thought they'd gotten scared, and they'd run."

"Scared?"

"Of Dern. Of being investigated for the robbery."

"So they took off, leaving you behind?"

"I was nineteen, Sheriff Moran—"

He interrupted me. "Harry."

"Okay," I said, feeling bashful (for goodness sake!). "Harry."

Something flickered in his eyes when I spoke his name, but he just nodded to prompt me to go on.

"I was working at a gas station to save money to get my own apartment. Dad didn't like that. Not the apartment part, working at the gas station. He didn't think it was safe. I usually did nights, because it paid more, and he'd do nights too, driving by to check things out, coming in to hang with me. Eventually, he understood my need to do it. Mom really understood it. She'd sing The Chicks' 'Wide Open Spaces' and say to Dad, 'We know what that's all about, don't we, Sonny-mine?'"

I took in another breath at that treasured memory, because Lord, did I love to hear my mother sing…and call my dad "Sonny-mine."

I let my breath out before I finished, "I was also taking online college courses to get my English degree. I wasn't sure if I wanted to be a teacher or a librarian."

Neither of those happened, because suddenly, I needed to figure out how to keep a house, pay utility bills and feed myself on a gas station attendant's salary.

"So, in other words, they didn't take you because they didn't want to interrupt your life," Harry boiled it down for me.

"Yes, I think so." I hoped so. "They planned. They took care of me. Like, they deeded this house to me." I drifted a hand in front of me. "They put my name on the car. They gave me power of attorney to get to their bank accounts. There wasn't much in them, but it helped when they…" I hated to say it, but I said it, "disappeared."

"And they didn't come back."

"They didn't come back," I confirmed.

"And you never heard from them?"

Oh God. Oh God. Oh God.

I was beginning to feel sick.

"No, I never heard from them," I told him.

"And you didn't report them missing?"

Oh God. Oh God. *Oh God.*

"Until recently," I began to remind him, "you weren't the sheriff, Sheriff Moran."

Understanding dawned on his face.

"They were being framed," I stated. "I know it." I didn't, but I was pretty danged sure of it. "Dern had a thing for Mom. Mom only had eyes for Dad. I don't know if he ever tried anything with her, but I sense he did, because she was really afraid of him. Dad was super ticked about it, but he was a handyman, not the county sheriff. And Dern was the kind of man you didn't pick a fight with, even if you were in the right. He was also the kind of man who got what he wanted, even if he had to deal dirty to get it."

"I know, Lillian," Harry said soothingly.

"I think,"—I lifted my chin—"I know that they're good no matter where they are because they're together. They might not know Dern isn't sheriff anymore. They might not know it's safe to come back."

This was all lame, and I knew Harry knew it by the look he was trying to hide on his face.

"And I've never had the money to hire a private investigator to find them," I declared.

That was an outright lie.

I didn't want to know what such a person would find.

My parents…they'd call.

They'd write.

I was in denial.

Epic denial.

Today, I had a feeling, I wasn't going to be able to inhabit that space any longer.

"We did it before," I said this defiantly, determined to hold on to hope until the bitter end. "We lived in LA before we moved here. We loved it there. Mom and Dad, they're both from the Midwest. They met when Mom accidentally rear-ended Dad. They got out of their cars, took one look at each other, and they were married a week later. They call it instalove these days. And it was. Mom would dig that term. She'd get a T-shirt with it and Dad's face on it, she'd loved it so much. After they got married, they moved to LA , had me, and it was all Disneyland and Knott's Berry Farm and Mom always getting excited because we could go see a movie in the Chinese Theater like it was any ole movie theater."

"That's sweet, Lillian, but I'm not sure what you meant when you said, 'we did it before,'" Harry noted.

"Upped stakes and left," I explained. "One day, in LA, we just upped stakes and left. Came up here. Dad almost immediately sold our car. I think they bought this house in cash. I was ten. They said it was time to slow down, find the quiet life. They didn't want to raise their daughter in the mean city."

"But you suspect different?"

I shook my head, but said, "I don't know. It was just so sudden. At first, I was mad about leaving California and my friends. But then we were here and it's so beautiful here, and they were so happy. It was impossible not to be happy with them."

Harry said nothing to that.

"What I'm trying to get at is, this isn't out of the norm for them. To decide to go and then just go."

Again...*lame!*

"And leave you behind," Harry said quietly.

I pressed my lips together before asserting, "If they have each other, they're fine."

Harry again was silent.

"Why are you asking about this now?" I demanded. "Especially if the statute of limitations has run out."

"The Dietrichs reported quite a bit of their property was stolen in that robbery. Guns, valuables, even vehicles," he told me.

It was my turn to be silent.

Harry shifted in his seat, and I did not at all like how uncomfortable he looked doing it.

He finally settled and stated, "One of the guns reported missing was recently found in Idaho."

"Okay..." I said, not getting it.

"Lillian..."

He didn't finish that.

A chill glided over my skin.

"What?" I whispered.

"I need to ask you for a DNA sample."

Ice flooded my veins.

"Why?" I pushed out.

"I'm so sorry, Lillian," he said gently. So, so gently, my stomach roiled. "The gun was found buried with two bodies."

I shot up and raced to the bathroom.

I landed on my knees in front of the toilet.

And I got sick.

THREE

I Can't Stop

Lillian

It was on heave two when my hair was pulled back to be held at my nape and a warm hand landed between my shoulders blades and started stroking my spine.

Great.

I was vomiting in front of Handsome Harry Moran.

"Get it out, honey," he murmured.

Great times two. I was now crying.

Puking and crying.

Two bodies.

I bucked and sobbed and heaved again, the trifecta of sad, mortifying and gross.

Eventually, there was nothing more coming out.

When I rested my forehead against the seat, Harry flushed the toilet and urged, "Stay there."

I wasn't going anywhere. Ever. I was never leaving that bathroom. Not ever.

Regrettably, he returned and ordered gently, "Sit back, Lillian."

I sat back and avoided his eyes.

I was embarrassed, yeah.

Mostly, I was destroyed.

He wiped my mouth with a wet cloth then handed me a La Croix.

The tab was already popped.

I took some in my mouth, swished it around, leaned in and spat it out in the toilet.

Harry flushed it again.

I sat back and took another drink then dashed at the wet that was leaking onto my cheeks.

God, I hated vomiting.

I could avoid Harry no longer, considering he sat on his ass in my tiny bathroom with me.

Yes.

He sat on his ass right there with me in my tiny bathroom.

When I finally caught his gaze, he said hopelessly, "Don't lose hope, Lillian. Those bodies have yet to be identified."

"I've been living in denial," I mumbled pitifully.

"Maybe. Maybe not."

"I'd sleep on an air mattress for the last sixteen years if I thought a PI could find my parents. I didn't…I couldn't…I—"

Harry saved me by cutting in. "Understandable."

"They'd call."

"All right."

"Or write."

"Okay, honey," he whispered.

My face scrunched, then I was sobbing again, but this time, doing it in Handsome Harry Moran's arms.

God, he was warm. Hard and strong and warm. I could burrow into him forever.

And that was just what I did.

Burrowed in.

I wanted to pull away. He had better things to do with his time than comforting a woman on the floor in her bathroom. Perps to bring to justice. Drugs to confiscate. Jaywalkers to warn. Stuff like that.

But I couldn't stop crying.

I was learning sixteen years of knowing—*knowing*—and not letting yourself believe pent up a lot of tears.

"We-we should contact those re-records people. Idiot woman l-lives in denial for s-s-sixteen years. I bet I beat them all by a mile," I said.

Harry's strong arms gave me a gentle squeeze. "Stop it, Lillian."

I shoved my forehead hard into his neck and murmured, "I always knew."

He rubbed my back and whispered, "Yeah."

We sat there, him holding me, me letting him hold me, and it seemed like we did it for a long time.

Eventually, it hit me that jaywalking was dangerous, and someone had to levy a warning on those who did it, so I pulled out of his arms, swiped at my face again and lied, "I'm okay."

Harry got to his feet in a smooth, agile move that I really wanted to appreciate, but he was pulling me up and I had to concentrate on not falling down again, not to mention, I didn't appreciate much right then.

"Is there someone you could call?" he asked when we were both standing in my tiny bathroom.

I nodded.

"Can I call them for you before I go?"

I shook my head. "I can do it. Do you want the, um…DNA sample now?"

"Maybe tomorrow. Can you come by the department?" he requested.

Another nod from me.

He reached into his pocket, pulled out a little holder that looked like it was made of baseball glove leather. He flipped it open and slid out a business card. He handed it to me and I took it.

"Call me and let me know when you can make it in. I'll take the sample personally."

That was nice and all, but I'd hurled in front of him. I'd cried into his uniform (I could see the mascara smears on his shoulder, *yikes!*). I didn't need to open my mouth and let him rub a Q-tip in it.

"You don't have to do that."

"We're in this together now, Lillian."

Tears filled my eyes.

I had friends.

I had my grandparents, all getting up there in years, but still living and doing it in Indiana.

But after my parents disappeared, I'd felt very alone.

Enter Willie and me making the stupidest decision of my life.

Now, Handsome Harry Moran was telling me we were in this together.

I couldn't hack it.

"Don't be nice to me," I warned.

Surprise slashed through his face. "Pardon?"

"You're going to make me cry again." I flipped out a hand. "Being a nice guy and all."

"I'm afraid I can't stop being that," he said.

"Fantastic," I mumbled, and he smiled.

There was no bright that could cut the dark that had very recently consumed my life. Or, I should say, very recently *re-*consumed it.

Except that smile.

He took me out of my amazement of that fact, and captivation with his smile, when he pushed, "You're going to get someone over here?"

I nodded.

He kept pushing. "And you're going to call me and tell me when you can come to the station?"

I nodded again.

"You'll get through this, Lillian."

I wanted to believe that.

But I wasn't so sure.

His voice dipped, and honest to God, the way it sounded, it felt like I was back in his arms. "I'll get you through it, honey."

"You're being nice," I warned.

He smiled again, reached out and touched the back of my hand like he was sending out a search party. He found what he was looking for, seeing as his fingers wrapped around mine and he pulled me out of the bathroom.

Still holding my hand, he led us to the great room and asked, "Where's your phone?"

I looked to the kitchen counter.

He drew me there.

When he stopped us by my phone, I looked up at him. "Are you going to wait for me to call Kay?"

Or Jenna, Janie or Molly.

"No, I just wanted you in your pretty kitchen with your pretty flowers before I leave you."

Oh my God!

This totally *sucked*!

Years, I'd been watching this man, thinking he was the bee's knees.

I did not need to find out my parents were (very likely) irretrievably gone after denying for nearly two decades my parents were gone and then find out how much of the bee's knees this guy was.

He read my annoyed expression, I knew, when his lips twitched and he muttered, "Sorry, I'm being nice again."

"It's irritating," I snapped, taking odd comfort in being peevish rather than being a slobbering, wailing mess.

He bit his lip, but that didn't stop his smirk.

I narrowed my eyes at it.

"I'll see you tomorrow," he stated.

Whatever.

"Hang in there, Lillian," he bid.

I switched targets and narrowed my eyes at his eyes.

"Right," he muttered, openly fighting a smile.

I watched him walk to the front door and I braced when he stopped at it and turned to me.

"I'm so sorry, honey," he said.

He. Was. Killing. Me.

"Go away," I returned.

"See you tomorrow," he repeated.

"Whatever," I replied, this time verbally.

He shot me another smile.

And then Handsome Harry Moran was gone.

FOUR

Sell His Soul

Harry

H arry's thoughts were all over the place on his drive out to metaphorically bang his head against the wall at the Zowkower compound.

He should be going back to the station. Getting his shit tight. Re-reading that email from Coeur D'Alene. Re-assessing what little they knew about the bones they'd found in that grave on the side of that mountain.

But he didn't because after meeting Lillian, it was now burned on his brain.

Man. Woman. Both in their mid to late forties.

Both died of gunshot wounds, and they knew that because they'd found the bullets in that hole with them, surmising they had once been in their bodies, along with bullets that had made the holes in the skulls.

He tried to rein it in, the varied directions his mind was leading him, but he could still feel Lillian's grief wetting his shirt, and Harry knew all about grief.

So he was struggling.

He'd been in this business a long time. You get to know people, how they think, how they work, the fucked-up shit they get up to, the stupid mistakes they make, the depths of denial they could dig.

It didn't take fifteen years in law enforcement to follow the trail of Dern dicking with Lillian's parents, a clear frame-up happening with the Dietrichs (only for any investigation into that being mysteriously dropped when the Rainiers couldn't be found), the Rainiers leaving town, and Lillian finding Willie, a good-looking bad guy with a way with the ladies, though he was the least of the trouble that was the mess of the Zowkowers.

But Harry had fifteen years of law enforcement and all of that tracked.

Something else tracked.

Something he didn't want to think about, but something he couldn't stop thinking about.

Twenty-five years he'd lived in that town with Lillian Rainier, and he'd never noticed her.

He was five years older than her, so he wouldn't have run into her at school.

She said she'd come to a town council meeting, which likely meant she regularly attended, as did many residents of Misted Pines, and he couldn't for the life of him place her there.

How he didn't notice a beautiful woman with long, thick auburn hair, sparkling green eyes and a fantastic ass, boiled down to two things.

First, from the moment he met her, he saw no woman other than the one he'd made his wife.

Second, a year into their marriage, his wife died, and when she did, he saw nothing and did nothing but take care of his dogs and do his job.

Christ, he knew it at the time, which was the reason he got so damned pissed about it, but now it was crystal clear that his buddy, Doc, who'd gotten up in his face a year ago about this, was right.

For all intents and purposes, Harry had died when Winnie did.

When Lillian opened her door, it felt like someone hit him with a defibrillator.

It got worse after walking into her house, seeing her comfortable living room that shouted *Home!* And her warm, busy kitchen that stated clearly someone cooked there and liked doing it.

Fuck, it even smelled like cinnamon, rosemary and yeast. Like she'd just made cookies, a roast *and* bread.

That kitchen was a kitchen any person on the planet would want to come home to.

That kitchen was the kitchen, especially with the woman it belonged to, any cop would sell his soul to call his.

Both the kitchen.

And the woman.

This took him to the next thing that was on his mind.

That being, Willie Zowkower homed in on a young woman who found herself suddenly alone, and very vulnerable. Harry had no doubt he charmed her, took her hand in marriage, and then got his rocks off by fucking with her for fifteen years.

And that pissed Harry off.

It pissed him off so much, it was the years of suffering his loss that eroded the extremes of his emotion, the years of working under Dern that honed his level of patience into a weapon, that made him not blind with rage about it.

Especially coupling Willie targeting Lillian with the fact that Dern had targeted Avery Rainier.

One thing Harry could not abide was a cop abusing his position.

He'd lived under that too, and he'd hated every fucking second of it.

But whatever happened that made Sonny and Avery Rainier run had followed them to Idaho, and Dern was a son of a bitch, but Harry didn't peg him as a murderer.

He had to get a lock on it.

He had no doubt Rita Zowkower, the matriarch of that clan—and considering the numerous run-ins they'd all had with her, she was known somewhat affectionately by LEOs as Ma Zow—was going to be the one who would open the door.

She was sweet as sugar to your face, lethal as a snake if you threatened one of her boys.

Going up against her, Harry had to have his shit together.

He had no idea if hyena mommas acted like lionesses, but if they did, Rita would be their queen.

She had five boys, Willie being the middle. And all those boys cut their teeth on everything from drag racing to joy riding to mailbox bashing to drunk driving, only to graduate to bar brawls and domestic disturbances, dealing, helping themselves to things that weren't theirs, and one of them (the only one incarcerated, so far) experimenting with cooking meth.

Although he had occasion to drive up the lane to the Zowkower place dozens of times in his career, as he did it this time, he saw something different.

Lillian didn't have a lot to work with. Harry had been in many houses like hers, and he knew what he saw was half of what she had. The rest were two bedrooms at the back.

But she'd made every inch of it an alluring safe haven.

Even her little bathroom, with its mix of exposed barn wood and white-painted shiplap on the walls, the claw-footed tub resting on ornate chrome feet under the back window, the droopy, fernlike trees growing out of pots in wicker baskets flanking the tub, the square bowl of a sink resting on top of a long vanity that was designed to make the most of the space, was welcoming and invited you to hang for a while.

Rita Zowkower had done the same with the eight-acre compound that was her domain.

If you didn't know who lived there, you wouldn't know this was the den of iniquity it was.

The house was essentially a massive log cabin broken up by a foundation of stone. Hearty landscaping was perfectly clipped and augmented by beds and borders of bright annual flowers.

He could see the fenced garden off to the side with late-growing pumpkins, squash and vegetables still verdant green. The fortified-against-predators chicken coop with fancy chickens right then pecking and tottering outside it. The pristine pole barn on the other side that Harry knew housed snowmobiles and ATVs.

Harry owned four acres south of town. He kept it shipshape, but it hadn't been a home since Winnie died. And he had to admit, Winnie was no homemaker.

They'd had a deal. He did the cooking, because he liked it, she did the cleaning, because she enjoyed seeing the results of her efforts. He took care of the land; she took care of the animals.

But there would never be any pots of button mums on his porch, or fresh flowers on his kitchen table, not because Winnie wasn't energy and adventure and light and love, but because that simply wasn't her thing.

She'd loved daisies, so they'd had another thing: Harry bringing her daisies once a week. It could be a Monday. It could be Saturday morning when he'd run out and grab some for her. But Winnie knew, once a week, she'd get daisies from her man.

So it was Harry that put the cut flowers in their home.

He wondered now, with the Zowkower place spread before him, what Lillian could create with his land.

And that was entirely fucked up.

She'd just learned there was a good likelihood she'd lost her parents for good.

And he was an emotional disaster.

As he drove up and parked next to a shiny-clean, silver Ford F-350, he spied the woman of the manor walking out the front door.

He knew she'd wear no makeup, but she had skin of a woman ten years younger. At her age, her hair couldn't be that healthy blonde naturally, but it looked it, and the attractive ponytail it was pulled back into appeared fashioned by a professional's hand.

Over a tank, she was wearing an old, oversized flannel shirt that had probably been her husband's, or one of her boys'. This topped jeans that had dirt on them, but they weren't dirty. All of this covered the trim, fit, average-tall body of a woman in her early sixties, but if you didn't know that, you'd think she was no older than her early forties.

He got out of his cruiser and started toward the walk, raising a friendly hand.

Rita crossed her arms and waited for him at the top of the steps but belied that closed posture by painting a welcoming smile on her face.

Or, maybe it actually was welcoming.

With Rita, you never knew.

"Well, sheriff, you sure know how to brighten a girl's day," she called when he got closer.

Rita Zowkower used everything at her disposal to keep her clan safe and free, including flattery and flirting.

He stopped at the foot of the front steps, wondering if he had rifles trained on him, though he didn't reckon he did. Her boys might be pissants, even her husband, but there wasn't a stupid bone in Rita's body. She'd never make that kind of mistake, no matter if Harry was there to haul one of her kin away. She'd figure out how to get him back without landing her clan in deeper water.

Or, like the son of hers they caught, she'd sacrifice him for the greater good of the whole but get him the best attorney money could buy so he wasn't away from the gang for long.

He already knew this visit was a wasted effort, but Harry was coming to terms with a lot of shit that day, apparently, including equating his mother's constant lament at how stubborn he was with just how long he held on to losing his wife.

He shook off that thought and noticed Rita had work gloves sticking out of her back pocket, and he wondered if he'd interrupted her gardening or burying a body.

Harry launched in with, "You probably know why I've come out this way."

"Told you before, don't mind sayin' it again, sheriff, my boy just upped and disappeared. Reported that to you months ago. Not sure he was even in this state when that assault occurred. Not sure where he is. Was hopin' you'd find him."

She did indeed file a missing person's report on Willie.

She did that the day after twenty witnesses reported they saw Willie beat the absolute shit out of a man at The Hole, a bar on the outskirts of town.

He now had more information, about bigamy, about Willie

leaving the country, he just had to be careful not to throw Lillian under the bus when he used it.

"This is what I've come out here about, Rita," Harry lied. "Don't want to get your hopes up, not certain how valid this information is, but got word Willie's up north."

Nothing showed on her face. Not surprise, not what he knew she was doing: running down the possible culprits who might have let this information slip.

"Up north?" she asked.

"Canada. Vancouver way."

Again she gave him nothing, except, "Not sure what my boy would be doin' up there. Got no family up that way."

"Well, facing an assault charge with a fair few witnesses who say it was him, on top of a drunk and disorderly and destruction of property, figure, with his record, he'd go about anywhere to escape the law."

There was a slight raise of her chin before, "Even an innocent man would flee, he fears his freedom taken away when he didn't do anything wrong."

Harry figured that was absolutely true, considering it appeared like Sonny and Avery Rainier did just that.

Harry lifted a boot and rested it on the step in front of him, but made no other move to get closer to her.

And then he did what he'd never done since it happened, something he was willing to use to get Willie Fucking Zowkower in one of his cells and on a path to justice for putting a man in the hospital and pulling shit with Lillian.

"Winnie and me," he started quietly, and Ma Zow came out when he saw her take a soft, indrawn breath and the skin around her eyes gentled, "we didn't have the time to start a family. But the way I loved her, I know the babies we would've made would be everything to me. Since I know I'd do the same for Winnie, I figure I'd do it for our kids, that being anything to keep them safe. Now it might go against the grain for you, thinking what's safest for your boy is for him to turn himself in and answer for what he's done."

When he saw the gentle seep out of her features, he changed tacks.

"Or follow the path of justice that man who spent three days in the hospital deserves and find himself exonerated and free to be with his family if he didn't do it. But things can get messy when we gotta call in other agencies, Rita, like me phoning up to Vancouver to get them to be on the lookout for your son. And if they find him, extradite him down here. Judges tend to get crotchety when someone strains the resources of an already thin law enforcement arm with an unnecessary and prolonged chase, paperwork, and all that shit. Things ease up a whole lot when someone comes forward to answer a few questions, or admit what they've done, apologize for it, and face up to the consequences of it."

It was a day of surprises, he noted, when it looked like she was considering this.

He gave it a beat.

She said nothing.

So he sighed and shared, "My next step is a call up to Vancouver. You think on what I've said. We've got our eyes peeled and we're gonna widen the net. One thing I reckon, we'll have Willie home soon."

Only then did she give him something.

Her mouth tightened as Harry took his foot off the step.

"You take care of yourself, Rita," he bid.

"You do the same, sheriff," she replied. And he had to hand it to her, there was warmth in her tone, like she meant those words.

Then again, maybe she did.

He jerked up his chin and headed to his cruiser.

Rita Zowkower remained on the porch even, Harry saw in his rearview mirror, as he drove down her lane, turned at the end, and only then did he lose sight of her.

FIVE

The Best in The Business

Harry

It was taxing even Harry's patience to sit at his desk and re-read the Dietrich robbery file, especially the notes of the interviews Dern conducted with Lillian.

Harry had read them before he met her, and they felt dirty to him then.

He read them now in a different light, and now they read as filth.

Dern had personally interviewed her at her home, which had to be daunting for Lillian, especially since he'd done it when her parents were at the station being interrogated, and she'd just been up all night doing a shift at work.

After her parents had run, Dern had then pulled her into the station, when that was entirely unnecessary.

It also was straight-up intimidating to a teenage witness who had no apparent connection to the crime outside her relationship with two suspects who had such a slender link to the offense, it couldn't even be described as a thread. Further, she'd never been in trouble with the law and was vulnerable, considering her parents were the surprise suspects in a crime and had disappeared.

And Dern had gone hard at her, clearly in an effort to break her in order to coerce her into saying something that would incriminate her parents.

He'd done this even though there were no witnesses placing Sonny or Avery Rainier at the scene, and Sonny's fingerprints being there were likely left after he did the many odd jobs that the Dietrichs themselves shared they'd hired him to do.

Although Sonny's prints were everywhere, they'd only found one of Avery's. And it was so obviously placed, it was laughable, and it demonstrated how untouchable Dern thought he was.

The Dietrichs had reported that Simon "Sonny" Rainier told them he was having money problems and had asked them for a loan. They'd further reported he'd not been happy when they'd turned him down. They'd shared his demeanor was aggressive and desperate.

They'd shared this when no one, even Lillian, who had access to their bank accounts, which had three thousand in checking, and seven thousand in savings and a money market at nearly ten, corroborated their story.

There had been no interviews conducted with informants that could tell them if Sonny or Avery dealt with local bookies, loan sharks or dealers to see if they had a debt that twenty grand couldn't cover. Nor was there any evidence in the file that the police had gone to any stores or suppliers Sonny or Avery might be in arrears with. No friends or clients came forward or reported under interview that Sonny or Avery had mentioned money issues, asked for a loan, or had gambling, drink or drug addictions. And pulling their credit card histories showed they paid them off in full, every month.

They obviously had a thing about debt, since they not only owned their home outright, they only had one car, and they owned that outright too.

Lillian had given her mother and father an alibi, a thorough one.

That evening, they were home and Lillian sensed nothing amiss.

Her mother had made hamburgers and homemade fries for dinner, and Lillian had helped. There were caramel chocolate brownies with ice cream for dessert, and Sonny made those.

They'd then watched TV, and Lillian had stayed up to study before she had to go to work. Her mother dropped her at work. Her protective father had called twice while she was at the gas station, and swung by to visit with her, sticking around for about forty-five minutes before he went home.

As usual, her mom was up and had breakfast ready for Lillian by the time Sonny went to get his daughter and bring her home.

Shortly after, both were picked up for questioning about the robbery.

The night of the robbery, the Dietrichs had been at a party, gone from six thirty, returning at twelve forty-five.

Lillian left for work at a quarter to eleven, and since Avery took her, the drop off caught on an outside camera at the gas station, it gave Sonny and Avery less than two hours to drive the twenty minutes to the Dietrichs, ransack their house, steal jewelry, crack open a safe and lift its contents, grab five rifles and four handguns, and drive away in a stolen Jeep and a Chevy Tahoe, at least one of them having to return to get their own vehicle, before the Dietrichs returned.

It wasn't an impossible crime, for, say, a career criminal.

A husband and wife finding themselves in money straits pulling it off, including cracking open a safe, was see-through it was so thin.

Sonny was caught on a surveillance camera inside the gas station, arriving at one twenty-seven, and he'd stayed, as Lillian had explained, until two-oh-eight.

Harry had viewed that surveillance video and saw a tall, handsome man with dark auburn hair who didn't seem to have a care in the world as he chatted with his girl, ate a pack of peanuts he bought at the station and chased them down with Fresca.

Watching that video made Harry's gut burn.

This was a man who worked hard, that work physical, and he loved his daughter so much, he was up at one in the morning and hanging with her at a gas station because he wanted to do what he could to keep her safe.

The man had to be out of his mind when he and his wife were forced to leave that daughter behind.

And Harry wouldn't even allow himself to contemplate what was going through their heads the moments before the bullets entered their brains.

The picture was forming, and Harry was seeing they didn't leave Lillian because they were all good just as long as they had each other.

They left her because they knew the danger would follow, and she was safer at home.

Preliminary interviews with Sonny and Avery done before they saw the writing on the wall and hauled ass, or got tweaked by what might turn out to be the severity of the situation if those bodies were actually them, and they again hauled ass, repeated the same things Lillian said...to the letter.

And no matter how Dern tried to wear her down, both of Lillian's interviews held up. There wasn't the slightest deviation in her story, or how it corroborated her parents'.

For some reason, Dern and/or the Dietrichs had targeted them.

What Harry needed to know was...why?

Did he think he could punish Avery not responding to his attentions by fucking with their lives?

Or was this something uglier, shadier, deeper?

Something that had to do with the Dietrichs, who were very clearly in on it, as they immediately pointed the finger at Sonny.

The statute of limitations may have long since expired on the robbery, but considering it wasn't investigated at the time, it had not expired on insurance fraud, and the Dietrichs had seen a big check after that robbery.

And murder had no statute.

Harry heard them coming before they arrived at the open door to his office, which had Harry reaching to his mouse and clicking to another window he'd opened earlier on his screen.

He quickly scanned his bank balance again, before he closed the screen.

And then Jason and Jesse Bohannan walked in.

He'd called them because a sixteen-year-old crime he couldn't move forward in any tangible way, one where there was no violence or loss of life, was not something he could, in good faith, spend his department's resources investigating.

At least, not until (or if) those bodies were identified and tied to a robbery in Misted Pines.

But he could spend his personal resources on Jace and Jesse investigating it.

What Harry knew was, whatever was going to happen, he was damn sure going to get a head start on it.

Seemed it turned out to be good he'd lived a shadow of his life, spending his money on his mortgage, gas for his truck, food that kept him healthy, dry cleaning for his uniforms, and a new pair of jeans and a few shirts every couple of years, because he had a good amount saved up.

Cade Bohannan's boys were just barely in their early thirties, but considering their father was their mentor, they were still the best in the business.

And they cost a whack.

They were twins, and Harry had learned a long time ago how to tell them apart.

Jesse was cocky as fuck and wore that like a badge of honor.

Jason was so confident, he didn't have to bother with any badge.

Other than that, they were identical.

"You called," Jesse drawled after he'd folded his long body in one of the chairs in front of Harry's desk, Jace doing the same in the chair beside him.

Harry flipped the Dietrich file closed and shoved it across his desk at them.

Jace leaned forward and took it.

"Robbery. Sixteen years ago," he began. "Clear evidence Dern was trying to frame a couple for the crime. He had a thing for the wife, she only had a thing for her husband. Could be, Dern didn't like that much and intended to show her who had the power."

Jace's lips got tight. Jesse's eyes got hard.

Like all of Fret County, the twins hadn't been shielded from Dern's corruption.

"They hightailed it and haven't been heard from since," Harry continued. "Until the cops in Coeur D'Alene ran the serial number on a gun they found in a grave alongside two sets of remains. That gun was reported stolen in that robbery."

"Fucking hell," Jason muttered.

"This have to do with Sonny and Avery?" Jesse asked, and Harry's back straightened.

"Did you know them?"

"Know their girl Lillian was the hot number in school," Jesse said. "She graduated before we got there, but her legend remained."

Harry could see that.

"And Dad dug Sonny," Jace shared. "Dad's a do-it-yourself kind of guy, but he'd call Sonny every once in a while, if he needed an extra man on a job he was doing around the house. It was a long time ago, you'd have to ask him, but think they'd share a drink on occasion."

"I do know Dad thought shit was off when they ghosted," Jesse added.

Harry scratched a conversation with Cade on his to-do list, but that already said a lot. Cade Bohannan was known as one of the best criminal profilers in history. If he had Sonny anywhere near his land, that meant Sonny Rainier was solid as a granite.

"Do you know Lillian?" Harry asked.

Jesse smirked.

Jason watched him closely.

Harry wasn't surprised at these reactions.

She was an attractive woman. He had a dick.

And these two shared one brain, but they both used far more of that organ than the vast majority of people. They were sharp, shrewd, and between their ex-cop, ex-FBI profiler father's tutelage and their natural God-given ability, they read practically any situation like it was typed in a book.

"*Know* her, know her, no," Jesse eventually answered. "Seen her around, absolutely."

"She got hooked up with Willie Z. Shocked the shit out of everyone. Then she took a half a breath and got shot of Willie Z, which no one found surprising," Jason put in.

He didn't need it, but that corroborated Lillian's story.

"If you're free, I need you in LA," Harry stated. "Lillian says they lived there before they moved up here. She said the move was sudden, they upped stakes and left and bought their house with cash in Misted Pines. Real estate was a damn sight cheaper back then, but not that cheap. I want to know why they took off from LA and how they had the resources to set up here in MP."

Jason looked surprised. "You think they did it?"

"As much as this guts me, for them, for Lillian, for anyone who cared about them, I think it's their remains that were found in that hole, and I want every fucking i dotted and every t crossed when we find the fucks who took a loving couple away from their beloved daughter, their lives ending with multiple bullets in their bodies, before that happened they knew their love affair was at its tragic end and their daughter was going to be alone in this world. I want them exonerated even before anyone thinks to throw shit at them. Which means, once you're done in LA, I want you in Idaho. Tell me when you're heading there. I'll let the locals know you're on my team."

"This deputized shit?" Jason asked.

"This is coming out of my pocket," Harry answered.

Jason's brows winged up. Jesse's shot down.

"Harry, we ain't cheap," Jesse said quietly. "We'll give you a discount, because you're a brother, but you're talking time, gas, maybe flights, maybe money to loosen tongues—"

Harry interrupted him. "At one thirty in the morning, Sonny would go to the gas station where Lillian worked just to keep her company and be sure she was safe."

Jesse shut his mouth, and this time, Jason's eyes got hard.

"If anyone has the barest fucking doubt that those two were

involved in the Dietrich mess, I want it washed away," Harry announced. "And I want answers for Lillian. She's waited sixteen years to find out what happened to her parents. That's long enough."

The twins exchanged a look, and Harry would give his left ball to know what that kind of thing meant between them, considering at the same time they looked back to Harry, and it seemed in the interim, silently, they'd agreed Jason was the one who would be tasked with asking the next question.

It came quiet, curious…and hopeful.

"You got something going on with her, man?"

"No," Harry answered.

"Dude," Jesse said. "Seen her around. She's smokin'."

"That didn't escape my attention," Harry told him.

"So…" Jace prompted.

"So, she's coming in tomorrow to give a DNA sample so we can see if those bodies are her parents. Been out of the game for a while, but still not sure that's when to make a play," Harry replied.

"But you want to make a play?" Jesse pushed.

Fuck him.

He had good friends. They cared. They worried.

And they could be pains in his ass.

"Let's just figure this shit out for her, yeah?" Harry requested.

This was met with several beats of silence before Jason raised the file.

"Can we take this, or do we gotta read it here and leave it here?"

"I want it here, but we'll make you copies," Harry replied.

He got two identical nods that came in sync.

Then they all got up and headed to the copy machine.

SIX

You're Welcome

Harry

Harry was about to drive by the parking spot, but since Polly, his assistant, was continuing to ignore his order to get rid of it, and the sign was still there, reserving it for him right at the front of the station, he swung into it.

He then scratched the takedown of that sign on top of his long list of shit to get done that morning.

He did this because he found it uncomfortable, having that privilege. And even though his office was situated at the front of the station, a short walk from the entry and reception bench, all his deputies and the staff parked in back.

Sure, this way he could go in and get to his office without having to traverse the back halls that included the locker rooms, an armory, equipment storage, the booking room, bathrooms, their interview room, interrogation rooms and dispatch.

However, parking in back was better than making such a public show of his position by sliding his cruiser in a reserved space out front.

Not to mention, he'd inherited that spot from Dern.

So that was enough to make Harry want it gone.

Considering his newly rearranged list of shit to do, he was pleased Polly did what Polly did every morning.

She met him at the front door.

As usual, she shoved an Aromacobana cup in his hand. He'd have no clue until he tasted it what was in it, though it was usually a latte, sometimes a chai. She mixed it up with flavorings because she said, "Someone has to put *some* excitement in your life, Harry. And until you figure it out, it's gonna be me." (It was safe to say the twins and Doc weren't the only ones who wanted Harry to get his head out of his ass about the loss of his wife and return to the land of the living.)

She opened her mouth, but he got there before her.

"Polly, I want that sign out front down by the end of the week."

She shut her mouth only to open it again and point out, "You sure parked your cruiser there."

"Because no one else would park there if I didn't," Harry retorted. "And I'm not gonna let a prime space like that go wasting."

She rolled her eyes on a big sigh.

He took a sip of his coffee.

It was Aromacobana' s famed Mexican, that being almond, vanilla, rice milk and cinnamon.

He moved to the swinging half door that led to the bullpen and Polly called out to him.

"Woman named Lillian Rainier is in your office."

Something in his chest tightened and he turned back to Polly.

Lillian hadn't phoned to let him know she was coming.

That thought added a gut lurch, and the feeling wasn't pleasant.

"She said she's supposed to give a DNA sample," Polly went on. "She said anyone could take it. I asked who requested it. She said you."

Polly moved his way, got close and lowered her voice when she finished.

"I got eyes. I got a brain. And I read romance novels. You wanted a sample, you'd have taken a kit with you or come back to get one since her house is just a block away. You wanted to see her again, you'd ask her to come to the station. So I threw a wrench in her works of trying to avoid you. You're welcome."

It fucked him, but he felt like hugging her.

"Oh, and by the way, I knew Sonny *and* Avery," she continued. "Leland kept me well out of that fiasco he had brewing. Not sure why you pulled that file and Lillian's here to give DNA, but I'll tell you something for nothing, they didn't do it. No way. Three things Sonny Rainier needed in his life, his wife, his girl, and a roof over his head. Four things Avery needed, her man, her daughter, a kitchen to cook food in and a garden to grow. Sonny didn't hunt. Didn't own a gun. Can't say he didn't have a violent bone in his body, because if someone hurt one of his two girls, hell would be paid. Avery was sunshine and rainbows, sang like a dream, and the only time I ever saw her down was when she caught Leland's eye, and he wouldn't let it go. They'd no sooner rob anyone and go on the run then cut the noses off their faces."

Normally, he had a rule.

Ask Polly first.

She knew all Leland was up to, and she hated it, just like he did. She knew more people in that county than he did, and she didn't keep what she knew to herself. She might have had a more finely tuned sense of justice even than Harry had, and that was saying something. She was, and had been for a long time, the most valuable asset in that department.

Why he didn't ask her about this, he didn't know.

Maybe because he hadn't met Lillian yet.

"You're heard," he said as he turned away again.

"Harry."

He turned back.

"That girl looks like she's been through the wringer. This about those bodies found in Idaho?" she asked.

"We can hope not," he said quietly.

Her eyes brightened with tears, and she whispered, "Damn."

Harry patted her shoulder, lifted his coffee and murmured, "Thanks," and then he made his way to his office.

Lillian was standing in front of his desk. She was wearing brown jeans, a black shirt, and a denim jacket, a casual outfit that still was flattering, stylish and made her look put together.

And she was staring at the picture of Winnie that was on the credenza behind his desk.

He braced for that to sting.

And then he braced against what it meant that it didn't.

What he didn't brace for was when he called, "Lillian," and she turned to him.

He'd left her in her pretty kitchen with her pretty flowers and a promise she'd phone a friend. She'd retreated to tetchiness in order to hold her shit together.

Obviously, after he left, it fell apart.

Polly wasn't wrong. She looked put through the wringer. Her eyes were swollen and bloodshot. Her skin was sallow. And her posture said she held the weight of the world in the pockets of her jean jacket.

"Hey," she greeted.

He stopped close to her, not as close as he'd like, but close enough to affect a kind of friendliness, even intimacy, in hopes of communicating support and empathy.

When he did, he smelled what he smelled yesterday, fresh green notes of jasmine and rose mixed with something musky and earthy, like a hint of patchouli.

In other words, she smelled like a garden, and he barely knew her, but he knew that was perfect for her.

"I take it you had a rough night," he noted.

"I look that good?" she quipped, no humor in those green eyes.

He sidestepped that and queried, "You call a friend?"

"Four of them. Two spent the night. Janie and Kay."

"Good," he muttered.

She looked around, suddenly avoiding his eyes, saying, "You're probably busy. Should we get this done?"

"We should. We will. Then I'm taking you to the Double D and feeding you."

Her gaze whipped to his.

"Sorry?" she asked.

"You eaten this morning?"

"I'm not hungry."

"Did you eat last night?"

Her lips thinned.

That meant no.

"I'm taking you to breakfast," he announced.

"Sheriff Moran—"

"I thought we agreed I was Harry yesterday," he pointed out.

She said nothing but at least what he said put some color in her cheeks.

"I told you I was going to get you through this," he reminded her. "And I'm going to get you through it."

"You're being nice again," she warned, tears shimmering in her eyes.

"Get used to it," he warned in return.

And then, before she could resist further, he took her hand, led her out of his office, and called for his deputy, Wade, to assist when he led her to an interview room to take the swabs.

SEVEN

Wanna Know a Secret?

Harry

H e knew it was a mistake by the time they were half a block down from the station heading toward the Double D.

It wasn't lost on Harry well before Dern's downfall that he was a popular guy.

Whether they liked it or not, people needed police.

You had a cop you didn't trust, you cleaved to the cop you did.

He also knew by the turnout at Winnie's funeral.

She was well-liked, but a lot of those people were there for him.

So, years later, Harry should have known that walking down the street with a beautiful woman, when he had not done something like that since Winnie died, was going to cause a stir in a small town where people got into other people's business like it was their job.

And he saw and felt a lot of eyes on them, most of them not trying to hide it.

But Lillian needed to eat, so he couldn't turn back.

And part of him, a part he wasn't quite at one with, a part he wasn't allowing fully to surface, but a part that was still there, thought they'd have to get used to it, so they might as well start now.

Including Lillian.

Though, to give Lillian a break, when they got to the diner, he led them to a booth at the side, not easily visible from the front windows.

They'd barely settled across from each other before Heidi, their waitress, was there.

She opened her mouth, took one look at Lillian after she pulled off her sunglasses, then Heidi's gaze shot to Harry.

Harry subtly shook his head.

Heidi's eyes grew melancholy before she blanked it and turned back to Lillian.

"Hey, Lill," she greeted cheerily. "The usual?"

And there it was.

Lillian lived her life, she was a part of Misted Pines, she had a usual for breakfast at the Double D, and Harry had been so out of it, he'd never noticed her.

Christ.

He wasn't ever going to share this shit with Doc. He'd never hear the end of it.

"I think I just want coffee," Lillian ordered.

"She'll have a full stack of cashew granola pancakes, and a side of bacon," Harry ordered for her.

Heidi pressed her lips together, but now her eyes were dancing.

"Harry, I can't eat all that," Lillian protested.

Harry worked out daily and ate healthy. He did this because his job demanded it. He did this because he represented the sheriff's department on the whole. And he did it because he didn't like to feel bloated, weighed down or lackadaisical, which eating shit made him feel.

His mother used to say he was Popeye; spinach gave him superpowers.

She was right.

He allowed himself to splurge seven days of the year: his birthday, the Fourth of July, Halloween (he had a weakness for candy), Thanksgiving, Christmas, New Year's and if he was invited to a Memorial Day party (which he always was).

In the meantime, he'd have a beer, or a drink, he'd chow down on a burger or dig into a steak, and he couldn't eat a baked potato without all the fixin's, but other than that, Harry ate clean.

"I'll finish what you don't eat," he said.

"I see you dragged in the competitor's product to mock us," Heidi noted, dipping her head to the Aromacobana cup he still held.

And he was glad she did, because it made Lillian emit a short chuckle.

"I got two sips left so I'll need another," he told Heidi.

"On it," Heidi said and walked away.

"I have some things for you," Lillian told him, taking his attention to her.

She was pulling an envelope out of her purse.

She slid it across the table to him. "Pictures of Mom and Dad. Just in case you need them for some reason." She hesitated, rolling her lips together. "I'll, um…want them back."

He took the envelope and tucked it carefully into his breast pocket, saying, "Don't worry, honey. I'll make certain you get them back."

She stared at his pocket like she was going to leap across the table and reclaim the envelope.

And Harry felt that with her. He knew how precious they became when pictures and possessions were all you had left of someone you loved.

She got a handle on it, though she didn't look him in the eye as she said, "I also talked to their dentist. Well, not to their actual dentist. He retired. But the practice is there. They think they might still have their records. I mean, they don't. Not at the office. But they might have them in a storage unit, and they said they'd send someone to look. I've given permission to send them to the station if they have them. I don't know if I actually needed to do that, but, I just…I don't know…"

"Felt the need to do something," he filled in for her.

"Yeah," she mumbled. She took a visible breath and asked, "Will that make things go faster?"

"Depends on if Idaho has Rapid DNA, which has cut DNA identification time down by a lot. Though, usually a dental ID goes faster. I just didn't expect after all this time—"

She cut him off. "I get it."

"Dentists usually only keep records for six years after a patient's last visit," Harry said quietly. "If they can locate them, we can significantly speed this up."

"Great," she replied, though she definitely didn't think it was great.

Heidi showed with their coffees, set them down, and again walked away.

"Otherwise, how are you hanging in there?" he asked.

"You have to ask?" she pointed to her eyes while still avoiding his. "I put cucumbers on them, and green tea bags when the cukes didn't work, and finally a cold cloth. And I still look like I ran eyes wide open through a dust storm."

"Crying is healing," he said.

"Well, I should be healed by now," she muttered, reaching for the cream and dropping some in her mug. She then slid it across the table toward him and finished, "But I'm not."

One thing Harry learned losing Winnie, and giving death notices, and attending funerals of people he knew, and victims he didn't, there was nothing anyone could say that made it better.

Nothing.

When you were stuck in grief, the only thing that helped even the slightest was knowing people were thinking of you and they gave a shit.

And he was doing that.

But fuck him, he wished he could do more.

"Though, you know, they were together," she said softly, stirring her coffee. "If it's them, that means they died together, and were buried together, and have been resting together ever since. And they'd want it like that."

She lifted her cup, took a sip, put it down, and finally gave him her direct gaze, and it absolutely gutted him to see the depths of sorrow dug deep there.

"It doesn't help a lot, but it helps a little," she concluded.

"That's good," he murmured, sipping his own coffee.

"Also, if it's them, knowing why they didn't get in touch. Just…" —she shrugged—"*knowing*. You hear people talk about closure. You watch those true crime shows and the victims' families and friends talking about getting answers, and how that helps. And now I can say I guess it does. I mean, we don't know yet, not for sure. But I just…I just…"—she cleared her throat—"I just can't help but think it'll feel better because I know where they are and I'll get them back. Not like I want, but they'll be back with me."

"That makes complete sense," Harry said. "And if it's them, we'll get them back as soon as we can."

Her lip quivered, as did her nostrils, but she sucked in a breath and got a lock on it.

Harry decided to move them out of this.

"Did you take off work today?"

Her head twitched like that was a surprise question, then she said, "No. I kinda make my own hours."

"What do you do?"

"I've got a property management company." Her lips tipped up just a tad. "That makes it sound fancy. It's not fancy. I don't have an office or anything. But I look after fourteen properties of people who have weekend or holiday places in and around MP. I rake the pine needles, make sure the appliances and furnace and water heater are running, the roof isn't leaking, rodents aren't getting in. I close them down for the winter, but head out regularly and have a look around to make sure all is good. And when they come, I go in and tidy them, turn on the furnace, stock them with groceries." She gave him a slightly bigger smile. "I don't do windows or toilets or hedge clippers. If they want a full clean, I work with my friend Kay's cleaning business, and Jenna's husband does landscaping, so if there's anything like that, I contract out to Trey. But I will run a vacuum or dust and wipe down counters."

She took another sip of coffee and Harry was pleased as hell she warmed to her theme and kept talking.

"I got a hankering to blow out the back wall of my house and give myself a proper master bedroom with walk-in closet and another bathroom, and on the other side a TV room or maybe a big mud room, so I took on some Vrbo and Airbnb properties."

She made a face and kept right on going.

"Found out real fast people treat other's possessions with a disrespect I wasn't expecting. And the owners of those are cheap as all heck. Kay also wouldn't take the cleaning jobs for what they wanted to pay, especially for the mess people left behind. Since most of them ran through every cleaning service in the county, Kay eventually got some of the business at her rates, not what they think her rates should be. But I was always getting calls at all hours about people being loud or doing stupid stuff, and neighbors getting mad, and renters breaking stuff that had to be fixed. It was a hassle, so I let those properties go."

Harry knew all about Vrbo and Airbnb renters, and she was not wrong. There were some real assholes who rented those properties, behaving like they rented a house on the moon that no one else would ever use, not something someone owned and gave a shit about with neighbors who had to put up with their crap.

"Did you get your master bedroom before you did?" Harry asked.

Lillian shook her head. "No. And just to say, I didn't manage to get my degree, but I did take a course in editing and proofreading. The property management thing wasn't exactly cutting it, so I had to find something that bridged the gap. I had some clients, independent authors. After I lost the vacation rentals, I picked up a few more writers. I'll be saving maybe another year, then I'll have enough to get that project done."

Like her parents, she saved, then when she had the cash, she'd take the plunge.

It was a smart way to live.

And learning all this gave Harry some reasons why he might not have noticed her, because part of her work was scattered across the county, and all of it was very solitary.

Seeing as it appeared they ran the course of that conversational line, he changed it.

"I went to see Rita Zowkower yesterday."

Her eyes got wide. "Really?"

"Is that a problem?" he asked.

Her gaze went vague while she thought about that.

"I haven't spoken directly to Rita in, God…I don't know how many years." Her attention refocused on him. "She blocked me on her phone ages ago."

"We're actively looking for Willie, Lillian, so I'm gonna ask again if that family has given you trouble."

"Rita runs those boys like a general," she told him something he knew. "But I'm no threat to her, and she doesn't have time for people who, in her estimation, don't matter. The minute I kicked Willie out, I ceased to matter. That said, I didn't matter much when Willie was with me, either."

Heidi showed again and put Lillian's pancakes and a plate of bacon in front of her.

Regardless of her protestations about not being hungry, Lillian grabbed the syrup and her knife and dug right in.

"You don't have to answer this, it's none of my business, but you and Willie don't seem like a fit," Harry noted.

Smearing whipped butter and pouring syrup at the same time, Lillian gave it up freely.

"I was out at the Halfway having drinks with Molly." She took her attention from her pancakes and gave him a small smile. "And yes, sheriff, I was underage."

"Think the statute of limitations on that has expired too," he joked, and was pleased as all hell that got him a full smile, and honest to God, he'd never seen a smile so damned pretty.

After giving him that, Lillian turned back to her food. "I really didn't want anything to do with him because, okay, he's good-looking, but he started chatting me up and it was clear he was on the make. So I shut it down. Somehow, he got my number and called to ask me out for coffee the next day. I don't know why. He was charming, and I was freaked about Mom and Dad being gone, feeling lonely, and I guess that made me stupid. So I went. Before we even finished half our coffee, he asked me to dinner the next night. There was something sweet about that, how obvious he was about liking to spend time with me, wanting more."

Harry never thought in his life Willie Zowkower would teach him something, but he sure as fuck filed that away.

She forked into her pancakes, took a bite, and after she swallowed, she looked at him and said, "I think it kinda reminded me of my parents. How keen he was to be with me. I fell in love fast, convinced what they found was what I found."

"Honey," he murmured sympathetically.

"I did love him, Harry," she replied quietly. "I mean, it was real. But I wanted what my parents had, and it wasn't that. Not to mention, Willie's family was constantly in our lives. They'd knock on the door at all hours. They were always trying to get him involved in stuff he never told me about, but I knew if it came from a knock at two in the morning, it wasn't right. He just,"—she flipped one hand one way, her fork the other—"couldn't say no."

She took another bite, put her fork down, went for a rasher of bacon, munched it and returned to him.

"Rita had a definite hierarchy in her family, and she expected me to take the role she assigned, that being letting Willie do what he wanted, support his brothers and father, and just cook the food for the table and keep her son satisfied in bed."

Holy fuck.

"Jesus, was she that open with that shit?" Harry asked.

"Entirely," Lillian answered. "This was not what my parents had, and Willie was too weak to stick up for me or put up boundaries. I eventually got fed up with it and kicked him out."

Harry snatched a piece of bacon and got another smile from her when he did.

Then she started talking again. "The thing that makes me sad about it is, in that family, Willie was the odd man out. I hurt for him, knowing he knew he didn't fit. I sometimes wonder if he fell so fast for me because I had my own house, and he thought he could escape. And honestly, it wouldn't surprise me if he did something blatant, something big that would make Rita send him on the run, doing it just for an excuse to get away from all the oppression."

Harry couldn't say he'd noticed Willie was the dark sheep, but he'd never been married to him.

What he could say was that none of the Zowkowers had ever done anything as brazen as fucking a man up with plenty of witnesses, necessitating him getting out of town fast, and staying out.

So what Lillian said definitely held merit.

On this thought, he saw movement out of the corner of his eye, looked that way and noted Kimmy, MP's lovable but crotchety and criminally (though, regrettably not officially) nosy loon, bearing down on them.

He gave her a look.

She shot one back.

Then her gaze turned to Lillian, who peered over her shoulder to see what had Harry's attention.

Kimmy took one look at Lillian and her swollen eyes, she stopped dead, pivoted and marched right out.

"Oh my God," Lillian breathed, and Harry looked to her to see her beautiful face filled with marvel. "We discovered a way to stop Kimmy from bellying all the way up in our business. I just have to learn to cry on cue."

He laughed softly and she smiled at him as he did.

She then frowned, but it was obviously fake.

She did this before she said, "You suck."

He nearly barked out a laugh, but instead asked, "Why's that?"

She pointed at her plate with her fork. "Because I was hungry."

"Not a fan of being wrong?" he teased.

The frown that earned was not fake.

"Not a fan of why you knew I was hungry."

He wasn't sure if she was talking about his job, or his understanding of grief due to his dead wife.

She told him. "MP is small, nothing in Fret County much bigger, but you sure do see your fair share of crap, don't you, sheriff?"

"I sure do, honey."

She scrunched her nose.

It was bottom line adorable.

He leaned into the table toward her. "Wanna know a secret?"

She nodded.

"It's going to make me sound insane."

"Sock it to me," she invited.

"There's not another job on Earth I'd want to do."

For a beat, her face froze.

Then it got soft, those startling green eyes of hers got warm, and she whispered, "On the floor of my tiny bathroom."

"What?"

"Nothing, Harry. Just...I see that because you're real good at it."

Jesus, why did that feel so damned fantastic?

"Thanks, sweetheart."

Pink hit Lillian's cheeks and she returned to her pancakes.

Harry let her.

And he watched her devour them as he sipped his coffee.

EIGHT

Dumplings

Lillian

The next evening—that being the evening the day after I had breakfast with Handsome Harry Moran at the Double D, one I enjoyed in spite of all that was happening (which was a miracle)—I lay with my back resting against the arm of my couch, my laptop in front of me, while Ronetta futzed about in my kitchen.

Ronetta was my next-door neighbor and had been since we moved in.

She had two kids who were young teenagers when we arrived in Misted Pines, both of whom had since moved away. Her daughter was now a high-flying casting director in LA. Her son was a vintner in Sonoma County, and he was a big deal. His wine was always winning awards.

Back in the day, Sherise and Shane were my babysitters.

And Shane was my first crush.

Ronetta also had a husband, George, who refused to retire because he was a lot like his wife. It'd be torture for him if he didn't have a busy schedule with lots to do.

They'd given me the idea to blow out the back of my house and add on, since they'd done it ages ago so Sherise and Shane could have their own rooms, George could have a man cave, and Ronnie could have a sunroom where she drank tea, watched birds, read books and gossiped with her gals on the phone.

It was important to note that Ronetta was one half of the whole who made up my role models.

She, like Mom (and Dad and George), was always busy. It was her personality.

Mom was all about the kids she watched and the garden she grew and keeping the house tidy and looking after her family. Nearly every day, she wore dresses because they were easy and a ponytail at her nape because that was easy too (though, she was what she called "a natural woman" (and she'd call herself that right before she sang the song, which was right before Dad would sweep her in his arms and slow dance with her while she sang it) so she rarely wore makeup).

Ronetta also had a nice garden, but cooking was her thing.

And she was always turned out. I didn't think I'd ever seen her without her hair and makeup perfect, her outfit just right, her shoes and purse and accessories coordinating like she styled movie stars.

She was also that woman you paid attention to so you could learn, because she always did the right thing.

She knew what to wear to the cinema, or to the town council meeting, or to the farmer's market, or to a fancy birthday party. She knew the perfect gift to buy her children's teachers or the perfect dish to bring to the potluck.

And she was that woman who entertained like she wrote the book on the subject. Just the right floral arrangements that had just the right amount of wow factor, nothing more, nothing less. Just the right hors d'oeuvres that were creative, unique and delicious. Just the right fold on the napkins that made them look elegant and told you she cared enough about you showing that she put in the extra effort. That supremely roasted prime rib sliced to perfection with a horseradish sauce you'd pay good money to have the recipe.

She could write style and etiquette books or create her own magazine. She was Martha Stewart in a braided-hair, petite, Black woman's body (and no shade on Martha, the woman built an empire and survived an epic takedown only to launch an even more epic comeback) except Ronetta was a lot less bossy, and a lot more sweet.

I adored her.

I put on makeup every day because of her, even if I was raking pine needles.

I wore cute outfits to go to the grocery store, because I so admired that she did the same.

She was a woman who knew she was worth taking care of herself, enjoying every facet of being a woman and not caring what anyone thought of that.

And since Mom and Dad left, she'd been my touchstone.

She was super tight with my mom. But be it my age at the time, or just that she was a mother, after they disappeared, and when we heard nothing, she slipped into that role for me and never showed how worried or scared she was about what was happening.

One could say she had an unfortunately not-very-unique perspective on what could befall people at the hands of dirty cops.

And now…

Well now, she knew what might be happening in Idaho.

So now she was in my kitchen, whipping up soul food I'd be eating for the next week, and doing what she did even when Mom and Dad were here.

Looking after me.

I was supposed to be proofing a book, something I couldn't concentrate on while Ronetta was in my kitchen, but I was faking it because she wanted me to get on with things while she saw to me.

But since I'd been faking it for a while, I decided she might be okay with me stopping.

So I looked over my shoulder and asked, "Is George coming over for dinner?"

She stopped mixing what I sensed was going to be dumplings to go into the chicken on the stove, glanced at her iWatch with its fancy tortoiseshell band, and replied, "He'll be here in about twenty."

George had also been tight with Dad. He was a dad, and he

looked after me too, but they'd been serious buds and he hadn't been as good at hiding his concern, then fear, and finally sadness when they vanished and never returned.

I was worried about George now, considering what the news might be.

I was worried about Ronetta too.

The Band-Aid we'd all carefully kept glued down was losing any hope at adhesive, and we all knew it.

I set my laptop aside, got up and walked to the kitchen.

"Can I do anything to help?" I offered.

"Did you get your words in?" she demanded.

Okay, so maybe Ronetta could be a bit bossy.

I hadn't, but I said, "Almost. I'll finish it later."

That appeared to be acceptable, I knew, because she turned to the pot, started dropping dumplings into the simmering broth, and she stated, "You can open the wine."

I went to the fridge to grab the bottle she'd brought over.

I nabbed my wine opener and was going at it when I requested, "Can I ask you a question?"

Spoon raised, bowl of dumpling batter in her other hand, she turned to me and declared, "Yes. Even with all that's going on, I think it's a good idea you phone our handsome sheriff and ask if he wants to go see a movie."

My throat got tight, and I could actually feel my eyes bug out.

She turned to the big pot, saying, "One thing that's for certain about your parents, no matter what news we get, while they had them, they lived their lives like every day mattered. If your momma wanted to sing, she sang. If your daddy wanted to take his girls on a hike, he told his client he'd fix their fence the next day, and he took his girls on a hike." She turned again and pointed a batter smeared wooden spoon at me. "You need to learn from that, girl."

"I'm not sure Harry—" I began.

That was as far as I got.

"Stop it," she ordered. "I've been paying close attention to that boy since he got hired. He wasn't like the rest. Had to admit, I got more than a few jollies at just how deep under Dern's skin

Harry Moran got, just by giving a damn about his job and doing it right. George and I opened a bottle of champagne when we heard he won his seat as sheriff, and since Dern was busy getting incarcerated, the man ran unopposed. We still drained that bottle dry."

"Ronetta—"

She spoke over me.

"So what I know is, he never took a pretty girl to breakfast after he gave her bad news."

Oh yes, the entire town was buzzing about that. I had a multitude of texts from Kay, Molly, Janie and Jenna about me going to the Double D with Handsome Harry Moran.

"I don't think now is the time to—"

"When *is* the time then?" she challenged just as the front door opened.

Guess George was early.

I looked to the door and watched his handsome face light up when he saw me, his full lips starting to curve into a smile, then he turned that to his wife, his smile died, and his brows formed a V.

"Woman, tell me you aren't giving our girl a lecture," he demanded, shutting the door behind him.

Ronetta returned to the pot. "I don't want to hear it from you."

"You didn't want to hear it from me last night when you were on about this," George said to his wife's back. Then to me, "Darlin', you take your time with Sheriff Moran. Boy's not stupid. He knows a good thing. He'll wait until you're ready."

It was like they thought something was happening with me and Harry.

Okay, in another universe, when I wasn't on the verge of experiencing another trauma as pertained to my parents, I might get into a zone where I was feeling this.

But Harry's wife had died years ago, and he was gorgeous. He could have any woman he wanted. He just never (ever) had a woman. Not after his wife.

If there was ever a confirmed bachelor (or in his case, bachelor widower), it was Harry.

"He's just looking out for me as we go through this identification process," I protested.

George's brows hit his hairline. Ronetta again turned to me and hers did the same.

"Seriously," I punctuated my statement.

Ronetta dumped the bowl with the dumpling batter residue in the sink, declaring, "I cannot with *all* my babies. Sherise is *too busy* to look for a man. It's not like the apparatus down there works until she's a hundred and fifty. She's gotta get *moving* if she's going to give me grandbabies. Shane's got his face in a wine vat half the time, and when he doesn't, he refuses to discuss anything with either of us, except us moving to Sonoma, which is *not* going to happen."

"To be fair, Ronnie," I cut in, "we've had two serial killers, a deranged fan who burned her celebrity author crush in a barn after shooting him and his wife, a serious sex scandal that exploded globally that involved not one, not two, not three, but *four* local couples, and a gaggle of women who formed a no-men-allowed coven and took over a housing development whose members were featured in an interview on Elsa Cohen's show on Netflix. Shane's far from crazy to be worried his mom and dad are right in the middle of all those messes."

"Well, things have calmed down since all that happened," Ronetta sniffed.

I didn't have the heart to remind her that they hadn't, seeing as we were awaiting the identification of two bodies who were probably my parents, and her dear friends.

But I saw it when it came to her anyway.

I felt George's change in vibe, but I was closer.

So I got to her first.

I pulled her into my arms.

"I'm good, I'm good," she muttered, resisting my hold.

"Stop it, you're not, I'm not. But I'm a big girl now, Ronnie, you don't have to hold the world at bay for me anymore. I can handle this." I took my arms from around her and framed her beloved face with my hands. "And I can handle it because *you* taught me how."

That did it.

Her face started collapsing, I drew her into my arms again, she pushed closer, and I felt her body buck with a sob.

George got near, gently pulled her from me and into his own arms, murmuring, "Mind the dumplin's, darlin'."

I nodded and did as he asked.

I gave them space, and now it was me futzing around my kitchen, looking for busy work while Ronetta, who wasn't big on showing emotion that didn't include joy, love, humor, encouragement, and when it was deserved, disappointment, pulled herself together.

I knew she'd gotten a handle on it when I heard her whisper, "I'll just go fix my face."

"You do that, love," George whispered back.

He was finishing my job with the wine when I walked to him with some glasses.

"If it's them, it's good we know," I said softly.

"You're right, doll," he muttered glumly, taking a glass from me and starting to pour.

I got into what I was going to ask Ronetta earlier.

"I haven't told my grandparents."

He shook his head. "You're right not to. Let's get the news. Save them from this awful..." His mouth tightened before he finished, "Waiting."

I felt it coming over me too, the return of the tears, because Mom and Dad would be so relieved about this.

Honestly, if they'd been told what would happen, I swear, they'd say, "Well, at least Ronnie and George are right next door."

And they would be right.

"We were so lucky to move in next to you," I whispered, and George looked at me, his familiar brown eyes startled. "*I* was so lucky."

Those eyes warmed.

He cupped my cheek and stroked the apple with his thumb. "That feeling is mutual, Lilly Bean."

The smile I gave him was trembly.

He took his hand away but kept hold on my gaze. "And for what it's worth, Sonny would be over the moon a man like Harry Moran was in his daughter's life. Dependable. Loyal. And he's proved to us all the depths of his love, sadly doing it after he lost his wife, but he also did it before. He doted on her and he didn't care who saw it. That's a real man, Lilly Bean. That's the kind of man your father would want for you."

Dang it!

The tears hit my eyes.

I was able to stop them from falling when Ronetta swept in, asking, "Is no one looking after my dumplings?"

I sniffed hard and raced to the pot.

I wasn't sure what I was supposed to do. She'd taught me to cook this dish when I was fourteen. Essentially, you just let them simmer.

But it took my attention elsewhere so Ronnie could do another thing Ronnie was adept at doing: demonstrating stealth love. She did this by coming up behind me, rubbing my back, then wrapping her fingers around my waist to give me a squeeze.

And then, before I could turn and catch her eyes, she left me and went to her husband for her glass of wine.

NINE

Let's Start Here

Harry

That same night, when his phone went, Harry was having a beer, his feet in warm socks resting on top of the old tree stump on his porch, a fleece jacket on, his three dogs lying around his rocking chair, his eyes to his empty stables, and his thoughts yet again on having them knocked down.

He looked at his phone screen expecting it to be Cade, considering he was right then on a lecture tour, his woman Delphine with him. He was doing courses for law enforcement officers down the east coast, returning in a couple of days.

Those two had a busy schedule, and Cade had said he'd call when he had time. But they'd exchanged some texts about the Sonny and Avery Rainier situation, and what Cade's boys said held true.

Cade knew Sonny, also Avery (just not as well), and he was dead set there was no chance they were involved in the Dietrich situation. So much so, at the time, he'd been preparing to wade in if Dern took it too far.

They hadn't been able to discuss it fully, and since Sonny was a friend of Cade's, Harry hadn't had the heart to share about the two bodies in Idaho.

But the call wasn't from Cade, or any of Harry's deputies sharing something had sparked off and he needed to head back into town, which comprised the vast majority of calls Harry received.

It was from Doc.

"Fuck," he muttered, knowing what this was about.

Doc wasn't a caller, he was a texter, usually.

Unless he had something to give Harry shit about.

Even knowing this, considering he was the sheriff, they were friends, and Doc, his woman and his son went through some serious shit last year, he took the call.

"Hey."

"Nadia wants her over for dinner."

Just as Harry suspected.

He blew out a sigh.

Nadia was Doc's (now pregnant) wife.

And Harry's breakfast with Lillian was one hundred percent making the rounds.

"We'll be nice," Doc said. "We won't scare her off."

"With her, it isn't that."

"Bullshit."

It was.

It was bullshit.

It was such bullshit, Harry had been wracking his brain for two days for some excuse to call Lillian, stop by her house, anything to get in touch with her, see how she was doing, try to make her smile.

As a matter of ongoing police work, but also as his only reason to talk to Lillian, he'd phoned her parents' dentist office to ask after their files, only to find it was "busy season" (whatever the fuck that meant) at the office and they hadn't had time to send anyone out to the storage unit to check. But considering the weighty matter at hand, they promised to do it the next day, even if it was a Saturday.

"Where did you find her?" Doc asked. "Jess says she's a knockout."

So it wasn't the breakfast for Doc, it was Jesse who had the big mouth.

"She's lived here decades."

"Whatever," Doc muttered. "Glad you're finally pulling your head out. Nadia's beside herself. She's got Ledge poring over cookbooks, trying to decide what to serve when you two show. And we can just say my eleven-year-old son is pretty pleased about this too, considering normally he'd probably break out in a rash if he even touched a cookbook."

"I met her because we're waiting on the identification of two sets of remains found in Idaho, and there's a very good chance they're her murdered parents," Harry told his friend.

"Fucking hell," Doc whispered.

"So…yeah. Now is not the time for me to make a move."

"You got too many scruples, brother," Doc said. "Most men would think now's the perfect time to make a move."

"I'm not most men, and that shit is fucked if most men think that way. She's vulnerable."

"This is what I know, Harry," Doc started. "Most men would look at this as a way to use a woman's weakness to get in her pants. And you're right. That's fucked and you are not most men. So if you're into this woman, it isn't about that. Or not just about that."

It wasn't.

Not *just*.

It had been a long dry spell since Winnie.

But even if that was the case, what he wasn't allowing himself to come to terms with, but he still knew it was there, was that wasn't all there was with what he felt for Lillian.

Though, he definitely felt it.

Definitely.

He could spend a very happy week just thinking about what it would feel like to have two handfuls of her sweet, round ass.

But that absolutely wasn't all this was about.

Doc continued, "And she lives in this town, she's gonna know that about you. So bottom line, we can't always pick our times. Sometimes, the time picks us."

It hit Harry then that Doc had met Nadia just months after Nadia's mother was brutally murdered by her father. And Doc was even more of a confirmed bachelor than Harry was.

But those two fell fast, fell hard, and stuck.

Cade and Delphine. His other friends Rus and Cin. And Doc and Nadia. All second chance, all later in life, all fell quick, and now all solid.

Shit.

"I get it, whatever you think you gotta do," Doc stated. "But you're a good man, Harry, and one thing I know is true, when the shit hits the fan, you need as many good people around you as you can get. Think about that."

Harry made no reply, because he was thinking about it.

"I'll tell Nadia she's got time to figure it out, and we'll see you when we see you," Doc concluded.

"I wouldn't say no to being invited over for Nadia's cooking in the meantime, or your beer brats," Harry replied.

Doc's voice held humor when he said, "Okay then, I'll talk with my woman and let you know. Later, Harry."

"Later, Doc."

They disconnected. Harry took a sip of his beer and resumed staring at the stables.

Winnie loved riding. They didn't have enough land for her to roam free, but they did have permission from their neighbors on both sides for her to ride their land, which was where he found her, on his neighbor's property to the east, after he came home from work, and she wasn't home and didn't come home or answer her phone.

But her horse came home without her.

Harry hadn't entered those stables since. His brother had taken care of selling the horses and all the tack. His father and brother had spread the hay in the field so it would return to the earth. And they'd closed those stables down. Harry hadn't even used them for storage.

They added value to the land. They were still in good nick.

But it was time for them to go.

On that thought, his phone buzzed against his thigh.

He glanced down at the screen to see an unknown number, and considering he was sheriff, he didn't have the luxury of ignoring it.

He put it to his ear. "Harry Moran."

"Hey, Harry," Lillian greeted.

Harry scooted back in his seat and took his feet off the stump, causing all three of his dogs to come alert.

"Hey," he replied. "Everything okay?"

"I just...do you have time? Is it all right for me to call you?"

Fuck yes to both questions.

"You can call me anytime. What's up?"

"I talked to George—" she began.

"George?" he asked, and damn, it came out sharp.

"My neighbor. Dad's best friend."

Okay then.

"You talked to him about what?" Harry inquired.

"Well, I haven't told my grandparents about what might be happening," she stated, but said no more.

"All right," he prompted.

"They're all still with us. And they're in Indiana." Again, she gave him that, but no more.

So he said, "Okay."

"They, you know, came out. Back when Mom and Dad took off. They used to come out a lot. They said it was because they had to replace the washer and dryer, or check on the roof, or fix the fence, which they did. Mostly, it was so they could look after me. They're older now, it isn't as easy, but I mean, obviously, they went through all of that with me."

"Yeah, honey," he said gently, deciding sitting out on his porch with the stables in his face was not how he wanted to have this conversation.

So he got up and his dogs got up with him. They all went into the house.

"I'm not telling them yet because we don't know anything yet," Lillian went on. "George said that's the right thing to do. I was just wondering if you agreed."

She knew he'd agree because her grandparents were probably at the very least in their seventies, they were too far away to provide the love and support Lillian needed right then, and if those bodies weren't Sonny and Avery, there was no reason to upset them.

This meant Lillian didn't want to know if he agreed.

She just wanted to talk to him.

Harry didn't even try to ignore the warmth that made him feel as he stretched out on his couch, his head to the armrest, and his dogs jockeyed for position on the floor beside him.

"It was the right thing to do," he assured her.

"Okay," she mumbled.

They lapsed into silence.

Christ, it'd been so long since he did this, he didn't know what the fuck to say. And he didn't want to talk about the files in the dentist's storage or anything about her parents that couldn't help but distress her.

Though, Lillian knew what to say.

"Do you want to go see a movie?"

Harry's entire body got tight.

Man, she put it right out there.

But it came out like she was blurting, and he knew that was true when she kept talking, doing it rapidly, at the same time backpedaling.

"Or is that not appropriate? With me being a witness and all. Or, um…you might not want to just because you might not want—"

He forced his muscles to relax and said softly, "Yes, Lillian, I definitely want to see a movie with you."

He could feel her relief come over the line and it made him smile.

Even so, he had to speak on.

"Though, first, you aren't a witness. You're a family member." What he left unsaid was *of two possible victims.* "That said, even if there's no policy against it in my department, it's still not entirely ethical that I take you out. If one of my deputies did this, we'd be having a conversation about his or her intentions."

"But, just to say, I asked *you* out."

That coaxed another smile out of him, but he said, "Yes, honey, but the bottom line is you're vulnerable at the moment, and it can be seen as me taking advantage of that."

"What people see and what is are different most of the time," she retorted. "But you're not Dern and everybody knows that. And honestly, it's not like half the town isn't gabbing about it already. So if you haven't received an avalanche of ethics complaints, we're probably good."

They probably were.

"I just want you to go in understanding where this is considering who you are and who I am."

"I understand," she said swiftly.

That didn't make him smile, it made him grin.

She really wanted to go out with him.

Since he wanted that too, he was all the way down.

"In for a penny, in for a pound," she mumbled, sounding nervous. And then she gave it to him. "Just so you know, this isn't a *he's my rescuer* situation. Just so you know…" There was a very long, heavy pause, then on a rush, "I've had a crush on you for a while."

Harry didn't know what to say to that, which was good, since she wasn't done talking.

"Not in a stalkery, euw kind of way. I mean, you're handsome. And, um…*tall*."

"Thanks," he choked out, trying hard not to bust out laughing.

"So, it stands to reason I would." Another lengthy pause. "Have a crush on you, that is."

"To put you out of your misery, sweetheart, I may have just met you a few days ago, so my crush hasn't lasted that long, but it's there."

"Really?" she whispered, so soft, so sweet, so hopeful, he felt it in his chest and his dick.

"Really," he whispered back.

"Can I go back to Willie and why I—?"

Oh no, they weren't going to do that.

"Lillian," he interrupted her. "Let's start here. You've had a life. I've had a life. And we can, and I hope we will, talk about those lives. I wouldn't pick how we met as how I'd like to meet a beautiful woman I'm very attracted to and would like to get to know better. But we don't have a choice but to work around that. So how about we stick with easy shit for a while and get into the heavier shit later?"

"That would be *awesome*," she breathed, causing Harry to grin again. "So what's easy shit?" she asked.

"I have no clue," he admitted.

He heard her soft, pretty laugh, and he wondered if her mother's singing was as musical as Lillian's laughter.

"So, I already checked, and tomorrow night the theater has a double bill of *Murder by Death* and *Knives Out*," she stated. "It starts at seven, and there's a half hour intermission, so it might be a late night."

"I'm an early to bed, early to rise guy, but I can make an exception on a Saturday."

"I'm an early to bed, early to rise girl, too."

"You wanna eat junk at the theater, or hit Luigi's for some pasta before?"

"Let's go for pasta before. I haven't been to Luigi's in ages."

That meant more time. Time to chat. Time to get comfortable with each other.

He was so fucking totally down.

They continued to talk while he sipped beer and envisioned her sitting on her comfortable-looking couch.

He told her about his dogs and asked if she liked animals.

She told him about her cat, who she'd had for fifteen years, getting it for some company right after her parents went missing, but it had died the year before, and, "I'm still not ready to replace her."

She also spoke about her parents missing like it was matter of fact, something Harry had no doubt it had become for her as the time stretched on.

But the loss of her pet openly gutted her, even if she lost her the year before.

Not that he wanted to even contemplate losing one of his

74

babies, but how much she cared for her cat said good things to Harry.

She told him she loved mysteries, both books and movies, so she'd been wanting to go to this double bill since it was announced.

He told her he obviously got off on mysteries, considering his job, which made her laugh that pretty laugh again.

She told him about Ronetta and George, her neighbors, and Sherise and Shane, their kids who had left the nest.

He told her his father had moved down to Arizona after retiring, and that his brother was in Olympia, practicing law.

There was discussion about what they'd get at Luigi's (she was going for the chicken piccata, he told her he'd get the caprese salad, which opened the door to her shoveling a slight amount of shit at him for finding the only somewhat healthy thing on the menu to eat). This led to them discussing their favorite restaurants in town, their favorite spots to hike, and them learning they shared a "favorite day." That being renting a boat and going out on one of their lakes and simply being out in the fresh air, on the water, doing nothing.

In other words, they laid the getting-to-know-you groundwork before Lillian told him she had some proofing to do on one of her client's manuscripts, so she had to let him go.

Once they got into the swing of it, there was something comforting and easy about shooting the shit with Lillian, hearing her voice in his ear, having her give him her time, giving it in return.

But work was work, so even if he didn't want to, he let her go.

Then he got up, taking his empty bottle to the sink to rinse out before putting it in the recycling.

His dogs followed him.

He turned, and giving distracted head scratches to his pups, it occurred to him he hadn't enjoyed a night at home since Winnie died.

Not one.

But that night, he wasn't alone with a drink, his dogs, and a game, a show or a book, the night dark and closing him into a quiet, lonely house that had once, long ago, been full of life.

That night, he'd had something a whole lot more.

And fuck, but he liked it.

On that thought, Harry gazed around his kitchen.

Even if his mom and dad had plans when they'd moved into that place, they hadn't gotten around to finishing them, so it hadn't been updated in decades, only the appliances replaced when the others gave out.

It was a kitchen that was all he'd known, since he bought this house and land from his father, and he grew up there.

It was a kitchen he didn't cook in very much, because he was a busy man with a busy job, and it sucked cooking for one.

A kitchen he didn't realize until right then he didn't like all that much. And it wasn't about Winnie. She'd mostly only been in it to make toast, pour a bowl of cereal, grab a mug of coffee, or eat the food he made her.

It was that it was the kitchen of someone who didn't give a fuck. The wallpaper was dated and looked like something out of *Stranger Things*. The countertops were nicked. The floor was linoleum, and it had held up, but it was butt-ugly.

It was a kitchen that was an indictment of the life he'd been living. The time he'd allowed grief to steal from him.

But standing there, after being asked out by a strong, sweet, beautiful woman, Harry refused to get mired down in these thoughts.

It was what it was.

But things were changing, *he* was changing.

And tomorrow, it would be Saturday.

Date night.

He was getting back in the game.

But he knew he wouldn't be if it wasn't Lillian doing it with him.

And he was all the way down with that too.

TEN

Fork Maneuvers

Harry

At five the next evening, Harry was in his office.
He'd received word that day the dentist practice was incorrect. They'd checked their unit, and Sonny and Avery's charts had been purged when their dentist retired, because they were old enough to be purged.

They apologized profusely, they'd wanted to help, but Harry expressed gratitude and reminded them they'd done nothing wrong.

They'd just have to wait for the DNA.

He'd come into town early (he was picking up Lillian in half an hour to take her to Luigi's) to check if he'd heard anything from Coeur D'Alene (he hadn't), or if there was any shit he had to deal with that he could get out of his way so he could hit the ground running on Monday.

There, he'd found a file on his desk with a Post-it on top from Rus, his friend, but also his lead detective, that said, *You're right. Shady. And worth a look. Let me know.*

It was one of the files they'd tagged as suspect from Dern's term.

Harry opened it, even if he'd already been through it closely.

He read it again.

It was the case of the apparent suicide of Clifford "Muggsy" Ballard.

Harry had been working at the department then, and by that time, the department had split down the middle. Men (and there were no women back then, not deputies, nor were there any people of color...at all) who were serious about the job were in Harry's camp, and the others who were there to get what they could out of a position of authority and power were in Dern's.

Harry had been one of two investigating deputies, the other one was in Dern's camp.

However, neither of them worked this file directly.

Unusually, only Dern worked it. And very quickly, it was ruled suicide.

Though Harry remembered it, not only because that was unusual, but also because a woman came in, had a loud argument with Dern, and came out, shouting, "You're a useless piece of dirt, sheriff!"

When Harry asked Polly who the woman was, he was told it was Muggsy's mother.

The file was slim, with just some photos of the scene that Harry had to admit, if you took ten citizens off the street, showed those to them and said, "You've got twenty seconds to decide what happened here," all ten would say it was a suicide.

However, the report was only three-quarters of a page long, and noted only *friends and acquaintances suggested deceased had shown recent signs of depression.*

Nothing else was done, including testing for GSR on the deceased's hand.

It was the ME's report that caught their eye.

Where she checked "suicide" on the report, there was an asterisk. And at the asterisk, it said *see notes in report about bruising.*

Harry had never seen anything like that.

Upon reading these notes, the medical examiner described the body had bruising and swelling about the face consistent with taking a beating, and defensive wounds on his arms. All of which happened very close to death, though in her estimation, not directly prior to it.

Anyone, but perhaps Dern, would think that was beyond hinky.

After studying the pictures in minute detail, with nothing jumping out at him except for the fact the man had experienced a beatdown before he died, Harry was about to close the file, shut down his computer and purge his thoughts on it (for now), deciding to sit down with Rus and discuss a way forward on Monday, when he sensed someone approaching down the hall.

He looked up to see Megan, the president of the town council, lifting a hand to knock on his doorframe.

"Hey," he greeted before her knuckles struck frame.

She dropped her hand and walked in. "Do I have to tell my sheriff how important it is to get regular rest and downtime, not because his work is anything but exemplary, but because he's my friend, and I feel the need to lecture him about looking after himself?"

Harry's gaze dropped to her smart suit, which meant she was either out on a Saturday seeing to work (she was in real estate) or seeing to town council business.

Therefore, he raised his brows to indicate her kettle calling out his pot.

She smiled and moved farther in. "I was on my way home to Dan when I saw you in here."

He needed to learn to close his blinds when he didn't want a well-meaning friend to detour into his office in order to tell him off.

"Just had something to check, then I'm headed out to dinner," he told her.

Her eyes lit with interest, but she only hummed, "Hmm."

With Megan, Harry wasn't going to go there.

He respected her, he liked her, and he had occasion to hang with her, mostly if he'd been asked over to Cade and Delphine's, because she was Delphine's closest friend, so if Harry was asked, it was likely Megan and Dan had been asked.

But she wasn't even close to his closest friend, nor was he hers.

So they weren't going to be discussing Lillian.

"Though, while you're here, we've finished the audit and there are going to be a couple of cases we'll be looking deeper into," he shared.

"As suspected," she mumbled irritably.

"Also, while we're offering advice," he started, doing it smiling at her so she'd know he took no offense, but also so she wouldn't take any with what he said next. "I'll repeat my concerns you're not running in the next election."

Megan shook her head. "You know my feelings about incumbency, Harry."

"Yes, I do," he retorted. "But before you, we had town council that was at best, mismanaged, at worst, and more accurately, it was managed with gross negligence. If you had another term, you'd have time to groom someone to take over."

"That's just it," she replied. "These political legacies are kind of like monarchies. In the end, you have one line holding most of the power. And they can become corrupt or complacent, which was what happened to the council before I shook it up. You know more than me that corruption needs to be stamped out. But people don't need complacency either. They need fresh ideas and energy. And even if the person you don't want gets elected, it's a good thing, because it encourages engagement. So I've no intention not only to run, but to groom someone to take over. It's time for new blood, Harry. And anyway," her eyes twinkled, "if I'm president of the town council, it'd make it hard to be a county commissioner."

After she delivered this litany, Harry found himself mostly repeating what Doc said to him the night before. "It's inconvenient you have too many scruples."

She smiled, hitched her purse strap more firmly on her shoulder and said, "I know it sounds like I'm contradicting myself, but I'm glad you're running for another term. It's my feeling a sheriff should be appointed by a group of people who understand he, or she, is fit to serve. What you do isn't and never should be considered political. So, even if you're running unopposed, I'm going to vote for you, but I'm going to pretend I'm doing it as a member of a group who knows what they're doing and appointing the right man for the job."

He lifted his chin to accept the compliment and decided not to tell her that was what all voters should be doing.

Her eyes again twinkled, "And I sure hope that dinner you're going to is with that pretty Rainier woman. I've referred some clients to her, and I've never regretted it. She's a good seed. I sadly wasn't around to see you escorting her down the sidewalk or chatting with her at the Double D, but from everything I've heard, you make a handsome couple."

"Tell Dan I said hey," Harry replied in order to share how he felt about discussing his dinner plans.

His reply only made Megan laugh, lift a hand, bid him to have a good weekend, and she walked out.

Harry checked his watch, then locked up the files, powered down his computer, and he went out and drove the block to Lillian's.

This was something he'd never do, but he didn't know if she'd be in comfortable shoes, and he didn't want to make her walk if she wasn't. The theater was only a few blocks away from her house, but Luigi's was a couple minutes' drive out of town and not walking distance.

So he parked outside her house and didn't miss the movement of the curtains in the window of the place next door.

Even if it was mildly annoying, he felt his lips quirk, because he suspected that was Ronetta (or George) and the affection with which Lillian spoke of them meant he didn't mind they were up in Lillian's business.

He knocked on her door and was surprised when, about five seconds later, it opened.

Harry sucked in breath.

Her thick, rich russet hair was down and filled with curls and body. Her makeup was more dramatic and way sexier than he'd seen her wear it. She had on a complicated, light peach, long-sleeved sweater that had a crisscross, halter-type thing at the neck, which gave a keyhole hint to cleavage and left a good amount of her shoulders bare. She wore this with white jeans that fit phenomenally tight and showed a slender inch of skin between the hem and the soft taupe booties she wore. The booties had a stacked heel and put her at a height where he, at six one, wouldn't have to bend his neck so far to kiss her (incidentally, he clocked her at around five eight).

Harry had no idea until right then the skin of a woman's shoulders and a half an inch of their shin were so fucking sexy, but Lillian proved this true.

"Hey," she puffed out, taking his attention to her face, which was flushed as he watched her eyes roaming his chest and then they dipped down, and she bit her lip.

Jesus Christ.

"Hey," he replied, before her staring at his crotch and biting her lip like that gave her more of a show in that area.

Her gaze sped to his and her cheeks flushed deeper.

"You look nice," she said, her voice husky.

"That's my line," he returned, and there it was, more pink in her cheeks.

"Come in while I"—she cleared her throat—"grab my jacket and purse."

He came in.

She closed the door and hustled to the kitchen table.

There were new flowers there.

He took his attention off them in order to take in the show of Lillian shrugging on a jean jacket, her ass swaying, her hand flipping the long sheath of her hair out of the collar. She grabbed a little bag, shoved her phone and keys in, and settled the strap on her shoulder.

She turned and made her way back, stopping in front of him.

"Shit part out of the way first," he said gently. "Your dentist doesn't have your parents' charts."

She made that cute scrunchy face, even if why she had to make it sucked.

"I know the folks at Coeur d'Alene aren't sitting on this. Cops don't like unidentified bodies. They're on it. We should hear soon, regardless," he assured.

She nodded.

He put a line under it by asking, "Have a good Saturday?"

"I cleaned my house. I paid bills. I did my grocery shopping. So now I can be all about you, and tomorrow, I can be all about an epic chillout."

"Doesn't sound like a fun day, but I'm all about you being all about me, considering I'm on track to be all about you." He enjoyed the renewed blush in her cheeks as he finished, "And a Sunday chillout is always good."

Her head tipped to the side, sending her gorgeous hair tumbling over her shoulder. "Do you let yourself have Sunday chillouts?"

"Afraid people don't refrain from doing stupid shit on Sundays. And they definitely don't refrain on Saturday nights."

"That means no."

"Yeah, it means no."

"And you still wouldn't want to do any other job but this?" she asked.

"And I still wouldn't want to do any other job but this," he confirmed.

She stared at him.

And then he grunted when she threw herself at him.

Automatically, his hands went to her waist, and his neck bent so he could look down at her.

Which put him in position for her to slide up on her toes and press her mouth to his.

He smelled jasmine and rose, felt a soft woman pressed down his front, and Jesus fuck, her lips fit perfectly against his.

For so many reasons, he wanted to have more finesse.

But this was Lillian, who still missed her cat a year after her passing, had fresh flowers in her kitchen, took beating after beating, kept her feet and kept going and had a laugh that sounded like a song.

And she'd thrown herself at him.

So he didn't have finesse in him.

His arms closed around her, his mouth opened, hers reciprocated, and he swept his tongue inside.

He felt warmth, tasted beautiful woman, his cock that had been stirring since he laid eyes on her woke up and his arms tightened, pulling her deeper into his body as he slanted his head and took even more from her.

Lillian pressed closer, arching into him, her fingers sliding into his hair, and she gave it.

At her touch, he groaned into her mouth.

All about giving as good as she got, she moaned in return.

They made out, hot and heavy, for too long before he broke it, but he didn't let her go.

Both of them breathing heavily, they stared into each other's heated eyes.

Fuck him, that green shone like emeralds when she was turned on, and that in turn was a massive turn on.

"Well," she said with a trembling voice, "it's good we did that. It won't be on our minds all through dinner and ruin the movies because that's all we're thinking about."

She was very wrong. Now that he knew what she tasted like and how good she could kiss, that was all he was going to be thinking about.

"And we have practice," she continued. "So we can just take up where we left off when you bring me home."

He couldn't stop it.

He busted out laughing, pulling her even closer, and after his head shot back with his humor, he shoved his face in her neck getting a nose full of jasmine and rose, and liking it.

She let him do that, and only when his laughter started waning did she whisper, "That feels nice."

He lifted his head and smiled down at her.

His smile faded when he saw how intent she looked.

Not serious.

Intent.

"I'm going to see about making you do that more often, Harry Moran," she said softly.

"I'm not going to argue with that, Lillian Rainier," he replied, also softly, making his own vow, silently, to do the same once he got her through whatever was going to come.

She touched his jaw, then bopped up to give him a peck on the lips before pulling from his arms, but taking his hand and leading him toward the door, saying, "I need to get fed. I also need to watch you eat tomatoes and basil. I've spent all day making up great quips about you wasting a perfectly good opportunity to splurge on carbs. I don't want to forget any."

"I'll take a bite of yours," he said, reaching to the door handle but not catching it because she stopped dead.

He turned to her.

"I don't share food," she declared.

"Bummer," he muttered on a tease.

"Okay, I'll share with you," she decreed instantly, evidence she was either a pushover, or she was a pushover for him.

The first one he didn't believe. Not with all she'd wrought all by herself in her thirty-five years.

The second one he'd take.

He opened the door, murmuring, "Obliged."

"But don't tell anyone," she warned. "I'm famous for my fork maneuvers."

He was chuckling as they stood out on her porch, and he waited for her to lock up after them.

"Fork maneuvers?" he asked.

She glanced up at him. "As in, spearing you if you try to nab something off my plate."

That earned more chuckles.

She locked her door and stowed her keys back in her purse.

He took her hand and guided her to his truck. He opened the door for her, helped her in, and closed it on her.

He glanced to her neighbor's house as he moved around the hood and saw Ronetta wasn't hiding behind a curtain anymore. She was standing in the window, arms crossed, staring at him. George was beside her.

Ronetta just stared.

George lifted two fingers to his eyes and then turned them around toward Harry.

Harry jutted his chin their way then dropped it to grin down at his boots.

The minute he got into his truck and turned the ignition, Lillian rolled her window down.

He looked to her.

She had her head out the window and was shouting, "Stop being weird!"

He burst out laughing again, but when he turned that way, he saw George disappear from the window.

Ronetta wasn't as easily cowed.

"Roll up your window, sweetheart, it's cold," Harry ordered as he put the truck in gear.

She did as told.

And Harry drove them to Luigi's.

ELEVEN

Time to Make Bread

Lillian

I woke up instantly knowing I felt refreshed...
And happy.

The second one took my attention because, as sad as it sounded, I didn't remember the last time I felt happy.

Really, truly, genuinely *happy*.

It was a miracle, especially in light of all that was going on.

And it was because my date with Harry had been *amazing*.

I turned to my side, curled my legs into my belly and aimed my eyes out my back window.

It was late, the sun fully out, so I had definitely slept in.

I saw the line of sunflowers I'd planted outside the window, and I again felt the loss of Sparkles, my cat, who was a morning cuddler.

I was seeing, with all that was happening, it was time to let her go and add to my family.

It was time to do a lot of things.

Primarily basking in the goodness of the memories of last night.

Just to say, Sheriff Harry Moran didn't mind looking at pictures of Sparkles (more than one of them), and I could tell he was totally sincere when he said how cute she was.

He also didn't hesitate pulling out his phone to show me snaps of his pups: the gray pit bull he'd confiscated during a case he was investigating and then kept, and his two chocolate labs, Linus and Lucy.

Yes, Harry liked *Peanuts*.

Another for his plus column (and FYI, so far, there didn't seem to be a minus column, but the plus column got longer and longer as the night wore on).

He told me more about his dad, and his younger brother, who was an attorney in Olympia, had been married for five years, and had given Harry a niece and nephew.

He also told me how close they all were. How the three men had a tradition to vacation together each year, just the Moran boys bonding, taking a long weekend on a houseboat on Lake Powell, or a full week fishing in the Florida Keys, whale watching in Maine or hiking in Alaska.

Though, his brother's family wasn't left out. Harry and his dad always went to them for Thanksgiving and Christmas (if Harry could get away from work, something he said he often didn't do so his married and partnered up deputies didn't have to work the holidays). He and his dad did this so the family didn't have to travel with two little kids or be away from home on the holidays.

And no matter what was going on at work, Harry never missed any of his niece or nephew's birthday parties.

I adored how close he was with them. I adored that he also had copious pictures of them on his phone and showed them proudly.

The only snag with this was when he shared his mother had passed away when he was eleven, "eaten up by cancer" (his words).

That meant the two most important women in his life had died way too young.

But even though I grabbed his hand after he shared that and gave it a strong squeeze, studying him closely as I did, he only smiled at me. It was soft and gorgeous, but it wasn't melancholy, just solemn.

Then again, he'd had a long time to get used to living with those losses.

Though, obviously, I didn't like he'd had to.

I shared more about Ronnie, George, Sherise and Shane, as well as Janie, Jenna, Molly and Kay, and yes, I scrolled through my phone to show him pictures too.

Conversation was never stilted, nor did it wax and wane.

I knew he skirted around too much talk of my parents, and I appreciated it, but other than that, he chatted freely about his work (or as freely as he could, some stuff he couldn't tell me), his friends (he was tight with Doc Riggs, Rus Lazarus, Jaeger Rhett and Cade Bohannan), and admitted openly he wouldn't be able to do his job without Polly Pickler.

And he asked questions about me and listened to my answers.

Further, he was interesting, always, but especially when he talked about his job.

He shared about Ray Andrews (MP's first serial killer), Richard Sandusky (the second one) and the whole sad affair that happened with the Whitaker family (the author and his wife who were murdered by his personal assistant, who turned out to be his lethal fan).

What Harry did for a living could be morbid, and definitely gloomy, but I could tell it fed something in him to do it, and it couldn't be denied that was attractive, and what he shared was fascinating.

He took a bite of my chicken piccata and warned me not to have dessert because, "Four and a half hours of movie watching means a visit to the concession stand." He also chuckled good-naturedly at my lame quips about him eating only his salad.

Through all this, he'd clearly found his groove after being out of practice with dating. He was teasy and flirty and made me feel pretty and desirable, the way his chocolate gaze heated when he caught sight of the skin of my shoulder, or got hungry, when it dropped to my mouth.

Gah!

It was *everything*!

More everything, after we left the restaurant. Even before we got there, it was clear I broke the seal on touch with our kiss, and I learned Harry was a touchy guy (I adored that too), and a gentleman to boot.

We held hands when we walked together or he put a gentle guiding touch on my waist, back or hip when he wanted me to be somewhere. He opened doors. He waited for me to precede him. He pulled my chair out for me. He reached out and tugged my hair playfully when he'd tease me. He paid for everything.

And he bought me a tub of popcorn and some Milk Duds during intermission (he had some popcorn, just a little bit, but no Milk Duds).

All of that was great.

All of that was perfect.

All of that was built on the foundation of the insanely delicious kiss we shared.

And all of it ended after we shared many more insanely delicious kisses just inside my closed door when he took me home.

We did all of that standing, necking, with a wee bit of mild groping, and there was something about it that was sweet and throwback and thoughtful as all heck. It was like, if we took one more step in, or moved the festivities to my couch, it would be pushing it too far, taking too much, and Harry wasn't about to do that.

This, what we were doing, was happening. We were both all in.

But Harry made it clear he was going to see to me while we explored it.

Mom and Dad and that unknown were underlying all of this, and if I allowed myself to think about it, I might start weeping again. Because he knew that, had a mind to it, and like he'd promised from the beginning, he was seeing me through it.

It was just that, now, there was an added, and very welcome, nuance to it.

Before he left, while we were trading swift, soft kisses in my open front door, I offered, "Wanna chill out with me tomorrow?"

"I was afraid you wouldn't ask," he replied, my belly melted, he kissed my nose and ordered, "Sleep in and text me when you wake up. We'll make plans."

"You don't *plan* chillouts, Harry," I educated.

He grinned (and *dang*, I loved his grin). "Right. We'll plan for you to show me how not to plan a chillout."

"Acceptable."

He gave me a squeeze, let me go, walked down my path, and then we had a staring contest with him leaned across the cab of his truck, making gestures for me to get inside and close the door, and me standing in my door, making gestures for him to drive away.

I lost this contest when Harry got out of his truck, went to the side of the hood and called in his authoritative, commanding voice, "Inside, Lillian! Lock the door!"

"All right, all right," I muttered, smiling to myself.

I went inside and locked the door.

I then walked to the window and watched him drive away before I turned and floated on air through my house, going through the motions of getting ready for bed.

Once in bed, I nodded right off (another miracle!) and slept like a baby.

That brought me to now, where I turned and took my phone off the magnetic thingie that displayed and charged it.

When I did, I saw I had a whole slew of texts from all of my girls, as well as group texts including all of the girls, a voicemail from Ronnie (she texted, but when she wanted to chat, she called).

And last, a text from Harry.

Hope you slept well. Hope you slept in. Call me when you get up. Later, sweetheart.

I giggled (actually *giggled*) with glee at waking up to a text from Handsome Harry Moran as I hit his name on the top of the text and then made the call.

It rang twice before he greeted, "Hey, honey."

There were background noises that sounded weird, but I replied, "Mornin', Harry."

"You sleep in?" he asked.

"Just woke up."

"Good," he muttered. Then louder, with those noises in the background trailing off, he said, "Lillian, I'm sorry. It's going to be a while before I can get to you. There was a car accident early this morning."

"Oh no," I whispered, upset someone was having a crappy morning, but wondering why one of his deputies couldn't deal with this so Harry could have some time off, something I'd noted in our talking last night he didn't seem to take much of.

"I'll call when this gets sorted, but it'll probably be a lot later."

"I can make us dinner," I suggested.

"Does a chillout day include cooking?" he asked, sounding curious.

Yeah, the man needed time off.

"Considering the fact my chillout vibe was leading down the path of baking cookies and bread today, yes."

"Right." He sounded distracted.

"I should let you go."

"Honey," he started, and I braced at his tone. "I wouldn't be here, I'd be getting ready to go there, but there was a fatality."

"*Oh no*," I repeated.

Well, that explained why Harry was wading in and not leaving it to his deputies.

"I'm sorry," Harry said. "I'll keep you in the know as the day goes on where I'm at."

"You don't need to apologize, Harry. Real quick, is there anything you don't eat? I mean, I get you're health conscious, but other than that."

"I don't tend to be picky."

"Great. Now I'll let you go. But I'm sorry this is how you started your Sunday."

"It's the job, sweetheart," he replied, again distracted.

"Okay. Talk soon," I said quickly. "Bye, Harry."

"Later, baby," he muttered and then rang off.

But I blinked.

Baby?

Oh my God!

Handsome Harry Moran called me *baby*.

It stunk Harry's Sunday began like this, but oddly, it also felt right, because it was him, it was what he did, he was fulfilling his calling.

It absolutely did *not* stink that he called me baby and I got to cook for him that night.

I lay in bed, mentally scanned my inventory of food, decided on a menu and also decided, if I was going to bake bread, I needed to get going.

This was when my phone vibrated.

I looked down at it, expecting Ronnie or one of the girls.

It was an unknown caller.

With all that was going on, I'd been picking up the unknown calls, just in case. Of course, this meant I got a lot of marketers and other people whose sad job it was to waste your time and annoy you.

I couldn't imagine, if there was news about Mom and Dad, Harry wouldn't intercept it and give it to me himself.

But you never knew.

So I braced and took the call.

"Hello?"

"Are you fucking kidding me?"

I shot to sitting in bed.

"Willie?" I whispered.

"Yeah, it's *Willie*, your fucking *husband*," he clipped.

"I—"

"You're dating *a cop*?"

"Willie—"

"*We're* a thing, Lillian. We're *the* thing."

I stared unseeing at my bedclothes because…

Was he insane?

"We're divorced," I snapped.

"Not my doing. *Hello*, woman. I did everything I could to stop your ass from pulling that off."

Oh my God!

"We were together for six months," I reminded him.

"Also not my doing."

"Yeah, because I *kicked you out*," I bit off.

"And again, *not my doing*," he gritted.

"You've been married twice since."

"Keeping tabs on me?" he drawled.

Lord!

"Leave me alone, Willie," I demanded. "We're over. We've been over for a decade and a half. We're so over, you can't describe it as over, because we didn't even begin."

"Oh, we began."

"Nope, I'm not doing this," I stated. "You're the past. A depressing, stupid past. And I'm beyond it."

"Lil—"

I didn't hear what he was going to say because I disconnected, then I blocked him.

Flipping heck.

Was he really going to do this?

After I had the best date of my life with maybe the best guy I ever met and in the middle of maybe (probably) learning my parents were dead?

No, not dead. Murdered.

Yes, he was going to do this. Because he was Willie Zowkower.

And worse, I was probably going to have to tell Ronnie and (eek!) George about it.

Even worse!

Harry and I were just beginning, but even so, I knew if I didn't tell him Willie had called, he'd be upset.

"Dang, damn, shit," I whispered. Then, "Ugh!" I grunted.

With that, I threw back the covers and pulled myself out of bed.

It was time to make bread.

TWELVE

Planted My Flag

Lillian

I t was three o'clock in the afternoon when I opened the door to Harry.

He was out of uniform, wearing jeans and a sweater that were more casual than what he wore last night, but no less attractive.

I didn't stare like I did (mortifyingly) the night before.

I was preoccupied by the pinched skin around his eyes.

He noticed me noticing and tried to throw me off the scent by rounding my waist with an arm and dropping a soft, hey-there kiss on my lips.

He smelled great and his lips felt even better, but his attempt didn't work.

When he tried to pull away, I curled my fingers into his sweater.

"That bad?" I asked, knowing the answer because of the word "fatality."

He tried to throw me off the scent again by saying, "I don't think there's a better smell in the world than baking bread, except your perfume."

This had me melting into him, but I tipped my head to the side, a nonverbal demand for him to share.

"Lillian, it's a lot," he whispered.

"Can I take this opportunity to remind you that my parents disappeared sixteen years ago, and I had help, I had support, but I survived it. I pivoted from the life I thought I'd have and made a life that's good. In other words, I'm not breakable, Harry."

He gave me a look that said everyone was breakable, and he'd know.

So I added, "If we're going to try to do this, I mean, like, explore us, and *we are*," I asserted, and was pleased to see some of the dreariness leave his gaze when I did. "It's your job. You've got to know you can unload on me about it."

"Okay, but maybe not on our second date."

Left unsaid, *While we're waiting for news about your parents.*

"It's our third date, I'm counting breakfast. No, it's our fourth. It was weird, but I figure if you vomit in front of a man, it's a date."

Some of the tightness dwindled around his eyes as he chuckled.

"Tell me," I urged softly.

"I had to do a death notice," he said quickly. "The wife was destroyed, but not surprised. Her husband had alcohol issues. We'd already picked him up for DUI twice, so he'd lost his license and shouldn't have been driving. He didn't negotiate a curve, ran off the road and slammed into someone's garage, went right through the wall, and totaled their car inside. He wasn't wearing his seatbelt. No one else was involved, but he not only had a wife, he also had three kids, all under the age of thirteen."

"Oh, Harry," I whispered, sliding my hand up to curl it around his neck.

He wrapped his other arm around me so he was holding me with both. "So maybe tell me about your day, because mine, until now, was shit."

Okay, scratch telling him Willie called off my list.

"I made oatmeal cinnamon cookies, which you don't have to eat, but you do have to take some into the station for your deputies. While doing this, I had an epic text session with all my girls about our date last night, and full disclosure, they're my girls so they now know you're a phenomenal kisser."

That got me another chuckle, and the strain around his eyes seemed to lessen further.

"Though, I've sworn them all to secrecy," I continued. "And you can trust that. It's not anybody's business how Sheriff Moran kisses, even if it would make him even more popular with his constituents. At least the female ones."

More chuckles from him as he shuffled me in, all the way to the kitchen, where he let me go so he could pop open the tin on the cookies.

Cinnamon goodness wafted up to mingle with the yeasty goodness of the baking bread.

"I've decided it's a splurge day," he said.

Fantastic.

I smiled huge at him.

He took it in, his gaze heating, then he dropped his mouth to mine and kissed it off.

When he lifted his head, breathily, I continued, "Ronnie came over and I endured a ten-minute I-told-you-so lecture from her, considering she was the one who encouraged me to ask you out for a movie."

His brows shot up. "She did?"

I nodded.

"Remind me to thank her when I meet her."

He said *when* he met her.

I smiled hugely at him again.

Then I finished, "I read a little bit. I baked bread. And I decided we're having taco salad for dinner."

"That sounds awesome."

"But now, I'm going to introduce you to *We Are Lady Parts* because it's hilarious and heartwarming and romantic and I'm sensing you need all of that."

"*We Are Lady Parts?*"

"It's a TV show from the UK about a Muslim women's punk rock band."

At my description of the show, he let out a surprised bark of laughter.

"Trust me, you'll be doing a lot of that while watching it," I promised him.

"Then cue it up, honey, because I could use a few laughs."

"You want something to drink first?"

"One of those La Croix?"

"You got it."

I moved to get his drink, and one for me.

Harry moved to the couch.

I went right in for the cuddle.

Harry welcomed it.

We snuggled in, and he did laugh, a whole lot. By the third episode, that skin around his eyes was clear and the tension in his body was gone.

So I felt like I'd climbed a mountain and planted my flag on top.

This feeling dug deeper as we worked together to make the taco salad, and ate it like any couple would, sitting in front of the TV.

It dug even deeper when Harry finally instigated our next make-out session on the couch, this one including far more groping, which proved I wasn't romanticizing what he gave me the day before, he really was that good with his mouth (and hands).

And it dug even deeper when Harry ended it, saying he had to get back to his dogs, and I knew he did, but he also was guiding this, he'd decided to take it slow, and I appreciated that, because it was what I needed.

At my door amid giving me lingering good-bye kisses, he said, "My turn to cook for you."

"You helped me cook this time."

"You can help me cook tomorrow night."

Tomorrow night.

I smiled at him and even I knew it was radiant.

He gave me yet another, very lingering good-bye kiss before he gave me a squeeze and walked to his truck, the bag with the tin of cookies and the loaf of bread I baked dangling from his hand.

We did the same you-go-inside, no-*you*-drive-away thing, but much shorter this time (I didn't want him to have to get out of his truck, so I let him win).

I closed the door, smiling inwardly and looking forward to meeting his dogs.

And I decided I could tell him about Willie later. Maybe on our fifth date.

Or our sixth.

Or maybe Willie would take a hint, and I wouldn't have to tell Harry at all.

THIRTEEN

Damned Cookie

Harry

The next morning, Harry dropped the tin of cookies in the staff kitchen.

It was light a few, the ones he and Lillian had eaten the night before, and the ones he'd put in a Stasher at home.

After his run that morning, he'd had eggs, bacon, and a thick slab of Lillian's bread, lightly toasted and slathered in butter. He took one bite and added grape jelly, because that flavorful, chewy bread needed jelly.

And right then, he walked down the back hall toward his office, and it wasn't lost on him his thoughts were light, as was his step, because he'd started his day shitty yesterday, and he could compartmentalize, he could get on with things, but no cop could escape the fact you carried a hint of every tragedy you processed or investigated with you. And in the beginning, after they'd just happened, they weighed heavy.

But Lillian took it from him, she cuddled with him, she fed him, she made him laugh.

She didn't erase it, but by damn, she sure as hell made it better.

He hadn't walked into this station feeling this unburdened since he lost his wife.

Two dates (or, he smiled to himself, in Lillian's estimation, four) and she gave him that.

Oh yeah, they were exploring this because she wasn't just gorgeous, soft, generous, a great cook with fantastic taste in movies and television who was strong and smart and tasted fantastic.

She didn't get loaded down with his job.

In the days before Winnie, he'd dated, and he'd done it while he was a deputy. He'd had colleagues share it took a certain kind of woman to marry a dedicated cop. And he'd learned that quickly when his job got in the way of him paying attention to them.

It was early days with Lillian, but she didn't throw a fit when he showed way later than they expected, and she'd noticed immediately the toll that crash had taken on him, and she set about doing something about it.

So yeah, fuck yeah, he hadn't felt this unencumbered coming to work for years.

And he fucking liked it.

So yeah again.

They were going to explore this.

To the fullest.

He shrugged off his jacket, hung it on a hook, settled behind his desk, turned on his computer, and Polly strolled in with his Aromacobana.

"Just so you know, I have to pay attention to catch you coming in, and then I have to bring you your coffee in your office," she griped in a roundabout way about the sign in the front being gone and Harry now parking out back.

"You used to watch for me to show out front, met me at reception, and now, I walk right by your office, and it's right next to mine," he pointed out, and added, "I've also told you repeatedly you don't have to buy me a coffee, but if you insist on doing it, I could just walk into your office and get it so you don't have to walk to mine."

"If I don't go to the front, I can't look over the boys and girls and make sure they're getting themselves settled and taking care of business," she retorted.

He usually arrived around morning shift change, and Polly was always in first, so he saw she'd want to do this, because Polly kept her finger on all of their pulses.

He should have known there was a method to her madness.

Even so.

"I'm not putting the sign back up," he warned.

She rolled her eyes.

Rus showed at the door carrying his own Aromacobana cup.

"Hey, Pol," he greeted her.

"Heya, Rus," she replied, then sashayed out.

Rus's attention came to Harry. "Know you just got in but wanted to know if you saw that file on Clifford Ballard."

Harry motioned for him to come in, Rus did and sat opposite Harry as Harry pulled out the file.

"At the time Ballard died, his mother came in and had a dustup with Dern. She left, shouting that he was a piece of dirt," Harry told him, plopping the case file between them.

"You good with me poking around?"

Rus was ex-FBI, just like Cade. But whereas Cade was a profiler, Rus had been a field agent, and a celebrated one. He hunted down the Crystal Killer, aka Richard Sandusky, even if, in the end, the man had essentially turned himself in.

During this, Rus had fallen for a local, so he left that life and started a new one in MP,

One could say, even if there was always someone doing some punk-ass shit in every corner of the country, things were a good deal quieter and less challenging in Fret County than working for the FBI.

In other words, Rus needed something to sink his teeth into, and he was raring to do it with the Ballard case.

"I'd start with his mom and then retrace Dern's steps with the friends who reported Ballard was showing signs of depression," Harry suggested. "Those read hinky to me."

Rus reached for the file. "They read the same to me."

"Also, if you got time, sniff around the Dietrichs."

Rus angled his head in question. "The Idaho bodies?"

"I don't know, but my gut tells me yes, and if it is a yes, I want to hit the ground running."

"'Spect you know, the station and the entire town are talking," Rus reported, referring to Lillian.

And that was Rus.

He didn't get up in Harry's business. But he'd be right there if Harry needed to share that business.

"I know," Harry sighed.

"Hear word she's gorgeous, hard-working, no-nonsense, sweet," Rus noted.

"Correct on all accounts."

Rus's gaze got intense. "Pleased for you, buddy."

"Thanks, man," Harry replied.

They both looked to the door when Polly filled it.

And neither of them liked the expression on her face.

"There's someone here who would like to talk to you, sheriff," she said.

She only called him sheriff if things needed to be official.

Rus immediately stood.

Harry nodded his head at Polly.

Rus left after exchanging a look with Harry, and he took the Ballard file with him.

Polly led an attractive woman in who Harry would peg being in her mid to late forties.

"I'll just leave you two to talk," Polly stated, surprisingly not introducing the woman.

She closed the door behind her.

Harry stood, rounded his desk and offered his hand. "I'm Harry Moran."

She took his hand but said, "I'm not going to tell you my name, because…"

She didn't finish that, and from her nervous demeanor, Harry didn't push it.

He swung out an arm to indicate she should sit. She did, and he resumed his own seat.

She started it. "I heard you're looking through old files. Dern's files."

His interest was already piqued, but it got even more so with that opener.

"Yes," he confirmed.

"Because you're, uh…looking into Dern, I, well my friends told me that I should come in and tell you something."

"And what would that be?" Harry asked casually, not applying too much pressure, even though he really wanted to know.

"I work in an…office. I…a while ago, I got a divorce. After I did, Leland Dern would come to my office, like…"—she shifted anxiously —"*repeatedly*. It made me uncomfortable. I was a single mom. But back then, I had a four-year-old, he's, erm…older now."

She rolled her shoulders and clenched her jaw.

Harry sat and waited, his gaze steady on her, keeping his hands from forming fists because he sensed where this was going.

Part of the mess that got Leland Dern's ass put in prison was not following through with the investigations of two deputies who had complaints of sexual coercion lodged against them.

Though, Dern doing anything of that nature himself was new.

He was not surprised at Lillian's report of her mother catching Dern's eye, and Dern throwing a tantrum because he got his feelings hurt, even to the point of instigating a frameup.

That was just the kind of guy he was.

But this kind of thing was ballsy, blatant…

And worst of all, it hinted at a pattern.

Being attracted to a woman you couldn't have was one thing. Being butt-hurt she didn't like you back came with the territory. It was just Dern who would act out egregiously on something like that.

Criminally stalking another one and using your deputies to help you was a-fucking-nother.

She continued, "It seemed like he was on the make. No, it didn't seem like it. He was. I mean, I met him only once, at the Hideaway.

I didn't even really process it at the time, except he was kind of…
skeevy."

Dern was all kinds of skeevy.

Harry nodded encouragingly.

"I don't know how he found out where I worked, but he did.
The more he showed, the more I tried to put him off, the more he
seemed to come after me, until I didn't have a choice. I'd had
enough, so I told my ex-husband about it. Obviously, we didn't get
along, but we shared our boy. Even if we didn't get along, he wasn't
happy about it either."

"All right," Harry said quietly.

She swallowed visibly then kept talking.

"Darrin…I mean, my ex, he went to speak to Dern to make him
back off. But this only caused Dern to…well, he…" she trailed off.

"He's not here anymore, ma'am," Harry reminded her. "And I
worked here for a decade when he did. I'm not sure there's much
you'll say that will surprise me. But it might be something I need to
know as we go about the business of cleaning up after him."

"Okay," she whispered, and it sounded almost pained.

Harry felt bile rise up his throat.

"Right, so after my ex had a word with him, things got really
bad," she relayed. "Both me and Darrin would have deputies
following us, pulling us over for the slightest infractions, like, they
said Darrin had a broken taillight, when he didn't. They said I was
supposedly going over the speed limit, when I swear I wasn't. Stuff
like that."

Harry felt a muscle in his jaw jump, but he just nodded.

"And he was still coming to my office. My boss got sick of it, and
she waded in. She went to Dern herself. I don't know what she did
or said, but after she talked to him, all of it stopped."

"Can I ask your boss's name and if I can talk to her?" Harry
requested.

The color ran out of her face, and she shook her head.

"He doesn't have that power anymore," Harry said quietly.

"You don't know. You're a guy. You're a cop. But all that lasted
months. It was really scary, sheriff. Utterly *terrifying*."

That muscle jumped in his jaw again.

"I got back together with Darrin," she shared. "I mean, it wasn't like I did it because I had to because of what Dern was doing. Dern messing with us reminded us of the connection we'd lost. Who we used to be. And Darrin is super protective. But that's beside the point. I hope we'd find our way back to each other anyway. It's just...Dern is not the kind of man you get on his bad side. And now Darrin and I also have a daughter, and it was just... Sheriff, it was just very, very scary."

"Leland Dern was tried for his abuses of office, and he served a year sentence and is now living somewhere else, so we can't try him again," Harry informed her. "If you'd go on record, it would just be more we'd have on him if something else springs up with this case audit. You absolutely do not have to make an official statement or lodge a complaint. It's your choice. But I'll be here if you change your mind."

"Lodge a complaint?"

"It's up to you, totally up to you, but we can investigate this, Dern and the former deputies who were involved in it, and we can press charges if there's evidence to support them."

"Now?" she asked. When he nodded, she noted, "But that was years ago."

"If a victim is too afraid to come forward to report a crime, the clock starts when the crime is reported."

"Whoa," she mumbled.

"I can promise you, I will investigate this to its fullest if that's what you want. It might not lead to anything, but I have a feeling there are a number of former deputies that are more than a little concerned about what our audit will bring, and it's a little bit of poetic justice when they used their position to terrify a woman and her husband, that they get some of that back. And I can assure you, if anyone did anything to you, you'd have the full force of this department at your back."

She rolled her lips together, but her eyes lit.

"Think about it," he urged.

She nodded. "I will. I'll think about it, and I'll talk to Darrin about it."

"I'm here, whatever you decide."

She studied him a beat before she declared, "You're so not him, it's not funny."

"Best compliment I could get," he replied.

A hesitant smile formed on her face before she stood. Harry stood with her, and he escorted her to the front door.

Once she was out, he prowled to Polly's office, entered and closed the door behind him.

"You know who she was?" he demanded.

Polly shook her head. "But I can guess."

Harry was thinking about that woman, who was still scared even though Dern no longer lived in their county, or any of the ones bordering it.

He was also thinking about Avery Rainier.

"How often did he pull that shit?" Harry asked.

"There were things he hid from me, Harry, and the boys did too. Just like he hid them from you. So I don't know. He scared them so bad, they wouldn't come to me. They'd not even go to Pete so Pete could come to me, and no one's afraid of talking to Pete."

Pete was her husband. He owned the Double D. And he, like Polly was a mom, was a dad to anyone who knew him.

"But I'd hear murmurings," she continued. "Some of the men, it went against the grain. But if your boss tells you to do something—"

"If your boss tells you to terrorize a woman and her husband because he wants to get into her pants and she won't let him, you quit, and then you report that boss to someone who can stop his shit," Harry ground out.

"I'm not excusing them, I'm explaining. And you're transferring, because of Av and your feelings for Lillian."

"Fuck yeah, I am," he clipped.

"He's gone, Harry," Polly said gently.

"You can't ever get that kind of stain out. She wouldn't make an official statement because she's *still* scared of Dern."

Polly's lips thinned.

"Fuck," Harry muttered.

"Go have a cookie," Polly suggested.

Christ.

"You run. You lift weights," she reminded him. "You're generally active all the time. You can have a cookie when it isn't Christmas, Harry Moran. You won't get a gut. Food is soothing."

"It's just when you think food is soothing, you get a gut."

"Not if a pretty woman made you cookies, and you eat just one, for heaven's sake."

Harry scowled at her.

"Go on, get a cookie and then get to work," she ordered.

Polly was totally the boss of this station, he just held the title.

Harry left and he didn't go to his office.

He went to get a damned cookie.

And fuck him, after he ate it, he felt better.

FOURTEEN

Marie Antoinette

Harry

That evening, his dogs going crazy told Harry Lillian had arrived.

He and his pups moved through his house and out to the front door. When he got to his porch, he saw her parking her dark-blue Subaru, which was at least seven years old, next to his truck.

His pups raced toward her car until Harry put his teeth to his lip and whistled.

They stopped dead and sat, long tails sweeping the grass, tongues lolling with excitement, eyes locked on Lillian getting out of her car.

His dogs were social, but Harry didn't often have company.

Something else that needed, and was going to (imminently), change.

Lillian had a bottle cradled in her arm with a big bow on it.

She shot a smile to him but moved right to his dogs. He knew she knew animals when she did it slowly, crouching a little and offering a hand low that they could smell.

Once they all got in a good sniff, he called, "Alright," and all three dogs got up and bounded around her.

He heard her laugh as she made her way to Harry at the same time giving pets to his dogs when they were within touching distance.

Harry stood at the top of the steps, with only enough space for her to wedge herself in front of him when she arrived.

This meant her smile was even bigger when she got to him.

He glanced at the bottle.

It was Jameson.

He raised his brows at her.

"Ronetta knows Sean Stoll's mom. She did the sleuth work for me," she explained.

Sean was one of his deputies.

"I didn't bring you anything when I came to yours for dinner," he pointed out.

"You don't live next to Ronnie. If she knew I came to your house without a host's gift, she might take me off her Christmas list."

Harry smiled.

Lillian returned the smile.

That was when Harry took the bottle from her, and then he kissed her.

The dogs milled around them as they did what they seemed to always do when they kissed, losing themselves to it, to each other, the world abating, it was just them, Harry and Lillian, in a universe that actually worked, and all of the shit of it just faded away.

And every time, the hunger deepened.

So now, it almost seemed desperate how greedy he was for her smell, her taste, her tits pressed to his chest, the feel of her fingers in his hair, and as ever, she gave as good as she got, communicating how voracious she was for what she could get from him.

This meant Harry had to stop it.

They weren't going there until after they had answers about her parents.

He was not going to be that guy.

So, no matter how hard it was, he stopped it, touched the tip of her nose with his and whispered, "Let's get you inside."

She looked a mix of disappointed and hazy, both of which he liked, but she nodded.

He took her hand and led her in.

He didn't plan on being curious about what she thought about his house, but he found himself watching her as he led her into the front room.

And he then found himself shocked when her eyes lit with pleasure.

He looked to the living room, one his parents had gotten to before his mom got sick.

Huge sectional. Stone walls. Big media center. Terracotta tile floors, Native woven rugs. Rustic wood coffee and end tables.

"Okay, if you told a Hollywood set designer, 'Design a living room for a hot guy rural Washington State sheriff,' they'd design this," she declared, recapturing his attention. "It's perfect. I love it. And I really have to teach you how to chill out. This is chillout central."

Harry turned back to the living room, suddenly seeing it differently.

Seeing it now as the room his mom designed so her boys could truck in from whatever they were doing outside, lay about, be comfortable, spill drinks and track mud and drop potato chip crumbles.

It wasn't ugly, if it was dated.

What it was, was sturdy, warm and welcoming.

He looked again to Lillian to see Smokey had claimed her.

But more, she'd claimed Smokey.

Another surprise.

People tended to be skittish around pit bulls, even if that breed was loyal and affectionate.

But not Lillian.

Before Harry got him, Smokey had been starved nearly to death, so he didn't trust easily.

But there he was, leaning against Lillian's leg while she scratched behind his ears.

Fuck. This woman.

He had to clear his throat before he spoke.

"Hungry?" he asked.

She nodded.

He moved her way, grabbed her hand and walked her to the kitchen.

He watched for her reaction to that room as well and saw what he expected to see this time. She masked her expression to hide she was unimpressed.

"I lived here growing up," he told her. "Bought it off Dad when he wanted to downsize, before he retired and moved to Arizona. Mom and Dad got this place as a fixer-upper. They did the important stuff first, putting on a new roof, installing a new furnace and water heater, kitting out the bathrooms, the living room, their boys' rooms. She got sick before they tackled the kitchen."

"Ah," she replied.

"Winnie wasn't a cook," he stated, and her gaze darted to his, shock that he put Winnie out there easily read in it. "And honestly, I didn't give much of a fuck about anything after I lost her."

"Harry," she whispered.

He set the bottle aside and gathered her into his arms.

"I know I said we'd keep it light," he began. "But I saw you staring at her picture in my office."

She immediately appeared uncomfortable.

"She lived," he said quietly, and her gaze grew intent on his. "I loved her. I married her. I was destroyed when I lost her. But that was years ago and something you need to know. I'm stubborn."

Her eyes got big at this admission, and she mumbled, "Um… okay."

"Being stubborn," he went on, "I held on to her loss longer than I should." He gave her a squeeze and warned, "I'm not over her, Lillian. I'll never be over her. I thought I was going to spend the rest of my life with her, but that isn't what fucks me about her breaking her neck when she was twenty-eight. What fucks me about it is she was hilarious. She was up for anything. She wanted to eat pizza in Italy and sushi in Japan and curry in India, and she never went to any of those places. It fucks me not only that we had a beautiful life together we didn't get to live, but *she* had a beautiful life *she* didn't get to live. That's what fucks me."

"I can imagine," Lillian whispered, still studying him intensely.

"She'll always be in my heart. But, not so recently, a friend told me Winnie would be pissed as shit I stopped living when she did. He was right. It took me until meeting you to understand how right he was."

Her body melted into his as her gaze on him warmed so much, the green in her eyes seemed to turn to liquid jade.

"But I need to be able to talk about her," Harry gently continued. "I don't want her to be the elephant in the room. I want her to be what she was. A woman I loved who I lost, and I hated that, but I'm still here."

She lifted a hand, stroked his jaw and said, "Okay, honey."

"Same with Mom," he pushed it.

She blinked then tucked her lips between her teeth.

He gave her a slight shake. "I saw your expression when I mentioned I lost her. It was a long time ago, and, sweetheart,"—he dipped his face closer to hers and his voice lower—"you know you never get over that either."

"No," she whispered. "You never do."

"You don't have to hurt for me because I was hurt. You've got enough on your plate right now. But, one way or the other, no one in this world escapes what I've experienced. It's just life."

"Okay," she repeated.

"So can we make lettuce wrapped burgers and Asian slaw?" he asked.

She scrunched her nose at the mention of lettuce wraps.

"I bought you a fresh bun at the bakery counter at the market, and I grabbed you a slice of carrot cake from Aromacobana," he told her.

Her eyes lit up.

He grinned at her.

Then he kissed her again, this time making it quick and closed-mouthed.

He let her go, poured her a glass of wine, and they got down to making dinner in his ugly-as-fuck kitchen while his dogs meandered around hoping they'd drop food to the outdated linoleum.

THERE WAS ONLY SO MUCH a man could take.

So, after they finished their second episode of their ongoing binge of *We Are Lady Parts*, and Lillian attacked him, they were now stretched on the couch, Harry's long body pressing Lillian's soft one into the cushions, their mouths fused.

And he had to end it, because things were getting out of hand.

They were doing this because Harry finally got his hand on Lillian's round ass.

He'd touched her, got his fingers under her top the night before, feeling the warm silk of her skin, going so far as to brush the side of her breast, but no farther.

But the instant his hand cupped a cheek of her ass over her jeans, she arched into him, pressing her hips to his, and his cock, hard and beginning to ache, got harder and definitely ached.

He broke the kiss but not the touch of their lips and whispered, "Baby."

Her eyes were hooded, hot, but when he said that word, her fingers that had been threaded in his hair, fisted in it, she tilted her head and again captured his mouth.

Her hunger flooded into him, and Harry ground his painfully restrained cock into her soft hips, swallowing her moan and groaning into her mouth.

Christ, he had to stop this.

He didn't stop it when her fingers brushed agonizingly against his dick while she frantically undid her jeans.

He pulled away again. "Lilly."

She kissed him again at the same time she captured his hand, tugging it around, up, and pressing it *in*, before her hand retreated.

Feeling the sleek, soaked folds between her legs, he grunted, his dick jerked, he instinctively circled her clit with more than a hint of pressure, and she tore her mouth from his, her neck arching, her back too, and she ground into his fingers as she whimpered.

Fucking *fuck*.

It took everything he had to cup her sex and whisper, "Baby, we need to slow this down."

She righted her head, her eyes now lost, lost to what they were doing, lost to him, and she begged, "Please don't."

"This is a big step," he reminded her.

"We're ready," she said instantly.

His lips tipped up. "I'm ready, but I need to be sure you are."

"Have you lost feeling in your fingers?" she demanded.

That surprised a laugh out of him.

"Harry, I'm not being funny," she snapped, impatient.

"Sweetheart."

"Harry."

"Lillian."

"*Harry*."

Experimentally, he circled her clit again.

Her eyes fluttered closed, her lips parted, and he felt his cock beading.

Okay then.

Fuck it.

He kissed her and he fingered her, and then he stopped kissing her so he could watch as he made her come.

And fucking hell, the show was *spectacular*.

As she recovered, he ran his lips along her jaw, down her neck, across her throat, and up to her ear, and when he felt her fingers relax in his hair and she started stroking it, he slid his hand out of her jeans.

He lifted his head and looked down at her.

She had just the barest sprinkle of freckles across her nose, her skin was rosy from her orgasm, her gaze hazy with it.

He already knew he could look at her for a lifetime.

But seeing her like this, he knew he could give that to her for a lifetime.

"Good?" he asked softly.

"Your turn," she said as answer.

He shook his head. "Unh-unh."

Her eyes narrowed. "Sorry?"

"I'm good," he stated.

"Uh…Harry, I can feel you're not."

He smiled at her. "It isn't a fatal condition."

"I know. But does it matter to you that I *want* to alleviate your… *condition*?" she asked.

"What matters to me is that I like spending time with you, I intend to spend a damned sight more of it, and as that time wears on, I don't want you to have that first reason to question my motives."

Her chin ducked into her neck in shock.

"So as I said, I'm good," he reiterated.

His body jerked as, abruptly, she caught his face in her hands.

"We'll wait," she said in a harsh whisper, feeling—so much fucking feeling—pouring out of her green eyes, deluging his body, his bones, his soul, all of which had felt so damned empty, so brittle, starting with losing his mom, watching his father and brother do it too, then finding Winnie, always so animated, lying so still on the ground among the pines. "We'll wait because you're such a danged good guy, I sense what you need is to wait. You couldn't live with not waiting. But just so you know, I'm ready whenever you are," she finished.

"I'll file that away," he whispered in return, but his wasn't harsh, it was low, heavy, but weighted with the good she was offering, like the bad he'd been carrying since he was eleven never existed.

"And I'll spend time trying to figure out how I found myself dating a super good guy at the same time wishing he was a little bad."

"Oh, I can be bad, sweetheart," he promised.

Her eyes rounded and she smacked his arm. "Don't be hot when you won't allow me to get you hotter."

"But I'm allowed to get *you* hotter."

"*Quid pro quo* from here on out," she sniffed.

Harry frowned. "I don't agree to that."

"It's not fair, I get me some and you don't let me give you anything."

"You are so very wrong I didn't get anything out of that, Lillian."

Her eyes got even rounder, and she smacked his arm even harder. "Stop being an even *better* guy, Harry," she demanded.

He started laughing.

"Oh my God, now I'm annoyed because the guy I'm dating is even more awesome than I thought. *And* he's a miracle man with his fingers."

"Wait 'til you get my mouth."

Her gaze thinned and she snapped, "Stop it, Harry."

"I'm also filing away that I need to make you come harder, it seems like it wears off quick," he teased.

For a second, she stiffened under him.

Then she dissolved into giggles.

Watching her laugh was almost better than watching her come.

"Another episode over carrot cake?" he suggested when her giggles diminished.

"Are you going to have a bite?"

He nodded.

"Okay then," she mumbled.

He angled to the side, did up her jeans, then pulled her up to sitting before he took his feet.

"Want some coffee too, baby?" he asked.

"Do you have herbal tea?"

He didn't, but Aromacobana had the good shit for sale, so he'd be getting some.

"Sorry," he muttered.

"That's okay. Decaf?" she asked.

"Definitely fell down on this job," he said.

"No you didn't. I've just always had trouble sleeping, even when I was a kid. So I don't drink caffeine after three in the afternoon."

Harry's neck tightened at learning this. "You've always had trouble sleeping?"

She nodded. "All my life. Though, the last two nights I dropped right off."

Now, learning that, his chest burned as he stared at her

She smirked at him and said, "So there, Harry. This is what I'm dealing with." She circled her hand in the air. "All the goodness that is you."

He reached, dragged her out of the couch, and kissed her hard and long, until they were both breathless.

"I'll get some tea at Aromacobana," he said when he broke it. "What's your favorite?"

"You suck," she lied wispily, still recovering from the kiss. "And anything. Mint. Chamomile. Hibiscus. Passionflower. One of their herbal blends."

"I'll get decaf too."

"And you suck even more."

He grinned at her.

She frowned at it. "Stop being hot."

"I'll try."

Her eyes lifted to his. "You'll fail."

He shrugged.

She rolled her eyes, touched her mouth to his and demanded, "Get me cake."

"As you wish, Marie Antoinette."

Another eye roll, but she ended this one smiling.

He put her back into his couch.

Smokey stayed with her, but Lucy and Linus came with Harry as he got his girl some cake.

FIFTEEN

Parental Link

Harry

Late the next afternoon, returning from Aromacobana with a bag full of herbal teas and a pouch of fancy decaf, his mind on the conversation he'd just had over coffee with Cade, he hit his office to see Rus on his way out of it.

His gaze went down to the bag in Harry's hand, then came up again to Harry's face, and he left it at that, even though Harry had been getting stick from everyone in the department for two days about that fucking tin of cookies.

Needless to say, if she was going for it, Lillian got his men's and women's approval through sugar, butter, oatmeal and cinnamon.

"Left you a note, was going to my desk to email," Rus explained why he was in Harry's office, even if Harry had an open-door policy.

The office wasn't his anyway, it was owned by the county.

"What's up?" Harry asked.

"Brief on Ballard...and the Dietrichs."

He read Rus's face, noting this detective dog had found a juicy bone, and Harry moved to the chair behind his desk.

Rus sat opposite him and waited for Harry to stow the bag before he launched in.

"Ballard's mother gave me an earful. And his friends gave more. Apparently, this guy was a sad sack. If life didn't bring him low on the regular, he made stupid decisions to get brought low. Kept losing jobs. His wife cheated on him. Then she left him and cleaned him out when she did. He'd regularly make shitty investments on dubious projects that didn't pan out. The thing was, he didn't let it get him down. He was well-liked. He was, according to more than one friend, 'that guy.' The one who'd help you move. The one who'd watch your dog while you were on vacation. The one who'd take you for a beer if your girlfriend dumped you."

"So suicide didn't jive with them," Harry deduced.

"Not at all," Rus replied. "It rarely does. People miss the signs loved ones are sending, or those loved ones do everything they can to mask the signs. But honest to God, Harry, that doesn't sound like what this is. This guy had lived through a lot and kept on rolling. He didn't hide any of it either. He was a talker. He shared. He bitched. When he had sorrows to drown, he did that publicly."

"Does anyone know if he was going through anything around his death?"

Rus shook his head. "He wasn't living the big life after his wife cleaned him out. One bedroom apartment. Job working for Stormy at the tire store. He wasn't dating anyone. But he'd just been to a friend's fortieth birthday party the day before, and several of the attendees remember he was what he usually was. The life of the party."

"Was he banged up when he went to this party?"

Rus shook his head. "Nope."

"Anyone have any idea about that?"

"All anyone could guess was that he was excited about some new scheme he said was going to make him rich, and it might have gone bad. They didn't know what it was or who was involved, but he swore he'd be buying lakefront property and a boat. No one thought anything about it at the time, because this was Muggsy's gig. He threw good money after bad constantly. Some even said this was why his wife strayed. He was so sure he was going to get rich quick, he got poor quicker and dragged her down with him."

Harry left the truth unspoken. That the woman could have left him without kicking him when he was down by cheating on him. But Rus knew that better than him, seeing as Rus's ex thought Rus needed a lesson about how little attention he was paying her, and she used fucking another man in their marital bed to teach it.

"The only thing that grabbed my attention from what they were saying," Rus went on, "whatever this new scheme was, it was different. He wasn't investing his own money. Whatever it was, he bragged he didn't have to lift a finger or hand over a dime, and he was going to be rolling in it."

He and Rus stared at each other then, because if something sounded too good to be true in that way, it was usually illegal.

"The statements Dern apparently took that said he was depressed?" Harry inquired.

"Every single person I talked to, outside Ballard's mother, said they never spoke to a cop, Dern or anyone else. And Dern didn't come to her, she went to Dern."

Fuck.

"You talk to the ex?" Harry asked.

"Got a call in to her asking for some time. Waiting for a call back."

Harry nodded. "What did the mother have to say about her visit to Dern?"

"That her son didn't kill himself," Rus answered. "Safe to say, she's still pissed, but she's relieved we're looking into it. She told me she has nothing against suicide. She made that very clear. It isn't like she's got any erroneous ideas that's some smear on their family or the job she did as a mother. She's simply adamant Ballard didn't take his own life. And only slightly less adamant that when Dern wasn't being 'infernally lazy,' her words, he was playing favorites. Cozying up and doing favors for people who would donate to his re-election campaign or let him borrow their condo at a ski resort. She said he didn't have time for someone he didn't think mattered, like Muggsy."

She wasn't wrong.

Even so.

"That doesn't explain why he took that case himself and closed it in a couple of days," Harry pointed out. "He had two deputies who investigated crimes, and he could have punted it to either of us."

"No, it doesn't explain it," Rus agreed.

"Talk to the medical examiner?" Harry asked.

"She's having a busy couple of days. We've set a time for tomorrow afternoon to talk. She's pulling her files to familiarize herself with this case, considering it was seven years ago."

"I'll want to know why she didn't test for GSR."

"That's on my list of questions for her."

Sensing that was as far as they could go on Ballard, Harry said, "Now the Dietrichs."

Rus leveled his gaze on Harry's. "They're gone."

Harry's neck started itching. "Gone?"

"No one at their house. Looks kept up, but the feel is it's deserted and has been awhile. I had a walk around. It also appears that someone took the time to shut it down. Blinds closed. Electric meter barely registering usage. Pads on the outdoor furniture stowed. Mrs. Dietrich doesn't work. Mr. Dietrich hasn't been into his office in months. Apparently, he's working remotely. He told his staff he's in Seattle because his mother is ill, and he needs to be closer to her. Problem with that, and what they don't know but I do, is his mother died eleven years ago."

"Fuck," Harry bit off.

"They got land, so their neighbors aren't close, but talked to several of the people on their road. No one has seen either Dietrich come or go in a good long while."

"I announced the audit last year, Rus. How long have they been gone?"

"His office reports he hasn't been coming in regularly for a good ten months, even though he does check in personally, but he does it randomly, and he doesn't stay long. A few hours, then he's gone."

"So they heard about the audit, knew their file might be flagged, possibly knew two dead bodies were in the mix, they shut shit down and took off, with Mr. Dietrich showing sporadically to keep his finger on the pulse."

"It's a theory."

"What's your theory?" Harry asked.

"Same as yours. So that's why I'll now be requesting resources to see if I can track these assholes."

"We have to wait for Idaho, Rus. Focus on Ballard."

"I'll focus on Ballard, at the same time get everything ready to submit, and if I have to, I'll do it on my own time, so when we hear from Idaho I can just hit enter and shit will be in motion."

Harry made a decision. "Not your own time, just do it."

Rus nodded.

"Just got done talking to Cade about this case," Harry shared. "He didn't have much to offer except for the fact the Dietrichs were big donors to Dern's election campaigns, and by Cade's estimation, this put Dern in their pocket. Considering Sonny and Avery were indicated, he started poking around and he didn't quit when they disappeared. While he was doing it, he heard rumblings that Dietrich was having some money problems. Sonny and Avery didn't get caught or come back, the case faded away, Cade stopped looking into it."

"So, possible insurance fraud," Rus deduced.

"Possible," Harry replied.

"I'll start sniffing around that too," Rus said.

"Good," Harry muttered. And then he told his friend, "What Lillian and I have started is serious."

Regardless that it was early in their relationship to make this declaration, Rus's lips tipped up.

"I'm trying to take it slow for her, but she's not making that easy," Harry continued sharing.

"I know how that feels. Cin attacked me in the middle of Brittanie's murder investigation. She knew the woman and loved her, I didn't. She was feeling big things. She needed that connection, maybe even needed to feel alive or to suck as much out of life as she could get." Another lip tip. "I was worried for her, but still happy to oblige, and in the end, it worked out pretty damned good for both of us."

Something to think about if Lillian continued to push toward getting his dick, which was something, it didn't have to be said, was hard as fuck to deny her.

"Cin knew her in school," Rus told him. "She was a couple years ahead, but she said Lillian was one of the 'smart kids' when she could have been one of the 'popular kids' because of how pretty she is. She entered writing competitions and worked on the school paper and the yearbook. They didn't run in the same crowd, but Cin liked her then, and she still does, even if they still don't run in the same circles."

None of this was surprising.

After sharing that, Rus rose from his chair, probably chomping at the bit to get some wheels in motion after two meaty cases finally landed on his desk. "Look forward to meeting her."

"Look forward to introducing you to her."

Rus inclined his head and said, "I got paperwork to fill out."

With that, he left, and Harry returned to his own work.

He was at it for half an hour before his phone on his desk lit up with a text from Lillian.

At store. Do you like farro?

He smiled because of her question and because, in about an hour, he was leaving to go home, change, get his dogs, then return to town to go to her house to make dinner with her.

It was her idea to invite the dogs.

Yes, he answered.

She came back with, *Salmon?*

Yes, but you don't have to get fancy.

I'm on a mission. Do you like macerated cabbage?

"Fuck it," he muttered, smiling through his words and calling her.

"Hey," she greeted.

"Hey back. Yes, I like cabbage. But salmon is expensive."

"Don't mess with my mojo," she bossed. "I saw a recipe I want to try. Do you like ginger?"

What she meant was, she looked up recipes for food he'd want to eat.

Christ, she'd been just down the block from him.

For years.

"Yes, honey, but—" Harry tried.

"A little heat? The recipe has red pepper flakes."

Harry started chuckling. "Yes, Lilly, though—"

"Persian cucumber?"

Harry stopped chuckling because he was laughing.

"I'm thinking yes on the cucumber and carrot," she mumbled into his laughter.

"Yes," he pushed out through it, just as his phone vibed in his hand with another call. "Hang on, a call is coming in."

"Okeydokey."

Okeydokey?

Christ.

Just down the block.

Fuck him.

He took his phone from his ear, looked at who was calling, and the blood suddenly flowed sluggish through his veins.

He pushed through it to go back to her and forced a light note into his voice. "Gotta take this. You going home soon?"

"Right after I check out."

"See you there, sweetheart."

"'Kay, Harry. Bye."

"Later, Lilly."

He disconnected from Lillian and quickly took the call coming in before it went to voicemail.

"Moran," he said.

"Harry?" a woman asked.

"Yeah, Lynda. You get word?"

"I'm sorry, Harry," Sergeant Lynda Westwood of the Coeur

D'Alene Police Department said. "They're yours. Parental DNA links to the sample you sent. We have Simon and Avery Rainier's bones in our morgue."

God damn…

Fuck.

SIXTEEN

Idaho

Harry

The first thing Harry did was quickly walk to Rus's desk and ask him if he'd go to Harry's house and let the dogs out after he left work and before he went home.

Rus took one look at his face, his lips thinned, then he asked, "Idaho?"

"Idaho," Harry answered.

"I'll let them out and bring them over to ours. That way, you won't have to worry about them tonight. As you know, Maddie loves them."

Maddie was Cin's daughter, and she did love Lucy, Linus and Smokey, and they loved her.

"Thanks, brother," Harry muttered. Then he tipped his head to Rus's computer and said, "Hit enter."

Rus nodded.

Harry went back to his office and got right on his phone.

Jason answered in two rings.

"We got shit," Jason said as greeting. "But we got so much shit, we're compiling it at the same time we gotta—"

"Those bones are Sonny's and Avery's."

"*Fuck*," Jace bit.

"So give it to me fast. What you got?" Harry demanded.

"We think we're onto something. Few days, we'll be home. Before that, just so you know, and Lillian probably didn't know this at the time, but the Rainier place in LA was broken into when Avery was home, Sonny was at work and Lillian was at school. She was okay, it was just a junkie looking for something to pawn so he could get his fix, and she reported she thought she scared him more than he scared her, but still, it tweaked her. Friends say Sonny wasn't much of a city boy, and the rat race of LA was beginning to wear on Avery too. They said the break-in was the last straw for Sonny. They had their place on the market within a week of the incident and took off the day it closed."

That was an explanation, but not a full one.

Before he could dig into that, Jace kept talking.

"Needless to say, property values in LA are a lot higher than in MP. The equity they had in their place, plus the fact it was known both Sonny and Avery didn't live beyond their means and regularly set money aside in savings, it's not a stretch they could buy a small two bedroom in Misted Pines."

That explained more.

"I hear you. But that's not exactly upping stakes and leaving," Harry pointed out.

"When I was ten, Dad could have had a for sale sign in the front yard for a year, and I probably wouldn't have noticed it, but I definitely would have pitched a fit if I knew Dad was going to sell our place. Better to say you're sorry than get in a discussion with a ten-year-old who doesn't want to leave her friends."

That tracked, though now they'd never really know why Sonny and Avery didn't share with their daughter they were moving.

"Right. So what are you on to?" Harry asked.

"I don't wanna say unless it doesn't pan out. But we think we got a lock on the hotel where Sonny and Avery stayed here in Coeur d'Alene."

So the twins were already in Idaho.

Fantastic.

He had no idea, after all this time, how the twins had managed to possibly track the Rainiers to a hotel, or why that might be important at this juncture. But he'd learned in dealing with the twins to give them their head and let them get on with it. The results rarely disappointed.

"I'm on my way to go tell Lillian the results of the tests," Harry shared. "You find anything, I want to know so I can decide if she'll want to know."

"You got it." There was a heavy pause before, "Don't envy you, brother. Take care of you while you take care of her."

"You're heard. Thanks, Jace. Later."

"Later."

They disconnected and Harry shut down.

He stopped in Polly's office on his way out.

"I'm gone," he told her.

He knew word had gotten around when her eyes were somber as she looked at him.

"I'm sorry, honey," she said gently. "So sorry for you and for Sonny and Av's girl."

He nodded, said no more, and noted a number of solemn eyes of his deputies and staff as he hoofed it out of the station.

He headed down the block, but he didn't go to Lillian's house.

He went to her neighbors.

He hit the doorbell and Ronetta opened it within seconds.

Tears hit her eyes the minute she clapped them on him.

"I need you," he said the instant he clapped his on her.

Her voice was throaty when she bid, "Come in, she's not home yet. I need to call George."

She stepped back. He stepped in. She closed the door and went to her phone. He went to the window to keep a lookout for Lillian's return.

He heard murmuring behind him.

It stopped and Ronetta was standing beside him.

"George is coming," she said.

He looked down at her.

"I'm so sorry," he whispered.

Her gaze rose to his. "Sometimes, the world doesn't make sense."

"No, it doesn't."

"You're poorer, never having met them," she declared.

"I know."

Her lip trembled.

Harry slid an arm around her shoulders.

She gave him her weight.

"She's going to come undone," Ronetta warned.

"Reckon so."

"George might too, just so you know. Sonny and my husband were two peas in a pod."

"Whatever you need me to do, I'll do it."

"Knew you were a good egg," she said under her breath.

That felt good, but Harry didn't reply.

Five minutes later, Lillian's Subaru rolled up the street and into her drive.

Harry looked back down at Ronetta. "George know to come next door?"

She nodded.

"Ready to go?" he asked.

She shook her head, but said, "Let's go."

He watched her draw in a deep breath, and only when she let it go did he take his arm from her shoulders, and they walked to the door, out it, across her lawn, and Lillian's.

They were walking up the front steps when Lillian opened her door.

Her gaze pinging between Harry and Ronetta, she otherwise didn't move out of the doorway.

He stopped in front of her, and before he could say anything, she seemed to be walking, or even falling, back.

Swiftly, Harry reached out to catch her, but instead, she listed forward, put her hand on his chest, and her touch seared right through his uniform, right into his skin, doing this like a brand, one he'd wear with honor for the rest of his life.

Then she collapsed into him.

And the sobs came.

SEVENTEEN

The Best Ones

Harry

Harry bent and picked Lillian up, carrying her into the house. He heard Ronetta close the door behind them as he walked Lillian to her couch and sat on it.

Considering her position in his arms, she landed in his lap. He intended to put her into the seat beside him, but her arms slid around his neck and she burrowed in close, so he left her where she was and tightened his hold on her.

Ronetta first put a box of tissues on the couch next to him, then she came back with two glasses of water and placed them on the tray on Lillian's ottoman. She retreated, but Harry heard her murmuring from the back hall, and he suspected she was making more calls.

He shifted to get more comfortable, and when he did, Lillian latched on to his hair and yanked her face out of his neck to look at him.

"Don't leave me," she breathed jaggedly, the serrated words dragging along his soul.

"I'm not going anywhere, honey," he whispered.

"I mean…" She sniffed, released her hold, hesitated, and asked, "Can someone look after your pups?"

He knew what she was asking.

"Got Rus on it already," he assured her.

Her face started to crumble, so he cupped her head and tucked it back into his neck.

It happened about ten minutes later, the thing that happened when you were loved and had good friends.

George showed first.

He took in what was happening on the couch and quickly tutted and wagged a finger when Lillian tried to move to get up and go to him.

He instead came to them, leaned in, kissed the side of her head and muttered, "Don't move a muscle. Stay right where you are. We got you, darlin'."

More tears came from Lillian, George's desolate, concerned gaze slid through Harry's as he straightened away, then he went to his wife.

Lillian's friend Jenna showed next. Molly came after. Janie and Kay came together.

Lillian had it under control by then, and Harry had pulled them out of the couch and put her on her feet.

After she allowed her friends to give her love, Ronetta claimed her and took her to the bathroom. Then they moved to another room, and Lillian came out with the mascara smears cleared away, her face shiny with moisturizer, and she'd changed out of her sweater and jeans into some loose drawstring pants, a tight cami and bulky cardigan with slippers on her feet.

George left for a few minutes and came back with a bottle of Macallan. He showed it to Harry across the room and Harry nodded. George poured him two fingers just as he liked it. Neat.

Ronetta got on making some macaroni and cheese. Molly got on to opening bottles of wine and pouring. The other women put Lillian's groceries away. Mark, Kay's husband, showed. Then Trey, Jenna's husband, showed.

And surprisingly, Rus showed.

When George opened the door to him, Harry moved in that direction and George moved out of the way.

Rus was carrying Harry's duffle.

"Got a clean uniform in my truck. Want me to put it in your office?" Rus asked.

Jesus, but he had good friends too.

He already had an extra uniform in his office, but he didn't get to answer, Ronetta was there.

"Bring it on up, son," she ordered.

Rus didn't wait for Harry to say anything. He handed Harry the duffle then hoofed it down to his SUV where Harry could see all three of his dogs in the back. He wanted to go down and give them pets, but he didn't want to confuse them, and more, leave Lillian, even just to walk down to the street for five minutes.

Rus returned with one of Harry's uniforms in dry-cleaner plastic, but again, Harry didn't take it. Ronetta did.

"Leave you to it," Rus said.

"Thanks, brother," Harry replied.

Rus dipped his chin, turned and walked away.

Harry shut the door and Ronetta was still there.

"Follow me," she said.

He did and she took him to the room beyond the bathroom, which would be the smaller of the two bedrooms in the house.

When they entered, Harry saw lots of soft colors, dried flowers, an ivory iron bed, and he knew this was Lillian's room, which meant in all of these years, she hadn't taken over her parents' room.

He felt a sharp pain in his chest at learning this.

"You can change in here," Ronetta said after hanging his uniform in Lillian's closet.

He looked down at her but didn't get a chance to exchange a glance. She was walking out.

And he was apparently spending the night.

He had zero problems with that.

Ronetta was right about something else. Lillian didn't need him hanging around in his sheriff's uniform.

He opened his duffle, pawed through it and saw Rus's experience with packing a go bag for his work in the FBI hadn't been lost in the few years he'd been out of that game.

Harry quickly changed into faded jeans, a sweater, and he put on the warm socks Rus added to the bag.

Then he headed back out.

Lillian came right to him when he showed, wrapping her arms around his middle and pressing her front to his side. Her hold was tight.

This told Harry he'd been correct in not going out to have some time with his dogs, she didn't like she'd lost sight of him. He took careful note of that.

And Harry didn't know her enough to know if all this company was a balm, or if she felt some ingrained need to play hostess when she needed to focus on other things.

Like she had all night, Ronetta took charge of this too.

Once the mac and cheese was in the oven, and a salad was in the fridge, with an ease and grace that even in the circumstances Harry found fascinating, she made her point.

So with lots of hugging and "I'll check in tomorrow" and "Try to get some sleep" and "If you need anything, you know how to find me," (with every single one of them, even the men, sending Harry speculative or grateful looks) her friends left.

Then came more hugging and murmured words, and Ronetta and George left, with George leaving behind the Macallan and Ronetta leaving behind her instructions to Harry about when to take out the mac and cheese.

Harry made sure Lillian had a full glass of wine, he grabbed what remained of his whisky, and he took them to the couch.

She cuddled close immediately.

Harry welcomed it and pulled her closer.

"It's stupid," she whispered into his neck.

"What's stupid, baby?" he whispered into her hair.

"Me crying and carrying on. I knew it. I've known it for years. They would never have left me behind."

"It's still a shock," he noted.

"I guess," she mumbled. "But even if in the meantime I honed my talents with denial to a sharp edge, if I didn't know it before, I would have known it when you first came to visit me."

He gave her a gentle admonishing shake. "You're allowed to react, now, sixteen years ago, sixteen years from now."

She pulled her head off his shoulder and looked at him. "I love Amina and Saira and Momtaz and Bisma and Ayesha, but I need to watch something mindless tonight."

She was talking about the characters in their show.

"We'll find something," he muttered.

"Do you mind staying with me?" she asked shyly.

Harry rounded her jaw with his hand and dipped close. "Honey, if you want me here, I wouldn't be anywhere else."

Wet filled her eyes again, she sucked in an audible breath and said, "Thanks."

"Are you gonna be able to eat mac and cheese?" he asked.

"Ronnie's mac and cheese is the awesomest," she told him something he could already tell by sight and smell. "But I'm not sure how my stomach would respond to something heavy."

"Salad?"

She curled her lip.

He smiled at her. "Want me to make you a sandwich?"

"Are you going to let me get away with having wine for dinner?"

"No."

Her lips turned down and she gave in. "So I'll have a little mac and cheese and some salad."

"All right, sweetheart."

He reached for her remote.

She snuggled into his side.

He found a home improvement show, they settled in, and he got up when it was time to get the dish out of the oven. He made them both a plate. After they ate, Lillian insisted on helping him wash up.

This commenced them taking in two hours of watching people extol the virtues of shiplap and fight over the price of tile, during which Lillian fell dead asleep against him.

He let her sleep another half an hour before he clicked off the TV and lifted her again in his arms.

She roused on the way to her bedroom.

Ronetta had taken care of things in there too, with a light on one of the bedside tables giving a soft glow.

When he set Lillian on her feet beside her bed, she gazed around vaguely, and he asked quietly, "Where can I find some blankets for the couch?"

Her head tipped back, she reached out and took his hand.

"Please stay with me?" she requested.

He didn't fight it, there was no purpose.

She wanted him there, that was where he'd be.

And incidentally, that was where he preferred to be.

"You get ready for bed first. I'll shut down the house."

She nodded.

Harry kissed her forehead then moved out of the room.

He heard her shuffling around as he checked windows, turned out lights and locked the door, at the same time he texted Rus.

Dogs good?

Fine, Rus replied. Then, *Lillian hanging in there?*

Yeah, Harry told him. Then, *You're a good friend, Rus.*

You'd know, Rus returned.

Yeah, Rus was a good friend.

He went to the bedroom to retrieve his dopp kit and the pajama bottoms Rus packed and saw Lillian curled up in bed, her pretty green eyes to him.

She looked cute tucked up under her white quilt, her thick, amazing auburn hair stark against the white pillowcases.

Cute and vulnerable and sweet and expectant, a little scared, a lot sad.

And right then, his.

His.

On this thought, Harry felt something move inside him.

No, it was more like a shift.

And then it locked into place.

Sturdy, strong.

Immovable.

His.

"Be right back," he said, his tone gruff.

Gratitude saturated her features, and what room it left, there was the slightest hint of peace.

In this time, the worst of her life, Harry being there gave her that hint of peace.

His.

Her head moved on her pillow with her nod.

He took his kit to the bathroom, did his thing and returned to Lillian.

She flicked back the covers.

He accepted the invitation, folding in beside her and reaching beyond her to turn out the light.

When the room was dark, he settled in, pulled the covers up high over them, then drew Lillian into his body. When he got her there, he tangled them up.

They lay there, tucked tight, for some time, and Lillian didn't fade back into sleep.

"If you have troubles getting to sleep, I should have kept us on the couch," Harry belatedly muttered.

Lillian pressed closer. "Oh no, honey, this is much better."

She was very right. He was just pleased she agreed.

He still wanted her to go back to sleep.

Harry stroked her back.

And then she told him where her thoughts were, which would be the same as his.

"Who would do that to them?"

Harry buried his face in the top of her hair, wishing he could promise her he'd find who murdered her parents. Wishing he could actually do that so she'd have answers and justice.

But sixteen years had passed. Evidence assuredly had been lost. Witnesses definitely had forgotten. And the ultimate crime didn't happen on his patch.

In other words, as much as it fucked him, Harry couldn't make that promise.

What he could say was, "I'll do everything I can to find out."

"Are you sure you're okay being here? Are the dogs okay by themselves for the night?"

"They're with Rus. Which means they're with Maddie, and she's probably feeding them raw filet mignon and they won't want to come home."

She laughed softly, it sounded genuine but out of practice, like that evening had lasted ten years and she hadn't felt mirth during any of them.

They fell silent.

Then Lillian whispered, "I'm so sorry you have to go through this with me."

"Lilly," he said sharply.

At his tone, he felt her head move and her gaze on him through the dark.

When he got the last, he stated, "I feel like the luckiest man on the planet that I get to be here for you while you go through this."

He wasn't lying.

This was who he was.

And at this very moment in his life, this was where he was made to be.

She pushed her face in his throat and whispered, "My good guy."

"Damn straight," he murmured.

Her fingers curled spasmodically against the skin of his back, like she could clutch it.

Then they loosened and pressed tight.

"'Night, Harry," she said.

"'Night, Lilly," he replied.

It took a while, but eventually Harry felt her relax in his hold as sleep claimed her.

Then, as it claimed him and he gathered Lillian even closer, he thought he'd never know what kind of woman a black hat would win.

What he knew for certain was the men who wore the white hats got the best ones.

EIGHTEEN

But You Will

Harry

It was unsurprising when Harry woke up the next day, he saw Lillian's head on his shoulder, and he knew she was already awake.

It had been so long, he gave himself a selfish moment to savor the feel of waking up with a beautiful woman pressed to him in bed. To feel her softness. Smell her scent. Support her weight.

In the night, they'd moved only so he'd fallen to his back and she'd cuddled to his side, but their legs were still tangled, and he had his arm around her, she had hers resting along his stomach.

This was probably why she sensed him awake and tipped her head back.

"Hey," she said softly.

He turned to his side and into her.

"Hey," he replied.

"Sleep okay?" she queried.

He nodded.

"Worth me wasting breath to ask if you did?" he inquired.

"Not really," she mumbled.

"Honey," he whispered.

"Though, it's been an enjoyable few hours, watching the sunrise illuminate your chest," she quipped. "You're pretty built, Sheriff Moran."

The position of the sun was a problem.

He'd slept in.

Harry didn't mention that. "That's good, since I work hard at it."

"I can tell."

He smiled at her.

"You make plans with Ronetta today?" he asked after what he overheard in snippets the evening before.

"Yeah," she said. "I have a couple of clients coming into town this weekend. Ronnie's coming with me to do a little tidying at their places. Then Jenna needs help at one of her greenhouses, so we're going to go over there."

This was the Lillian he was getting to know. She preferred to be busy.

"Want me over tonight?" he asked.

She gave him a squeeze. "Yes, please."

"Then I'll be over tonight."

Her expression turned thoughtful. "Maybe I should go to you. Even pooches think that Daddy is better than any filet mignon."

"If you're cool with it, I can bring them here."

He knew the answer. She'd already invited them. He just didn't remind her why they didn't come.

But he was surprised at how her eyes lit up. It wasn't her usual blinding radiance, but he'd take it.

"That'd be awesome," she agreed.

He nestled her closer before he had to say, "I can tell by the position of the sun I'm running late, so I need to get going."

"It's good work is only a five-minute walk away, then," she replied.

This was something interesting to consider, and blindsiding him, Harry found himself considering it.

He didn't live far from the department. Fifteen minutes, if traffic was good. Twenty if it was tourist season or the equivalent of rush hour in Misted Pines.

But twenty to thirty extra minutes in any day was a boon.

Lillian took him out of his thoughts when she made a move, saying, "I'll go first in the bathroom so I can brush my teeth, then make you coffee."

He kept her where she was.

When her gaze landed on his, he ordered, "You stay here and try to sleep more."

"Harry," she said quietly. "I'll never get back to sleep, and I'm better when I've got something to do. Let me make you coffee. And toast? Maybe some eggs?"

Since he already knew this about her, he acquiesced. "Something in my stomach would be good."

She nodded, moved in for a swift kiss, then she rolled out of bed.

Harry didn't.

He used that time to fully take in her space. The wanton femininity of it. The muted floral pattern of the curtains at the window. The ornate gilt on the small vintage mirror on the wall. Not one but two dried flower arrangements on the white chest that served as her bedside table. The big, soft spray of the massive dry bouquet in its creamy pot on the windowsill. The elegant sweep of wispy white drapes that hung on the wall at the sides of the headboard to frame the bed.

The soft sheets.

The plethora of pillows.

Lillian made every inch of her space…*Lillian*.

It was her, so easy to look at, so pleasing to the eye, you missed how much work she put into making it what it was.

Harry was a guy. He didn't want to worry about taking off his boots or smoothing a bedspread just right.

But somehow he knew he'd break his back to keep what Lillian made *Lillian* just as it was supposed to be.

On this thought, he heard her call, "I'm out," and he knew the bathroom was free.

He rolled out of bed.

Rus hadn't only packed Harry's toothbrush, paste and floss, he packed his shampoo, shower wash, shaver and comb.

Definitely a deft hand with a go bag.

Harry took his uniform and an extra pair of skivvies to the bathroom, did his morning thing, dressed, left his bathroom stuff where it was, took his pajamas back to the duffle, shoved everything in, pinned on his badge and tucked his pens in his breast pocket, grabbed his boots and duffle and walked out.

He dumped his stuff by the couch and moved to the kitchen.

Lillian had a mug waiting for him by the coffeemaker.

He claimed it, took a sip and headed to where she was scrambling cheesy eggs at the stove. There was a plate with buttered toast at the ready.

"Looks good," he said.

"I like that you're here and I get to cook for you."

Harry accepted that velvet blow gladly.

She tipped her head back to look up at him. "But I'm going to lose my feminist card having said that, so don't tell anybody."

"Are you a feminist?" he asked.

She appeared confused. "Well...yeah."

He smiled at her. "Don't worry, sweetheart. I liked you at my place so I could cook for you too. All equal."

"*Shoo*," she joked.

He kissed the side of her head.

She let him, then took the skillet off the burner and scraped all the eggs on the plate by the toast.

"None for you?" he asked.

She handed him the plate and reached for her mug. "I'm just going to have toast."

He didn't argue, it wasn't the time. And anyway, Ronetta would soon be in the picture, the handoff complete, and she would look after their girl.

He took his food to the table. Lillian came with him.

He ate. She sipped coffee.

He used that time again to savor. Savor having someone close as you went about your morning. Savor sitting at a table eating while she sipped her coffee. Savor the fall of her hair on her shoulders and the way her cardigan had slipped off one.

But Harry knew this was something else for her, having him there.

And he savored that too.

She waited until he was done and washing it down with the last of his joe before she asked, "When can I get them back?"

He reached out and took her hand before he told her about the rest of the conversation he had with Lynda.

"The police have processed everything they need to process, and they'll be released within twenty-four to forty-eight hours. The minute we get word, I'll be dispatching Wade Dickerson, one of my best deputies, to go get them."

Wet trembled at the edges of her eyes, as did her voice, when she said, "Thanks, Harry."

"They're also investigating this."

"Okay."

"We'll be giving them everything we have, and we'll be investigating here."

She nodded.

"And I have Jason and Jesse Bohannan in Idaho. They'll be turning over rocks too."

Her brows slid up. "Cade Bohannan's boys?"

"Yes. They're private investigators. Sometimes, they work as consultants with my crew."

That last wasn't a lie, it was just that it wasn't the department that was going to pay their invoices this time.

"I hear about cold cases being solved these days," she fished.

His hold on her tightened. "I'm not going to encourage you to hope, I'm also not going to tell you there is no hope. What I'm going to say is that sixteen years puts law enforcement at a significant disadvantage, but that doesn't mean it's impossible."

She studied him a beat before she said, "Thank you for being honest."

"Always."

"Can I be needy for a second?" she requested.

He moved his hand so their fingers were laced together and chided, "You're not being needy, honey. This is as serious as shit can get. Just tell me what you need, and I'll do what I can to give it to you."

He watched her fight to control her emotion, before she said, "Okay, then, can you pack heavy and bring a ton of dog food? I don't…" She popped her head to the side like she got a sudden pain in her neck before she finished, "It's soothing, having you around."

"And you want to be home."

"I want to be in *our* home."

He knew what she meant.

"You didn't move into their room," he whispered.

"I haven't touched their room," she whispered back.

Goddamn it.

Honed her talents with denial.

Knowing this, Harry mentally pledged to keep an eye on her. She was like a prey animal, adept at hiding vulnerability.

"I'm here as long as you need me."

"Thanks, Harry." She was still whispering.

He got up and moved to her, savoring again while he watched her tilt her head back as he bent low to touch his mouth to hers.

"I gotta get going," he said, wishing he didn't, but important shit had to get done, and with the most important of it, they'd already lost sixteen years. They couldn't lose another day.

"Do you want me to make you another coffee in a travel mug?" Lillian offered.

"No, Polly will have an Aromacobana for me."

"Okay."

"I'll check in during the day."

"You don't have—"

"It'll be to look in on you, but mostly it'll be for me."

She studied him for another few beats then said, "Stuff happens to you that really sucks, at the same time stuff happens that's really awesome. It's confusing, but whatever. Thanks for being so awesome, Harry."

"I don't think you're getting this," he told her.

"What?" she asked.

He didn't answer.

He said, "But you will."

He gave her another kiss, then went to put on his boots. He grabbed his duffle. Returned for one last kiss and a "See you later."

He waited for her eyes to warm at his words, and only then did he walk out the door.

He didn't saunter to the station. In fact, it took effort to stop himself from jogging.

Polly met him at reception.

She handed him his coffee.

He handed her his duffle and requested, "Can you drop that in my office?"

"Sure thing, Harry. How is she?"

"Demolished, but getting on with it."

"That's Sonny and Avery," Polly mumbled and bustled away.

Harry went direct to Rus's desk, their eyes locked the short journey.

"Wanna take a field trip?" he asked his detective.

"Where we goin'?" Rus returned.

"I'm feeling a convo with Leland Dern."

Slowly, Rus smiled.

NINETEEN

Messed-up Ways

Harry

It was a haul to Dern's remote, tiny A-frame in the pines two counties away.

So when they parked outside of it, the first thing Harry did was pull out his phone and text Lillian.

Hanging in there?

"I think he likes you," Rus noted.

Harry looked to Rus, then he followed the direction of Rus's attention and saw, on the small front deck of the A-frame, Dern was now standing there, the barrel of a shotgun resting on his shoulder, in his other hand, the lead attached to the collar of a rottweiler.

Rus didn't like to carry a gun, but he'd been doing this for a while, so he didn't leave the station without one, at least one in his vehicle.

This meant when he got out of their cruiser, he swung his gun belt on.

Harry unsnapped the strap on his weapon before he got out, and he kept his hand resting on the butt as he waited for Rus to join him, and he kept it there as they started up the walk.

The dog barked and strained the leash.

Dern shouted, "You're trespassing!"

Both the men stopped five feet from the foot of the steps to the deck.

"Can have a chat here or can take you to the station. We don't have Uber in MP yet. Jerry's still running his taxi service, though, gotta say, it'd probably be a helluva fare to get back," Harry said.

"You got no cause to take me to the station," Dern retorted.

"How sure are you about that?" Harry asked.

His dog was strong and raring to take a bite out of Harry and Rus. So much so, he pulled Dern a good foot toward the edge of the deck before Dern again gained control over him.

"Not feeling you have control over that animal and are clearly using him as a threat. It would haunt me to my dying day if I had to shoot your dog, but I will, you don't put him inside," Harry warned. "And leave your shotgun in there when you do."

"Got nothin' to say to you," Dern returned.

"Okay then, let me tell you, we're looking at murder and you're indicated. So, now you know why we're here, you gonna stick with that?"

The color fled Dern's face.

Harry kept at him. "Now, I don't think you pulled any of the triggers, but I do think it wouldn't be tough to find my way to believing you were an accessory or aided and abetted, either before or after the fact..." he paused for effect, "on all three."

When Harry said "three," Dern started looking sick.

This, unfortunately, could mean anything.

Harry had cleaned house when he took over. That meant he gave the officers on staff the opportunity to pull their shit tight or get out. Some left. Some Harry knew were useless, so he found reasons to let them go.

Some of them, Harry also knew, were still close to Dern.

Therefore, Harry had no doubt Dern knew they were looking at his cases. He had no doubt Dern would know they'd find something. And he had no doubt, as a former cop, that the time Dern did in prison was probably not very fun.

He could just be tweaked about anything that even hinted at a road back there.

Or he could be involved in one—or three—murders, and he knew it.

"So I suggest you put your fucking dog in your house, leave the gun in there too, and have a chat with me and my detective," Harry concluded.

Dern, being Dern, wasted a good minute of their time by having a staring contest with Harry.

This pissed him off, because he'd felt his phone vibrate, so he knew Lillian had replied, and he didn't want to be standing there for an hour having a staring contest. He wanted to get this done so he could read and reply to it.

Dern finally turned and moved to the door of his house.

Harry pulled out his phone and checked his texts.

Yeah, honey. Want anything special for dinner? She asked.

We'll do that farro thing, he replied.

He was able to read her *OK* before Dern returned.

Harry shoved his phone back in his pocket.

Rus muttered, "She good?" under his breath.

Harry nodded, his attention on Dern.

Dern led with, "I see you're trumping up more charges like landing my ass in prison and taking my office wasn't enough for you."

He and Rus discussed this on the long ride out there.

They decided not to let the Rainier situation slip, because Rus's poking around might have been reported to Gerald and Michelle Dietrich, and they were already spooked enough, but they still had ties to MP. He didn't need them to vanish.

So they decided on Ballard and to leave Dern guessing about the rest.

"You wanna tell me why you didn't assign Muggsy Ballard's case to me or Roy?"

"Who?" Dern demanded.

"Roy, your other detective. Remember him?"

"No, I remember Roy. Of course I remember Roy," Dern spat. "What's the case?"

"Muggsy Ballard. Given name Clifford," Harry told him.

"No clue who that is," Dern replied.

"Suicide," Rus chimed in. "Who somehow got the shit kicked out of him before he allegedly blew his own brains out."

"And no GSR test was ordered," Harry added.

"And no friend or family member noted suicidal tendencies, ideations or depression," Rus put in. "Though the case file says they did."

"But the dead guy had a dream to get rich fast, and he dealt with some shady characters to do it," Harry said. "In fact, at the time he died, he was waiting for a deal to make good that he was sure would get him a house on the lake."

"Right, that loser," Dern muttered.

Both men on his walk shifted with annoyed agitation.

"Roy had a full plate," Dern stated. "He did the legwork, asked me to tie up loose ends and put it to bed. Only reason why I was the investigator on record."

This was news, and not how Harry remembered it.

It was also suspicious, and bottom line suspect police work. You investigated a case, you signed your fucking name to it.

But like Polly said, all sorts of shit went down at the station that they hid from Harry. The two camps were staunchly divided by then. Half the deputies didn't talk to the other half. Roy, for instance, on the regular avoided Harry like he was contagious.

"What loose ends did you tie up?" Rus asked.

"Fuck if I know," Dern replied. "That was years ago." His gaze narrowed on Harry. "But Roy was a good cop, one who didn't deserve to lose his job. Probably just had to look it over before I signed off."

Roy was a lazy ass who would never pass a physical, if Dern did what Harry did and made his deputies, even his investigators, pass one once a year.

This was eventually how Harry was able to get rid of him. The man refused to give up his daily burgers and malts from The Double

D, and as such, couldn't run around the high school track without doubling over halfway. Harry gave him an extra three months to get in some semblance of shape and try again, but he'd failed again.

Roy had gone so far as to take it to the union, arguing an investigator didn't need to pass a fitness exam.

Since it was policy, and he was given three months before the first exam, and another three months to try to pass the second, he'd lost his appeal.

That said, Dern was also a lazy ass, so it wouldn't surprise him at all if Dern didn't even read the report before he signed off on it and filed it away, leaving a mother and a bunch of friends with no answers as to the death of someone they cared about.

"Ballard's mother seemed to make herself pretty clear when she confronted you about the results of your investigation," Rus pointed out.

"Doesn't say a lot about her, she let her son get to that point," Dern retorted. "They act out like that when they know they got some blame. And at least *I*"—he shot a shitty look at Harry—"went to bat for my boy and didn't let some hysterical woman sway me into questioning his abilities."

Harry didn't rise to the bait.

"What else you got?" Dern sneered.

"We're not at liberty to discuss an active murder investigation," Harry told him, and Dern tried to hold the sneer, but the color was not returning to his face. "Though, I wouldn't go anywhere."

"You had something on me, you wouldn't waste a trip out here to *chat*," Dern spewed. "You'd haul me in. So I know you got dick."

Harry took one step forward, and talking low, his gaze fastened on his ex-boss, he said, "No, Leland. We've found countless cases of shoddy police work, which, fortunately for you, we can't do anything about. We've also got fifteen cases you need to be really, *really* worried about, because the first two we reopened put your ass in a sling. So I reckon the next thirteen aren't gonna go much better for you."

Harry indicated where he was standing with a flick of his hand and finished.

"Consider this me scratching at the last dregs of respect I had for you, not that there was much to begin with. Get in touch with your attorneys, because this is the most comfortable *chat* you're likely going to have with me."

"Fuck you, Moran," Dern clipped.

"Always a pleasure," Harry replied.

He turned, caught Rus's gaze, and they walked back to the cruiser.

They got in, and after Harry re-snapped the strap on his weapon, he pulled out his phone.

Are we good with wine? He sent to Lillian.

She and her women had gone through three bottles the night before.

He hit the button to fire up the engine and took one last look at Dern's small A-frame.

The man had been married twice, and one of the many pluses of living in a small town was that word got around about men like Dern, so most of the women in town knew to keep well away. This being why he only had the two ex-wives.

Dern had been found guilty of misappropriation of funds by a public official, and eight counts of gross misdemeanor. The judge had been kind in sentencing, but not with the fines. Dern had to pay forty-five grand in fines, on top of legal fees, all this on top of losing his employment.

Harry knew it cleaned him out. Dern leaving MP wasn't just about him tucking tail and running. He'd had to sell his house to cover his financial liabilities.

He was alone. Disgraced. And if not broke, close to it. Too old to be a cop, too publicly corrupt to run for sheriff in another county.

"Cautionary tale," Rus said.

"Too right," Harry agreed.

"That's the first time I met that guy, and from what I'd heard, I knew he was an ass, but, Jesus. He exceeded expectations."

"Yep," Harry agreed again.

"You knew him, your take on that?" Rus asked.

"He knows he left behind a load of dirt. He just doesn't know if we have enough to bury him with it." Rus made no response, so Harry queried, "Your take not knowing him?"

"Tweaked right the fuck out."

"Mm-hmm," Harry hummed.

His phone vibed and he looked down at it.

I'll get some in, came from Lillian.

I'll get some, he returned.

Then he put the cruiser in gear and reversed out of Dern's drive.

His phone vibed when he stopped to switch to drive.

I'm getting it or I'm forcing you to eat a brownie after dinner.

He smiled.

You win, he shot off before he switched gears and set them on their way.

"Shit works out in really fucking messed-up ways," Rus remarked.

Harry glanced at him. "What do you mean?"

"I came to town because a young woman was brutally murdered. I stayed in town because, regardless of that, it's a great place to live. And, not incidentally in the slightest, I fell in love with this beautiful woman you all kept hidden up in your forest on the side of a mountain. Something I should thank you all for, since it meant when I found her, I could claim her."

Harry chuckled.

Rus went on, "You met Lillian because her parents were murdered. And now you're smiling at some text on your phone, and I've never seen you smile at your phone. So like I said, shit works out in fucked-up ways."

"Not sure it does everywhere, but that seems to be the case in MP."

"Absolutely."

Yeah.

Absolutely.

Rus pulled out his own phone, probably to text Cin.

And Harry drove them back to Misted Pines.

TWENTY

Petty-ass Shit

Harry

When they got back to the station, Rus headed in Karen's direction. She was one of Harry's deputies, and when Harry wasn't partnering up with Rus, Rus partnered up with Karen.

They were going out to find Roy Farrell to ask a few questions.

Harry headed to his office to get whatever admin shit that was undoubtedly waiting for him out of the way so he could go with Rus later to meet the medical examiner.

On his way, Polly came out of her office and waylaid him.

"Got word from Idaho," she said. "As you asked, I sent Wade to go get Sonny and Avery. He left about an hour ago."

Harry took a breath into his nose and nodded.

"Also sent all we had on the Dietrich robbery to them. It was embarrassing, what little I sent, but I sent it," she continued.

Embarrassment for an administration that wasn't of their making was going to be the least of their concerns as they cleaned up Dern's mess.

"Thanks, Polly," he replied.

She moved into her office.

Harry went to his, sat behind his desk, and as he powered up his computer, he pulled out his phone and called Lillian.

"Hey," she greeted.

"Hey," he returned. "Where are you?"

"At Jenna's greenhouse."

"Is Ronetta with you?"

"Yeah, her and Trey." Her tone had turned cautious. "What's up?"

"They've released your parents, honey," he told her. "I need to know where Wade should take them when he gets back from Coeur d'Alene. He'll be back tomorrow."

"Oh my God, I didn't—" she started.

Harry heard Ronetta in the background. "What's happening?"

"Mom and Dad are coming home," Lillian told her. "We've been running around. I didn't think—"

"Hand me your phone, Lilly Bean," Ronetta ordered.

Lilly Bean.

Cute.

There was a handoff, and then Ronetta said, "Hello, Harry."

"Hey there, Ronetta."

"You can take Sonny and Av to Pullman's Mortuary Chapel. They're expecting them."

"They are?" Lillian asked in the background.

"It's all taken care of," Ronetta told her.

Harry then heard nothing but a faraway sobbing hiccup.

"Ronetta," he called tersely.

"Trey's got her, Harry," Ronetta said in his ear. "She' s a little choked up. I made some calls last night. It's mostly arranged. I didn't know we'd get them back this fast, so I didn't mention it to Lillian. She's pulling it together. I'll go over everything with her now."

"Right."

"Harry…" She said no more, but he sensed she was moving somewhere private and that didn't make him happy.

"Ronetta," he repeated sharply.

"Okay, we called Lillian's grandparents this morning."

Shit.

"Needless to say, they were upset," Ronetta continued. "Though, unlike Lillian, I sense not really surprised. That said, they've been hiding a few things from Lillian, probably because they wanted her to think they'd be there if she needed them."

This made Harry even less happy. "What are they hiding?"

"Her grandpa Rainier isn't getting around real great, at this point, essentially wheelchair bound, and he gets tired very quickly. Grandma Rainier is dealing with dementia. And her grandma Nowak's diabetes means she has to have dialysis several times a week."

Harry was mildly ticked. "That's a lot to hide."

"I agree, though I also understand," Ronetta replied. "Lillian has taken more than her fair share of licks. But this means they can't make it to Sonny and Av's services." A pause then, "I sense this also has to do with how devastated they are at the news. Even though they weren't surprised, I got the feeling they also couldn't hack it. Some of us, answers and closure help. Some of us, we wish we never knew. They're all in their eighties. This is a blow for anyone, but for them, it's not a memory you want to be making when you're at that time in your life."

He could understand that.

"Lillian told them she's going to go out there for Thanksgiving," Ronetta went on. "They'll do something to memorialize Sonny and Av then."

"How'd she handle all of that?" Harry asked.

"Well, she didn't do cartwheels, but I felt a little relief. Bearing your own grief is a heavy enough load. Looking after your elderly grandparents and adding theirs is too much. Not that our Lilly Bean wouldn't stand strong, just that would be asking a lot."

"Agreed," Harry grunted.

"Thanksgiving in Indiana with some time between the news and then will be a much better way to spend time together."

"Again, agreed," Harry replied.

"Hang on, she wants the phone," Ronetta said.

Another handoff and he had Lillian back.

"I'm okay," she assured, sounding a little husky, but other than that, like she said, okay. "I just…it gets overwhelming, having such good friends."

"I know, baby," he murmured.

"Did Ronetta tell you about my grandfolks?"

"Yeah, sweetheart. It's probably for the best, yes?"

"This might sound weird, but I don't think Mom or Dad would want them there. I don't think they'd even want me, Ronnie and George or Shane and Sherise there. They weren't about being sad. They were about…everything else other than that."

"I definitely got that from what everyone says about them."

"So I guess, in a way, this is working out as it should."

"Good way to look at it."

She put a line under that, asking, "What time will you be over tonight?"

"Gotta get the dogs, get some things packed. I'm aiming for six. Cool?"

"Definitely cool. See you then."

"Yeah, sweetheart. See you then."

They disconnected, and Harry was able to deal with some email before he heard a commotion out in the hall.

He got up and was heading to the door when he heard Polly say, "Now is not the time, Kimmy."

Shit.

Kimmy wasn't only the town's lovable, nosy curmudgeon, she was their local conspiracy theorist.

Reopening old cases, dead residents being found a state away, was candy to Kimmy.

He hit the door to see Polly barring Kimmy in the hall.

"It's okay, Polly."

And it was because this was part of his job. He never had time for it, but he always had to make time.

Polly looked over her shoulder at him.

"Harry," she said by way of protest.

He looked beyond her at Kimmy, who was wearing a green and

red plaid sweatshirt with a headband in her hair that had a puffy Christmas tree sticking out of the top.

The tree illuminated, and he knew this because right then, the tiny lights on it were lit.

In this getup, especially seeing someone wearing it in late September, most people would have trouble taking the woman seriously.

Since it felt like he'd known Kimmy Milford his entire life, and he'd never seen her in anything but some incarnation of that outfit, Harry didn't even blink.

"Kimmy, you have something to report?" Harry asked her.

Kimmy shot Polly a look and huffed by her. Harry moved out of the way so she could enter his office.

As he followed her, he was surprised to see she didn't settle into a seat so she could share in detail her ideas about what was happening and put every effort into pumping Harry for information she could disseminate freely, doing this adding her own spin to anything Harry would say (not that he was going to say a damned thing).

He was also surprised when she started it off by stating, "I'm not gonna take a lot of your time, Harry. 'Spect you got better things to do."

He stopped by the side of his desk and crossed his arms on his chest. "What you got for me, Kimmy?"

"I heard about the Rainiers. I kinda knew Av. She liked Christmas."

Kimmy ran the local holiday shop, and no surprise to anyone, her specialty was Christmas.

"Her girl likes it too," Kimmy went on. "She decorates some of the houses she looks after as well. I know her a lot better."

Harry had no doubt Lillian put on a show at Christmas.

"I'm just gonna say, Michelle Dietrich always kitted out their place at Christmastime," Kimmy reported.

That got Harry's attention.

Kimmy kept going.

"She was always buying new gear to shake it up. But that year, the Christmas before the Rainiers went missing, and everyone was talking about them maybe stealing a bunch of stuff before they did, Michelle asked to do Christmas on account. Told me she'd pay me, just invoice her. I never did that kind of thing, but she was a good customer. She did it up big for Halloween too. So I made an exception."

"And you invoiced her," Harry guessed.

"Yeah, and she didn't pay it. Like, *months*, Harry, she didn't pay. I sent reminder after reminder, then I started calling her. She got pissy at me. Told me she was just busy. She'd get to writing me a check. She couldn't believe how rude I was being when she'd always been such a loyal customer. Now, we're talkin' I delivered a truckload of Christmas to her house in November, and I don't do deliveries either, and the next May, she still owes me thousands of dollars. It wasn't like I demanded a check the next day, but just to say, I never sent Christmas on account to *anybody*. I did her a favor. She dragged her feet for six damned months."

"Did she eventually pay you?"

"Yeah, she came in, nose right up in the air, handed me the cash and told me, since I didn't value my customers, she was going to go to Spokane or Seattle to do her Christmas from then on. Woman never stepped foot in my shop again. Gotta say, it was a loss to my bottom line, but not my peace of mind."

Harry felt his pulse thump.

"She paid in cash?" Harry asked.

"Three-thousand-five-hundred-some-odd dollars in cash," Kimmy confirmed. "I keep my receipts, Harry. Would have to dig, may take some time, but you need it, bet I'd be able to find it."

"I don't know if I need it, Kimmy, but it won't hurt to have it," he told her.

"Then I'll get on it."

Harry narrowed his eyes on her. "That all you got?"

She jerked up her head. "What's concrete that I know. But you want rumor and innuendo?"

Fuck yeah, he wanted everything he could get on Gerald and Michelle Dietrich.

"Hit me," he invited.

Kimmy didn't hesitate.

"Gerald and Michelle made an art of in-your-face living large. They wanted everyone to know they were the haves, and the rest of us poor suckers were the have-nots. They both came from money, and I guess that crap is ingrained in people like that."

Not all of them, but some, definitely.

Kimmy continued, "So they weren't big on letting that reputation slip, even if, around that time, they were living large everywhere 'on account.' It wasn't only me they strung along, waiting to get paid. And it wasn't only me they threw attitude at for expecting money for goods and services rendered, pulling the 'loyal customer, how dare you' card. They sure did quiet that all down once they got stuff sorted, though. They burned a lot of bridges, but it wasn't that. It was like, they were suddenly being careful not to bring any attention to themselves."

It sucked, but the truth of it was, rumor and innuendo often uncovered the nasty shit.

As Kimmy just proved.

"And you're absolutely certain all of this happened around the time the Rainiers disappeared," Harry pushed.

She gave him one nod. "Absolutely. Wasn't long after, Michelle came in with her cash. Now, I know some time has passed, but we didn't have serial killers hanging around back then and no sex tape scandals were going down. It wasn't usual for people to get robbed and other people to go missing. So I remember."

That worked for him.

"You know who they had these accounts with?" Harry asked.

"I'll go back to my shop and write you a list. Then I'll get on that receipt."

"It'd be appreciated, Kimmy."

She gave him a salute that was so smart, it had the Christmas tree on top of her skull wobbling, then she trudged out.

Harry stared at the door, thinking insurance fraud was so fucking on the table.

The shit of it was—with what was reported missing, which meant the claim paid out was hundreds of thousands of dollars—

this would land the Dietrichs into the felony arena for fraud, and that carried prison time as well as fines. He'd seen people kill for much less.

But as far as he knew, that couple had their rough patch, got beyond it and carried on with their lives. They might have been quieter about it, but they did it.

So, if Lillian's parents lost their lives in that deal, whittling this down, the Dietrichs took those lives for the sole purpose of not only not wanting to sort their shit out in a legal way, but also not wanting to lose face.

And that was some petty-ass shit.

Harry stood still, having to take a second to calm himself down so he didn't do something man-stupid, like throwing his computer through the window.

When he got a lock on it, he sat down and called Rus.

First, he wanted to know where the fuck the Dietrichs were.

And second, he was allocating Rus not only Karen, but Sean, because once Kimmy gave him her list, they were going to run down everyone on it.

And then keep digging.

TWENTY-ONE

Under the Bus

Harry

Later that afternoon, Harry was standing outside the county morgue, waiting on Rus to show.

He was also texting the twins.

At the same time, he was structuring dual investigations in his head. One that went after answers for Muggsy Ballard's family, and the other that would hopefully find justice for Sonny, Avery and Lillian.

He had responsibility for an entire county. Though it wasn't anywhere near overpopulated, they had a lot of tourist traffic, and considering the state of human nature, once the Ray Andrews deal happened, that tourist traffic ratcheted up significantly, and on top of all that had gone down since, it hadn't diminished.

This was good for the town of Misted Pines. It was bad for law enforcement.

In other words, his deputies didn't twiddle their thumbs.

But he only had one investigator, outside himself, and that was normally all right, considering it was Rus, and he was literally one of the best in the business.

Now, though, Harry also had thirteen other cases they needed to run shit down on.

Wade had never made any murmurings of sitting the detective's exam, but Karen and Sean had.

Wade had been on staff the longest, and Harry trusted him with his life.

But he needed to carve out some time to encourage all of his deputies to look toward future advancement.

Harry could see it would be tough to think about that when the person you'd be working with was a decorated ex-FBI agent who had closing some seriously high-profile cases on his resume.

For some, it was in their nature to compete, and that worked for a department when the win was closing cases. However, you never wanted to set yourself up to lose, and being a newbie going up against the best would be daunting even for the most competitive person.

For others, imposter syndrome could take hold, and you had to be too on the ball when investigating to doubt your every move and decision.

But they were in the thick of it and would be for a while.

He needed to promote somebody.

This was his thought when he saw Rus walking up the sidewalk.

When Rus met him, Harry asked, "Find Roy?"

"Left work early with a migraine. No one answered at home."

Goddamn it.

"Dern called him," Harry bit off.

"Dern called him, and worse, Harry, the guy ghosted when he did."

"So we don't think this is hinky, it just fucking is," Harry summed it up.

Rus looked to the building behind Harry. "I sure hope Pfeiffer isn't involved in this shit."

Harry did too. As far as he knew, Dr. Theresa Pfeiffer, Fret County Medical Examiner, was a straight arrow.

But Harry sadly didn't know everything.

They went into the building and directly to Pfeiffer's office.

She was sitting at her desk, eating a sandwich.

Harry had no clue, with the smell of this place and the work that was done in it, how she could eat there, but again, he didn't know everything.

She looked up when she noticed them in the doorway. "Hey, boys. Come in."

They moved in, took seats across from her, and Harry set the Ballard file he'd brought with him on his lap.

Sandwich still in hand, she adjusted stuff on her desk until she pulled out her own file. She flicked it open and scanned it.

"Clifford Ballard, right?" she asked.

"Yeah. Suicide. But—" That was as far as Harry got before Theresa's gaze shot to his.

"Suicide?" she asked.

Harry looked to Rus to see Rus's eyes on him.

He turned back to Theresa. "Suicide."

"I didn't determine suicide. I determined suspected homicide. *Strongly* suspected homicide." She closed the file, picked it up and tossed it several inches so it plopped in front of Harry. "There was trace GSR on him, but only because the man was shot. No significant GSR on his hand that would indicate he pulled the trigger. We all know how GSR works, so that doesn't mean he didn't. But with the trace GSR, either he was around another gun or guns that were discharged, or the gun was not in his hand when the bullet went into his brain."

Harry felt chills creep over his skin as he reached for the file.

He opened it leaning toward Rus so they both could read it.

But he didn't have to read it. He could see immediately that it wasn't what they had in their file.

Harry took his department's file and tossed it in front of her.

"Our report reads differently," he told her.

She kept hold on his gaze a beat before she opened it.

It didn't take long before her face got red. Very red. *Pissed* red. Fuck.

"That's my signature. That even looks like my writing," she

stated, attention still on the file. It lifted to Harry. "But that is not my report."

She tossed her sandwich on some waxed paper on her desk, brushed her hands together and sat back angrily.

"Honestly, when I pulled this, had a look at it and remembered the case, I got annoyed because I hadn't heard anything was happening with it," she said. "But then I remembered Roy was looking into it, and that man could barely find his shoelaces, so it didn't surprise me he couldn't find a murderer."

"So you remember Roy. Did Dern have anything to do with this case?" Harry asked.

She shook her head. "I vaguely remember thinking that poor soul was in trouble because you weren't on rotation to catch his case, rather than Roy, but by that time, Dern had so divorced himself from any real police work, I don't know if I'd seen him in my morgue for years."

"So all you remember is Roy," Harry pushed.

"All I remember is Roy, Harry," she replied. "But it was years ago. Still, I can say with some certainty that I didn't deal at all with Dern on this case. I sent my report to Roy, then I had other bodies to deal with, and I'm afraid to say, I didn't think about it much, outside feeling sad that obviously Roy hadn't solved it, since I heard nothing else about it."

She returned her attention to the file in front of her, bent close to it, then opened some drawers, rummaging through them until she found a magnifying glass.

She took it to the report, inspecting it closely in a variety of places, and her face got red again.

She tossed the magnifying glass on the report testily and stated, "That signature has been traced. You'd have to get an expert's opinion, but there's a carefulness to it that isn't mine and looking closely at it, you can see the outline of my signature underneath. In fact, there's a carefulness to all the writing. Also, you can see some Wite-Out marks. Someone emptied a copy of another report with Wite-Out, forged this one and traced my signature over the top."

"Can I?" Harry asked.

She flung an irritable hand to the file in front of her. Harry gave the one he had to Rus and grabbed theirs and the magnifying glass.

Again, he leaned to the side so Rus could follow with him.

The base form was over-copied in the first place.

But with the glass it was easy to see small breaks in lines and ghosts of impressions of words that were there before, which the naked eye wouldn't see or would identify as a smudge or a bad copy of the original form.

"Son of a bitch," Rus muttered.

Harry yanked out his phone and made a call.

"You got me," Polly answered.

"Polly, send two deputies to sit on Roy Farrell's place. Inconspicuous. I don't want them made, and Roy might be able to make them. The minute he comes home or there's any sign of life in his house, they go in and get him. I want him at the station as soon as we can find his ass."

"You got it," she said.

"Polly," he called before she hung up.

"Yeah, Harry?"

"Also put a BOLO out on that asshole."

"You got that too."

"And while we're ratcheting shit up, I want regular drive-bys, day and night, at the Dietrichs' home and office."

"Got that as well."

She hesitated, and when Harry said no more, she hung up.

Harry shoved his phone back in his pocket and returned to Theresa.

"Can we have a copy of the actual report?" he gritted.

"My freaking pleasure," she stated, rising from her chair.

He handed it to her, and she stormed out.

Harry turned to Rus. "I don't think Dern knew about this. This was Roy."

"This was Roy," Rus agreed. "Roy taking advantage of a chief officer who didn't pay dick attention."

"At the same time punting it to him so if anyone asked questions, Dern was the investigator on record."

"Threw his buddy right under the bus."

Harry wanted to find some pleasure in the fact that one of Dern's loyal soldiers set him up like that, but he couldn't.

Because now he also had a seven-year-old murder on his hands, and he had to find some way to break it to Muggsy Ballard's mother that his department had wholly failed her and her son in the sense that there was an active cover-up of his murder which no one had noticed until now.

"Shit," Harry muttered.

"Yeah," Rus sighed. "Fuckin' *shit*."

TWENTY-TWO

Time Portal

Harry

R us dropped him at home so Harry could leave his cruiser at the station and drive his truck to Lillian's.

Rus was then going to his place to get the dogs and bring them back into town.

Harry had told him he didn't have to drive all the way out to Bonner Mountain and back in when Harry could fetch his pups, but Rus insisted.

"With all this shit swirling, your time is gonna be limited, and whatever free time you got, you need for Lillian. I can bring the dogs in, and then Maddie and I can have dinner at the Double D."

He and Lillian were both getting an education on the loyalty they'd earned, and Harry was grateful for it.

Now, he'd packed heavy, had enough dog food in his truck to last weeks, the dogs had their own go bag of rawhides and toys, but before he took off for Lillian's, he hit go on a number he hadn't touched in years.

Dern didn't answer, it went to voicemail.

Not a surprise when he would've seen Harry's name come up on his screen.

But Harry didn't hesitate to leave a message.

"Weird how Roy Farrell developed a migraine to take him home from work today, then he didn't actually go home. But just so you know, we discovered the ME's report on Clifford Ballard was falsified. Theresa ruled it a homicide, not a suicide. You're the investigator on record, Leland. You signed off on a doctored file. Farrell fucked you. He positioned you real good, then he *fucked you hard*. Good for you that you'd take your boys' backs, but they're leaving you swinging. Think on that."

He ended the call, and carrying the last bag from his house, the one with his pups' water and food bowls, Harry headed out to his truck.

He was halfway back to town when his dash told him he had a call from Jesse.

He found a place to swing in so he could give it the attention it deserved, parked in a spot at the back of the lot at the grocery store, and he took the call.

"Jesse," he greeted.

"Harry, you got time?"

Never.

For this, though, absolutely.

"Yeah."

"Right. We did our thing in LA. Jace said he briefed you on that?"

"Briefly," Harry said.

"Well, nothing strange. They had reasons to find the quiet life. All we got on them there was all we'd get if we asked around MP. Good folk. Solid folk. Likeable folk. They were remembered and there was worry they seemed to drop off the face of the earth, since they'd been keeping in touch. Particularly Avery. Apparently, the woman wrote a helluvan entertaining Christmas letter."

Everything...absolutely everything he'd learned about the Rainiers stated clear they were good, kind, loving, hardworking, decent people.

And they ended up in an unmarked grave on the side of a mountain a state away.

Fuck him.

"They had valid concerns," Harry muttered what they now knew too well.

"When we got to Idaho," Jesse continued, "we worked on the idea that it was Sonny and Avery's destination. That they were going to report what they knew here, out of Washington State, to law enforcement that was enough removed, Leland Dern might not brush shoulders with them at a local convention."

"Safe assumption," Harry murmured.

"So we figured they got a hotel room."

"Right."

"Fortunately, not only was Avery a knockout, Sonny wasn't tough to look at either. Found a woman who remembered Sonny."

Fucking hell.

"No shit?" Harry asked.

"Part was he was good-looking. Part was, her dad remembered both of them. They run a mom-and-pop motel, a lot like our Blue Mountain. Clean, the proprietors give a shit, but not expensive. The woman we talked to was next gen, but she worked there back then, remembered her father talking about it. Had to wait until she could get in touch with him. They retired. Went down to New Mexico."

"Okay," Harry said.

"She got in touch with him, he got in touch with us. And this dude still remembered Sonny and Avery."

Fuck, these guys were good.

"What'd he say?" Harry asked.

"We hit the mother lode, Harry."

Harry closed his eyes as relief, and the first flicker of hope surged through him.

He opened them and urged, "Hit me with it."

"He said he wasn't surprised someone was poking around, because when his daughter phoned him, and he tuned into the local Coeur d'Alene news and saw two bodies were found, he and his wife were debating calling the cops due to remembering Sonny and Avery."

They made an impression. An impression that lasted sixteen years and was the first thought these people had when bodies were found.

The hallmark of a good witness statement.

Harry stared unseeing at the parking lot he was in, and he listened hard.

"The dude said they were memorable first because they looked straight out of Hollywood. He said he'd never seen such a good-looking couple. After he got over that, he noticed they were acting odd. Not like they were on the run, more like they were *being chased*."

"Fuck," Harry whispered.

"Yeah," Jess agreed. "Then, they made the request to check out very early, and asked if they could just leave their key in the room so they didn't have to disturb anybody with checkout. Onward from this, feeling tweaked about their demeanor, that night, this guy recalls seeing a man in a car in his parking lot, parked across the lot from their room. He was just sitting there, and not a patron, so this guy went out to ask him what he was doing. The minute the hotel owner started to approach, the man in the car put his headlights on and drove away. Due to the headlights, the owner didn't get a good look at his face."

"What'd you get on this car and this guy?"

"Only that it was for sure a white male, dark hair, beard, youngish. Twenties, maybe early thirties at a stretch. And the car had Washington plates. It was a Ford sedan, he thinks dark blue or black, but that was all he got before the guy was gone."

"He remember any digits on that plate?"

"Unfortunately, no."

"Still puts someone from around here, there," Harry said.

"Yeah, it does. But that isn't all."

Harry felt his blood start to heat, the good kind of that shit happening.

The kind you got when all leads seemed to have run dry, and then suddenly a window opened and you had your pick of them.

Jesse continued, "This dude told us he was surprised when the maid went in the next day, and they hadn't checked out. All of their belongings were still there. They didn't come back that day or check out the next, and considering this was all fishy, he reported it to the cops. But at the time, the cops had no interest in it. He did, and thought something was off, so he carefully packed their belongings and put them in storage."

Harry felt his blood pressure spike, again, the good kind of that happening.

"Where they've remained for sixteen years," Jesse concluded.

"Jesus Christ, Jess," Harry swore, fighting back the urge to punch his roof in elation.

"I know, man. The daughter took us back there, her dad was on FaceTime, helped us dig them out from under a decade and a half of familial and business debris. We called the cops, met Sergeant Westwood. She and her team came and got the stuff. But she let us stick around when they opened those cases. In Avery's suitcase there were two journals. The entries aren't extensive until the last few weeks of their lives. We didn't get to read them, but thanks to you telling her we're on your team, Westwood's letting us come in and have a look after the evidence is processed. We got a one o'clock appointment with her tomorrow. Still, she said she's gonna keep you in the know, so you might hear from her before you hear from us."

He'd be a little later to Lillian's, because Westwood was his next call.

"You see anything while she was flipping through?"

"This won't surprise you, but I'd keep a close eye on the Dietrichs. Saw that name more than a few times. I'd also expect a call from the Feds. This crosses state lines. Westwood doesn't have a dick to swing, but she's easily read as not that kind of cop. She doesn't give a shit sixteen years have gone by. She's pissed as fuck someone buried bodies in her beautiful town, and even more pissed they killed them there. She'd call in the Canadian Mounties if she thought they'd help her nail whoever did this."

That was the impression he got from Westwood.

"Wade's probably there by now. He's bringing back the remains," Harry told him.

"We know. He gave us a call. We're having dinner tonight."

"Lillian wants her parents back, but I want Wade to go with you when you look at what's in those suitcases and those journals."

"You want me to relay that, or are you gonna do it?"

"I'll text him. First, I gotta call Westwood."

"Great."

He had one more question, for the investigation, and for Lillian.

"This hotel keep registration records?"

"The daughter dug those out too and handed them over. The dad said they were there one night."

More than likely, the night they died.

So at least Lillian would have a date to put on a gravestone.

"I'm gonna pay you, but even so, I owe you both one," Harry stated.

"Harry, I heard about the cookies. You don't owe us dick."

Those fucking cookies.

Harry had no chance to respond, Jess hung up on him.

Harry immediately called Lynda.

"Figured I'd hear from you," she said as greeting.

"Jess reported in."

"I was about ten minutes from calling you. Lab's still processing. Once I get my hands on them, if it takes me two weeks, I'm going to read every word in those journals. But we're on hold. Feds are sending some guys. There's gonna be the usual jockeying that masks itself as coordinating. But I'll cut through that crap as fast as I can and get this shit rolling."

"Appreciated, Lynda. And I'd appreciate it if my deputy who's there to get Sonny and Avery could sit in when you let Jess and Jace look at those journals."

"Is he hot too? Because I'm married, and those boys are too young for me, but still, I've got urges that are detrimental to my continued holy matrimony."

If Misted Pines did a bachelor auction for the animal rescue, they'd be funded indefinitely if Jason and Jesse participated.

"Bohannan stock is special," Harry replied.

"Yeah. I've heard of their dad. Anyone with a badge has heard of their dad. Then again, you all have been having some pretty public problems for a few years, and he was dragged into it, and he isn't hard on the eyes either, so I might have paid a bit more attention than I normally would, and normally I'd be all kinds of interested."

"Time to scratch a vacation to Misted Pines on your calendar."

"Thanks, no. No offense, but people get dead there in ugly ways, and your people even get dead *here* in ugly ways."

He couldn't argue that.

"One way or another, Harry," she continued, "you're in this. Best I can, I'll treat this like your desk is next to mine. First up, your man will come back with copies of those journals."

"Then I'll scratch it on my calendar to drive out there and buy you a steak."

"That's a date I'll keep."

"Great, Lynda, but I gotta give full disclosure here. I'll be overseeing, but I'm romantically involved with Sonny and Avery Rainier's daughter. I'm gonna have to punt this to my detective, Rus Lazarus. He'll be lead on what comes out of Misted Pines."

No nonsense Sergeant Lynda Westwood said only, "You're heard. Anything else?"

"Nope."

"Right then. Later, Harry."

"Later, Lynda."

He shot a text off to Wade before he swung back on the road on his way to Lillian's house.

He debated what to tell her.

The existence of her parents' things was going to be a big deal. The journals, even bigger. Just that they were there to be had, not getting into the fact that they've opened up a time portal to sixteen years in the past.

But depending on what light they shed, she wouldn't get them back, more than likely, until the investigation was closed, and maybe not even then.

That said, that morning they had nothing but two bodies and theories, and now they had physical evidence and witnesses.

So it messed with his head to give her hope when this all might lead to nothing.

But Harry was going to tell her.

TWENTY-THREE

You're You

Lillian

When I heard Harry pull up in my drive, I hustled out the side door to the garage and hit the garage door opener.

What I always thought was hilariously Americana, my house was tiny, and my garage was nearly as big as my house. Set back on the lot, it was two-car with a massive storage room and a laundry room at the back.

Easy for Harry to park his truck next to my Subaru, even if he had one of those big duallies.

When he got out, he came right around to me, tugged me into his arms and dropped a sweet, light kiss on my lips.

I'd had Ronetta all day, Trey and Jenna part of it, texts and phone calls from people I cared about telling me I was in their thoughts.

But until right then, standing in Harry's arms, I'd been riding an undercurrent of feeling everything was wrong. The air smelled wrong, the sky looked wrong, food tasted wrong.

And now everything felt right.

"What can I help bring in?" I asked.

He let me go (alas), turned and opened his passenger side door. He handed me a couple of carrier bags.

He then shifted to the back door and hefted two thirty-pound bags of dog food on his shoulder.

He'd totally earned all the many swells and plains of muscles in his chest (and arms, I couldn't forget those arms).

"I'll leave one of these out here. If you could get water sorted for them,"—he tipped his head toward what I was holding—"their bowls are in there, that'd be good."

"Gotcha," I replied and went in.

While I was unpacking the dog stuff, Harry came in and out, leaving one of the sacks of dog food, then returning with his duffle and a number of hangers covered in clear plastic containing his uniforms draped over his shoulder.

He stopped and looked down at the new doggie station I'd created. There were three brown and cream checked mats that had been personalized, one said LUCY, another LINUS and the last SMOKEY. Now, all those mats had stainless steel bowls filled with water on them.

Slowly, Harry turned to look at me.

"I wanted them to know they're welcome," I explained.

A number of things happened in my body when his expression changed. I'd seen a version of that look on his face a lot the night before, and that morning, but there was an added nuance that, yes, even where I was right then in my life, made my nipples bead.

And he hadn't seen the dog beds I'd bought yet.

"How did you get them personalized in a day?" he asked.

"Jenna does that in house. I called her this morning, she had them ready by the time we swung by this afternoon."

Still carrying his duffle and uniforms, he came to me, and I got another light kiss.

He then started across the room but stopped dead again when he saw the three big, fleecy, pillowy beds, which were the new décor in the living room.

His neck twisted so he could look at me, and that expression on his face was about a million times stronger.

"Did you also buy filet mignon?" he asked.

"I knew I forgot something," I joked.

He smiled then returned on his journey to my bedroom.

I followed him.

He dropped the duffle.

I opened the door to my closet where there was now a couple of feet of extra space, and several free hangers.

"You can put your uniforms there," I told him.

Harry did that.

When he did, I stated, "Okay, this is also not stalkery euw. While you're with me, you're more than welcome to live out of your duffle bag. But…" I moved to my dresser and opened the second drawer, the one I'd emptied earlier. "You can also unpack so you'll feel more at home. No pressure," I said hurriedly. "I'm not making any statements or being weird or—"

I stopped talking when Harry walked up to me and put his fingers to my lips.

"You're tidy," he said quietly, dropping his hand. "I get it. You don't want my shit all over the floor."

This was very true. I was very tidy.

And okay, this was a big thing for me, especially now, when I needed my space like I needed my space.

But I also needed Harry.

Though, it was more, since I didn't need Harry to *think* I was needy, latching on to him and sending what we were exploring into the stratosphere way too soon because I was raw and emotional and, well…*needy*.

I bit my lip.

"I can unpack, Lillian, it isn't a big deal," he said.

I studied him closely. "You sure?"

"Honey."

That was all he said.

I had a feeling he thought that word communicated more than it actually did, so regrettably, I had to ask him what he thought it communicated.

"Is that confirmation you're sure?"

"Is there something here beyond the something we both know all too well is happening here?" he asked in return.

Hunh?

"I'm not following," I admitted.

"Lillian, we both know why I'm here. We both also know I need to be here how you need me to be here. So if you need things a certain way, there isn't anything to be nervous about. So, is there something else that's making you nervous?"

I was seeing why he was so good at what he did for a living.

I was also reminded how new we were, because we hadn't gotten to the point of talking about things like this.

Or, I hadn't.

"I dated someone not too long ago. We were together for a while. I was ready for more. He'd been burned pretty bad by someone else, and he wasn't. I think I got too pushy and that's when things ended."

"How long were you together?"

"A year and a half."

His face softened. "That's not too long to start to get pushy, sweetheart."

"I didn't think so," I mumbled.

"Who was it?"

My body gave a slight jerk, because he'd told me he was friends with Doc Riggs.

And Doc Riggs shared something important in common with my ex-boyfriend.

"Stormy Tennant," I told him.

"Ah," he replied.

But yeah.

Ah.

Stormy had totally been screwed over by a woman, as had Doc Riggs, seeing as it was the same woman who screwed them both over.

They each got something really good out of it. But even so, what she did was unconscionable.

"I liked him a lot." And thought I'd loved him, but I was reconsidering that these days. "But I got it."

"Yeah," Harry agreed. "Though I feel for him about why he'd be skittish to commit, and it led him to doing something stupid, like letting a fantastic woman slip through his fingers. But I'm feeling selfish, so I'm glad he did."

Right.

Time to kiss him and do it hard.

I threw myself at him and did just that.

We were still doing it when my doorbell rang.

"That's probably Rus with the dogs," he muttered against my lips.

That would be the only thing I'd be glad forced us to stop necking. Animals made a home.

I totally needed to hit the rescue.

Harry took my hand, led me to the front door, and he was right. He opened it and a very handsome man I knew was the FBI guy who came to deal with the Brittanie Iverson murder and then stayed, stood there next to Lucinda Bonner's adorable daughter.

The girl had hold of Lucy's leash. The man had Smokey's and Linus's.

All three of the dogs were straining toward their daddy.

"Come in," Harry invited as he shuffled us out of the way.

A doggie fracas ensued as they did, leashes were unclipped, dogs got excited, pets and ear rubs were extended, Harry got them under control, and then finally they settled down enough to put noses to the ground and suss out their new space.

"Right." Harry slid his arm around my shoulders. "Rus, Maddie, this is Lillian. Lillian, this is my friend Rus and his stepdaughter, Madden."

"We don't call me that, Harry," Maddie informed him. "Rus is my second dad, and I'm his second daughter." She looked to me. "On account he has another one older than me. But she and me are just sisters even though we've got different mothers..." A pause then, "And fathers."

"I like that way of looking at it," I told her.

I liked more the consummately satisfied and doting expression Rus had on his face when his "second daughter" said all of this.

"Sabrina, my sister, is graduating college next year and she's gonna move to Misted Pines," Maddie went on to share. "She says she likes the fresh air and all the wildflowers we get. But mostly she likes Jason Bohannan."

"Well, those are all good reasons, on top of having her dad close, and her sister."

I clamped my mouth shut after I said that. The feel of the room changed, Harry's arm tightened, and I watched Maddie's face turn sad.

And being a kid, she just went for it.

"Rus told me about your mom and dad. I'm sorry."

"Thanks, honey," I mumbled.

"I had another sister once," she announced. "She didn't have the same mom and dad as me either. Her name was Brittanie."

I stiffened at learning she thought of that poor murdered woman as her sister and just how a little kid might process that kind of loss. I was a big kid, and I was struggling.

Maddie again didn't hesitate to put it out there.

"We put her ashes in the river, and she floated away. I'd *so* rather have Brittanie around so I could do her hair like she used to let me do, but it felt good, watching her float away like that. I don't know why, and Mom says I shouldn't question it, just let it feel good. And until I watched her float away, knowing she was gone, I didn't feel good at all. So I decided to do that. Just let it feel good, I mean."

"It works that way, I guess," I replied.

"Well, I hope you feel better when you, uh…do whatever you're gonna do with your mom and dad."

"I hope so too."

Harry butted in. "Maddie, can you help Lillian get the dogs sorted while I talk to Rus outside for a bit?"

Maddie looked up at him. "Sure, Harry."

Harry's arm gave me a squeeze, so I looked up at him too, but I got a kiss on my nose and a whispered, "Be right back, baby."

I loved it when he said that.

It wasn't hard to figure out why. It was because I knew he'd actually be back, and two people I cared about left and never returned.

But I didn't have it in me to analyze this too much. Not then.

I just rested in the knowledge I knew he'd be back.

Though, what Maddie said was food for thought, because it felt good, and truthfully, there was no reason to question it.

The men went out, leaving me with Maddie.

"I don't think the dogs need much sorting," Maddie remarked.

I gazed around.

Smokey was drinking out of the dish on Lucy's mat. Lucy was lying on one of the new dog beds. Linus was up on the sectional, exploring.

"They do this a lot, you know," Maddie said.

I turned to her, thinking she was referring to the dogs. "Do what?"

"Rus and Harry 'talking outside.' They do that a lot."

I bet they did.

"Do you want a drink? I also have snacks," I offered.

She shook her head then came closer to me when Smokey came to me, sat down and rested his muscled bulk against my leg.

She petted Smokey's head. "Rus and me are having burgers and shakes at the Double D." She grinned up at me. "I get a lot of father and daughter nights, seeing as I have two dads."

I hid the feeling that someone had punched me in the heart at the reminder I'd never again share a burger and a shake with my dad (or my mom) and said, "That's awesome."

She frowned. "I'm not being careful with you like Rus told me to."

"You're fine, honey," I assured quickly. "It's the worst, but we both know that. You can be super, extra careful, and it's still going to hurt for a while."

"It *is* the worst," she agreed. "I was real glad Rus was around when it happened to us. I got him, but Mom got him too. She loved Brittanie like me."

"I'm understanding that," I told her, my thoughts moving to Harry.

She smiled. "I know. I heard Mom talking to Gram. Everybody's real happy Harry found his good girl. Like, Harry's the best guy in town, outside my dad, and Rus, and my uncle Porter, and maybe the Bohannan twins, oh, also Mr. Bohanan, and I can't forget Mr. Riggs."

I grinned at her as her list kept getting longer.

She finally ended it. "So Harry'd need to find the best girl. And everyone in town thinks you're her."

That didn't feel like a punch in the heart.

It felt like the warmth of a blanket.

"Wow, thanks," I replied.

"Smokey thinks so too," she said.

I looked down at Smokey, and like he felt my attention, he panted up at me.

I gave him deeper scratches behind his ear.

He licked my wrist.

The door opened and Harry came in, but Rus just swung his torso in.

"Ready to eat, kid?" he asked Maddie.

"Yeah," she replied, then she surprised me by bopping into my space and giving me a quick hug.

She let me go and bopped toward the door, but she left me feeling better. Not as right as I felt when I was in Harry's arms, but kids had superpowers they didn't know they had. And Maddie just used hers on me.

"Nice to meet you, Lillian," Rus said.

"Thanks for looking after the dogs and bringing them over. And enjoy your Double D," I returned.

"No problem and will do."

Maddie had completed the hug she gave Harry and waved at me as Rus made room for her to walk out the door.

Harry closed it on them.

"She's a sweet kid," I observed.

"The best," he replied and came to me.

When he did, all the dogs came to both of us and bustled around.

But Harry was only about me. I knew this when he slid his arms around me, not losing contact with my gaze.

Yeah, there it was again.

I was grounded. I was safe. I was with a good man.

This was right.

"Wanna start dinner?" I asked.

"I have something to share first," he told me.

Uh-oh.

"Is it something bad?" I asked hesitantly.

"No. It's something we hope will be really good."

Oh my God.

He said "we."

Like police "we?"

"What?"

He let me go but again took my hand, and this time he led me to the couch. He sat us down, doing this close. The dogs continued to bustle around, and Harry gave some distracted head strokes, but again, his attention didn't leave me.

Then he told me about suitcases and journals and a motel owner who remembered my parents.

He finished with, "I don't want to get your hopes up. But when an ongoing crime crosses state lines, the FBI is automatically called in. This means you have the Fret County Sheriff's Department, Coeur d'Alene Police and the FBI looking into it. We had very little to go on, Lilly. We now have something to follow. Your mom's journals could be key. I was very worried how this investigation would go, honey. I'm feeling a fuck ton better about it now."

"Mom journaled," I whispered.

"Yeah," he said.

"For as long as I knew. She told me she liked to 'get it all down, even if it's the bad stuff, doll baby, get it out, put it away, but mostly if it's the good.' That's what she'd say."

Harry took my hand in both of his, and I was so wound up in the knowledge there were suitcases, journals in my mom's hand, journals sharing her thoughts, it took me a bit to realize he was saying nothing but playing with my fingers.

"Harry?" I called.

My breath caught when his brown eyes came to mine.

They were burning.

"I need to find these fucks for you," he said, his deep voice abrasive, rubbing over my skin like sandpaper.

Even so, that strength of feeling soothed some rough spots.

I caught his hands in both of mine.

"You can only do what you can do," I said quietly.

"I have to withdraw from actively being involved in this investigation. I'm with you. I'm not impartial. It could cause problems down the line."

Oh, my good guy.

"It's okay. I get it. You have to do what's right," I reminded him. "You're you. That's what you do."

"We've got something now, Lilly, and we're gonna follow it until it leads to answers for you."

"Honestly, honey, you don't have to try to make me feel better by making promises you're worried you can't keep."

His fingers tightened around mine. "We're gonna follow it until it leads to answers, Lillian."

"Okay, baby," I whispered.

He stared at me, the heat in his eyes warming my heart.

Then I watched as he wrestled the depth of his emotion under control, the heat turned to a warm glow, and he said, "Let's make dinner."

I smiled, leaned in for a kiss, pulled back and agreed, "Let's make dinner."

TWENTY-FOUR

The Deep Stuff

Lillian

"So, Stormy. Anyone else?" Harry asked.

We were lying in the dark in my bed, limbs entangled, dogs ignoring their new beds seeing as I knew Smokey lay on the rug beside me, and Lucy and Linus were on the other side by Harry.

Harry liked the salmon farro veggie bowls with spicy ginger, sesame and soy sauce we made (shocker: so did I). While we ate, and after we cleaned up, we watched some cooking shows.

But we went to bed early, even earlier than I would normally, and I was usually in bed with a book by nine.

I knew why now.

We were chatting in the dark about deeper stuff we needed to know, in a safe space for both of us (or at least I hoped Harry thought it was safe).

And Harry was affecting a maneuver to take my mind off other things before I fell asleep.

It wouldn't work, but the thought was sweet.

"There was a lot of dating," I told him. "I met someone really nice who I liked a lot once, but he was here on a fishing trip. He lives in Oregon. We did the long-distance thing for nearly a year. Then he met someone closer to home."

"And he ended it?"

It was so lovely how his question sounded entirely disbelieving, like someone ending things with me was unfathomable to him.

Oh yes, that was very lovely.

"No, he gave me an ultimatum. Either I move there, or he moves on. I wasn't going to move there…" I blew out a breath, "for obvious reasons."

See?

No matter what he tried, my mind would circle back to my parents.

"He couldn't move?" Harry pulled things back on target.

"He could. He was a systems engineer. He worked remote for a company based in San Francisco. He could live anywhere. But he liked where he lived, I liked where I lived, I wasn't going to leave if my parents might come back, and he exposed the dick within by not getting that. Not to mention, every woman knows, you don't shake up your entire life and move for a man. I mean, at least not one who hasn't committed to you. And the whole 'I found someone else, you better stake your claim or I'll move on' thing was totally uncool." My eyes wandered to the strong column of his throat illuminated by moonlight, and I mumbled, "I think I dodged a bullet with that guy."

Harry's hands smoothed up my back. "I know you did."

I focused on Harry's hands and silently agreed. Wholeheartedly.

"You?" I asked. Then I dipped my voice, "I mean, outside of Winnie."

"No one."

I blinked in the dark. "No one?"

He tightened his arms around me. "No one."

Was he for real?

I harked back to try to remember when I heard he'd lost his wife.

I wasn't sure, but I thought it was around eight years ago.

So again…

Was he for real?

"You mean not like anyone to, um…you know, even, uh…clear out the waterworks?"

For a second, he just lay there.

Then he busted out laughing.

I liked the sound. I liked how his doing it felt, his long body in my bed making it shake. I liked just feeling that long body tremble with humor.

But I liked how he automatically tucked me even closer when he did it best of all.

He was still chuckling when he asked, "Clear out the waterworks?"

"I sense you know what I mean," I replied tartly.

"I know what you mean, sweetheart."

Yep, still chuckling.

"I thought you guys needed that," I remarked.

He sobered when he replied, "No. Some guys need women to think we need it so they can play on a woman's guilt and innate nature to nurture so she'll give it up to him. Men can go without. Especially those who understand sex is meaningful, they had a relationship that was the most meaningful thing in their lives, and they know anything less would be a pale imitation, mocking what they know they can have if they find the right person. I have the equipment and the imagination to take care of myself in the meantime, and I did."

There it was.

The perfect scheme to get my mind off all that was happening.

Putting in it visions of Harry's amazing chest flexing and swelling as he jacked off.

Harry shifted, and I felt his nose skim my jaw until his lips were at my ear.

"I'll demonstrate for you someday," he whispered there.

Oh my.

Proof my good guy could be bad.

I shivered, wanting that "someday" to be now.

On that thought, I let my hands roam his skin.

He was so warm and hard everywhere, but his skin was so soft.

Harry settled his head back on the pillows, offering, "I'll take you there, honey, if you want me to, be happy to do that for you, but I'm not going there."

My hands stilled. "What if I want to take you there?"

And I did. Big time. Since it felt like I'd been wanting Harry Moran for a lifetime.

But especially now, considering I knew how long it had been for him.

I mean, I pretty much thought he held some sorcery, because he was just that magnificent, but that was a super long wait for anybody.

"I know you want to take me there," Harry replied. "I hope you know how hard it is to deny letting you do it. But it can't happen now."

He pressed into me so I fell to my back and his long, strong body was mostly on top of mine.

"This position doesn't help, Harry," I informed him.

Another chuckle, this one lower, sexier, which also didn't help.

Then he said, "Let's get you through the next couple of days."

I huffed.

"If I can make it, you can make it," he challenged.

"It really is inconvenient, the strong handle you have on your ethics and morals," I grumbled.

He kissed my neck and said there, "Promise to make it worth it."

"Again, not helping, Harry Moran," I told the dark ceiling.

The shadow of his head obscured that view. "You've lived too long with questions, now you have an answer. I know how that answer feels, especially considering the permanence of it. The fact there's nothing you can do to change it. The fact you'd give everything to change it. Now I'm asking you to trust me to navigate you through the worst of it."

Well, that put a damper on the raging libido ignited by having Harry's partially clothed body in my bed.

"I'm sorry you lost her," I whispered.

"I know you are, baby."

KRISTEN ASHLEY

"Even if it means, if you didn't, you wouldn't be here."

"I know."

"I'm sorry you understand what I'm going through too, losing Winnie, and your mom."

"I know, Lilly."

"And I'm not going to think you're taking advantage," I assured him. "In fact, I'm worried you'll think I'm taking advantage of you."

I watched his shadowed head twitch. "Taking advantage of me?"

"Dragging your uniforms here, your dogs here, sixty pounds of dog food."

"Lilly—"

"It's got to be a pain."

"Am I acting like it's a pain?"

I thought about it, then said, "No. But you wouldn't."

"All right, let's do this," he stated in a way, even if I wasn't sure what "this" was, I was both excited to find out and scared shitless.

I didn't get the chance to voice my dichotomy of emotions at his announcement.

He "did this."

"I wouldn't be here if I didn't want to be here. Expanding on that, I'm very aware of what's being communicated that I'm here. If I wasn't serious about what we're doing, if I wasn't into you, if I didn't want to know you better, if I wasn't in a place I was ready and willing to put in that work, and aware I was doing it and what I was saying by doing it, I wouldn't be here. But I'm here, Lillian. My dogs are here. My uniforms are here. My shampoo is here. This is not a hardship. I'm not making a sacrifice. I'm not racking up brownie points. I'm doing what I need to do for a woman I care about who is going through a seriously shit time. You are not taking advantage of me. If we were casual, or I had doubts, or I simply wasn't sure, believe me, I would not be here. I would not make that statement. But again...*I'm here.*"

He was there.

Right there.

And I wasn't breathing.

"Now, are you with me on that?" he demanded.

"Yes," I wheezed.

"Finally," he muttered, like he'd been trying to convince me of something for millennia, and it took me that long to believe him.

Therefore, my eyes grew squinty. "You'll have to cut me some slack. I found you during that seriously shit time. I don't want you to think I'm some emotional leech or something."

"My job is dealing with people in their shittiest times," he reminded me. "I've met those kinds of emotional leeches. I know you aren't that."

"Well...good, I guess." I said, like it wasn't.

His shadowed head angled to the side. "Are we sliding into an argument about how much I like you and am glad we met so I could be here for you, and me knowing you're not an emotional leech?"

"No."

But...yeah.

I was still kind of snapping.

"Christ, she wants my dick," he muttered like I wasn't there.

"Well...yeah." Totally still snapping. "Harry, have you seen your body?"

Another moment of stillness before his laughter boomed through the room.

I slapped part of that fabulous body, particularly his pectoral.

"Girls need it too," I declared.

His face dipped close. "Are you gonna play on my guilt and my innate nature to protect and provide to get yourself some of my cock?"

"Will it work?"

"No."

I huffed again.

Harry chuckled again but shifted us, so he was on his back, and I was draped down his side (again, this was not making things better!).

His fingers then sifted into my hair, and he started playing.

I was beginning to think he might be a bit of a tease.

Then again, it certainly took my mind off other things.

"Let's talk about something else," he suggested.

"Like what?" I asked.

"Whatever you want," he offered.

"Okay, do you like cats?"

"Yes."

"But you like dogs better?"

"I'm active and my dogs run with me. I've got a little land, and they like roaming it with me. If Smokey was a cat being starved by a useless bitch I'm very glad moved out of my county, he'd be at my house living the good life with someone who gets he needs food and clean litter and love. I don't like dogs better. They just fit my life better. Do you like cats better?"

"I had to hustle when Mom and Dad left. For the first few years, I had two jobs and was lonely, so I got a cat because I didn't have the time I needed to devote to training a dog and looking after him."

It was then I remembered something, with all that was happening, that had totally slipped my mind.

So I shared, "That reminds me. I forgot to tell you Willie called me the other day."

I found myself suddenly sitting in bed with Harry since he jack-knifed up and took me with him.

"What?" he demanded.

"Willie called the other day."

"When?" he bit off.

"Um…" I tried to remember when he called. "Sunday morning. After our first date. Wait, I mean, our fourth."

Or was it our third?

I got another moment of silence from Harry, but this one wasn't a precursor to him laughing, I knew, because the air was heavy and snagged.

"Harry?" I called.

His voice was low and vibrating when he asked, "Why didn't you tell me?"

"Someone died in a car accident," I reminded him.

"Again, why didn't you tell me?"

"You'd had a shitty day."

"Four days have elapsed since then."

"Well, I don't think I have to mention I then got my own supremely shitty news."

With another sudden movement, I was on my back again, and Harry was on me.

Full on me this time.

"Okay, honey, I need you to pay close attention," he started.

Oh, I was paying close attention all right. Having Harry's weight on me felt *amazing*.

"Lillian, you with me?" he called.

I forced my focus on him.

No, my focus was totally *on him*, all of him. So instead, I forced my focus on what he was saying.

"Right here."

"Never, sweetheart, *never*, no matter what shit I'm dealing with at work, do you bury shit you're dealing with. Never keep it from me. Never."

Oh my God.

Could I take him being more awesome?

"Okay, Harry," I whispered.

"Do I need to say the word 'never' again?" he asked.

"No, Harry," I promised.

"He called before we found out about your parents," he noted.

"Yes," I confirmed.

"What did he say?"

Oh boy.

Harry must have felt my hesitance, because his voice got kind of scary when he repeated, "What did he say?"

"Well, he found out we're dating, and he was mad."

"He was mad," Harry repeated dully, like he didn't get it.

I knew how he felt.

Ugh!

"He said he was my husband, and we were a thing."

"But you're divorced."

"Very."

"And it was over after you kicked him out."

"So over. Totally over. We redefined the word 'over,' we were so totally over after I kicked him out."

Maybe I went a little overboard on that, but nothing in it was untrue.

"He didn't try to come back?" Harry asked.

"He did. But Shane had graduated from college by then and was home, putting in applications to find a job. He got some of his buddies to go with him to pay Willie a visit. They shared how they felt about Willie bugging me. Shane then found a job and went to California, but his buddies were still in town. They all played football at MP High. In other words, they were guys you didn't mess with. And although after their visit Willie tried calling and sending flowers and gifts and stuff, eventually, he quit, and I thought it was over."

"But he doesn't think it's over."

"He said the reason I couldn't find him to divorce him was so I couldn't divorce him."

"And yet he's been married twice since?"

"That's what I heard. But I haven't talked to Willie personally since Shane warned him off."

"Has he gotten in touch since Sunday?"

"No."

Harry rolled off me and onto his back.

I turned to my side and got up on my forearm to see him rubbing his face with both hands.

"You seem more upset about this than I was," I noted worriedly.

He stopped rubbing his face. "If any of the Zowkowers get anywhere near you, I want you to tell me immediately."

"You're kind of freaking me out, Harry," I whispered.

His hand darted out, catching me at the back of my neck and pulling me close.

"That's the point I'm making. You tell me, I worry about it, and you don't."

"I know the Zowkowers are bad news, but I was never a part of that."

"I know."

"Willie just probably heard about us, because everyone was talking, and he knows you're the kind of guy I'd get serious about, so he got territorial, because he's an idiot."

"If he knew about me, he'd know about Storm, and this didn't happen then?"

I sighed. "Harry, everyone knows what Angelica did to Stormy. So everyone knows it's going to take a while for him to get over that and trust women again, if he ever does. With him, I fell into the trap of 'I can fix him, I'll show him how awesome I am, and he'll get it.' Needless to say, he didn't get it."

Harry swept his thumb out to stroke the side of my neck.

"We're getting into a lot of deep shit tonight, baby, but unfortunately, the time picked itself."

Oh Lord.

"What?" I asked.

"I don't want to freak you."

Oh Lord!

"What?" I breathed.

"I know myself," he announced.

"Okay," I said when he said no more.

"For me, this is a lot more than I'm into you and I want to get to know you better. I've processed through both of those. For me, the man I am, the woman you are, what's happening to you, I'm your man, and you are my woman."

I stopped breathing.

You are my woman.

Oh *Lord.*

"So," he went on, sounding vaguely uncomfortable, "your ex-husband dicking with you at all would get a rise out of me. This happening right before you found out about your parents triggers something in me that's a bit more extreme."

"W-what's that?" I asked.

"Remember I mentioned that nature to provide and protect?"

195

I nodded.

"Well, the protect part goes into overdrive."

And…

There it was.

I knew.

I knew before.

Way before.

I mean, Harry Moran was gorgeous, but it wasn't that.

Everyone knew he worked twice as hard when he worked for Dern, because he tried to do good in the face of bad. And everyone knew he still kept working twice as hard to prove the Dern tenure was over and people could trust the sheriff and his team.

Everyone also knew how much he'd loved his wife, even before he was forced to grieve her.

Everyone knew everything about the man who was Harry Moran.

And all of *that* was why I had a crush on him.

Because…

Because…

He was my dad.

Harry was his own unique version of the man Simon Rainier was.

A simple man, but that didn't quite cover the facts that he was a good man, a smart man, a noble man, a thoughtful man, a man who had a deep capacity to love.

In other words, my dad.

And the minute I clapped eyes on Harry, just like my mom, I knew he was the man for me.

I just had to wait until he was ready.

And now he was ready.

So now, what he was saying was, like my dad was when he met my mom, Harry was *mine*.

I'd found it, what I was looking for.

I'd found what they had.

Oh dang.

I was going to cry again.

I shoved my face in his throat.

He wrapped both arms around me, and I felt him lift his head so he could say in my hair, "I don't want to scare you with that. That's just where I'm at. We're still going to go slow."

"I'm not scared," I said into his skin. "I just don't know how to deal with all I've lost and all I've gained all at the same time."

His arms around me spasmed.

I turned my head so I could rest my cheek on his shoulder and snaked my arm around his flat belly. "I'll tell you if Willie or any of the Zowkowers contact me."

"Okay, Lilly," he murmured.

"This is it, isn't it?" I whispered, hope heavy in my tone.

He knew what I was asking, I knew with how tight he held me before he loosened his hold.

"This is it, sweetheart. You okay with that?"

I hadn't been okay for sixteen years.

Now, I knew they were gone and would never come back, not really. Just what was left of them would.

But I was more than okay.

And they would be okay, knowing how okay I was.

"So okay, we're redefining the word okay with how okay I am," I said.

I felt his body relax.

"I wish you knew them," I whispered.

"I wish I did too," he returned my whisper.

"I think Maddie's right. Ronnie told me all she has planned for them, and it's perfect. I think when it happens, it'll help a lot."

"Rus was worried she was too forthright. They try to encourage that with her, but sometimes it's the wrong time."

"She wasn't too forthright. Kids are smarter than we give them credit for, and if we'd just listen, we'd know it."

"Yeah." He caught a lock of my hair and started twirling it. "You want kids?"

Oh, we were definitely getting into the deep stuff.

"Yeah."

"How many?"

"Two, maybe three. You?"

"Two." He tugged playfully on my hair. "Maybe three."

I smiled against his shoulder.

"Boys? Girls? You care?" I asked.

"Healthy," he answered.

And there I was...

So, so deep.

And it was warm and safe down there with Harry, not exposed and alone with the storms of life buffeting me at random.

I wondered if Mom felt like this the entire time she had Dad, but even wondering, I knew she did.

I knew something else too.

They'd worry about me. They'd hate to leave me.

But they went together, and I knew into my soul there was peace in that for them, because neither of them had to live without the other for more than instants.

And I found peace with that.

It didn't mean I was *at peace* with how they were taken.

But there was peace in that.

More peace came when Harry spoke again.

"Though, I'd want them in sports, no matter the gender," he went on. "Or some extracurricular activity. Definitely there will be a strict limit on screentime."

"Totally. They need to be outside. Or doing something. Music or crafts or whatever."

"Yeah."

We were oh-so deep, and we stayed deep, talking about kids, how Harry liked how close to his work my house was, how he wasn't tied to his, even if he grew up there, because of all that he'd lost there.

We talked about giving it a little time, and cleaning out my parents' room together, and redoing it, so we could lay them to rest in my house too.

We talked about me meeting his dad, his brother, his sister-in-law and his niece and nephew. We further talked about how cute that niece and nephew were.

We talked about how he'd meet the only brother and sister I'd ever had, Shane and Sherise, because they were coming up for the memorial.

We talked until I got drowsy, and Harry turned into me so we were both on our sides, he was snuggling me close and murmuring, "Go to sleep, baby."

So that was when he stopped talking, because I did as Harry asked, and within moments, I fell fast asleep.

TWENTY-FIVE

Waiting to Drop

Harry

The next morning, Lillian was at his side, his dogs at her house snoozing on their new beds (except Linus, who was up on the couch, something Harry allowed at home, and Lillian made clear she allowed too, even if her couch was a lot nicer than his). They were snoozing because he'd taken them on a run.

Now, Harry and Lillian were walking into Aromacobana together because this was what Lillian described as her daily splurge.

She hadn't woken before him that day.

In fact, he got up, put on his running clothes, took his dogs out and ran a few miles, came back and fed them, showered, and made himself a coffee before she stumbled out, sleepy-eyed, wild-haired and adorable.

She hadn't had a lot of sleep the night before, so Harry was pleased as fuck she was getting caught up.

He was more pleased she was there with him, where he was at in his head with where they were in their relationship.

What he wasn't pleased about was Willie Zowkower deciding to fuck with her again.

But that wasn't going to be for Lillian.

No.

Harry would take care of that.

After she crashed sleepily into him and he held her for a few minutes, he said, "Get dressed, sweetheart, let's go to Aromacobana."

She nodded, pushed her face into his chest like it was an added hug, then she pulled away and did as he asked.

Now they were there, everyone in the coffee joint was watching them, and he didn't give a shit.

They got their coffees, she got a croissant, and they were back out on the sidewalk when he asked, "Plans for the day?"

"I need to dive deep into this manuscript so I can get it back to my author. The services for Mom and Dad are Saturday. I'll want to spend time with Shane and Sherise while they're here. I need a clear slate."

"Right."

"And I'll be popping to Jenna's. She's doing the flowers for the service. She wants to show me what she has in mind. Ronnie is coming with me."

"Okay."

They had their arms around each other's waists, and she used hers to give him a squeeze. "I'm also making dinner for my guy."

"Wait for me, we'll cook together."

She looked up at him. "I take it there's no set getting-home time for Sheriff Moran."

He gave her another squeeze. "No, honey, but I'll stay in touch during the day so you'll have a sense of when my day will be done."

She nodded.

They crossed the street.

They were passing Kimmy's Christmas store when Kimmy came out, indicating she'd probably been at the window watching everything and as such, clocking them going to Aromacobana, as well as clocking them coming back.

He was about to say something to get her to back off, but she handed Lillian a big, fancy, shiny candy cane with thin swirls of green mixed with thinner ones of white cut with a slender gold.

"Hammond's caramel apple. The crème de la crème of candy canes. Avery's favorite," Kimmy declared.

Harry heard Lillian's sharp indrawn breath, but Kimmy just patted her shoulder awkwardly, gave Harry big eyes, and disappeared back into her store.

Harry set them to walking again.

"Alex is so totally a moron," she said in an undertone.

"Who's Alex?" he asked.

"The guy who wouldn't move to Misted Pines from Oregon."

"Yup, totally a moron," Harry agreed, though why Harry thought he was a moron and why Lillian did were very different.

They kept walking, almost by the front door of the department, except she stopped.

He looked down at her. "I'm walking you home."

"It's not even a full block away."

"I'm walking you home," he repeated.

She leaned into him, wrapping both her arms around him, even with one hand holding a coffee and the other a croissant and a candy cane.

"You know how you *need* to see to me?" she asked.

He knew where this was going.

"Lillian—"

"Well, I *need* to drop you off at work and know you're where you need to be, and not doing something you don't need to be doing, that being walking me a block home."

"Honey—"

She got up on her toes, kissed him quiet and rolled back to her feet. "Go do good."

He bent and kissed her deeper, and longer, broke it and gave in, murmuring, "Later, beautiful."

She smiled at him, and he was happy as fuck to see it reached her eyes. "Later, handsome."

They broke off and he watched until she turned the corner onto her block.

He went in and activity in the bullpen obviously recommenced after everyone in it had stopped to watch Harry and Lillian through the front windows.

Polly was by the door in the reception bench holding an Aroma-cobana cup and beaming at him.

He moved to her, slid a coffee out of the two-cup carrier he had, handed it to her, then took the one she had and put it in the carrier.

"Things are changing," he announced. "Lillian likes to go to the coffee shop every morning. That means I'll be bringing you one every day."

"I'm awesome with change," Polly replied.

Harry couldn't stop his grin.

It died before he said, "I want everyone gathered. Two hours. Not the crew that did nights, but anyone that's off, call them in. We're having a department-wide briefing."

"You got it."

Polly took off.

Harry went to Rus's desk.

He took the other coffee out of the carrier and handed it to him.

"For looking after the dogs."

"You didn't have to, but I'll take it," Rus replied, proving his words by taking a sip.

Harry retrieved the other coffee, dumped the carrier in Rus's trash and took his own sip.

"Like I said last night, you're lead on the Rainiers," Harry started it. "Polly's calling everyone in. I'll deal with schedules. I'll figure out overtime. But whatever you need, you're gonna get."

"Already talked to the agents assigned in Idaho. They got things they've gotta go over there. Then they'll be out here. Hopefully by the time they get here, we'll have something meaty to give them."

Hopefully.

Harry nodded. "When Wade gets back, I'll want him with you. You've got him and Karen. I'm taking Sean for the Ballard case."

Rus nodded.

"You feel good about any of this?" Harry asked.

"I felt a whole lot better when I heard about the journals, but something is fucking with me."

Christ, he was glad he wasn't the only one feeling that.

"You know what that is?" Harry queried.

"No. If I figure it out, I'll tell you. But I get the feeling we're just scratching the surface of something."

"People have killed for far less than to cover up fraud, Rus," Harry said, even though he felt the same thing.

"Maybe it's that we've only sunk our teeth into two of those flagged files, and we're already up to our necks," Rus guessed.

Maybe.

Maybe that audit landed his entire department under a mountain of shit it was going to take effort, time and perseverance to dig out of. A great deal of all three.

Or maybe there was another shoe hovering, waiting to drop.

"I'll be ready for the briefing," Rus ended it. "All I added to Ballard's file is on your desk. Of note, the ex-wife still hasn't gotten back to me."

"Thanks, brother," Harry replied.

Rus jutted up his chin and turned back to his desk.

Harry went to his office and started his day.

TWENTY-SIX

Not Yet

Harry

"M aybe your deputy might want to step out," Stormy said irately when Sean and Harry walked into his office at the tire store later that morning.

Harry took in Storm's angry face, he looked to Sean, he guessed what this was about, then he said low, "Just for a few minutes."

Sean's alert eyes went between Harry and Stormy, and he replied, "Right outside the door."

He then stepped out, closing the door behind him.

Stormy didn't make him wait for it.

"If you're going to finally pull your thumb out, dip your toe back in the pool and find yourself some, leave Lillian out of it."

"Think you know me better than that, Stormy," Harry said, with practiced patience, keeping his calm.

Storm looked out the grimy window behind his desk, and Harry took in a man who fucked up and only recently realized it.

"I know you know about me and Lillian, do you know about her parents?" Harry asked.

"Yeah," Storm grunted. "Word's all over town."

"We got a problem here?" Harry kept at him, and Storm looked back his way. "Because I hope we don't. Lillian told me you two were together. She understands it wasn't the right time for you, and she doesn't hold any ill will. But that's then, this is now, things have changed, and she doesn't need anyone giving her anything else to be upset about."

Like her fucking ex-husband.

"I wouldn't hurt Lillian," Stormy asserted.

"Then we're good."

It took him a beat, then Harry watched the tension leak out of Stormy's shoulders before he said, "I was happy to see you at Doc and Nadia's the last few parties they threw, Harry. It's good to see you out of uniform and having a life. And you're right. I know the man you are. I just hope you know where your head is at and don't set your sights on Lillian until after you've knocked off the dust and want to get serious, brother. And I say that also saying, if you do that and it works for you two like it didn't work for us, honest to Christ, it'll suck, because straight up, I still have feelings for her. Angelica did a number on me and Lillian paid for it. But I'll back your play because you deserve a good woman, and she deserves a good man."

"I'm not knocking off dust with Lillian, man," Harry replied, focusing on that, instead of all the rest Storm said, and losing hold on his patience.

"I know that too, and that's why this fuckin' sucks. Because I'm happy for you, for her, and I fucked up. Now she knows what's happened to her parents—"

He abruptly stopped talking.

But fucking hell, Harry got where this was coming from, and he felt him.

"You can still be there for her," Harry advised. "The services are Saturday. Come to them. It'll mean a lot."

Storm looked to his shoes and muttered, "Yeah."

Harry gave him some time.

Stormy took it, then, still muttering, "Angelica did me so fucking dirty, got the best thing in the world out of it, but until I heard about you and Lillian, heard what happened to her parents, I didn't realize the number she did on my head." He turned again to the window. "You don't want to hear this, but fuck me, I didn't think I could get more pissed at Angelica, but I am, since, because of her, I didn't recognize what I had with Lill, and now I'm out."

He was so totally out.

Harry said nothing, even if he felt more for him, because Harry got it.

Holding on to his grief meant he didn't even notice Lillian until she was right in front of his face.

Years, he'd lost. *They'd* lost.

But he was in a way better place than Stormy.

He gave the man more time, before he requested, "Can I call my deputy back in?"

Stormy looked at him. "Yeah."

Harry opened the door.

Sean entered and closed it behind him again.

"We're here about Muggsy Ballard," Harry told him and watched Stormy's dark brows shoot together. "He worked for you, yeah?"

"Yeah. Worked for me, and he was a friend."

"Tight?"

"Everyone who knew Muggsy was tight with him. He was that guy," Stormy replied.

"He was working for you when he died," Harry noted to confirm.

"Yeah," Storm said.

"Good worker?"

"Absolutely. He'd do anything for you. Was in early. Would stay late. Pissed me off because he never wanted to let me down, so he came in once with a flu, then half my guys got the fuckin' flu and called in sick for a week. But that was how Muggsy's mind worked. First thought, don't let a brother down. The rest of the thoughts didn't occur to him."

Harry glanced at Sean to give him a chance at the floor.

Sean took it.

"Close to his death, did he seem to have any issues?"

Storm shook his head. "I'm no psychologist, but Muggsy took a lot of falls in his life, most of them by his own design, but he always got up. Never knew a man who could dust off the seat of his pants and get on with it like Muggsy could."

"We're now aware that Muggsy didn't commit suicide," Harry told him.

For a beat, Stormy froze.

Then his irritability came back, tenfold.

"You are fucking kidding me," he bit out.

"I wish I was."

"Dern fucked that up?" Stormy demanded.

All Harry would say was, "We flagged his case in the audit. There were some inconsistencies. We're treating it as a homicide now."

"His ma know?"

That was the last stop they had made, and it went a lot better than Harry imagined it would, simply because she was beside herself someone was finally taking her concerns seriously.

"She knows," Harry told him. "So, again, I'm going to reiterate Sean's question. Was he having any issues when he died that you know of?"

"He was pretty certain he was gonna come into some big money, but then again, Muggsy was always certain he was going to come into some money."

"You know what that deal was about?" Sean asked.

Stormy shook his head, but a ghost of a fond smile was on his mouth. "That was Muggsy. He was such a fucking goofball. He'd be all about these sweet deals he was convinced were so sweet, he never said dick to anybody about them, because he didn't want anyone to horn him out of the action. Then nothing would come of them, or he'd lose his whole fuckin' shirt, and his pants, shoes, and boxers. But nothing stopped him. He was the eternal optimist."

"Do you know if Muggsy owned a gun?" Sean kept at it.

The gun was a thing, since Muggsy didn't have one registered to him, and the one found at the scene had not been sufficiently processed, and making matters worse, they had no idea where it was.

"If he did, he'd have sold it," Stormy said. "Man worked hard, but he was an idiot with money, so he always had money problems."

"We're cobbled by lost time, Storm," Harry reminded him. "Anything you can remember, even if you don't think it's a big deal, anything that might give us a lead, you call me or Sean at the station. Yeah?"

Storm jerked up his chin. "I'll think about it. Got some men who are still here that worked with him. I'll pull them in, you can talk to them before you go."

"We'd appreciate that," Harry said, and he and Sean moved out of the way so Stormy could get to the door.

He stopped in it and looked at Harry. "Around the time he died, he was pretty pissed Cheryl had moved on."

Cheryl had been Muggsy's wife.

"Pissed? Not upset? Depressed?" Harry asked.

"Fuck no," Stormy answered. "Totally not. She'd hooked up with a dude Muggs hated. Don't think you were best buds with him either."

Harry's body twitched. "I know him?"

"You worked with him. He was a deputy. Karl Abernathy."

Harry heard the crash of the shoe dropping, he just didn't know what it meant.

What he knew was, he didn't talk with men in Dern's camp, mostly because they didn't talk to him.

But Harry actively detested Karl Abernathy.

He wasn't just a shit cop, he was a shit individual.

Harry kept his voice carefully modulated when he asked, "She was with Karl?"

"Not with him anymore, as far as I know, but she was then. As you know, as well as the rest of us, Karl was one of Dern's goons. Got his jollies by fucking with people. Muggs wasn't the only one who hated him. If they knew him or had the misfortune to run into him, pretty much everyone hated him." Storm's gaze thinned on Harry. "This pertinent?"

"Since we're reopening an investigation seven years down the line, everything is pertinent," Harry hedged.

Stormy kept staring at him. When Harry gave him no more, he left the office.

Harry looked to Sean. "We need to talk to Cheryl Ballard ASAP. And we need to track down Karl. He quit the minute Dern was out. He was before your time, but you heard of him?"

"You got skin my color, or you have female parts, you knew all about Karl Abernathy, and you avoided him."

Goddamn fuck.

"Don't know what to say, Sean," Harry said.

"Nothing for you to say, Harry," Sean replied. "Not you who's a racist piece of shit with a badge."

No, he wasn't, which begged the question why no one said anything to him about this.

But that was victim blaming. They probably thought Harry was as powerless to do anything about it as they were.

Until girls started dying, then Harry'd had enough.

"You know anything else about him?" Harry asked.

"Know he's a bigot. Know he was a dirty cop. Know he had his nose far up Dern's ass. Know he expected, as in demanded, the cop discount anywhere he went, that being getting food and coffee and donuts and shit for free. Most of the schlubs that were tight with Dern were just lazy, liked playing cops and robbers but didn't spend much time being actual cops, but they still got a paycheck for it. Abernathy was the worst of the lot. Not even sure Dern knew what garbage he was. Just doubt, even if he knew, he'd care."

At least Harry knew all of that.

But he'd been powerless to do anything about it.

"The female parts thing you said?"

Sean shook his head. "I don't know. Just rumors. The thing is, Harry, if he busted our chops, pulled us over driving while Black, if he took it further, he'd have to deal with you. So he just busted our chops. Being fair about this, he'd dick with anybody if he felt like it, and it didn't matter the color of your skin. Women, though…"

"What?" Harry pushed.

"I have no proof of this, but heard word, BJs extorted for getting out of tickets."

It took Harry a lot longer than it normally did for him not to lose his fucking mind.

"I thought you knew," Sean said quietly.

"I did not fucking know," Harry returned furiously. "He was the first one to quit."

"I see it. You the boss, man, if you learned of his shit, he'd be so fucked, he wouldn't get himself unfucked for years. But he might get a whole lot more fucked in ways he really didn't like in prison."

"He wasn't one of the ones women came forward to report when we went through that shit when Dern was ousted," Harry pointed out.

"You and me both know, women hesitate or don't come forward at all. Someone like Abernathy, I could see they'd be shit scared, even if he wasn't a deputy anymore. The man had one serious mean streak."

"Christ, get on the phone with Polly," Harry ordered. "I want Cheryl in my station, and I want Karl in my station. And if they have to arrest either one of them to do it, then they arrest them."

"For what?"

"We'll start with obstruction of justice, and we'll figure it out from there."

"You think they know something?" Sean asked, pulling out his phone.

"I think Roy and Karl were friends. I think Muggsy Ballard didn't like his ex-wife with Karl, and it doesn't matter what a nice guy everyone says he was, they also say he did stupid shit all the time. I think Karl would put up with his girlfriend's ex giving him grief for about five seconds before he did whatever the fuck he wanted to do about it. And I think he was a cop back then, a cop who thought he could do whatever the fuck he wanted at all times. I think that might have gotten out of hand, Karl called Roy, they figured a way out of it, and if anyone asked questions, they set Dern up to take the fall. That's what I think. What I can prove, though, is nothing close to that. Not yet."

Sean nodded and got on his phone.

Harry pulled his out too, and he made a call.

Dern didn't pick up, and again, Harry was good with leaving a voicemail.

"So, in less than a day pursuing our homicide investigation, we've learned that Muggsy Ballard's ex-wife was dating Karl Abernathy. I'm sure you remember Karl. I'm sure you remember Karl and Roy were tight. So now it seems like two of your boys set you up to get fucked over. You got something for me that might help us figure this shit out, you might think of making a return to Misted Pines. And maybe you do that before that return becomes mandatory."

He ended the call and looked out Stormy's grubby window.

They were so fucking neck deep in Dern's incompetent shit.

Harry just had to hope he could keep their heads above it.

Or they'd drown in it.

TWENTY-SEVEN

Coors and Sundresses

Harry

That afternoon, Harry was in his office with Rus, running the day down.

The crux of what both of them had was dick.

No one knew where the Dietrichs were.

They had a son, Gerald Jr., who lived in Virginia, was some kind of lobbyist in DC, who did answer his phone.

And he reported he hadn't heard from his parents in weeks but reiterated the lie they were in Seattle seeing to a relative. He wasn't stupid enough to claim his grandma was still alive. He told Karen it was some great aunt once removed or some shit.

He then probably got right on his parents and told them they were fucked, but Harry's team couldn't do anything about that.

Pressure sometimes worked. Sometimes, people who did tremendously stupid shit smartened up when it went south, and their best bet was to sort it out or it would just get worse.

But it usually had to get pretty damned bad for them to pull their heads out of their asses.

The condo they told people they'd bought in Seattle to live in to look after Gerald Dietrich's mother was not a condo they owned or lived in. As such, no one in his office knew where he was. But they did know, if he got in touch, they were to report it and tell Dietrich he needed to get in contact with the Fret County Sheriff immediately.

Deputies spent the day running down Kimmy's list of businesses that the Dietrichs received goods and services from on account.

All of them reported the same thing Kimmy did. Non-payment for months, promises of restitution, weaponizing their attitude and entitlement to get people to back off, eventually making the debt good paying cash and not doing business with them again.

In fact, it seemed the Dietrichs ended up only living and maybe doing their grocery shopping in MP, otherwise, they'd burned all their bridges at shops, bars, restaurants, even the golf club.

A few of these vendors and businesses had threatened legal action, and got close to it, but Gerald and Michelle ponied up before that happened.

And this added pressure might have been why they took things to extremes.

Kimmy's word was corroborated about living quiet too.

The Dietrichs might take most of their custom out of town, but deputies were told by a number of people, after the public money problems, the alleged robbery and the Rainiers going missing, the Dietrichs kept a low profile.

He worked at his export business, dealing mostly in sporting goods, with a focus on hunting gear and air rifles. She had a few friends she'd visit. Both came from money to begin with.

Other than that, they didn't pull their Lord and Lady of Misted Pines bullshit at all.

Not since the Rainiers disappeared.

And now that the file was reopened, they were gone.

That said a lot to Harry, and it said the same thing to Rus.

Rus was hitting up banks and credit cards. Gerald and Michelle had two vehicles under license, and they had alerts out to other agencies to pick them up as persons of interest in a violent crime if their cars were spotted, and they were waiting for warrants to track cell phones.

Fortunately, the Feds were all up in this, and they could get shit done a lot faster than the locals.

It was the same with Cheryl Ballard, Karl Abernathy and Roy Farrell, just without federal backup.

Cheryl had called in sick the last two days at the bookkeeping firm where she worked.

Abernathy had put out a PI shingle in a neighboring town, and he wasn't in his office when Harry's deputies swung around. Harry had not bumped up against him since he left, so he figured Abernathy was doing cheating spouse cases, if he was getting any casework at all considering how little he was liked, and the state of his office. It was in a strip mall, and a

Google search Harry did on it showed a façade that wasn't anything to get excited about.

Farrell had called in sick that day.

They too had alerts on them and their vehicles, and Sean was working on warrants for Abernathy and Farrell's bank records and cell phones.

Tomorrow, they'd dig into friends, family and co-workers.

Unfortunately, all these fucks were going to make them work for it.

Harry just hoped something came of it.

They were wrapping things up when the screen lit on his phone with a call from Jason.

He glanced at Rus, who was staring at Harry's phone.

Then he took the call and put it on speaker.

"Hey, Jace," he greeted. "You're on speaker and Rus is with me."

"I'm here with Jess and Lynda, and you're on speaker too," he said. "Wade left. We told him we'd brief you. He wanted to get on the road with the Rainiers."

Harry mentally made a note to tell Polly to call Pullman's and give them a heads up.

"You have a look at those journals?" Harry asked.

"Yeah, we fuckin' did," Lynda's voice came over the line.

Harry again looked to Rus. Rus's mouth was tight.

So was Harry's.

He loosened it to remark, "I sense anger."

"These were good people, guess you know," Lynda sniped. "I wanna say I love my husband that much, but Avery Rainier loved her husband like she met him the day before and Cupid got cute. And I suspect you know she thought her daughter filled every day with rainbows."

Harry clenched his teeth.

Jason took over.

"The entries aren't long, not until the last few weeks. Just thoughts, feelings, things she wanted to remember, sometimes stuff she wanted to bitch about. Then she got into specifics. Apparently, Dietrich was a good client of Sonny's. Though, how he was often annoyed Avery. She wrote in her journal they expected Sonny to be at their beck and call. She wrote she wouldn't put it past them to call at two in the morning if they woke up cold and turned up the furnace, and the temperature didn't rise within seconds. She also wrote that Sonny didn't mind. He said it kept him in Coors and his two girls in sundresses."

Harry closed his eyes.

Coors and sundresses.

Fuck.

He opened them when Jace kept talking. "Thing was, Gerald Dietrich stopped paying Sonny's invoices."

Again, he caught Rus's eyes, because they knew all about that.

Jace kept going.

"The amount in arrears got pretty extreme, Sonny went to collect what he was owed and overheard Gerald talking to someone he thought was Leland Dern, seeing as there was a sheriff's cruiser in the drive and he knew Dern was tight with Dietrich. They were talking about the financial jam Dietrich was in and how, if some things disappeared, the insurance company could help him out. Sonny told Avery Dietrich also spoke of finding a 'fall guy.'"

"Goddamn it," Harry gritted.

"My thoughts exactly," Lynda agreed heatedly.

Jace came back to them.

"Sonny put this together, came home, and he and Avery didn't know what to do about it considering they couldn't report it to Dern. However, they realized very quickly that Gerald somehow found out Sonny overheard, or they just picked him as their fall guy, and as such, they both noted Gerald and his wife Michelle, not to mention Dern, seemed to be stalking them over the next few days. Worried that Sonny was going to be set up, and the 'long arm of Leland Dern' meant they'd have to go farther afield to find law enforcement to report this to, they quickly made worst-case-scenario arrangements for Lillian. They were proved right. Dern hauled them in to question them about the robbery. Once they were released, they took off."

Dern picked Sonny, Harry knew it.

He picked him because he had his eye on Avery.

"Hang on a second," he said to his phone, then hit the intercom button to Polly.

"Yeah, Harry?" she answered.

"Get a call in to whoever has jurisdiction where Dern lives. We need to start coordinating who's going to go get his ass. I want him in an interrogation room as soon as feasibly possible."

"On it," she said.

He went back to the crew in Idaho. "I can confirm that the Dietrichs were paid out for the insurance claim on the robbery. I can also confirm they were spreading cash around town to make good on debts they'd racked up, which I can assume was cash they had for selling their own stolen property."

"Fuckin' assholes," Jess muttered in the background.

"We got more," Lynda said. "There were prints on the gun found in that grave. We ran them through AFIS. No hits. Your ex-sheriff would be in the system, so he's out on that, since we also got confirmation that the bullets in the bodies came from that gun."

He knew Dern didn't pull the trigger.

Now he just wondered if Dern knew who did.

"Also, Sonny's wallet and Avery's purse have not been found,"

Lynda reported. "The plate they registered at the hotel for their car put it as a rental. It was found abandoned within a couple of days of them disappearing from the motel and returned to the rental car agency. Nothing came of that. It was in good nick, and they'd paid for it for a week up front, so the rental company didn't make a fuss. Why no one asked further questions about the people who rented it, I have no clue. Except for the fact that request would go to your sheriff, so maybe they did, and those inquiries died in Fret County. We sent more boys out to where the bodies were found to have a better look around to see if we can find the wallet and purse."

"Right," Harry said.

"We got motive with that journal, but big gaping holes every-where," Lynda stated. "Why didn't they go direct to the police? Why did they leave the motel? Why were they up on that mountain? The missing purse, wallet. And who was in that parking lot the owner saw? We got people canvassing. Long time ago, not many folks in those areas are the same now as they were then. We're trying to track down anyone who worked in that area to see if memories can be jogged. Sonny and Avery had to eat. Maybe a waitress remembers them. And maybe she'll remember a white guy with dark hair and a beard too. Maybe pigs will fly, but I don't mind my bacon raining from above. Bacon's bacon. I'll take it as I can get it."

"Good, Lynda," Harry muttered, thinking she was hilarious, and he liked how invested she was in this, but he was also feeling what he rarely felt in this job, no matter how tragic or hectic or frus-trating it could get.

Heavy.

So fucking heavy.

Coors and sundresses and the words of a woman in her journal, sharing how much she loved her husband, twenty plus years down the line of being with him.

Fuck.

Him.

"One other thing," Jace said. "In Avery's suitcase, there was a letter with postage on it. It's addressed to Lillian. They had to open it, and it explains they had to leave to keep themselves and her safe.

They couldn't tell her they were going, or why, also to keep her safe, but Avery promised they'd be in touch soon and they'd come back as soon as they could."

If they'd posted that letter, she would have known.

If they'd posted that letter, she could have found her way to some honest cop who might have found answers for her sooner.

If they'd posted that letter, she wouldn't have had to live sixteen years, wondering, scared, trying to hold on to hope, and honing her skills with denial.

This news gutted Harry so completely, he had to put an elbow to his desk and his forehead in his hand.

"Wade has copies of the journal and the letter," Jess entered the conversation. "And I know this won't make you feel any better, but they made Coeur D'Alene the day they left Misted Pines. They were only running for a day, Harry, before they were caught. But they were only running for a day. It's not much of anything, but it's still something."

He was right.

It wasn't much of anything.

They were one sleep away from hitting a police department and setting their life to rights.

But at least Lillian's parents weren't out of their minds with worry, hunted for days, or even weeks, before they were found and relieved of their lives.

So it totally wasn't much of anything.

But it was still something.

TWENTY-EIGHT

May Eighteenth

Harry

Harry stood in the observation room next to Cade Bohannan, both of them in the same stance— arms crossed on chests, legs planted, eyes to the one-way window—while Rus worked Dern.

Dern knew the score, so he had his attorney with him.

But it didn't matter.

Dern's ass would be in one of Harry's cells, because the Feds were coming, and they wanted a go at him too.

"Just gotta run this down," Rus said, scanning the papers on the table before him. "All right, late in the evening on May sixteenth, Gerald and Michelle Dietrich reported a burglary at their home." He looked to Dern. "Yes?"

"Don't have access to my old files, you do." Dern tipped his head to the file open in front of Rus. "So you tell me."

"According to your own notes, that's confirmed," Rus stated. "Solely upon Gerald Dietrich indicating Simon Rainier was having financial problems, early on the morning of May seventeenth, you picked up Simon and his wife Avery, regardless of the fact they had twenty thousand dollars in the bank, they carried no debt, even to the point they owned their home and car outright, no one else, family nor friends, reported they were in financial crisis, and no one reported they had issues with drugs, drink, or gambling. Oh, and neither of them had a record. Last, they both had alibis, not only alibiing each other, but their daughter alibiing them. But you still did not conduct an interview at their home, you took them to the station for an interrogation. To your recollection, do I have that right?"

"Don't know why we're talkin' about this. It was fuckin' years ago," Dern bit.

"Do I have that right?" Rus pushed.

"Sonny Rainier's prints were all over the Dietrich home."

"You didn't know that at the time, because he had no record. His prints weren't in the system. Neither were his wife's. But his prints could be explained because he was their handyman, and they used his services liberally."

"Avery's prints were too."

"One print. *One*. A thumb print on the safe," Rus pointed out.

"And the safe was broken into."

"Avery ran an at-home daycare. Again, she didn't have a record. How did she learn how to break open a safe?" Rus inquired.

"Her husband was a handyman," Dern spat.

"So Sonny's stupid enough to leave his prints everywhere, but Avery's careful, though not careful enough, and leaves one single print in the most incriminating location she can leave it. Is that what you're saying?" Rus queried.

"That's what we found," Dern said, and he smirked. "And then they ran, so what does that tell you?"

Harry's already tight neck muscles got tighter at Dern still pointing his filthy fucking finger at Lillian's parents.

And Christ, that fucking *smirk*, he wanted it to remove it from his face.

Physically.

"Okay then," Rus said easily, making it clear why he was in there with Dern, and Harry wasn't. Rus looked back down at the file and kept his eyes there. "You also interviewed their nineteen-year-old daughter, Lillian, at her home that same day."

"If you say so."

Rus looked at him. "You did. Her parents were released with a warning not to leave town. Upon attempting to pick them up for another interrogation after you got their prints and compared them to the ones at the scene, on May nineteenth, you found they'd skipped town. On that same day, you brought Lillian Rainier to the station and interrogated her for five hours. She repeatedly made the same statement she made on her first interview, a statement that fully corroborated the ones of her parents."

Dern said nothing, just glared at Rus.

"What did you do on May eighteenth?" Rus asked.

Dern's eyebrows twitched, and as far as Harry could read, they did this in confusion and surprise at the question.

"Again, what did you do May eighteenth?" Rus pressed.

"And *again*, I'll say that was a long fuckin' time ago. So, fuck if I remember," Dern replied.

"I just ran a timeline down for you," Rus pointed out. "May sixteenth, a major crime was reported, cars, guns, jewelry and other valuables to the tune of several hundred thousand dollars were missing. May seventeenth, you interrogated two suspects and interviewed their daughter. May nineteenth, you received word there was more evidence to indicate your suspects did it, you went to pick them up, they were gone, you interrogated their daughter. There's a day missing there, Leland. This isn't LA county. You didn't have fifty robberies reported every day. You must remember what happened that day."

"Well, I don't," Dern clipped.

Harry tensed.

And Rus went for it.

"That's really too bad, since the night of May eighteenth, someone murdered Simon and Avery Rainier in Idaho."

Dern's entire body bucked in his chair, his eyes went huge, and his attorney held up a hand Rus's way.

"I want a moment alone with my client," he demanded.

"Take all the time you need," Rus told him, gathering the file and standing. "He's not going anywhere. The Feds are on their way, and they want time with him. We'll be getting to that tomorrow."

"You're holding him?" the attorney asked.

Rus shot the attorney a penetrating scowl. "I got a clear frameup, obvious insurance fraud and two dead bodies, and the man sitting here who was found guilty of corrupting his office was the lead investigator on the case. Hell yes, I'm holding him."

"Nothing's clear or obvious," the attorney retorted. "Sounds to me my client had purpose to pursue the Rainiers."

"Then you don't know your client had a reputation for harassing and badgering women he found attractive, using the resources of this department to punish those who didn't fall for his charms. And Avery Rainier was one of those women."

The attorney's face got red.

Rus turned to Dern, and an expression came over Rus's face the like Harry had never seen on his friend, and it gave even him a shiver.

"She wanted nothing to do with you not just because you're all the nasty that's you, but because she loved her husband. For some twisted reason, you couldn't handle that. So you set Sonny up. You set Avery up. You picked them. *You.* And you delivered them to the Dietrichs. Which means you're responsible for their deaths, you miserable fuck."

With that, Rus left the room.

Harry and Cade turned to the door, so they saw Rus enter the observation room with them.

His eyes went right to Cade, but Harry's didn't.

"You good?" he asked Rus.

"I need a shower," Rus answered.

Harry got him.

"Your take?" Rus asked Cade.

"Well, we know the man's a narcissist," Cade began. "But narcissists know right from wrong. They just have the ability to twist

223

a wrong into a right if it serves their purpose. That said, murder is extreme for them. Emotional and physical abuse of significant others, loved ones, common. Murder, it can happen, but not as common."

"We know he didn't pull the trigger, Cade," Rus said. "How did you feel about what you saw in there?"

"He had no idea Sonny and Av were dead," Cade answered. "And he's freaked right now, blustering for all he's worth, because he's got Ballard's situation hanging over his head, and now this." Cade glanced at the window. "I don't know." He came back to the men in the room. "If I had to call it, I'd say he was fucking with Sonny and Avery just so there'd be something to report to the insurance company so the Dietrichs could get a payout. But also because they got on his bad side, and that's the man he is. He'd know there wouldn't be enough evidence to push through an arrest, and definitely not a conviction. There's so much reasonable doubt over the little they had, a lawyer fresh from passing the bar would get them off, a prosecutor would know that and therefore wouldn't touch it. The fuck of it is, Sonny and Avery didn't know it."

Yeah.

That was the fuck of it.

Or at least one huge fuck of the many fucks of it.

"He could have planted something, something more than the obvious plant of the thumbprint, if he really wanted to get nasty," Cade went on. "But I don't see it. The goal was to get his friends out of a financial situation. That happened. How Sonny and Avery ended up dead is not going to come from Dern, because he had no idea it went that far."

"Did you know the Dietrichs?" Rus asked.

Cade shook his head. "Of them. It's a small town. They got around. But we never met."

"You know Muggsy Ballard?" Harry put in.

Cade shook his head again. "Nope. Though I know Roy Farrell was a waste of space. And I know Karl Abernathy gave me a wide berth, which was suspicious. But that's all I got for you on that."

Harry blew out a sigh and said, "Thanks for coming in, Cade."

"Anytime, and anything for Sonny and Av, Harry. Anything," Cade replied.

Harry nodded.

Cade took off.

"I'll be sure he's processed then I'll get home," Rus said. "Nothing more we can do, so you get home too."

There was one other thing Harry had to do, and it was time to do it so he could get to Lillian.

He and Rus said their goodnights, and Harry headed to his office.

He closed the door and got his phone out.

He then made the call.

A couple of rings, Rita Zowkower answered.

"Hey there, Harry. You hear something about my boy?"

"Actually, yeah, Rita. He called his ex-wife a few days ago and made some statements to her that made her uncomfortable."

Silence, then, "You mean he called *your girlfriend.*"

"One and the same," Harry returned. "Now, just sayin', I know you're worried about him and don't know where he is. But just in case you know someone who can get word to him, remind him he's got three warrants for his arrest in Fret County. If he's seen around here for any reason, odds are, he's going to be a guest of the state for a good while."

That got him only silence.

"You there, Rita?" he called.

"I'm here, sheriff," she said. "Haven't talked to my boy in a while, but, you know, his ex-wife just took a blow, and she meant the world to him. He might get in touch with his momma so I'd send her flowers or somethin', and I'll share what you said if he does."

"Appreciate you. And maybe refrain on the flowers, Rita. Lillian is going through it right now, she doesn't have a lot of fond memories about her time as a Zowkower, it'd be the kindest thing you could do not to remind her of them."

It came tight when she said, "You're heard."

"Obliged. You have a good evening."

"Same to you, sheriff."

They disconnected, and seeing as that was all he could do unless he could get Willie's ass in one of his cells, Harry shut down his office and walked to Lillian's.

TWENTY-NINE

Chicken Tetrazzini

Harry

T he minute Harry walked through Lillian's front door, he saw the town of Misted Pines had gotten on it that day.

This came in the form of flower arrangements dotting pretty much every surface in Lillian's living room and kitchen.

Proof, Sonny and Avery were good people who were missed.

Proof, the first half of that, Lillian was too.

All his dogs came out to greet him, and Harry immediately felt a tightness enter his chest, because they came out of her parents' bedroom.

"Lilly?" he called.

"Back here," she called in return.

Yep, she was in their bedroom.

Shit.

He gave three rubdowns, then, with fur brushing his legs, he headed to the hall and through the open door that had yet to be open any time Harry was there.

He discovered two things.

One, Lillian decorated like her mother. It was a little dated, but the same cozy femininity was all over this room, and Harry wondered if Sonny enjoyed being surrounded by Avery as much as Harry enjoyed the same from Lillian.

He reckoned Sonny did.

He also found Lillian curled up on their bed.

She got up on a forearm and said, "Don't worry. I actually come in here a lot. Well, not a lot, but I do come in here when I get to missing them too much. It still smells like them."

She wasn't wrong.

It was vague, but even so, Harry scented lilies, which wasn't a surprise, and something spicy and musky.

Her mom's perfume and her father's cologne or aftershave.

This didn't make his chest any less tight.

She patted the bed.

He went and sat on it, then he tucked her hair behind her ear and said quietly, "Got some deliveries, I saw."

"Front porch was covered with them when I got home from Jenna's," she reported. "And we have so many casseroles, Ronetta and George had to put some in their fridge." She frowned exaggeratedly. "Alas, I gave them a thorough inspection, and none of them are Harry Moran Hot Body Approved."

He smiled at her. "I'm in the mood for comfort food."

She tipped her head to the side. "Bad day?"

He took in a deep breath, moved so he was twisted, resting both his forearms on the bed so his face was close to hers, and he told her about the journals and Dern.

He ended it with, "There's a letter for you too, baby, from your mom. She explained things. She just didn't get around to posting it. I'll have it all tomorrow and we'll find a time you can look at it."

It was shaky, and her eyes were bright, but she said, "Okay, Harry."

"They died May eighteenth, honey," he said gently.

She closed her eyes and dropped her head.

Harry inched closer and put his lips to her hair.

"Why does it feel good, knowing that?" she asked the comforter.

"Don't know," he said to her hair. "But if it does, just feel it."

Harry pulled back when she lifted her head. "That's the day they left."

She remembered.

Of course she would.

He nodded.

"They didn't mess around, whoever killed them," she remarked.

Linus, with bad timing, jumped up on the bed, and Harry ordered, "Off."

"No," Lillian protested. "They've been hanging with me. Mom and Dad loved animals. We had dogs all while I was growing up. The last one died about a year before they left. He was Dad's buddy. There were times the only good thing about all of that was that Bentley was gone before Dad was. Bentley wouldn't have been able to handle it."

"However you want it, Lilly," Harry replied.

"I got stuff to make a stir fry, but there's a chicken tetrazzini casserole that's been calling my name since I peeled back the foil."

"I'll go turn on the oven."

He made to stand, but she caught his wrist, so he stilled.

"I'm okay," she stated.

"You don't have to be," he returned.

"I know, but I want you to understand, I'm okay. Don't think anything about me being in here. I've been missing them forever, I'll keep missing them. I'm kind of…coming to terms, I guess. Maybe I'm searching for things to help me. Like the fact they died together, and I know that would bring them peace. Not a lot, but it'd be there. Like people are going to know now, not that they didn't before, but they'll for sure know Mom and Dad didn't have anything to do with that robbery. I hate that they're dead. I hate how they died. But I'm coping."

"Do we have to have the conversation again about how I don't think you're an emotional leech?" he teased.

Her lips tipped up. "No." Then her fingers tightened around his wrist. "I just like you, and I know you're going balls to the wall for me, so while you're doing that, I don't want you to worry about me at the same time."

"That's gonna happen anyway."

She let out a sad sigh.

"Put yourself in my shoes, where would you be at?" he asked.

It took a beat, but her eyes lit, and she replied, "I get you."

"So can I do my job, which I'd do anyway, and worry about my girl, something else I'd do anyway, and eat so many carbs I might throw up?"

"You can do the first two and half of the last one. Throwing up sucks."

He smiled, moved in to give her a quick kiss, then he left her where she was to turn on the oven.

Since he was in the kitchen, all three dogs came with him.

When he got out stuff to make a salad, Lucy and Linus remained.

But Smokey headed back to his girl.

THE NEXT MORNING, they were walking to Aromacobana when Lillian asked, "Did your dad ever remarry?"

Fuck.

He'd been so busy, he hadn't gotten in touch with his father or brother yet.

He knew both worried about him, he knew both would be thrilled he was finally getting back to life after losing Winnie.

And he knew they'd be pissed as shit that Lillian was who Lillian was going to be to him, and her parents' memorial happened, and he hadn't let them know.

And the memorial was tomorrow.

Shit.

"Is that too personal of a question?" she asked, pulling his attention back to her.

"Not at all," he assured. "I just realized I haven't called to tell them I met this great woman, and I need to get on that."

She smiled up at him.

He returned it and said, "And yes, Dad remarried. A couple of years after Mom died. It didn't work, mostly because she was a bitch. I wasn't a big fan. Josh wasn't either. They were married three years, then divorced. I think it spooked Dad. He did so well the first time, and the second was such a fail, he wasn't going to go there again. He's got a lady friend in Arizona. She'd been burned, he'd been burned, so they each have their own places. But they spend a lot of time together, go on cruises, shit like that. I've met her. Her name is Caroline. She's a good one."

They stopped to wait to cross the street, and once they were over, she mumbled. "I wonder."

"You wonder what?"

She looked up at him. "If this wicked stepmother might have been another reason you didn't try to find someone sooner after Winnie."

Harry had never thought of that, but it made sense.

"It's not the only reason, sweetheart," he said. "But yeah. Mom was a hard act to follow. Winnie definitely was too." He pulled her tighter to his side. "Though, I found her eventually."

She shot him another smile.

And it was then, Harry realized, the night before, she told no lies.

She wasn't skipping to the coffee joint and singing Taylor Swift songs, but she seemed lighter, quicker to smile, and the smiles were genuine.

He'd only known her with the cloud hanging over her.

He was looking forward to what he'd get when he got her out from under it.

What he knew was, he was going to like it.

And that was all in their messed-up world that Harry, down to his bones, *knew.*

However Lillian Rainier came to him, he was going to like it.

THIRTY

The Pain Was Real

Harry

L ate that same morning, after listening to some relief when Harry shared his news about meeting Lillian, Harry then got the kind of talking to he hadn't received since he was about eleven from his father. This talking to was about Harry calling to share he was seeing someone he wanted his father to meet the day before her murdered parents' memorial.

Onward from that, happiness from his brother, until Josh learned what was going to happen the next day, which meant Josh said, "Fuckin' hell, Harry. Give a man at least forty-eight hours to find a babysitter."

To which Harry told his brother they didn't have to come, and they could meet Lillian later, maybe at Christmas.

And now Harry was again in the observation room at the station.

Rus was in interrogation along with Special Agents Patterson and Bakshi, Dern and Dern's attorney.

"Now, weird thing is," Agent Patterson was saying, "we've been on this,"—he looked to his partner—"what we got logged on this case, Fatima? Twenty-six whole hours?"

"Around there," Bakshi replied casually.

Patterson went back to Dern. "Twenty-six hours. And in those twenty-six hours, we uncovered the fact that Gerald Dietrich made a bad investment, and to cover those losses, he made another one. It was the Great Recession. Shit like that was happening to a whole bunch of folks. But this put his boxers in a bunch, and they were squeezing his balls tight, especially considering he and his wife didn't think that maybe, money was scarce all of a sudden, they might want to cut back on the Chanel and fresh-flown-in Maine lobster. I mean, you all got lobster right here in the Puget Sound. That's a diss to the locals for sure."

Dern sat there, working hard at keeping his face a mask of nothing.

Then again, Harry understood it would be difficult since he'd spent the night in a cell it used to be him who provided that accommodation, so he didn't wake up in a good mood. And now he was being spoken down to by a special agent from the Federal Bureau of Investigations.

"This put them in a lot of debt. *A lot,*" Patterson stressed. "Though, the hefty insurance payment helped them out with that. Thing is, they seemed to get out from under it *before* they got that check."

Dern said nothing.

"So, we're looking at their finances," Patterson continued, "and imagine our surprise, after that robbery but before they got their insurance payout, they suddenly have much less overhead. Now, this isn't unheard of if you're in financial straits, but a man and a woman gotta eat, and get their highlights touched up, and there were no longer any credit or debit transactions for things like groceries, gas, hair stylists and barbers, or meals out."

"Maybe they went on a diet," Bakshi suggested.

"Maybe," Patterson said, his attention not leaving Dern. "Or maybe they were paying in cash."

Dern looked to the table.

"Then, doing some more poking around," Patterson kept at him, "we got a hit on a domestic dispute. Happened years ago. *Years*. Man brandishing a gun at his girlfriend in Olympia. Strange thing was, when they ran that gun, it wasn't registered to him. It was registered to a Gerald Dietrich and reported stolen. When asked where he got it, he said he bought it from an online site. That site has since closed down. But we sent some agents to talk to this gentleman, and he changed his tune when the FBI knocked on his door. Suddenly, he remembered where he got that gun, and several others. And damned if the man didn't describe the guy he bought the guns from as a man who looks exactly like Gerald Dietrich."

Dern continued to look at the table.

"Now, you were here, working that case, my question is, how we got all this in a little over a day, and in that day, we also had a sleep, took a long drive, and personally, I accomplished a very gratifying shit, so how on earth did all of this slip right by you?" Patterson asked.

Dern's attorney shifted awkwardly.

Dern didn't move or speak.

"Now we got two dead bodies. A husband and wife. A father and mother." Patterson's tone was deteriorating. "A man and a woman who were just living their lives, paying their taxes, raising their girl, keeping their home, doing their jobs, and suddenly, their asses are hauled in by the local sheriff, aspersions cast on their characters for a crime it would be clear to any imbecile they *did not commit*."

Dern reacted to that: he seemed in pain. Whether it indicated he carried guilt for what befell the Rainiers, or he understood at the very least, his reputation, which couldn't stand another hit, was going to be tarnished beyond repair, Harry didn't know.

But the pain was real.

"They went on the run, and gotta say," Patterson didn't let up, "I don't blame them. The caliber of law enforcement in this county, I would have gone somewhere else to find help too."

More reaction.

Dern's face got red.

"And they got *this close*,"—Patterson held up a thumb and forefinger a centimeter apart—"to being able to report to someone what was going down, clear their names, shed light on the guilty, and they...got...*dead*. And the day after their bodies were buried in an unmarked grave on the side of a mountain, you..."—he jabbed a meaty finger at Dern—"*you* hauled their teenage daughter to your station, and you went at her like she was sitting on the plans of a *fucking terrorist attack*."

Patterson was about to lose it, and his partner knew it, so she chimed in.

"You got any ideas how that might have happened to Sonny and Avery?" she asked.

"None whatsoever," Dern replied, but it sounded like it came around a frog in his throat.

"You got an alibi for where you were May eighteen of that year?" Bashki went on.

Dern glared at her. "I was here, working the Dietrich case."

"I'd like to reiterate the fact that my client had reason to suspect —" the attorney started.

"Shut the fuck up," Patterson bit out.

Yeah, definitely losing it.

He turned to Dern. "I can barely stand to look at you. And before I hurl, I gotta take a break from being in the same room with you."

With that, he got up and stormed out.

"Maybe it's time for all of us to take a break," Bakshi drawled.

She and Rus got up and left too, just not as dramatically.

Patterson joined Harry in observation, and they waited until the other two did the same before Patterson unleashed.

"The fuck of it is, we got nothin' on that asshole," he clipped. "It fucks me, but his lawyer is right. He set it up so interrogating the Rainiers seemed the logical step. How he did it, no. But I can't arrest someone for being an overly zealous cop and a dickweed, as much as I'd fuckin' like to."

"We might be able to find some links between the Dietrichs and Dern," Bakshi said. "But all we have is Avery Rainier's journal saying a Fret County sheriff's cruiser was in the Dietrichs' drive, and Sonny *thought* it was Dern, not that he saw him. She recorded Dern followed them, but it was also known he had a thing for her, so we might be able to contend stalking, but she's gone, so there's nothing we can do with that. We can't place Dern in Idaho, but I bet in this station, there's evidence to place Dern as being in Misted Pines the day they died. Dern's financials do not show an influx of cash, or anything hinky, that would say he got something out of the sale of the stolen items or the insurance payout. Unless we get another miracle like those journals, all we got on him is shitty police work with no follow through, and he's essentially already been tried and found guilty for doing that, he did his time and paid his fine."

"So you're saying we've got to cut him loose," Rus boiled it down.

"I want another crack at him," Patterson said.

"And after that, you'll have to cut him loose," Bakshi added. "I think he's coated in the filth of this. I think he was in on it. But I don't think he knew how far it'd gone."

Rus and Harry exchanged a look.

But this was where they were at.

With all of it.

Farrell, Ballard and Abernathy were all no-shows at work that day, with Ballard calling in again, but Farrell just not showing. Knocking on the doors of their homes garnered nothing.

Sean, Wade and Karen were out, talking to friends, family and co-workers.

And with regular shit to do on top of all this, he didn't have the staff to sit on Farrell's, Abernathy's or Cheryl Ballard's residences, and had to rely on random drive-bys and door knocking.

So until they got a hit on the Dietrichs, or had time to plow through what would come in now they had their warrants on the Ballard case, they were dead in the water.

"I need calories, that diner we passed got pie?" Patterson asked.

"If they have their Dutch apple, get two scoops of à la mode," Rus suggested.

Patterson jerked up his chin and prowled out.

"I better go with him so he doesn't arrest someone for looking at him funny," Bakshi joked. "We'll be back in an hour."

Rus and Harry nodded. She took off.

Rus turned to the window, and Harry followed his gaze.

Heads close, Dern and his attorney were conferring.

Or, his attorney was talking fast and Dern was listening.

"If I had to guess, that attorney is telling him not to open his mouth and say another word, ride it out, don't offer an opening, and he'll get him home," Rus guessed.

"Definitely," Harry agreed. "And it isn't enough, not near enough, but he's in a hell right now that we don't get, but it's the worst thing for him. He spent the night in what he considers one of his own cells, and if he had any support, any respect, anyone thought he got a raw deal, with this, all that's going to fade away. Everything he was, was tied up in being the elected sheriff of Fret County. Now he's the bad cop. The lazy cop. The corrupt cop. The dirty cop. The man indirectly responsible for the deaths of two of his citizens. He's got no authority. He's nobody's hero. If he had any delusions of a comeback, that dream is dead. He can't twist it, even in his own head. He's a stain on the history of this department. He knows it. He's gotta live with it. And he's gonna die knowing that's his legacy."

"Well, there I was, all ready to have a shitty day, and you just made my week," Rus joked.

Harry smiled at him.

Rus looked back to the window. "If that's all we got, I'll take it."

"That's all we got," Harry said to the window. "And along with me knowing he'll burn in hell for all he did, especially how it ended for Sonny and Avery, I'll take it too."

THIRTY-ONE

Her Family Was Home

Harry

With Dern released and headed home, no word on anyone they were looking for, and a mild headache fomenting between his eyes from looking at Dern's bank records to see if he could find something the Feds missed (they wouldn't get Farrell's or Abernathy's until next week), Harry took off, maybe for the first time in his career, fifteen minutes before five.

Five minutes later, he walked through Lillian's front door and stopped dead.

His dogs greeted him, but Harry was stuck on the tall, built, handsome Black man holding his woman close in his arms.

A beautiful, willowy Black woman was sitting at the table eating chicken tetrazzini, and everyone had clearly decided it was five o'clock somewhere, because the wine was out, and it looked like it'd been out for a while.

Ronetta rounded out the crew.

"Harry!" Lillian cried excitedly and broke from the Adonis's hold to dash to him. She gave him a hug and a quick peck on the lips, then took his hand, dragged him in and said, "Come and meet Shane and Sherise."

He only slightly relaxed at the confirmation of what he'd already guessed: this was who she thought of as her brother and sister.

The slightly part of that was, she'd also told him Shane was her first crush, not to mention, Shane was frowning at Harry in a way Harry wasn't thrilled about.

And now that he saw them, he remembered them both. He went to school with them.

Harry played baseball, not football, like Shane did, so they didn't run in the same circles.

But now, he for sure remembered Sherise, who was the most popular girl in her class, and Harry had graduated by then, but if he remembered correctly, she was homecoming queen.

It helped Shane's mood when Sherise gave him a brilliant smile and a kiss on the cheek. Shane's frown faded a little when he saw the familiar and affectionate manner in which Ronetta greeted him.

But the handshake he got from Shane might have fractured a few bones.

Maybe Lillian was Shane's crush too.

"Harry, wine, beer, whisky?" Ronetta asked as if he'd walked into her house.

Then again, he suspected he did.

This was all family here, and that happened.

"Beer's good," Harry said.

"Want me to warm you up some tetrazzini?" Lillian offered.

He looked down at her. "Are you eating?"

"I was thinking of diving into the beef enchilada casserole," Lillian said.

"Alfredo gnocchi," Sherise put in her vote, even still stuffing her face with the tetrazzini.

"We're freezing Lillian and Harry's casseroles," Ronetta decreed. "I already told you I'm making my fried fish and corn-bread tonight." She looked to Harry. "I made my banana pudding for you, Harry. Something healthy."

Harry couldn't stop his chuckle, because bananas were a power food, but not sandwiched between layers of pudding, whipped cream and Nilla Wafers.

"Can we talk outside?" Shane asked him.

Sherise rolled her eyes at Lillian.

Lillian smiled.

Ronetta topped up her wine.

"Sure," Harry said.

Since he was closer, Harry led the way.

Though, Shane walked all the way to the garden gate with Harry following before he stopped.

"I'm sure you get what I wanna talk about," Shane announced.

"Yeah," Harry said. "And there are three different law enforcement agencies—"

"No, man," Shane cut him off irritably. "You're *living* with Lillian and you two have been dating for only a week?"

Ah.

"No, I'm not living with Lillian. I'm staying with her. At her request," Harry corrected.

"And you two have been dating for only a week?" Shane reiterated.

"She loves you. So I'm going to try to be respectful when I say, Lillian's a grown woman, this is her choice, this is what we decided as a couple, and this is what's happening. I appreciate your concern, and I can assure you, I'm very aware our relationship is new. It might not make sense to you with how you're seeing it, but we're juggling getting to know each other with what's going on with Lillian, and I'm taking it as slow as I can considering the circumstances."

"Not slow enough, since you describe the two of you as a couple."

"Well, we are, and I'll let Lillian explain that to you if she wants."

"She has family right next door."

"She wants me right by her side."

Shane's handsome features pinched. "And that sure works for you."

"Listen, Shane, this isn't really your business—"

That made Shane's eyes flash. "The fuck?"

Definitely Lillian's big older brother.

"But I'm going to tell you anyway," Harry kept on like Shane hadn't interrupted, "because if I had a sister, I'd be like you. I'm here. My dogs are here. I'm where she needs me. But we haven't made love yet because I'm also *very* aware of her emotions right now, and I'm seeing to those."

Shane's chin jerked into his neck at Harry's frank disclosure, but Harry wasn't done.

"Now you tell me, you have the shitty timing of meeting one of the best women you've known a week before she finds out her parents were murdered, she found some balm in you being around, what would you do?"

Shane glowered at him for several very long beats.

He stopped doing that to glance at the house.

Then he dropped his head, lifted a hand, rubbed the back of his neck before he straightened and looked at Harry.

"I'm being a dick," he said softly. "But Sonny was like a dad to me. Avery was pure sunshine, and my second mom. And I gotta tell you, I'm pissed as fuck what happened to them."

"I get you."

"Be honest, how's Lilly Bean doing with this?"

"She's strong, but she talks, she cries, she has times I can see it come over her. But she's hanging in there."

"Don't let Mom fool you," he warned. "She's gonna be the backbone of all this, but she's suffering too."

"I'll keep an eye."

"Now, back to what you were saying, you all have any clue who would do this?"

"What has Lillian shared?"

"I just got home maybe twenty minutes ago. I didn't want to ask."

Harry nodded and ran it down.

"Fuck. After all this time, you got more than I expected you would," Shane remarked.

"We don't have a shooter, but we got a lot of people looking for him, whoever the fuck he is, and I swear to you, if there's any chance in hell of finding that guy, we're gonna find him. And we're gonna nail him."

Shane studied Harry a moment before he said, "I believe you." He shot another glance at the house and finished, "We should probably go inside."

Harry looked over his shoulder to see Ronetta, hands on hips, looking annoyed, standing in the window with Sherise, who, when she got Harry's attention, lifted her hand and did a finger wave. Lillian was there too, but she was bent over like she was petting one of the dogs.

They walked in, and the instant Shane closed the door, Sherise declared, "So, *Mom*, just in case you want to give me more guff about not giving you grandchildren, hark!" she cried, using her hands to indicate Shane like she was advertising a bottle of shampoo. "Feast your eyes on my big brother, who scares all my suitors away by having various versions of *a talk outside*." She clasped her hands in front of her and aimed fake moon eyes at Harry. "Please don't leave, Harry, no matter what badass bullshit Shane just treated you to."

"Language," Ronetta snapped.

"Mom, I'm thirty-eight years old," Sherise snapped back.

"You're never too old to respect your mother," Ronetta returned.

Shane was grinning hugely as he picked up a wineglass and took a sip.

Then he made a face. "Who bought this?"

"Not everyone can afford fifty-dollar bottles of wine, Shane," Sherise stated.

"I give a discount to family, Sherise," Shane returned. "How much did this cost?" he asked Lillian.

She sucked in her lips and refused to answer.

"Jesus Christ, you got it off the five-dollar shelf," Shane accused.

Ronetta cupped her ear and asked the ceiling, "Did I just hear my beloved son take the Lord's only begotten son's name in vain? Please tell me I did not. Pretty please."

Lillian came to Harry and handed him a beer. Then she claimed him from the side with her arm around his waist, so he slid his around her shoulders.

He took a sip and watched her face.

And fuck yeah.

The lightness was there.

There were two integral pieces missing who would always be lost to her.

But her family was home.

"OH MY GOD, THE SUNFLOWER WAR!" Sherise yelled.

Lillian giggled. "We could barely get into our houses when Mom and Ronnie were trying to outdo each other with sunflowers."

"The stalks of those are rough as hell. Think I lived a whole month coated in Neosporin," Shane put in.

"I can only say I was sure glad it was petunias the next year," George stated.

"Av won," Ronetta sniffed. "Av always won."

"And you always beat her with the better cornbread," Lillian said, then she took a bite of the same.

They were sitting around George and Ronetta's dining room table, eating fried fish, green beans, some carrot and turnip mash that Harry thought would suck, but was phenomenal, and corn-bread, which Lillian was right, it was the best he'd ever tasted.

And Harry was paying close attention, because conversation had moved to remembrances of Sonny and Avery, and he wanted to make sure Lillian was cool with it.

But Lillian was not only cool with it, she was blossoming under it.

He caught Shane's gaze, and Shane gave him a nod, sharing he was having a mind too.

So Harry looked to George, who tipped his head to the side to acknowledge he was on the lookout as well.

"I thought I'd never want to look at another sunflower after that year," Sherise said, then her voice changed. "But now, they're my favorite flower."

Harry tensed, he sensed Shane and George tensing.

But Lillian just reached out a hand across the table, Sherise took it, and they held on, with fingers and gazes, before they broke and Lillian said, "Remember when Mom got it in her head to have a chicken coop?"

Sherise burst out laughing, Ronetta chuckled, even Shane and George smiled.

And George said, "By the time she finally gave up on that, Sonny was running out of excuses as to why he couldn't build one for her. He wanted to spend his weekends cleaning up chicken poop like he wanted his fingernails pulled out at the roots. He kept coming over and asking me for new excuses she might buy, and damned if I wasn't running out of them too."

"I'll tell you what, if I had a rooster waking me up at the crack of dawn, there'd be some super fresh fried chicken on my dinner table that night," Ronetta declared.

And everyone was laughing.

"Think that's the only thing Sonny ever refused her," Ronetta whispered to her plate.

Lillian slouched to the side and hit Harry.

Harry wrapped an arm around her shoulders.

"He spoiled her something rotten, didn't he?" Lillian asked.

"Every damn day of his life, baby girl," George answered. "Every damn day."

Sherise sniffled.

Shane grabbed hold of his sister like Harry had Lillian.

"I miss her singing," Sherise said.

"I miss his really bad jokes," Shane said.

"I just miss my friends," George said.

"Well, they left us Lillian. And they left us a bucketload of good memories," Ronetta stated into what had become maudlin. "They left us with the way they lived with us, nothing but good and happy."

Harry took his wineglass and lifted it but said nothing.

"Hear. Hear," George said it for him, lifting his own.

Everyone grabbed their glasses.

"To Sonny and Av," George made the toast. "The best neighbors you could have. The best friends you could have. The best people there could be. I had a family of four when they moved in next door, but the minute they did, we all had a family of seven. Now they might be gone, but our family remains strong, and they'll always be a part of it."

"To Sonny and Av!" everyone said.

They all drank.

Lillian turned her head to give Harry's jaw a kiss, then straightened in her chair.

And they all ate great food in the company of family.

HARRY SURROUNDED her with him in her bed before he gave it to her.

So Lillian sat between his legs, his arms around her middle, as she read the last message her mother had for her.

There was an explanation of why they left her behind.

There was also a message of love.

Lillian didn't say anything for much longer than Harry knew it took her to read the letter.

Then he watched as she ran her fingertips over the words, like she could touch her mom again through her cursive.

"Will I get the original back?" she asked.

It was evidence, and likely not important enough not to be released, but in the unlikely event it was deemed so, he silently vowed he'd get it back for her anyway.

"Yes," he said.

"I wish…" She didn't finish that.

Harry gave her a squeeze. "What do you wish, sweetheart?"

"That she'd sent this. That they'd gone direct to the police department. That they'd kept driving. That they'd hidden in their room and never left." Her voice grew small. "That they were still here."

So he didn't lose hold on her, Harry moved her hair out of his way with his chin and buried his face in her neck.

"Thank you for bringing me a copy of this, Harry," she whispered.

As his response, he kissed her neck and lifted away.

She was now holding the letter to her chest, and she leaned back into him.

"And thank you for not letting Shane scare you away," she went on, lightening the mood, but keeping her mother's letter clasped to her.

"He wasn't as tough as all that, just worried about you."

"He's a good guy. I wish he'd find a great woman to marry and make babies so Ronetta won't complain about it anymore."

"And you'd get to spoil his babies," Harry added.

"Well, there is that," she replied.

Harry smiled as he remarked, "I think Sherise better get on that first."

"What Ronnie doesn't know is, Sherise doesn't want kids. It's kind of one of the reasons why she hasn't found a man."

"Why doesn't she want kids?" Harry asked.

Lillian shrugged and tilted her head back so it was on his shoulder and she could look at him.

"She's always been really ambitious. And she eats life. I don't think I've ever heard her say no to any invitation that came her way." A small smile hit her mouth. "Except kids. But she's up for anything. I think she just doesn't want them to slow her down." She pushed up just a bit and whispered like she was sharing a secret, because she was, "And don't tell, but she's been with someone for almost a year. It's pretty serious. They're looking at places to move in together. He doesn't want kids either. This is why Sherise isn't bringing him home to meet Ronnie and George. Because Ronnie will try to talk them into it. Oh, and also, so Shane won't talk to him *outside* and scare him off."

Harry chuckled.

She settled back in.

They lapsed into silence that was surprisingly comfortable.

Then she asked, "Do you think it would be weird to sleep with this letter under my pillow?"

"Not even a little bit."

"You're such a good guy, Harry," she whispered again, this time, though, it wasn't a secret.

They talked. They readjusted and got under the covers. Lillian smoothed the letter out under her pillow. Harry doused the lights.

They tangled up, and it took Lillian a while, but she finally fell asleep.

So Harry did too.

THE NEXT AFTERNOON, in the small, mostly Black-attended Baptist chapel in town, it was standing room only.

Lillian had elected to have Sonny and Avery's remains put in one urn, which from everything he'd heard about them, seemed apropos. That urn was on a pedestal at the front flanked by large, pretty autumn sprays of butterscotch mums, red gerbera daisies and big green leaves.

And sunflowers.

Off to the side stood a posterboard size picture of a handsome, auburn-haired man with his arms around a beautiful, blonde, green-eyed woman. They were outside. The sun was shining in their hair. She was bent double, her arms tucked to her front, her head back, her eyes sparkling, her gorgeous face full of laughter. He was behind her, bent into her, his arms wrapped around her, fingers curled around her wrists, looking at the camera, smiling.

She was wearing a sundress.

The pastor spoke of them as if he knew them, and Harry wondered if this was Ronetta and George's church, or all of their church. He and Lillian hadn't had time yet to discuss religion.

He'd wanted to stand off to the side, but Ronetta was having none of it.

This meant he was in the front pew between Lillian and Ronetta, George, Sherise and Shane rounding out their row.

When the pastor opened it up, numerous people came forward to share their love and amusing stories about Sonny and Avery, speaking with such respect and affection, it felt like the sixteen years had melted away and all they were relaying happened just last week.

When that ended, the choir in their robes stood up, and a young Black woman came forward as the pianist struck the first chords.

Lillian instantly tightened, sharing whatever this was, it wasn't expected.

And then the young woman, accompanied by the choir, started singing "(You Make Me Feel Like) A Natural Woman."

Lillian's arm flashed in front of him, and as if she was expecting it, Ronetta caught her hand.

And they held tight.

The singer didn't have the talent of Aretha Franklin, but nobody did.

She still kicked that song's ass.

When it was over, Ronetta and Lillian broke only so Lillian could blow a kiss to the singer.

The girl smiled and returned to her place in the choir.

So yeah, maybe this was Lillian's church.

The pastor invited everyone to the fellowship hall, and they stood from their bench.

No one in the chapel moved as Harry led Lillian out of the pew into the aisle. He held, because she held, until George and Ronetta, Sherise and Shane joined them.

Then they walked down the aisle together.

Harry saw them in the back: Josh, his wife, Amanda, Harry's dad *and* Caroline.

Jesus, his dad caught a plane from Arizona and dragged Caroline up with him.

He dipped his chin to them, hoping the look he gave them expressed the depths of his gratitude at their gesture, and he led his group into the fellowship hall.

Jenna and Janie, Molly and Kay were bustling around a table

filled with finger foods, and Trey and Mark were still shoving soft drinks and waters into tubs of ice.

With Lillian latching on to him, Harry stood with her as she received her parents' friends and acquaintances, and hers, nodding, giving hugs, accepting cheek kisses and hand clasps.

It seemed the entire Misted Pines football team, circa Shane's tenure there, shook his hand after they all gave Lillian tight hugs. Cade and Delphine gave their condolences. Rus, Cin and Madden as well. Even Doc, Nadia and Ledger showed, and Harry knew Lillian hadn't yet met any of them, and they didn't know Sonny and Avery. Same with his buddy, Jaeger, Madden's father, Cin's ex, who came with Rus, Cin and his girl, but he also showed to support Harry's new woman.

And Stormy took Harry's advice. It wasn't the most comfortable thing Harry ever did, standing beside his woman while her ex held her close (and for a fucking long time), but he got through it due to the expression on Lillian's face stating plain how much it meant.

Though, she understandably looked confused when his family arrived at them.

"Sweetheart, I want you to meet my dad, Greg, his partner, Caroline, my brother Josh, and my sister-in-law, Amanda," Harry introduced.

"Oh, wow," she whispered. "I...this is unexpected."

"Would have liked to meet you with a cup of Amanda's world-famous eggnog in my hand, but Harry called, and this is gonna have to do," his dad said, going right in for a kiss on her cheek.

"No pressure," Amanda added, coming in for a cheek brush after his dad moved away. "We have rooms at the Pinetop. And Caroline and I've got spa appointments."

"I'm staying with Lillian, you should stay at home," Harry invited, releasing Josh's hand and craning his neck to kiss Amanda's cheek.

"Caroline and Amanda have been on about this spa for the last two hours, so, I don't think so," Josh replied, then he smiled gently at Lillian and went in for his own cheek kiss. When he came away, he looked to Harry, "Brother, you and me have damn good taste."

"Hello," Ronetta butted in, which Harry translated to *You're taking up too much of Lillian's time, people I don't know, move along.*

"Ronnie." Lillian gestured to his family. "These are Harry's people. His dad, Greg, and Greg's partner, Caroline, and Harry's brother and sister-in-law, Josh and Amanda."

"Oh my!" Ronetta exclaimed. "Honored guests. Thank goodness I doubled up my baked bean recipe for dinner tonight."

"Her beans are *the greatest*," Lillian added.

"We're not here to intrude," Caroline protested. "We're just—"

"Oh now, I don't think so," Ronetta cut in, waving her hand in front of her face. Then she leaned in and whispered, "Come with me. Pastor Charles doesn't allow alcoholic beverages for the masses, but he's allowed me a stash."

Like a shot, Caroline and Amanda followed Ronetta, leaving Harry's dad and Josh behind.

"Really, stay at the house," Harry repeated his invitation.

"We have a suite with a view of the lake and a couple of days without the kids, so if you think I'll be able to pry Amanda away from that, you clearly don't know my wife," Josh replied.

"You have guests," his dad said to Lillian. "We'll visit more later, darlin'."

"It's really so lovely that you came," she returned.

"This is going to make me sound unhinged,"—his father's gaze shifted to Harry and then back to Lillian, making a point even in the circumstances she couldn't misconstrue—"but I wouldn't miss it for the world."

Lillian gave him a soft, sweet smile.

His father took her hand, patted it, then he and Josh moved away.

It took another half an hour for the people who were left to share their thoughts and condolences, and finally Harry had Lillian to himself.

"How you doing?" he asked.

"Mom sang that song to Dad," she belatedly explained the unusual memorial music choice.

"Figured it was something like that."

"I love it that your family showed. That's so crazy sweet."

"Like Amanda said, no pressure, honey. They're laid back and the holidays are around the corner. Plenty of time to get to know them then."

"Do you honestly think Ronetta is going to let them get away with a stealth visit, in and out, without her feeding them?"

Harry grinned at her.

Her eyes warmed as they dropped to his mouth.

Then her gaze moved to the room like she was looking for something.

She found it, because she waved at someone.

He turned that way and saw Madden waving back.

"They were gone so long, I'm going to keep them with me for a while," Lillian said so quietly, he had to lean in to hear her.

"Makes sense."

She turned to him. "And then I'll figure it out. Maybe I'll keep them with me forever. Maybe I'll spread them in the wildflower field Dad used to take Mom on hikes to, because she loved it so much."

"Your choice," Harry pointed out the obvious. "From what I hear about them, they'll want you to make it and trust you'll make the right one."

She leaned into him, and Harry suddenly had to brace, because she gave him all of her weight.

"I'm so glad you're here, Harry. *Right here.*"

"Wouldn't be anywhere else."

"I don't think I'll ever wear black again."

She was wearing a simple, body-skimming, modest dress that was very attractive, suited her figure, and was perfectly appropriate for the occasion. She told him Ronetta bought it for her.

And she looked good in it.

But black was not her color.

"Again, your choice, but you look gorgeous. You're the perfect mix of your mom and dad."

"Perfect mix," she whispered, slid her arms around him, and pressed her cheek to the lapel of his suit jacket.

He dropped a kiss on her head.

"Hungry?" he asked there.

"How long do you think we have to stay here?" she asked in return.

"You want me to take you away right now, we're gone. But I reckon Ronetta knows the protocol."

He was right.

She did.

Because twenty minutes later, Lillian and Harry were in his truck with an urn...

And a massive posterboard picture of two people in love.

THIRTY-TWO

Cleansing and Warm

Harry

The next morning, Harry came out of the bathroom wearing jeans, a long-sleeved tee, his hair wet and combed back, his feet bare.

He hit Lillian's great room to see Linus and Lucy flat out on their beds, but Smokey was sprawled on the floor next to the chair Lillian was sitting in at the kitchen table.

Not a surprise. He and his pups had run five miles that morning.

Lillian was wearing sleep shorts, a tight cami, a slouchy cardigan, with equally slouchy big socks on her feet.

She had one heel up to the seat, the other foot on the floor, and her finger was through the handle of a mug of coffee. Her eyes were drowsy, her hair a sleep-tangled mess, and she was a mix of totally adorable and imminently fuckable.

Her somnolent green gaze came to him, then it went to the kitchen counter.

Harry looked there and saw a steaming mug of coffee by the Nespresso.

She'd timed it to have it hot and ready for him when he got out of the shower.

Christ, he wanted to go right to her.

But he knew that wasn't wise. They were fresh off the memorial. They had plans in about an hour to meet up with everyone (including his family and hers) at the Double D for brunch, and as such, yet again, the time wasn't right.

So Harry took her invitation of coffee as his excuse not to drag her back to her bedroom.

He was hips against the counter, heel of one palm on it, sipping her kickass coffee, when she said, "Caroline called. They checked and they've got openings for facials and massages at the Pinetop. She asked if Ronetta, Sherise and I want to join them this afternoon. I called Ronnie, and they were all in. I hope it's okay that I said yes."

"Of course it's okay, baby," he murmured.

"I've never been to the Pinetop spa," she told him. Then she mumbled, "I've never actually been to a spa."

Harry could see that. In spite of it all, she'd made a beautiful life, but it wasn't a surprise it didn't include regular spa visits, or any at all.

But it was high time she added those kinds of things to her busy schedule.

"You gonna get a facial or a massage?" he asked.

"Massage," she told him.

Perfect, he thought.

"Good," he said.

They both took sips.

"You feeling okay?" he asked.

"Are you asking if I'm hungover?" she returned.

Ronetta and George had hosted Lillian's extended crew, including all her best girls, their men, and Harry's family. She served up baked beans and potato salad, with George wrapped up in a fleece manning the grill out back and filling burger orders. Ronetta had jam cake and ice cream for dessert.

And the wine, beer and cocktails had flowed freely.

Everyone had changed into something comfortable before going over, and it got to be like a party. There was laughter. Phone numbers were exchanged. Future plans were made.

And Ronetta gave Harry a tour of her sunroom, which rested across the entire back of their house. This meant he walked through the length of it, seeing they might have cut their long backyard in half, but they'd doubled the footprint of the house, giving everyone their own space—including their kids when they'd been at home—and then some.

It gave Harry food for thought.

"Yes," he answered Lillian's question.

"Nothing the Double D's French toast won't fix," she told him. Her lips quirked and she remarked, "Your dad seemed really excited to tuck into their biscuits and gravy."

"When he comes up, we usually meet at Josh and Amanda's. He hasn't been back to MP in…" Harry thought about it, "since I won the election."

"I'm glad he's taking advantage of being home."

Harry smiled at her.

Her eyes warmed when he did.

Then they wandered.

They caught on something, and she noted, "I've been forgetting to turn down the furnace."

He glanced where her eyes were aimed, saw nothing, and asked, "Sorry?"

She sipped again and shared, "I like to turn down the furnace at night. Sleep snuggly." She gave him a look he felt in his crotch on the word "snuggly," before she continued, "It also helps with the gas bill. But I've been forgetting."

He turned again to the wall, and it was then he saw an old dial thermostat he was shocked as shit still worked, considering it had to have been installed in the seventies.

"While you're at the spa, I'll go by Mackey's." Mackey's was the local hardware store. "Get you a thermostat you can program and control on your phone. I'll set it up, have that taken care of before you get back from the Pinetop."

She said nothing. Didn't protest. There was no *you don't have to do that* or *that's too much*, and when Harry returned his attention to her, his body locked.

Lillian had rested her cheek on her knee, but her gaze was on him, a look on her face he'd seen nuances of since he'd met her, but the feeling behind it was full force now, nothing buried, nothing hidden, nothing restrained, and it hit him like a rocket.

There was gratitude, and such depth of affection, it felt like it filled the room, he was swimming in it, and the waters were cleansing and warm.

And he'd been reborn.

Harry's mug crashed on the counter, and in two long strides, his swift movements making Smokey jerk up, he was at Lillian.

She'd lifted her head, and he pulled her mug out of her hold, set it on the kitchen table, caught her at the back of the neck and bent to take her mouth.

She opened immediately at the insistence of his tongue, and on his first stroke, she mewed into his mouth. The sound and feel sent a shock of heat through his body straight to his dick, and he sliced an arm around her back and yanked her out of her chair.

But it was Lillian who wrapped her arms tight around his neck and plastered her body to his.

It wasn't the time.

Though, it was.

They both knew it.

They hungered for this, needed to feed from it, the effort at keeping it at bay had drained both of them, and they had to fill up, doing it taking from the other.

Which was why Harry and Lillian both angled their heads, and the kiss became carnal.

She pulled his tee up at the back, and when her nails scored along the skin there, Harry grunted and grasped her waist.

He picked her up, turned her, put her on her ass on the edge of the kitchen table, then bent over her so her back was to it.

She wrapped her legs around his hips, and fuck...

Fuck...

That felt so goddamned good, he grunted into her mouth and slid his hands up her sides to her tits, where he used both thumbs to drag hard at her nipples.

She dug her feet in as leverage and rubbed herself against his stiff cock.

Jesus, he needed inside her.

And she needed him inside her.

Her drapes and blinds were open. He had to get her to her room.

This was happening.

His phone vibrated at his ass.

They both stilled, but Harry did it while groaning.

He couldn't ignore it.

It wasn't about his job. For Lillian, right now, that could wait.

It was that it could be something about her parents' case.

He broke the kiss and rested his forehead against hers, their heavy breaths mingling.

When he opened his eyes and lifted away, he saw loss in hers for a moment, but her gaze moved over his face, and something entirely feminine, exquisitely possessive and excruciatingly satisfied entered her expression.

And then she smirked, and that burned through his cock too.

She knew exactly what she did to him, and she liked it.

It was safe to say, Harry not only liked it too, he liked that she did.

"Better get that, honey," she purred.

His dick twitched at the tone of her voice.

Fuck.

He didn't move other than to pull the phone out of his pocket and look at the screen.

It was his father.

That wouldn't have anything to do with Sonny and Avery, but his dad had no reason to call, and Harry was a cop. Something souring in his gut told him to take it.

"Hey, Dad," he greeted.

"Harry. Son," his father replied.

Harry straightened, taking Lillian with him so she was sitting on the edge of the table, but his attention drifted over her head as he focused on his father.

"Everything cool?" he asked hesitantly, because he could already tell it was not.

"Harry, I brought Caro around to the house to show it to her, and, son, you need to come out here." His father paused, then, "Don't bring Lillian."

Shit.

"But call one of your deputies to come with you," his dad finished.

Shit.

THIRTY-THREE

Not Thinking Good Thoughts

Harry

H arry pulled up beside his dad's rental car.

Caroline was in it, maybe because autumn had taken firm hold and the morning was chilly.

Maybe because of what Harry saw across the front of his house.

He reckoned it was the second one, considering the pallor of her face and the weak smile she aimed in his direction.

His father was standing several feet from the foot of the steps.

Harry got out and joined him.

Once there, he stared at the bright red spray paint, in huge letters, spelling out BACK OFF!!!!!!

And yes, there were six exclamation points.

All the front windows had been smashed in, some shards on the porch, but Harry could tell right away that most of the breakage would be inside, meaning someone had thrown something through them from the outside.

"Got an idea of who did this?" his dad asked tightly.

He had three, and to be gender inclusive, four.

Karl Abernathy.

Roy Farrell.

Cheryl Ballard.

And Willie Zowkower.

He was a cop, so he had cameras, and he focused on the one he had pointed at his front door.

It was covered in red paint.

He pulled out his phone and opened up the camera app.

He hadn't sprung for the system that sent motion sensor notifications. He didn't have much to steal, he lived among the wildlife, and critters would constantly trip the sensors, and in being forced to contemplate it in that very moment, he'd been riding a lowkey ambivalence to his home since he lost Winnie.

In essence, he didn't give much of a shit.

Like now.

He wasn't upset at the damage.

He was annoyed with the message.

He scrolled through footage of when his camera was activated. He saw some racoon activity.

And then there he was.

Definitely a he.

Cheryl was out.

Dark clothes. A balaclava covering his face and hair. He kept his head down as he approached, then lifted a gloved hand, fingers spread over his face, which effectively hid any features the ski mask might expose, and then there was nothing but the nozzle of the spray can. Any footage after was just dark.

Willie Zowkower was tallish, maybe an inch or two shorter than Harry, and lean but muscular.

Roy Farrell was average height, now on the wrong side of middle age, and he carried quite a bit of extra weight.

Karl Abernathy was firm on the short side, stocky, and he used to be bulky with muscle.

Harry had always wondered if Abernathy's short stature was one of the reasons he was such an asshole.

The man in the video had a hint of a gut, but his shoulders were broad, and he was at most, five six.

And Harry would recognize that puggish gait anywhere.

His phone vibrated in his hand as he replayed the video, and he saw it was a call from Trey.

Goddamn it.

They'd exchanged numbers the evening before. Trey and Mark had told him they'd had to dump the commissioner of their fantasy football league when, on the first game of the season, he changed his lineup illegally. They appointed a new commissioner but hadn't found anyone to replace him. They invited Harry to tap in and take his picks.

Harry had never been in a fantasy football league, even if he was a football fan. This was because, as noted, the last eight years, he hadn't done much of anything but his job. Doc had pulled him out of the prison he'd created for himself, but that only meant he hit up a few of the frequent parties Doc and Nadia threw.

Other than that, and recently finding Lillian, he hadn't pushed it further.

Even knowing he didn't have the time, he'd accepted the invitation, partly because he was going to be a part of her crew now, he liked these men, and this was as an official of an invitation of friendship as men could extend, partly because he was a fan of football, but also because it was high time he got a fucking life.

But he didn't think Trey was calling because he was rabid for Harry to get in his picks.

He glanced at his father, stepped away and took the call.

"Hey, Trey," he said.

"Hey, Harry. You got a second?"

No.

"Yeah."

"Listen, okay, this is gonna be weird," Trey began. "I didn't want to get into it with you yesterday, for obvious reasons, but Friday, Jenna got a call at the store. It was from Willie."

Fucking *shit*.

"Yeah?" Harry prompted.

"Lillian's ex. Like, *way* ex," Trey informed him.

"I know," Harry said.

"He wanted to order flowers sent to Lill, and he told Jenna to pick whatever she thought Lill would like from her shop and make a basket or something. Budget five hundred bucks. Jenna told him that wasn't appropriate, but he insisted. Said he'd call someone else to send her something if Jenna didn't do it, but he knew Lillian would prefer Jenna got the business. She took the order but decided not to fill it. Or, she's going to, but she's going to send it to the old folks' home and make someone's day there, because she knows Lill wouldn't be a big fan of Willie horning in right now. That said, she also could send it, just anonymously, and when it's a better time, tell Lill it was from Willie."

Harry had little doubt Rita called her son and told him to lay off.

And Harry didn't like what it said when a son who'd toed the line his entire life kept stepping over it in very visible ways.

Especially now, when he was imposing himself on Lillian's life in a manner that Harry, the man in it, felt like he was staking some kind of claim in order to make some kind of unwelcome comeback.

"I can't tell Jenna how to run her business," Harry told him. "But I can confirm something you both know, this gesture would not be welcome by Lillian, now or in the future, anonymously or not."

"Yeah," Trey muttered.

"How did he pay for it?" Harry asked.

"Credit card."

Harry turned to watch Wade rolling up in his cruiser.

"He's got three warrants out for him in Fret County, Trey," Harry said. "I'd appreciate getting the credit card number."

"I'll text it to you."

"Obliged."

"We'll figure it out on this end, Harry. But you saying what we're thinking, Jenna can just refund him in a few days. If he gets shitty, he can talk to me."

Trey was no joke. He came off as a lovable teddy bear, but everyone knew you didn't poke a bear.

"Great, Trey. And thanks for calling."

"No problem."

By this time, Wade was walking to him, his eyes on the house.

"Karl Abernathy," Harry told him when Wade stopped at his side.

"Fucker," Wade said in an undertone.

It was more than that.

A lot more than that.

Harry snapped a photo then opened up his text string to Rus.

Hate to interrupt your Sunday, but this happened. Got Abernathy on video doing it. Face obscured, but it's him.

He sent the photo.

Then he saved the video and sent that.

Feeling heat, Rus pointed out the obvious.

Yep, Harry confirmed.

I'll go get some plywood. You take care of Lillian. I'll contact Wade or Karen and process the scene, then board up the windows.

Wade's here. Lillian has a spa appointment this afternoon. I'll be back to help. There won't be anything, he wore gloves and a ski mask, but we'll process anyway.

Figures. But gotcha. Later.

Harry shoved the phone in his back pocket. He sent his father a reassuring smile when he caught his concerned look, though he knew his father wasn't reassured.

"I'm not thinking good thoughts," Wade said.

"Nope," Harry agreed.

"This isn't about a file audit and shitty police work," Wade noted.

"Nope," Harry again agreed.

"I'll go get my camera," Wade sighed.

"Appreciated," Harry said.

That was when Harry stood, staring at his house, making the decision that if he and Lillian went the distance—which they would —they'd move in here for as long as it took to blow out the back of her place and add on enough rooms for two to three kids, and whatever extra space she wanted.

They'd then sell this place to pay it off, and if there was extra, start college and wedding funds.

He also stared at it knowing this was only the beginning.

A man who didn't know right from wrong was running scared.

Harry wasn't that kind of man, but he dealt with them nearly every day.

There were three doors available to him.

Obviously, Abernathy wasn't going to pick door one, come clean.

Equally obviously, he wasn't going to pick door two, which was get out of town and as far away as possible.

He'd picked door number three, because he was far more familiar with what lay beyond it.

Threats and intimidation, going at both hard, then harder, until he got what he wanted.

Harry wouldn't normally give two fucks about this.

But he did now.

Because he had Lillian.

He had something to lose.

And so did she.

THIRTY-FOUR

One of The Many

Harry

That evening, they'd had dinner with Harry's family at The Lodge, then went to the Squirrel's Nest for an after-dinner drink before Harry knew (and put it instantly out of his mind) his father wanted his woman alone in a hotel room, the same with his brother, so those four took off to the Pinetop.

Josh and Amanda were leaving early the next morning because Josh had some appointments in the afternoon he hadn't had time to reschedule.

His dad and Caroline were staying an extra few days so Greg could commune with some of his old buddies and introduce them to Caroline.

And Harry knew he and Lillian shared the same thing on their minds when he pulled Lillian's coat off her shoulders, exposing the figure-hugging sweater dress she was wearing under it, a dress that had dicked with his dick all night (her high heeled boots just added insult to injury, though, this was the kind of pain Harry was never going to complain about), and she said, "I'm not sure Greg and

Caroline are feeling the whole, I've-been-burned-you've-been-burned-let's-keep-this-casual thing anymore."

"Getting the same feeling," he remarked, taking her coat to the hall closet.

"Are you okay with that?" she asked, her gaze intent on him.

"Couldn't be happier," Harry answered. "As you can tell, Caroline is an amazing woman. She makes Dad happy. So, yeah. They make things official, however they do it, I'm all for it."

Her intensity cleared, she shot him a soft smile and joked, "Moran men on the move."

He returned her smile and hung up her coat before he shrugged off his leather one and did the same with it.

"Feeling one last whisky?" she asked.

He was feeling recommencing what they'd been interrupted doing that morning, but since they'd had the intrusion, he was also feeling he should give it another couple of days.

"No, I'm good."

"I'm going to make some tea, want some of that?" she offered.

He didn't normally drink tea.

But he was living his life again, so what the hell.

"Sure."

She grabbed the copper kettle from her stove and took it to the sink.

She then blindsided him. "Want to share what's got you wound up since you took off this morning?"

He noticed her tenseness then, something she'd also been hiding until she asked that question.

"It isn't about your mom and dad," he assured.

She put the kettle on the stove, switched on the burner, then turned to him and raised her brows.

They'd made so many inquiries, it wasn't a secret they'd reopened Muggsy Ballard's case.

But Harry had been coasting on brunch plans, her spa appointment, contacting his insurance agent, putting up plywood and sweeping up glass, installing a thermostat (among other things), and Lilly and him changing into something nicer to go to The

Lodge as his ploys not to share what his dad had discovered that morning.

He couldn't dodge it any longer.

"We've reopened a case that was deemed a suicide, but it was a homicide, and the person that's implicated is feeling antsy. He vandalized my house."

"Oh, Harry," she whispered.

But he watched carefully, and he didn't see fear permeating her features.

First, there was obvious upset on Harry's behalf.

Then, anger.

"Who would do something like that?" she snapped.

Her eyes got big when it came over her, remembering that question was one she was waiting on an answer to for her tragedy.

Therefore, Harry went to her and pulled her into his arms. She rested her hands on his chest.

"This is the first time something like this has happened. We got him on video. I know who he is. It's just finding him now," he told her.

"Okay," she replied.

"Normally, even the stupidest criminals know not to directly dick with a law enforcement officer in this way," Harry went on.

"If you know who this guy is, do you know if he's stupider than the stupidest criminal?" she asked.

He smiled at her. "He's not the brightest bulb in the box. But he might think he can intimidate me. Though, he also knows me, so he probably knows that's not going to happen."

"So..." she let that trail to prompt him to go on.

"If I had to guess, he definitely knows we're looking for him. He knows what he did, even if we don't understand the full extent of it yet. He's running scared and he's the kind of guy who would act out rather than do the right thing."

She slid her hands up to his neck and remarked, "You've got a very complicated job, Harry Moran." She used her thumbs to stroke the sides of his throat. "You sure it doesn't weigh on you?"

"I never said it didn't, honey," he told her gently. "I just said there's nothing else I'd want to do. Some days are like today, irritating and frustrating. The thing I know is that humans will never stop doing that kind of shit."

He had to go on carefully, but he'd already learned this was Lillian Rainier. Simon and Avery had raised a strong, smart, loving girl who could take some serious licks.

So he went on.

"But then we get those days we can give answers to people who need them and justice for people who deserve it. There isn't a job out there that doesn't come with some heavy, Lilly. Maybe mine is heavier some days, but in the end, it's worth it."

She had that look on her face again, the one she wore that morning, and he thought it was about what he'd just said, and perhaps it was.

But there was more.

"You gave me more than a thermostat today, Harry," she noted.

He did.

She had a new doorbell with a camera and there was also a camera on the side door that led to the backyard from her garage.

"It's basic safety these days, sweetheart."

It was the truth, but there was more.

She knew there was more because she cocked her head.

"And I'm not taking any chances," Harry continued. "I know Ronetta comes and goes as she pleases, but I'm going to ask you to lock your doors when you're home from now on. You should do it anyway. I just want to be careful. I can get you new locks so Ronetta and George, and anyone you want can get in with just a fingerprint."

"That might be kinda fun," she replied.

He was glad she was going to look at it that way.

The kettle whistled and she slid out of his hold to go get some mugs and a box of tea.

After she'd set everything up and poured the water, she handed him a mug.

"Peppermint," she explained. "The massage therapist told me I had some crazy knots in my muscles, and I might get a little nauseous because she released some toxins. She wasn't wrong. I feel kind of queasy. Mint helps."

"You got Epsom salts?" he asked.

She shook her head, cautiously sipping, then she said, "Wait. Someone sent a basket of bath stuff after they heard about Mom and Dad. I think there were some salts in that."

"I'll draw you a bath, put in the salts. They leech out the toxins, and it'll help you relax."

As answer, she slid her fingers up into his hair and put pressure on his scalp, but Harry didn't make her try too hard to bend his neck as she came up on her toes and pressed her mouth tight to his.

Harry initiated tongue, Lillian instantly responded, but this wasn't one of their kisses that fed their fire.

It was thorough, but languid and sweet.

Lillian had had a good day surrounded by family and people who cared. She'd had a massage, and that, coupled with a hot bath, would hopefully help her sleep, and that was what Harry wanted for her.

So this kiss was about intimacy, closeness, togetherness.

This was one of the many types of kisses they'd share thousands of over the decades. A late-evening lazy kiss that said everything, but didn't have to lead to anything.

Harry absolutely wanted to guide their relationship to the next level.

But right now, this was precisely what both of them needed.

And this was what they had.

Later, while Lillian was in the bath, Harry had the game on and his dogs around him.

And he found he actually liked peppermint tea.

THIRTY-FIVE

See Clear

Harry

Early the next afternoon, Harry was returning to the station from talking to the staff at the bookkeeping firm where Cheryl Ballard worked.

She hadn't called in sick that day, she was just a no-show, and her boss and co-workers were getting worried about law enforcement visits and Cheryl's continued absence.

Harry made it worse, because the sheriff coming to call was a strengthening sign things were really not good.

He'd learned what Sean had learned when he'd come out days earlier.

Cheryl Ballard was liked. She was a good employee. Dependable, normally.

Though, one woman who Harry deemed as closer to Cheryl than the others, and as such, she was someone who was cottoning on to the situation, shared Cheryl had very bad taste in men.

This wasn't news to Harry, and it, along with everything else they weren't getting meant they were no closer to anything on any of what they were investigating.

The cops in Idaho hadn't found Sonny's purse or Avery's wallet.

Jason and Jesse had been poking around, but along with their inquiries, and those of the police in Coeur d'Alene, they'd been unable to find anyone other than the motel owners who remembered them. Jason and Jesse decided that well had run dry and they were going to return to help dig into things in MP.

No word from the Dietrichs.

Because of this, Rus started putting more pressure on the son in DC, and in return Gerald Jr. started getting nasty, claiming police harassment and throwing barbs "because I know how you all work in Fret County."

Fortunately, Rus didn't easily get his feelings hurt, and he didn't hold back about how choppy the water was where his parents were wading, and if they didn't do themselves a few favors, the riptide would carry them away.

Unfortunately, what made up his job was nine parts hard slog paperwork, running down leads that came to nothing, filtering through what they had to see if they had anything (and often finding they didn't), painstakingly going through data and information, and waiting, with only one part being them getting their man (or woman)—that was, if they ever did.

They were neck deep in that shit now, working old cases which made all of it worse.

They just had to have patience and persevere.

The fortunate part was, Harry had a good deal of experience with both of those.

It was on this thought a call came in.

It was from Polly.

He took it. "Hey, Polly."

"Heya, Harry. Karen just briefed me, she's off somewhere with Rus now, so she wanted me to touch base with you. They ran down that credit card number. The card belongs to a woman named Tamara Barbeau. She lives up in Vancouver. Karen gave her a call, and Tamara had a lot to say."

"And what's that?"

"She said her husband just upped and left a few days ago. The thing is, he took a bunch of stuff when he did. Her emergency stash of money. Some necklace her granny gave her that she treasures. But it's also worth some cash. Even swiped the money out of her purse, along with her credit card."

From what Trey said, it sounded like Jenna had run that purchase, so obviously the card hadn't been reported yet.

Even so, he queried, "Did she report this stuff stolen?"

"She said he could get into pickles. She thought he was maybe just in another pickle, he'd figure it out like he normally does and come home. A little girl talk with Karen, this seems to be a thing with her man. Taking money, precious and valuable items would go missing, he'd get hold of her ATM card and make withdrawals. Karen obviously was a little surprised Tamara put up with this, but Tamara said she loved him, and once he got his life sorted out, it'd all be good. We can say she wasn't really happy when she heard he was using her card to buy his ex-wife flowers and gifts."

"One guess, her husband is Willie Zowkower."

"No, her husband is John Berringer. But when Karen asked for a description, John sounded a whole lot like Willie. So Karen sent a photo of Willie, and whaddaya know? Her husband married her under a false identity. We can just say Tamara wasn't thrilled to learn that either."

Jesus, what was Willie up to?

"Karen run down John Berringer with the Vancouver police?" Harry asked.

"She said she's going to get on that when she gets back."

Maybe instinct, maybe just practice in taking in his surroundings at all times, Harry turned his head, and at what he saw, he lightened his foot on the accelerator.

"Right, I'm headed back to the station," he told Polly, even if he had just decided on a detour. "I can't touch that investigation either, so let Karen know you're going to keep some fires burning while she's out in the field, and you call Vancouver and see if they've had any run-ins with a John Berringer. Be sure to link it with our earlier inquiries about Willie Zowkower."

"Will do, Harry. See you soon."

"See you," Harry said as he swung into a spot at the side of Frick Park.

This park was going to be one of Megan's many lasting legacies.

At the end of Main Street, the site had once been a thriving department store, which had gone out of business when Harry was just a kid. Nothing really took there, because the space was so vast. There were murmurings of a variety of different projects, turning it into apartments, or condos, or breaking it up and making it a kind of mall.

Nothing ever came of it, and in the meantime, the building became derelict and was eventually condemned.

It didn't look bad from the outside, but it was a ghostly reminder of a once thriving local business that had been edged out by chains and eventually online shopping.

With Megan's magic, she got the property transferred to the town, the building was demolished, a public vote had been instigated, and the people of Misted Pines decided to honor Eliza Frick, Misted Pines's illustrious suffragette, who also happened to be a staunch prohibitionist.

Prohibition had been an epic fail, but the results of Eliza's efforts cleared Main Street of the bars and bordellos that had been their main feature since the West was being won, opening it to shops, cafes, tea rooms, and eventually their cinema and more.

In the end, Eliza was the architect of what became of Misted Pines, which had once been a den of sin frequented by trappers, hunters, gold and silver prospectors, and railroad workers. To that day, there wasn't a single bar close to the town center, and that meant it was peaceful in the evenings, and sleepy in the late evenings, and for the most part, safe.

Now that park had a border of low hedges, lawns of thick grass, graveled pathways to a center feature of a fountain surrounded by flowers and urns, this ringed by benches that had been donated by local businesses and prominent families.

Misted Pines's infamous coven unsurprisingly maintained it, clipping the hedges, de-weeding and fertilizing the lawns, and planting the flowers. Come March, hyacinths and daffodils poked through the retreating snow. Tulips came next. Through the summer months, there were riots of flowers in the beds and hanging from the lampposts.

MP citizens picnicked there. They fed the birds there. They walked their dogs there.

But now, the foliage had been cleared and Harry knew they were preparing to decorate it for Halloween.

Also now, Ronetta sat alone on a bench by the fountain.

Harry debated whether to get out of his cruiser, but remembering what Shane said, he did.

He walked up to her and was standing beside her before she started and peered up at him.

Tears were tracking down her face.

"Didn't mean to startle you," he said quietly.

She dabbed at her cheeks with a hankie, and that almost made Harry smile, because Ronetta was the only woman he knew who carried a hankie.

"Lost in thought," she replied.

"I can leave you to it, if you like," he offered. "I can also stay."

It took her a moment to decide before she patted the bench beside her.

Harry sat down.

The fountain was still gurgling. They'd turn it off soon and drain it, so the freeze wouldn't ruin the pipes. It'd eventually be filled with pumpkins and corn stalks or some Halloween/Thanksgiving/autumn design scheme, those being replaced by Christmas decorations.

But right then, even with the traffic going by on Main Street, the sound of the water made the space tranquil.

Harry kept his eyes on it.

Ronetta did too.

"I have a very good marriage," Ronetta shared. "God smiled down on me when He pushed George in my path. But a marriage is always a marriage."

He knew what she was saying.

Harry's marriage had lasted only a year before Winnie broke her neck in that fall from her horse.

In the intervening time, he'd enshrined what they had, so in his memories, every second of it was light and laughter and love.

The truth of it was, Winnie had a foul temper. She sometimes wasn't good at communicating and was terrible with confrontation, until she was ready to explode, and then she let loose.

On his side of things, Harry got pissed she let it go so far rather than just being honest with him about shit that bothered her. So his response wasn't remotely healthy either.

They'd been young. They'd find their way eventually. Harry knew it down to his bones.

It didn't make their marriage any less strong or loving.

It just wasn't perfect.

"I'm the middle, have an older brother, and a younger one," Ronetta told him. "No sisters. Until Avery."

Damn.

He knew it, but there it was.

He took her hand.

Her fingers curled tight.

"She loved George completely," she went on. "So anything I could say when I complained about the little, stupid stuff, it didn't bother her a bit. It didn't turn her mind on George. She just listened. She was a safe place for me to let stuff go. She was a safe place for George that I could do it. I gave that same back with her and Sonny."

Harry said nothing.

"When my momma used to work my nerves, because she could be bossy," Ronetta continued. "When Shane and Sherise would get up to mischief. She was my sounding board. She was my touchstone. And I had the honor of giving that back to her."

Harry remained silent.

"It wasn't just having someone to complain to. I cannot tell you how much she used to make me laugh. We shared recipes. She helped me in my garden. I showed her how to bake bread. We had a tradition at Christmastime. She and Sonny and Lillian would come over and we'd eat and trim the tree, then George, Shane, Sherise and I would go over, and we'd have dessert and trim their tree. They've been gone so long, but Christmas has never been the same. Nothing has been the same. And now, even though I always knew in my heart they'd never go without keeping in contact with Lillian, George, me, so I knew something was terribly wrong, and it had to be something like this, I know nothing ever will be."

Harry kept hold of her hand and remained silent.

"Lord, I miss her," Ronetta whispered.

Harry let her hand go and wrapped an arm around her.

She melted into his side and rested her head on his shoulder.

They sat that way for long minutes before Ronetta spoke again.

"I'll tell you what, George and I were beside ourselves when Lillian got mixed up with that Zowkower boy. George especially. He thought he'd failed Sonny. Shane was livid. Sherise was worried. It was torture, living next door to Lillian making that big of a mistake. Will say, that boy had stars in his eyes every time he looked at her."

Harry was careful not to react.

Ronetta kept going.

"But he was bad news. No backbone. That family strayed far away from the straight and narrow, and more often than not, it walked right up to our girl's door, and he didn't do a thing about it. I cannot tell you the relief we felt when she got shot of him. We should have expected it, one thing Lillian always had was a good head on her shoulders. Both her parents gave her that. But there was relief all the same." She gave Harry's knee a squeeze. "We haven't had any of those feelings recently."

"I'm not certain I can express how much that means to me," Harry murmured the god's honest truth.

"No need, son," she replied. "You get stars in your eyes, you can't see. You're not a man who gets stars in his eyes. You see clear. That's the hallmark a relationship will work. You can't make it work if you don't see your partner clear."

Having said that, she straightened from his shoulder, tucked her hankie in her sweater sleeve and sniffled, indicating her moment of mourning and leaning on someone had passed.

"You're the bedrock of all of them," Harry pointed out. "But you're allowed to have a reaction to all that's happening."

She finally looked at him. "Oh, I know."

"What I'm saying is, they're strong too, and they all worry about you."

A small smile hit her lips. "I know that too. That's family, Harry. All of it is. I suspect you know that as well as me, what with your dad and brother coming at such short notice to be sure someone was seeing to you while you see to Lillian."

"So Dad grumbled about that to you," Harry observed.

Her smile got bigger. "Nothing left when our kids are grown, and we've raised them right, but to find little things to moan about. Just serves to remind us how little those things are, and what good jobs we've done in raising our kids."

Harry smiled back. "So that's how it goes."

"That's how it goes." She gave his knee another squeeze and her face got very serious. No, *stern*. "And I hope you figure that out sooner rather than later so I can hold some babies in my arms before I'm too old to open a can a soup, which will already be indication I'm too old, if I can't make my own danged soup."

Now he and Lillian were going to get it.

He didn't mind in the slightest, which was why he chuckled.

She stood and he came up with her.

She then took both of his hands and tipped her head back to catch his eyes.

And she dealt an unexpected blow when she stated, "My heart clean broke for you when you lost your wife."

"It was a long time ago," he reminded her.

She gave his hands a squeeze. "I know, honey. Just saying, I'm not the only bedrock around here. I thank God every day I found a good man and he's been mine for a long time, and if God keeps smiling on us, he'll stay that way. I don't know what you're going through, finding your love, and then years down the road, running into the next one. I just know it all has to be a lot for you, especially how it's happening."

"I stopped to give you a shoulder to cry on, not the other way around," he quipped.

That got him another smile, then she said, "Just know, Harry, I see you. George sees you. Shane and Sherise see you. And in case you're not getting it, I'll make it official and welcome you to the family."

That meant so much to Harry, he released her hands so he could hug her.

She relaxed into his embrace and hugged him back.

When they stepped away, he asked, "You walk here?"

"Yes. Needed a constitutional."

"You want a ride home?"

Her gaze warmed, or he should say it warmed more. "No, darlin'. I want to pop into Kimmy's and see what Halloween stuff she's put out."

Harry nodded, bent and kissed her cheek.

When he straightened, she lifted a hand to lightly pat his.

"Stay warm," he bid. "And see you later."

"That you will, Harry. That you definitely will."

He smiled at her again.

And then Harry left Ronetta in a park that memorialized a strong, honest, honorable woman who made a difference in her life.

Which seemed fitting.

THIRTY-SIX

Where This Is Going

Harry

Harry was in his office, dealing with email, thinking one thing he knew for certain about his future. When he retired, he wasn't going to have a fucking email.

He sensed someone coming, looked up and saw Sean knock on the frame of his door.

Harry did not like the expression on his deputy's face.

"Hey, Sean," he greeted.

Sean knew that was the invitation it was, and he entered Harry's office.

He sat across from Harry and said, "As you asked, ran down the gun found in Clifford Ballard's hand."

Harry was stunned. "You found it?"

"Yep."

"How did you find it?" Harry asked, shocked he had, since there was no record of what happened to it in the case file, and no record of it in their evidence locker.

"Those morons gave it to Ballard's mother."

Harry had no idea what to think of that, it was so wrong in so many ways.

First, through ballistics testing, it was proved to be the instrument of Ballard's death, which turned out to be a homicide, and considering there was definitely a cover-up, not "losing" it or finding some other way to sully the path to using it as evidence was so fucking stupid, Harry didn't know how to process it.

Second, giving it to the victim's mother like it actually was her son's property (when it wasn't), and it was the weapon that took his life was...

Harry couldn't find words to describe it.

Stupid. Cruel. Insane. Inept.

Those were the words that sprang to mind.

For fucks' sake, with the minutest amount of scrutiny, this wasn't anywhere near a successful cover-up. It was only Dern's negligence that meant it had gone on this long.

"Ran the serials, Harry," Sean cut into his thoughts.

Harry nodded for him to go on.

"Chased it back...here," Sean said.

Harry stared even as he felt his pulse stutter.

"Here?"

"Missing from the evidence locker." Sean's eyes dropped to the stack of files they had yet to dive into that had been pulled in the audit. "It was the weapon that shot Terence Dinklage."

This being why the shooting of Terence Dinklage, a man who didn't die, but he did lose the use of his legs, had been pulled in the audit. The weapon missing from the evidence locker.

That crime had never been solved, regardless that Terence reported he had an ongoing and escalating dispute with his neighbor about the eastern boundary of his property.

After one of many heated arguments about that very thing, later that day, when Terence was on his riding mower, mowing an area of his eight acres that was close to that boundary, he'd been shot in the back.

Two days later, the gun had been found in a dumpster in town and turned in by a traveling hippie who had been dumpster diving behind the Double D, foraging for food.

It was registered to Dinklage's neighbor, Albert Tremblay, who had conveniently reported it stolen a week before the incident.

However, this was another case Harry had pulled, because he questioned the veracity of the dates this theft was reported, considering it was entirely too coincidental, and one thing cops hated and many flatly refused to believe in were coincidences.

No prints were found on the weapon.

The case hadn't tanked because the gun had disappeared from the Fret County evidence locker. No matter how adamant Dinklage was that it was Tremblay who shot him, he'd been shot in the back. He didn't see the shooter. And Tremblay's wife reported he was in all that afternoon, watching a Mariners game on TV.

Another sheriff might have pushed it, dug deeper, but Dern didn't.

Worse, Farrell was lead on both cases. This could either explain the lazy detective work or be another indication Farrell was bent.

This incident occurred about six months before Ballard was shot.

And tracing that weapon back to their evidence locker meant the only real likelihood of who could get their hands on it was a cop.

Following that thread, it shone the light even brighter on Abernathy, or as an outside possibility, Farrell as the shooter in the Ballard case.

"You know what this means?" he asked Sean.

Sean winced, as any good cop would when confronted with the actions of a bad one.

"Yeah," he replied.

Harry pulled the stack of files closer and yanked out Tremblay's theft and Dinklage's shooting.

He tossed them on his desk in front of Sean and said, "Look through those. Then talk with Dinklage and Tremblay. Specifically Tremblay, and find people who know him. I want to know all about the dispute those two had. I also want to know if he has any ties to Dern, Farrell or Abernathy."

"You mean, start from the beginning?" Sean asked, sounding surprised.

"When I had time, I was going to talk to you, Wade and Karen. We need at least another investigator, with the growth in this county, it'd be better to have more. This means I need one, or all of you, to sit the detective's exam."

"We got money for that?"

Harry tapped the stack. "We're up to our necks, Sean, and I suspect that isn't going to end anytime soon. I'll find the money to promote when you pass."

"You think I'm ready for that?"

Sean was one of Harry's hires. He'd done three years as a beat cop in Seattle before his wife got pregnant, and both of them decided they wanted to raise their kids somewhere safer and quieter than the big city, and not incidentally, Sean's job would be safer too.

This meant he had seven years of police work under his belt.

"I'm not sure why you're questioning it," Harry remarked.

"I thought you'd go for Wade."

"As I said, this county is growing. Rus is the best at what he does, but he's not Superman." Harry indicated his computer with his hand. "And I've got to have half a mind to budgets, liaising with town councils and the County Commission, and twenty other admin tasks I can't let slide. I've got a jail to run, traffic to maintain, warrants to serve, a courthouse to keep safe, parole officers to support. It's time to promote, and you three have what it takes, so I want you three to consider this and make a decision." He tipped his head to the two files. "You can start with those. I want Rus focused, and considering I don't have a conflict of interest with anyone in those cases, you can run things with me. But yes. You're ready for it. And yes, I want you to start with the basics on those files and work up."

Harry leaned into his forearms on his desk and finished it.

"Link that gun to Abernathy or Farrell. Link Tremblay to Dern or Farrell. Connect the dots." He sat back. "If there are no dots to connect, find what dots there are and show them to me. I'll super-vise, but you're driving on this one, Sean. Let's get some good work done."

Sean nodded, one side of his lips lifting up, before he took the files and walked out of Harry's office.

He nearly ran into Harrys' dad as he left.

"Sorry," Sean said.

"Takes two to tango," Greg Moran replied good-naturedly.

Sean smiled at Harry's dad, nodded to him and disappeared.

Greg came in.

"Surprised you can walk straight, considering you've spent the afternoon with your crew at The Hole," Harry joked as he watched his father take a seat.

"My boy's the sheriff. Not feeling like getting a DUI. It might be embarrassing for him."

Harry grinned. "Obliged."

"Caro's going to stay another day, as planned. I'm gonna run her into Seattle, then come back, stay at the old place," his dad announced.

Harry wasn't a fan of that.

And he saw that his father wasn't over his concern of the day before.

"Dad—"

"No, Harry," Greg cut him off. "You still got my old shotguns. I'll replace the camera with something that gives me a heads-up I got company. I'll oversee the replacement of the windows once the insurance company gets itself sorted. Though, I reckon whatever weaselly-assed coward pulled that shit, he did it because he knew you weren't there. Probably not gonna pull any more shit if some-one's there."

"And he might," Harry pointed out.

"So he'll get some buckshot in him if he does," Greg returned.

As sheriff, no matter he wouldn't mind Karl Abernathy running from a shotgun pointed at him, he couldn't condone anyone pointing a shotgun at anybody.

"Dad—" Harry tried again.

"Let me save you the time and trouble," Greg interrupted. "You can talk, and you can talk some more, I'm not going anywhere, but I am gonna stay there. This is not about me doubting you can handle yourself or your job. I know you can handle both. This is deeper, and we both know it."

Harry wasn't sure what he was talking about.

"Care to explain?" he invited.

"One, Lillian's it for you."

No hesitation, Harry nodded to confirm.

"You two gonna have kids?"

Harry nodded again.

"Well, I've had discussions with Caro. I like the weather down there, but I hate missing out on my boys' lives and watching my grandbabies grow up. I told her I wanted to become a snowbird, find something small somewhere up here so I'm closer to you both for half a year. If you and Lillian move on with what you got, that move is definitely going to happen. Caroline came to Phoenix with her ex when her kids were in grade school. They're all close, though obviously not the ex."

When his dad smiled, Harry smiled back.

Greg kept talking.

"She gets all the good stuff all the time. But she says she'll be happy to spend six months up here with me. Gets her out of grandma duties, something she loves, but I'll be frank, one of her daughters takes advantage. Acts like Caro has no life outside looking after her kids. She can't pull that shit if Caro is fifteen hundred miles away."

Harry didn't say anything, even if he thought it sucked one of Caroline's daughters was thoughtless and treated her mom like that.

His father did say something.

"I got love and memories in that house, Harry. I raised my two sons in that house. I may have lost my wife while we were there, but I did right by our boys there. Josh and I spoke, and he feels the same. We see the writing on the wall. You've cared for it, but you don't care for it."

Harry opened his mouth, but his dad kept talking.

"We understand. Absolutely. But Josh and me want to buy it from you, pull down the stables, put up something we can put toys in, ATVs, snowmobiles, a boat. Spruce up the house. New kitchen. New décor. Amanda and Caroline would love digging into that. I come up in the summer, got a place to stay that's closer to my boys, real close to you, and Josh has a weekend getaway where he can take his family." A heavy pause and then, "And you're shot of it, and what you lost there, but maybe we can make it into something different, for us, for you, so we all can make new memories and keep it in the family."

"You know Lillian and I are very new," Harry warned.

His father's brown eyes grew intent. "I know you. I see her. I know that's true, and I know where this is going. And I'll admit, that's part of it. For me and for Caroline. Lillian lost her father. I'm a father. You're not. You don't get what it feels like, even though I don't know her all that well, to know she's a woman alone in this world without her dad. Caroline feels the same about Lillian losing her mom. I know Ronetta and George fill those shoes. But you can't have enough people looking out for you."

Fuck, but Harry loved his dad.

And Caroline was a damn fine woman.

Greg wasn't finished.

"And I will be beholden to her until my dying day for making you see there's life after Winnie."

Harry felt his chest squeeze.

His father kept going, but this time, his voice lowered.

"I loved that girl like a daughter. She was perfect for you. I miss her to this day. I hurt for you...to this day. I will say, I was a little concerned, what with you meeting Lillian during this sad time, and what that might mean, you being you and what you do for a living."

Harry spoke, and his tone was steely. "It isn't that."

"I know, son," Greg said quietly. "Again, when you're a father, you'll get it. You worry about pretty much everything, especially if it has to do with your child's happiness. Even if I met her at her parents' memorial, I saw right away it wasn't that. Is she leaning on you? Yes. Are you a man who doesn't feel right if he isn't strong enough for the people he cares about to lean on? Yes again. But it's very obviously not about that. And even if I didn't notice it, the way Ronetta and George are with you two, I would have gotten it."

Greg took a moment, and Harry let him, before his dad hit him with it.

"Lillian isn't a thing like Winnie. Doesn't look like her. Doesn't act like her. I don't know how you did it, Harry. But you found another wonderful woman who's perfect for you."

Harry didn't realize he was holding his breath until his father said that, and he let it out.

Greg went on, "It isn't like the buyback of the house has to happen tomorrow. But I don't want some asshole to get it in his head that maybe he can trip your trigger faster, say he burns the place down or something. And I want more time with you. I miss my son. I want to get to know Lillian better. And frankly, Harry, I miss home."

What could he say to that?

"We'll talk about it more later, but if you stay there, I want those cameras installed."

Greg Moran grinned.

"Caroline's going to come up with you?" Harry asked leadingly.

Greg shrugged. "We both thought we could keep it casual. We both were wrong. One of the reasons I can work with Josh on the buyback is because I'm selling the house down in Phoenix and we're moving in together."

Harry's smile was broad at learning that news.

"I dig that for you, Dad," Harry told him, his words loaded with feeling.

"I dig it too," Greg replied, smiling his own wide smile.

"We should talk about dinner tonight, if Caroline's leaving the day after tomorrow."

"She has an evening flight. We've got time. We can do dinner tomorrow night. But I think Lillian needs a break from everyone up in her face and space. They all got good intentions, but we both know, Harry, shit happens, but life goes on. You have to settle into life getting on, because you're not always going to have people around to distract you." More intent in his gaze. "And you have to have the space to deal with it without distractions."

Harry couldn't agree more. He'd learned that lesson the hard way, distracting himself with work, and not getting on with life.

Lillian hadn't complained.

The memorial was behind them. Lillian had placed the urn on a chest in her living room with the original picture of her parents that had been enlarged for the service resting in a fancy frame beside it. Sherise had left that morning. Shane had an afternoon flight he was probably on right then.

The stage was set.

Lillian had to get back to real life.

"I might be with you at the house," Harry told his father.

His dad burst out laughing.

When it started to wane, Harry stated, "I'm just staying with Lillian due to what's been happening."

"You try to leave that girl, go ahead, see what happens," Greg suggested, sounding like just the thought was hilarious.

"You were right earlier, Dad, she needs space."

"From *me*, Caro, people sending her flowers and covering her in casseroles. Not you, boy. Christ."

"Again, we haven't even been together a month."

They'd barely been together two weeks, and only that if he was looking at it like Lillian did, and their first "date" was the first day they met.

"If I've told you this once, I've told you the story a million times. Yor mother opened the door to me when I picked her up on our first date, she smiled at me, and I knew I was going to marry her. You just know. You knew with Winnie. You know with Lillian. And I'm telling you, son, no matter what's going on, she isn't missing she knows it with you."

"I'm aware. We've discussed this," Harry shared. "But she still needs—"

"You."

"Dad—"

Greg shook his head. "You do what you gotta do to make it right

287

in that head of yours. Part of me is proud you've got such a firm grip on right and wrong. Part of me wonders where we went wrong with how stubborn you are. But you'll see."

Harry decided it wasn't worth the effort to discuss it further.

"Right. We'll see. So dinner tomorrow night?"

"At the Bon Amie. I'll make reservations," Greg decided, then mumbled, "I hope they still have those pork chops."

"They do," Harry confirmed.

"Right," Greg replied. "Say, seven o'clock? Talk to Lillian. Let us know. And if George and Ronetta want to join, they're welcome."

Harry nodded.

His dad stood.

And again, Greg didn't hesitate to hit him with it.

"Love you, boy."

This was something about his father that always pierced Harry right through the heart.

Greg Moran never let the bullshit ideals of masculinity get in the way of sharing what he was feeling. Josh and Harry always knew they were loved, not only because their father showed it, but because he told them.

He'd noticed Josh did the same with his wife and his kids. His children were young, two and four, but Josh said it, often and with feeling.

And when Harry had people to love, he did too.

"Love you too, Dad," Harry replied.

That was when Greg treated his son to something else he'd never been stingy with.

A look of unadulterated pride.

And with that, Greg Moran walked out of his boy's office.

THIRTY-SEVEN

So Harry

Lillian

"This is stupid," I said nervously into the phone.

"Girl, it is *not* stupid," Sherise replied.

I was sitting cross-legged in the middle of my bed, and Harry had texted ten minutes ago saying he'd be home in ten minutes.

The time was nigh for me to abort, if I was going to abort.

Oh Lord.

I totally wanted to abort.

"I think he's the kind of guy who likes control," I told Sherise.

"I think he's the kind of guy who would lasso the moon if you decided you wanted it on a lead, so you need to be very clear to communicate what you want," Sherise told me, her words making my blood sing and making me forget (for a few seconds) I was in the throes of a panic attack.

It didn't take long for me to remember my panic attack.

"He's got a thing about being very clear he's not taking advantage of me."

"I love that," Sherise returned. "Though, I doubt he'll mind you take advantage of him."

I was going to say something, but the dogs, who were keeping me company lazing around on the floor by the bed, all shot to their feet, and Smokey let out a low woof.

"Lill?" Harry called, and the dogs raced out of the room.

As for me, my heart started racing for two reasons.

First, it was too late to turn back now.

Second, that was the first time he called me Lill. I loved it when he shortened my name to Lilly, but now I was wondering if I didn't love Lill more.

"He's home," I whispered to Sherise.

"Bye," Sherise said, then immediately hung up.

God!

"Lilly?" Harry called again, but from closer.

I twisted to put my phone on the nightstand.

I'd just twisted back when I saw Harry, still as a statue, standing in the door, his eyes glued to me.

Dang, he was handsome in his uniform.

"Uh…hey," I greeted.

For a second, he remained frozen.

Then, right in the door, he bent and pulled off his boots and socks.

He took a step in unbuttoning his cuffs.

Another step, he unbuttoned his shirt at the collar, put his hands behind his neck and pulled it off, badge and pens in the chest pocket and all.

One more step, he was beside the bed and off went his T-shirt.

Instantly, I became sopping wet (full disclosure, that started happening the second I saw him in the doorway).

Now it was me who was frozen with Handsome Harry Moran standing shirtless in my bedroom, his magnificent chest on display.

We stared at each other (okay, we did that after I made the superhuman effort to tear my eyes off his chest).

Then he lunged.

His long, heavy, hard body covered mine, and he kissed me.

I knew immediately this was different.

This wasn't hunger. This wasn't carnal.

This was voracious. It was unbridled.

His kiss was consuming. There wasn't room to think. Only to feel.

And damn, was I feeling things.

So many things.

Including his hands moving up my sides, his callouses catching on the chiffon and lace of my nightie, something so masculine, so Harry, just that made me quiver.

He suddenly gripped it, broke the kiss, and my arms were up, my hair was flying, as he pulled it off and tossed it aside.

He didn't even look at my body. He came in for another kiss, and I hadn't found myself in the seconds our lips weren't fused, but I lost myself in his kiss again anyway.

His mouth moved from mine, down my neck, my chest, his hand curled around my breast, his lips closed over my nipple, and he drew so deeply, my pussy clenched, my back arched, and I whimpered.

He sucked and he sucked, and he sucked harder as I moaned, gliding my fingers in his hair, eventually losing control as the sensations he was causing overwhelmed me, and I fisted it in my fingers.

He moved to the other breast and did the same, his thumb dragging roughly across the nipple he left behind, doing this over and over again.

Oh my God, I was going to come with just this.

On that thought, Harry returned his attention to my mouth, and he was kissing me dizzy again, but his hand was tracking with intent over my ribs, the swell of my belly, and he didn't mess around. No teasing, he dug right into the waistband of my panties, over the triangle of hair, and his fingers slid through my drenched folds.

Sensation rocketing through me, I mewed, but Harry growled at encountering what he was doing to me, and his weight left me.

I made a noise of protest that was cut short as, with no ado whatsoever (delicious!), Harry dragged my cute panties down my legs and threw them off the bed.

And then I watched in stupefied, turned-on fascination as his upper body undulated in a downward motion at the same time he grabbed the backs of my thighs.

He ended up on his stomach on the bed, my thighs thrown over his shoulders, I got a single second of the ridiculously sexy vision of his thick dark hair between my legs, then his mouth was on me.

I dug my heels in his back, my head in the pillows as Harry went at me with his mouth.

And that was the only way to describe it.

He went at me.

Good Lord.

He really knew how to do this.

"Harry," I panted, squirming and arching and rubbing against him.

It was going to happen, I was going to come, and it was going to be *insane*.

Harry stopped eating me.

No!

My head shot up.

"Honey," I whimpered.

"Shh," he soothed, now even sexier, looking up my body at me, the brown in his eyes liquid chocolate. He was using one finger to circle my clit in a maddening way that was both sweet and hot, but not hot enough.

"I—"

He dipped in again and fed.

Yes.

It didn't take long before he took me there again.

And right before I slid over the edge, he stopped, moved up and kissed my mound.

And again, my head shot up.

"Baby," I begged.

He grinned.

Oh my God!

I was going to kill him.

I was about to tell him that when he went down on me again.

Oh yes, this was good. So good. *Soooooooo sooooo* good.

He stopped again.

"Harry!" I snapped.

But this time, he left the bed, and I knew by the look on his face playtime was over for Harry (and I already knew it was *way* over for me).

I knew it more when he undid his uniform trousers and pulled them down with his boxer briefs.

And I got a full view of the entirety of what made Handsome Harry Moran, *Handsome Harry Moran*.

His cock wasn't too long, it wasn't too thick.

It was *just right*.

And those thighs?

I shivered.

He stepped free of his trousers and hesitated.

I didn't understand why, then I did.

Knowing his history, I'd planned for this, thinking with the way he wanted to take care of me (no matter what scrumptiousness happened on my kitchen table the day before), he might not have planned, so he might not be prepared.

I reached under the pillow, pulled the line of condoms out, sat up and gave it to him.

"Christ, baby," he said, his voice deep, guttural, so much so, it was like an exquisite touch.

I didn't have to encourage him to get a move on. He tore one of the condoms off the strip, and like he'd done it just yesterday, the day before, and every day of his life, he ripped it open and slid it on.

Seriously, how could I almost orgasm watching a man roll on a condom?

I didn't know, I just knew I almost did watching Harry handle his cock.

Then I wasn't thinking about that, or anything, because Harry was joining me in bed, parting my legs, lifting them high, settling between them on top of me.

He kissed me, light and sweet, before he raised his head.

I could feel him hard between my legs, and I was wondering

why he didn't get on with it like I very much needed him to, when he whispered, "Ready?"

I looked at him, and it was only then I could feel him straining to stay in control.

He was ready, more than ready, but he was holding to be sure I was.

And I knew then what I'd pretty much known since he held my hair back while I threw up and then sat with me in my little bathroom.

I would love this man until my dying breath.

"Ready," I whispered back.

He put his hand between us, took hold of himself, and I felt the head of his cock glide through my wet. He caught, and his eyes holding mine, slowly, so impeccably slowly, he slid in, and in, until he was seated fully, filling me.

And there was all the proof I needed.

Harry was right, I knew it already, and we weren't even finished.

Sex became beautifully, unbearably, magnificently meaningful when you did it with the person you loved.

It was so gorgeous. So perfect. So everything, I caught his head in both hands and stared into his eyes before I pulled him down and kissed him.

He kissed me back and moved inside me.

At first it was controlled, each thrust designed for optimal buildup of pleasure, an adjustment of the hips, and he'd give me something new, another one, and he'd hit deeper.

I loved it. It was awesome.

But I needed more.

I wrapped a calf around his thigh, pulled the other leg back further, and he slid in deeper.

He grunted.

I ran my nails up his spine.

Harry growled, a noise so primal, so predatory, everything I had clenched around him.

And that was when he *unleashed*.

Ah yes.

There it was.

We kissed. We touched. We scraped. We scratched. We bit. We clutched. We licked.

And Harry fucked me.

Hard.

It had been building since I saw him standing at the door, but when it finally hit me, my climax came as a surprise. Maybe because it was an explosion so intense, I saw starbursts and felt nothing but Harry's cock pounding inside me, his mouth greedy for my moans, one hand gripping the back of my neck, the other one doing the same to my hip to hold me steady to take his increasingly powerful drives.

And my orgasm kept coming.

And coming.

And it continued to do so even as his head snapped back, his grunt shook the room, he planted himself to the root, shoved his face in my neck and his powerful body shuddered on top of me.

I was coming down, stroking him.

He was coming down, giving me all his weight.

Then he rolled, I was on top, and my face was in his throat.

My body rose and fell with his deep breaths, my pants listed over his skin, his hands smoothed over my bottom, my back.

And finally, he wrapped his arms around me, they went tight, and he was hugging me.

Harry just ate me, fucked me hard, made me come harder, and now he was hugging me.

Hugging me!

God, that was so *Harry.*

"Good?" he asked.

Oh so *fucking* good.

I lifted my head. "If you have to ask, I didn't do it right."

He smiled at me, and my heart skipped a beat.

He was just so beautiful.

So *Harry.*

"You did it very right, baby," he whispered.

I dropped my head and kissed him.

Harry returned the kiss as he rolled us to our sides.

He ended it by landing a soft peck on my nose and murmuring, "Be right back."

I felt the warmth of those words as he got out of bed but pulled the covers out from under me, red rose petals flying then drifting, and he tugged them over me.

I got to watch via candlelight as Harry walked from the room.

His chest? Fabulous.

Thighs? Amazing.

Cock? Sheer perfection.

But his back and ass?

Lord, help me.

I curled my knees up and snuggled into the bed, taking in the light of the multitude of candles I'd lit all around the room. The scent of the petals I'd strewn. And I saw the champagne in the big bowl of ice with the two champagne glasses sitting beside it on Harry's nightstand. I didn't have a champagne bucket, but that bowl worked perfectly.

So okay.

The scene I'd set wasn't original.

So maybe it was a bit goofy.

So it was also totally obvious.

It worked.

Splendidly.

I grinned.

Harry came back, and I gladly took in the show, until he lifted the covers and got in bed beside me.

He gathered me close, tangled us up, but his hands roamed, feeling an impossible mixture of still greedy, affectionate and soothing.

If he could do it, I could do it.

So I did.

"It was Sherise's idea," I blurted, throwing my girl right under the bus with this whole seduction scene.

His brows went up.

"Just to say, she came up with it because I was over waiting," I pointed out the obvious.

He chuckled, and man, I loved to feel when he did that. "I didn't miss that."

"I sense you like control, but you know, a girl's gotta do what a girl's gotta do."

"Was I complaining?" he asked.

"No," I answered.

I didn't think it was physically possible for him to pull me closer, but he did.

And he said quietly, "You were ready. I was ready. It happened. It was phenomenal. It's gonna happen again, soon, and go a lot slower, and I know that'll be phenomenal too. So it's not all good. It's more than good. In other words, don't worry about it, sweetheart."

"'Kay," I mumbled, feeling like preening not only at his use of the word *phenomenal*, but also that it was going to happen again… *soon*.

That said.

"You hungry?" I queried.

"I honest to God couldn't face another casserole."

I laughed and snuggled against him. "I've got some finger foods planned. If you open the champagne, I'll go get them."

"I'll go get them."

Of course he'd offer.

New thermostat.

Doorbell camera.

Drawing me a bath.

So Harry.

I gave him a kiss and said softly, "There are a few finishing touches. Five minutes. Okay?"

He nodded, but he kissed me, and since it was a good one (like all of them), it lasted awhile before he let me go.

I slid out of bed, found my nightie (pink, with a stretchy lace bodice, a short scarf-hemmed, see-through skirt and matching string bikini panties—I'd bought it ages ago with the thought of using it on Stormy in a last-ditch effort to keep him, something I didn't do, so now it was all Harry's). I pulled it on, found the panties and slid them on too.

"The panties are moot at this juncture, baby," Harry noted in a gruff voice from the bed.

I turned to him to see him watching me, his eyes again molten chocolate.

So...

Yeah.

My man could be naughty, what with thinking his woman would wander around the kitchen commando in a nightie with a see-through skirt.

"A girl shouldn't be *too* easy," I kidded, which of course made him burst out laughing, since obviously I was bottom-line easy, considering I essentially threw myself at him, without the throwing part, but adding rose petals.

I loved the sound of his laugh, so I was smiling as I went to the kitchen.

The dogs followed me around (I was preparing food, so they would, but I'd learned Harry's pups liked company, if he hadn't tired them out and they weren't sleeping it off).

I had a plate full of strawberries, grapes, crudité, rolled cured meats, olives, cashews and almonds. I had another plate of toasted baguette slices and feta mixed with cream cheese. I nuked the spicy honey, drizzled it on the cheese, sprinkled the chopped pistachios on top, grabbed some napkins and the other plate and headed back to the bedroom.

I'd heard the cork pop while I was in the kitchen, and Harry had the champagne poured by the time I returned.

He was under the covers, but sitting up, his chest still a feast for my eyes while I put our edible feast on the bed.

I rounded it and got in beside him. Once I'd settled, he handed me my champagne.

"Should we toast?" I asked.

"What would your toast be?" he asked in return.

"Um..." I bit my lip.

His face grew wolfish, and, *damn*...

I didn't know he had that kind of look in him.

But...

Nice.

"How about, to a great fuck and many more to come," he teased.

I raised my glass, laughing. "I will totally toast to that."

He grinned at me, we clinked, drank, and for my part, I watched closely as he reached for a feta piece, took a bite, then his eyes came to me and they warmed.

"Delicious, sweetheart, and this is perfect," he said softly, tipping his head to the plates.

"Glad you like it," I replied.

"I mean all of it, Lilly," he kept at it. "All of it is absolutely perfect."

Oh God.

My sweet Harry.

"Glad you like it," I repeated, but this time it came out husky.

His gaze dropped to my lips.

I felt a rustling, heard a snuffling and looked to the side of the bed to see Smokey's snout doing some doggie exploring.

"I know you love me, pooch, but I know you want prosciutto right now more than your next breath, and you can't have any until Daddy's done with it," I told him as I reached out a hand to stroke his head.

"I don't give them human food, Lilly," Harry said gently.

I frowned at him.

He smiled at me. "I don't want them begging."

I made it obvious as I turned back to Smokey, before I glanced to Harry's side of the bed where two chocolate snouts were also doing some exploring around the edge, then raised my eyes to Harry.

"A dog is gonna dog," I stated.

Harry started laughing again, maybe not as strong as before, but I still loved it.

I sipped then grabbed my own cheese-smeared piece of bread

and ate it. I'd seen the recipe on Instagram, and since it was quick and easy but looked delish, I gave it a go.

I was right. It was delish.

"Dad came by the station today," Harry said.

"Yeah?" I asked, popping an olive in my mouth.

"He's making reservations for Bon Amie tomorrow night. Caroline's last night in town. You good with that?"

Because it was expensive, I'd only been to the restaurant at Bon Amie once, on a date. Though I'd gone to the burlesque show they had in the basement more than once, because it was awesome and the perfect girls' night out.

"That'd be great."

"They've invited Ronetta and George."

"I'll get in touch with Ronnie tomorrow and see if they're free."

"And Dad told me he's selling his house in Phoenix and moving in with Caroline."

This made me so happy for Greg and Caroline, as well as Harry, I beamed at him.

His brown eyes twinkled.

Yes, it made Harry happy.

"He's also going to buy back the house, with Josh, and they're going to live up here for half the year. He misses his sons, his grandkids, and apparently Caroline's daughter takes advantage of Grandma, and she needs a break."

That wasn't cool of Caroline's daughter, but I was stuck on the first part of what he said.

"He's going to buy back the house?"

"Yeah," Harry said, popping a grape in his mouth. After he swallowed, he went on. "With Josh. They're going to collect toys. A boat. ATVs. Josh is going to use it as a weekend place." With that, he bit into a roll of genoa salami.

"*Your* house?" I pushed.

He focused on me.

"Don't you kind of need your house?" I asked.

"I do. And then, eventually, I won't," he stated.

My pulse picked up.

We stared at each other.

But really, nothing needed to be said.

Honestly, if he was a terrible lover, I'd see if we could work on that, and I'd put in as much effort as was needed.

But he wasn't.

He was as great in bed as he was everywhere else.

So, yeah.

Nothing needed to be said.

"I love that for you," I told him.

I watched the tension leave his shoulders, and he grabbed another piece of shmeared toasted baguette.

"Dad as well as Josh being around more often, I love it too."

"So, a good day," I noted, though it was a question.

"Sean found some evidence that's leading us further down the path of finding some answers on the Ballard case. I'm not surprised at the answer we're getting, even if it sucks. So yeah, a good day."

I knew he couldn't tell me why it sucked, but I loved he could talk to me in the way he could about his work, and he did.

And I really loved both of us having a good day.

Just to say, I loved practically everything, if it had to do with Harry.

I told him about my day. "I had an author reach out to me. I'm a fan of hers. She wants me to proof for her. She publishes four books a year. I have the time, and it'll be a nice bump in income."

"Awesome, honey," he said through a small smile.

"Totally," I agreed.

We lapsed into chatting about our days, about Harry's father's and brother's plans to update and redecorate the house. I nearly accosted him when I caught the warmth in his eyes after I told him I spent half an hour with the dogs throwing tennis balls in the back-yard. And I almost did it again when I asked him if he'd help me decorate for Halloween that weekend (no surprise, he said yes).

Harry made me remain in bed when he took the plates back to the kitchen. I refilled the glasses while he was gone (and yes, my drapes and blinds were open at the front, so Harry put on his trousers, though he did it commando...*yum*).

But we didn't drink the recharged champagne (at first), because Harry had other things on his mind when he returned.

Or one thing. Singular.

Me.

He did as he said he would, and our second time was slower. I got to get him in my mouth. He went down on me again. He took his time taking me there, and naturally, for me to take him to the same place.

But once we got there, it was no less spectacular.

We finished the night sipping champagne and whispering to each other.

I didn't like waste, but we didn't finish the bottle, because good nibbles, champagne, two orgasms, and all that was Harry, I got drowsy.

Harry blew out the candles, cuddled me close, and within minutes, I was dead asleep.

And all night long, in Harry's arms, I slept like a baby.

THIRTY-EIGHT

The Dogs Are Settled

Harry

L illian had already found hers.

In fact, her sleek, tight cunt rippling around his dick with her orgasm milked his to fruition, he buried himself deep, shot into the condom and groaned into her neck.

She clutched him tight with her arms and legs, considering he was fucking her against the wall of her bedroom, sweaty from the sex and the run from which he'd just returned.

So the seal being broken meant he couldn't even look into her cute drowsy eyes and take in her mass of messy bedhead hair and not fuck her against the wall.

Jesus.

In fact, the last three days had been a fuck fest.

Mornings, either when he woke, or she woke, or this time after he got back from his run. Evenings, she jumped him the minute he walked through the door. Always again before sleep. And once, she'd woken him up in the middle of the night with her hands moving on him.

Fortunately, she loved it and egged him on, and he loved it and did the same.

But now, he was dripping with sweat.

He still didn't move.

He simply held her, as she held him, another habit they'd formed after sex.

He understood why it happened.

They both knew when you found something special, you held on.

Unfortunately, they both had busy days, so they couldn't do it forever.

"You good?" he whispered against her skin.

"Awesome," she did not whisper.

He smiled, pulled her off his dick and held her as he set her on her feet, and he kept doing it until he knew she was steady.

She looked up at him and there was no drowsiness in her eyes.

They were sated, happy, bright and sexy with what they'd just shared.

And yeah.

He wanted to fuck her again.

Another yeah.

He found something really fucking special.

"I'll get your coffee ready while you shower," she said.

"You don't have to make me coffee every day, honey," he told her.

"I wouldn't do it if I had to," she replied.

With no reason to discuss it further, he gave her another smile, a kiss, then he moved away, pulling his joggers up over his dick (he'd only yanked them down in front in order to put on a condom and drill her—totally, they'd broken the seal).

They headed out.

She went to the kitchen.

He went to the bathroom.

Not long later, he came out carrying his boots but otherwise fully dressed, to see her, also fully dressed for their trip to Aromacobana, which would come after he made himself a smoothie or some oatmeal.

She was at the kitchen table with her laptop, a mug of coffee, and Lucy and Smokey crashed out around her chair. Linus was snoozing in his bed.

This was when Harry instigated another ritual they'd made.

He went right to her. She tipped her head back to get his touch on the lips.

He then went to the Nespresso to grab his readied mug.

He set his oatmeal up and put it in the microwave, then rested his hips against the counter and took a sip of coffee.

And since the weekend was now around the corner, he asked, "What does Halloween decorating mean to you?"

She tossed him a grin. "Just some corn stalks, pumpkins, and about a hundred bats flying across the front of the house."

"A hundred?" he teased.

"Okay, more like seventy-five."

He chuckled.

The microwave binged.

He grabbed a spoon, his bowl, and he took them and his mug to the table, sitting catty-corner to her.

Lucy adjusted so she had her head on his foot.

He stirred his oatmeal and got into what he didn't want to get into.

But he had to.

"We need to talk about where we're at."

Her startled eyes came to him.

"Where we're at?" she asked.

Harry went carefully. "Dad's at the house. The new windows are in, the cameras have been installed. It isn't that."

He knew she understood where he was going when her expression changed.

She didn't seem panicked.

She seemed upset.

Even so, he asked, "Are you good with me going home?"

"Do you want to go home?" she returned.

"That isn't an answer to my question," he replied gently.

"I didn't think—" She looked away.

"You didn't think what?" he pressed.

"I thought…" She didn't finish that either.

"You thought what, Lilly?" he asked softly.

She took a breath then returned to him. "The dogs are settled here."

For a second, Harry didn't move.

Then he busted out laughing.

"Harry." He could tell by the snap in her voice, she didn't think anything was funny.

With effort, he got control of himself and stirred his oatmeal, saying, "So I'm not going home."

"Maybe you can go home when your dad heads back to Phoenix," she suggested.

He was so not ever going home.

Because he *was* home.

With Lilly.

Wherever that would be.

"Maybe," he muttered, still smiling and shoving oatmeal in his mouth.

"Anyway, you're busy with important work, so you don't need to be driving all the way out there and back. You need the extra time to solve cases and keep the peace in Misted Pines," she declared.

He chuckled around a mouth full of oatmeal but said nothing.

Sure, the extra twenty to thirty minutes worked for him in a big way.

But she wasn't fooling anybody.

"I'm going to need to do laundry, or you're going to have to free up more than just a drawer," he said.

"You're welcome to use my machines but bring more stuff anyway. Laundry is a drag."

Harry was so not going home.

He kept smiling.

Lillian kept sipping.

It took her a bit before she said shyly, "I thought we'd decided."

"We did, honey," he replied. "I just thought, with this so new, you might want some space for a while."

"I've had space. I'm good," she told him.

He gave her a soft smile, and she returned the same.

Harry went back to his oatmeal.

Eventually, he took his bowl to the sink, rinsed it, put it in the dishwasher, downed the last of his coffee and put the mug in the dishwasher along with the one Lillian handed him.

He put on his boots. She put on her Adidas. They added the element that had now become another habit since Harry knew the dogs would behave for her, and they put on their leashes.

And then they officially started their day.

That being Harry, Lillian and their pups heading to Aromacobana.

THIRTY-NINE

Jawas

Harry

"So, boiling it down," Sean was saying to Harry in his office later that morning, "Albert Tremblay is an asshole. None of his neighbors like him. Couldn't find anyone in the entirety of MP who had much good to say about him. They all think he shot Dinklage. Their dispute went away after Dinklage came home from the hospital in a wheelchair, but everyone thinks that's not because he felt bad someone did that to Dinklage. Instead, he didn't want any more attention on their argument because it was motive for shooting the man."

Harry tapped the back of a pen against the notebook in front of him as he listened to his deputy.

"In other words, in a snit after they had words, he took Dinklage's legs then he gave up on the property dispute," Sean concluded. "But I couldn't place Tremblay as a bud of Dern, Farrell or Abernathy. The gun going missing seems to be about it being available to do Ballard, nothing to do with Dinklage and Tremblay. Apparently, this guy is such a cantankerous dick, he wasn't even tight with a guy like Dern."

"What about the gun reported missing just a week before it was used to shoot his neighbor?" Harry asked.

"He's adamant it was stolen on that day. His wife is adamant it was stolen, also on that day. And by the way, they're a perfect pair. She's got an attitude too. Though, they couldn't quite explain why it was the *only* thing they reported stolen. I don't know about the dates, Harry. Maybe he gave Farrell some money to fudge them in the report. Maybe Farrell didn't get the date correct when he was writing it. The problem with that is, we can't find Farrell to ask just how dirty or stupid he was."

This was a problem.

Nothing was giving with anything.

Abernathy was smoke. Cheryl Ballard was too. As was Farrell. Nothing from the Dietrichs.

Rus had reported the alleged fraud to the insurance company, and they were investigating as well, so there had to be more pressure on that couple, if they could get word to them that was happening.

But they'd been through bank records. Any cell phones registered to any of their suspects had either run out of battery (likely after they were dumped or left behind) or been turned off. No credit card use, though, both Abernathy and Ballard had withdrawn large amounts of cash from their bank accounts before disappearing. In fact, Abernathy had drained his.

No sightings.

No contact with anyone.

No fucking anything.

This was what Harry expected out of this investigation.

This was what he feared he'd be giving Lillian.

What was fucking with him was, it wasn't just his operation that was on this. The FBI had a vastly wider reach.

And still nothing.

"You want me to keep at this?" Sean asked, holding up the files.

"Is there a next step?" Harry quizzed.

"Yes. Talk to Farrell," Sean gave the right answer, it just wasn't an answer they could do anything about.

Harry sighed.

Then he changed the subject. "The NTN video exams are coming up."

"I applied."

Harry smiled.

"So did Karen," Sean told him.

Good, Harry thought.

"Wade isn't feeling it," Sean went on, telling Harry something he already knew since, in the intervening time, he'd had the same discussion with Karen and Wade that he had with Sean.

Wade liked the beat, the streets, the cruiser and working one on one with people. There were cops who preferred to make a difference that way, and Wade was one of them.

He'd already been promoted to sergeant.

It was time to think about lieutenant.

"Seems I got until February to find some money for you and Karen," Harry said. *And for a promotion for Wade*, he thought.

Oral boards happened in the first six weeks of the new year.

"My woman is thrilled," Sean said. "She says we'll save enough from not having to dry clean my uniforms, we can take a cruise."

Harry wore a uniform and required his deputies to do so. He also required them to be cleaned and carefully pressed.

Rus wore army green or khaki cargo pants and a long-sleeved polo or fleece with a Fret County Sheriff badge stitched on the chest.

Harry considered a more official version of that for the entire team, because it was more comfortable, easier to move in, friendlier to look at for the average citizen and a lot easier to maintain. But he didn't want to make that decision so soon after Dern was ousted. He needed the authoritative visual. He needed to make a statement he and his crew took their jobs seriously.

Which meant now, it was still not the time to make the change, with the cases they were investigating reminding people of Dern's tenure.

But he took the note from Sean.

Expenses like that on a cop's pay could dig deep.

He and Sean finished their meeting, Sean took off, and Harry opened the folder that had Abernathy's and Farrell's bank records in it. Rus had gone over them, and there were some anomalies he wanted Harry to look at.

He saw Rus had highlighted some line items, but he didn't get that far because his phone screen lit up with a call from Lillian.

She didn't often call, she texted, so his brows drew together as he took it.

"Hey, sweetheart."

"Okay," she whispered, and his back went straight at the pitch of her voice. "A nugget to file away. Apparently, Kimmy keeps track of when the citizens of Misted Pines decorate their houses for the holidays."

He relaxed.

"How do you know that?" he asked.

"She knows my schedule is this weekend, so she came over and told me my bats were lame, then she dragged me to her shop, and she wants me to buy these things that look like black net Jawas, but their eyes are lit all over their bodies, and they have a witch's hat."

"Jawas?"

"From *Star Wars*. Hang on, I'll send you a photo."

He knew he lost her and his phone vibed with a text.

He got the image, and she was correct. They looked like black net Jawas with witches' hats.

When he heard her talking again, he put the phone back to his ear.

"...less than twenty dollars each. She says I need five."

"Get three."

"You think?"

"Are the bats black?"

"Yes."

"So get three and some orange lights." The lights in the Jawa witches were orange. "I'll string them around the porch."

"Oh my God, I see your vision," she breathed with excitement.

Fuck, he loved hearing that.

"Harry says we need orange lights," he heard her say in a

normal voice, and he knew she was no longer talking to him. "And three Jawas."

"They aren't Jawas!" he heard Kimmy shout. "And you need five."

"Harry says three."

A jostling on the phone and then he had Kimmy. "Three isn't enough. They're witches, not wise men."

"Lillian's front yard isn't that big."

"It's big enough for five. You aren't forming a coven, or you'd need thirteen."

"Three, Kimmy."

"Four," she haggled.

But his attention was taken by Polly standing at the door.

And yet again, another member of his team was wearing an expression he didn't like.

Though this one was more about him not getting it.

"I have to go, Kimmy," he said.

"Gotcha," she stated quickly. "I'll tell Lillian."

Then she disconnected.

Polly walked in.

"What's going on?" Harry asked.

"That lady who came in the other day?" she asked as answer.

"What lady?"

"The one who came to share that Leland harassed her."

Harry felt a mild spike in adrenaline, pleased she was back, hopefully to lodge a complaint.

"She's back?"

"Her and nine other women."

Harry didn't move.

Polly came closer. "They're filing complaints against Leland, for harassment, and Karl Abernathy, for coercion-based sexual assault."

Harry stood immediately from his chair.

He stalked out of his office with Polly at his back, down the hall, and only stopped when he saw the entirety of his bullpen taken up with deputies talking to women.

Rus wasn't there, likely because he'd taken someone to the inter-view room for privacy.

The woman who'd come previously glanced up at him.

There was determination in her eyes and softness in her features.

"This is about Avery," Polly whispered.

Yes.

Word had gotten around about what had happened to the Rainiers.

"This is about Avery," Harry said.

The woman released his gaze as she answered a question Raul posed to her.

"If any of these deputies needs my office for privacy, it's open," he said.

"You got it, Harry," Polly replied, wading into the bullpen.

Harry returned to his office to lock his computer screen and put away anything anyone shouldn't see if his office was needed.

Sean knocked on the door. He had a carefully composed expres-sion on his face that Harry knew was him keeping a lock on losing his mind at what these women had been forced to endure. He also had a woman hovering behind him.

Harry nodded and walked out, closing the door.

His phone vibrated in his hand.

He looked at the screen.

It was Wade.

He took the call.

"What's up?" he asked.

"Did the usual drive-by Farrell's house, got flagged down by a neighbor. She asked me to check something out. Harry, I need another unit and permission to enter his garage under exigent circumstances."

Harry walked swiftly toward the back of the station. "What are the circumstances?"

"Something's dead in there, Harry. I'm standing at the door, and even outside, I can smell it."

Fuck.

"Wait for me. I'm on my way. We have a situation at the station, everyone here is busy. Call dispatch to send a unit out to you."

"Got it."

"Be there soon."

"Later, Harry."

He disconnected.

Harry pushed out the back door, jogged to his cruiser, pulled himself in, took the time to text Rus what was going on.

And then he headed to Roy Farrell's house.

FORTY

I'm Going to Find You

Harry

Harry stood in Roy Farrell's living room, letting the feeling of dread that had been creeping since he gagged his way through walking up to a very dead Farrell in his car move over him.

The living room was clean. Not just tidy, *clean.*

Floors vacuumed. No dust on the furniture. Even the fucking pillows were fluffed.

The kitchen, an entirely different story.

Dirty dishes in the sink. A full dishwasher that hadn't been started. Crumbs and spills on the counter. Coffee forming mold in the coffeemaker.

Same with the bedroom and laundry room.

Unmade bed. Dirty clothes on the floor. Overflowing hampers in the laundry room.

Harry didn't move even as Rus made his way into the house.

They exchanged a glance, and Harry stayed where he was as Rus conducted his own inspection.

Eventually, Rus came to stand at his side.

"Theresa says carbon monoxide poisoning," Rus shared.

"She'll find sedatives in his stomach."

"She will?"

Harry crouched.

Rus crouched with him.

Harry pointed under the couch. "Karl missed one."

"Fuck," Rus said, and Harry knew Rus saw the little blue pill there.

They both straightened.

"Struggle in here," Rus caught on quick and started to run it down. "Farrell in shit shape, Abernathy got him subdued, forced the pills in him, waited for him to go unconscious, took him out to his car, started it up. Death would seem like suicide, even the sedatives wouldn't bely that. You find a note?"

"Nope."

"No note. Man's got children. He'd explain. Clean in here, the rest of the house is a mess," Rus kept on. "He swept away prints, DNA, but he wasn't smart enough to go through the rest of the house. Instead, this is like a neon sign that says, 'something happened in here.'"

"Theresa notice any bruising that might indicate he was in a struggle?" Harry asked.

"She didn't say. But she was just strapping him to the gurney when I arrived. She'll find out more when she gets him on her table."

Harry stared at a living room that was far less attractive than the one his mom and dad left him and Winnie, even if it was less dated.

Roy Farrell had cheated on his wife repeatedly. She kept taking him back. Until she couldn't hack it anymore.

She left, taking the kids with her.

Through water cooler talk, Harry knew Farrell fought for full custody, just to be an asshole, and bitched about it constantly, because attorneys cost a fortune.

In the end, they shared custody, and that was all Harry knew about it, especially the last nearly four years when Farrell had been out of the department.

Then again, there were two kids' rooms in that house, and it didn't look like they'd been touched in years. Doing the mental math, his son was close to graduation, his daughter also in high school, and both rooms were still little kids' rooms no teenager would be caught dead in.

It didn't take an investigator's power of deduction to theorize that the kids were about as fond of their dad being a cheating loser as their mother was. They got older, they found ways to stay away from him.

Farrell ended his life working security at Box and Save, MP's big box store. He was head of it, but it had to be a pay cut. It was definitely a status drop.

Could be, he just couldn't afford to feed three mouths when he was so intent to stuff so much into one.

"You have a look at those bank statements?" Rus asked.

Harry turned to him. "Abernathy's?"

Rus nodded.

"Been kind of busy, what'd you see?"

"Consistent deposits. Cash. Five hundred here, a thousand there. Nothing the IRS would ask questions about. But also not on any schedule. Sometimes months would go by, nothing. Then there'd be random deposits for a few months, then nothing again. Though, over the years, that shit was adding up."

"To what?"

"Last count, around forty K."

Harry whistled.

"I called the bank. Asked them to dig back further, give me everything they got," Rus said.

"Bribes?" Harry asked.

Rus shrugged. "My guess, yes. We've heard no word he had alternate employment, unless he took cash under the table. Though, why the man would be stupid enough to deposit them, I have no idea. But if that's the case, he's been on the take or hiding income from the IRS for at least the last seven years, even after he quit the department and before Ballard was killed."

Abruptly, Harry felt his throat close.

Now he knew what it meant when that shoe dropped.

They'd been working together long enough, Rus instantly went alert.

"What are you thinking?" he asked.

"Even after he quit?" Harry asked back.

"Yeah. Actually, there were more then."

"And before Ballard was killed?"

Rus fell silent.

Then his body jerked when his mind hit the same plain Harry's was on.

"Get on the bank, Rus. Expedite that shit," Harry said.

"Saw a picture of him," Rus replied. "Dark hair. White guy. Beard."

Dark hair, white guy, always wore a beard.

Goddamn it.

"He's shit scared," Rus said quietly.

"He's shit scared," Harry agreed.

"Cheryl Ballard is even more scared. She knows."

"She knows," Harry stated.

"And if he can find her, she's next."

"Yep. She's next," Harry said. "I'll talk to Theresa. If there's anyone in line before Farrell, I'll owe her a marker to get them bumped. I want Farrell's death declared a homicide. I want it everywhere we're looking for Karl Abernathy as a person of interest in four homicides. I want the Dietrichs' son to understand we're now worried for their safety, and they need to come in so we can see to it. I want Cheryl Ballard's next of kin to know the same thing. And I want Dern, Patterson and Bakshi back in my interrogation room."

"Abernathy's also wanted for two cases of sexual assault, along with five of attempted sexual assault."

At this news, fury coursed through Harry's body, and he had no choice but to stand there and let it burn down deep.

"Abernathy committed the robbery at the Dietrichs' behest," Rus spoke the words out loud.

"He committed the robbery," Harry agreed.

"He framed Sonny and Avery."

"He framed Sonny and Avery either because Dern was involved

and wanted it that way, or for the reason he tracked Sonny and Avery to Idaho, something Dern knew nothing about. Because Karl thought Sonny saw him at the Dietrichs," Harry confirmed.

"And he killed them there," Rus repeated.

"Yup."

"And he's been blackmailing the Dietrichs since then," Rus kept running it down.

"Mm-hmm."

"He left the gun with the bodies so if they were found, the Dietrichs would be tagged, because this asshole is all about the frameup and covering his ass," Rus continued.

"Right again."

"The prints on the gun will be one of the Dietrichs', because it was their gun, and he wouldn't have wiped it in order that he could tag them if it came down to it."

Harry nodded.

"He told Cheryl, somehow Muggsy found out, Muggsy wanted in on the action, that was going to be his big payday."

"And Karl took him out, Roy covered for him, and now Karl is cleaning up after himself," Harry finished it.

"Fuck," Rus said.

"Oh yeah," Harry agreed.

Rus walked away, pulling his phone out of his pocket.

Harry crouched again and looked at the little blue pill.

"I'm going to find you, you motherfucker," he whispered.

Then he stood and prowled out of that fetid house right to his cruiser.

FORTY-ONE

The Natives Are Restless

Harry

"He's got bruising around the torso consistent with receiving repeated blows, a particularly nasty one on the back of his thigh, and he took some hits to his genitalia, and as we both know, that would incapacitate even the fittest man," Theresa said in his ear. "And this gent was far from the fittest man."

Early that evening, Harry stood in his office, staring unseeing out of his window toward Main Street, and listening to the ME give a preliminary report on Roy Farrell.

"He was dead before the contusions could fully form," she went on. "But they aren't older and faded. They were just rising. I haven't cut him open yet, but from what I'm seeing on a visual inspection, I'm already leaning toward foul play."

Fucking perfect.

"Gotcha," Harry replied.

"I'll dig in now. You'll have my full report tomorrow."

Now was late. It was after five o'clock.

He was struggling because he wanted to tell her to go home and let murder wait until tomorrow.

But there was so much riding on this.

For Lillian.

In the end, Harry was powerless to do anything but say, "We'll run with what you've already given us. Go home. We can wait on the full report."

"Harry, Rus has briefed me on your theory about this, and I know about the cookies. I'm working late tonight," she retorted.

Christ, but it worked in that moment to be reminded how inherently good most people were when you were faced with someone who seemed to have no soul.

"Owe you one, Theresa."

"My job, Harry. Talk later."

"You got it."

They hung up and Harry continued to stare out the window.

He was unusually antsy, impatient.

He was this because Karl Abernathy was clearly rattled, a man like that rattled was proving beyond messy, and Harry didn't want anyone else dead.

And he wanted Lillian to know who killed her parents so she could fully close that chapter of her life and get on with it free from the burden of carrying that mystery.

"Harry?"

He turned and saw Megan in his doorway.

He expected this.

In fact, he was surprised it took this long.

"Hey, Megan," he greeted.

She came in and stopped in front of his desk. "I suspect you know the natives are restless."

He crossed his arms on his chest and said nothing.

Because…yeah.

To be fair, if he was a civilian, he would be too.

But for fuck's sake.

"The coven is up in my face about the outing of Dern and Karl Abernathy's reign of terror," Megan shared. "I did explain we duly elected a new sheriff some years ago, and he does not run his department in the same manner. They still want heads rolling. As much as part of me understands who they are and why they became what they became, they're still a serious thorn in my side. But with all honesty, they aren't the only ones who are super freaking ticked about the stuff that's surfacing in Misted Pines."

"Dern is scheduled to return to this station tomorrow at one o'clock with his attorney to answer questions about the complaints lodged today, along with speaking again to the FBI about the murders of the Rainiers. We have accounts of three further abuses of office, and if he knew the fucked-up shit Abernathy was up to, and he didn't put a stop to it, that's going to go worse for him. He's already done time for shit like this, Megan, but make no mistake, when he comes in tomorrow, and after we get whatever we can out of him, I'm gonna charge him for three counts of criminal stalking and harassment."

She nodded.

"And we are going balls to the wall to find Abernathy," he told her.

She nodded again.

"If you need to call a town council meeting so people feel they're informed and we have things in hand, and I have to attend and report, I will, but I won't like it. It goes without saying, I'm not thrilled about what's surfacing in Misted Pines either, but unlike them, it's my job to do something about it. I intend to do that. I need time to do it. But I also have a life."

Her lips twitched before she said, "I'll buy you as much time as I can."

It was Harry who nodded then.

She shifted to leave but turned back. "And I cannot tell you how happy it makes me that you have a life outside this office, Harry."

Harry pulled in breath through his nose then tipped his head at her.

She smiled fully at him and walked out.

Harry engaged his phone and made a call.

Jess answered after one ring. "We're on it."

"Abernathy?" Harry asked.

Polly appeared in his door.

He shook his head at her.

"Yeah," Jess answered.

"You got anything?" Harry queried, watching Polly walk to his desk to grab a pen and a Post-it pad.

"Nothing so far," Jess informed him. "But we're looking. We get anything to feed to you, we'll do it."

Polly stuck the Post-it on his desk phone, and it said LINE 1 ASAP.

She then turned and walked out.

"Thanks, Jess," Harry said. "I've got another call. If we get anything, you'll get it. You might hear from me, Rus, Karen or Sean."

"Got it."

Harry lowered his voice. "I want him run to ground, Jess."

"You're heard, Harry. We're on it. Later, brother."

"Later, Jess."

Harry dropped his phone on his desk, pulled off the Post-it, picked up the receiver of his landline and hit line one.

"Harry Moran," he answered.

"Sheriff Moran, this is Special Agent Leticia Sanford, Seattle Bureau, FBI."

Harry felt his brow crease. "What can I do for you, Special Agent Sanford?"

"Got word you were looking for John Berringer, aka Paul Masterson, aka Lucas Harmon, birth name William Anthony Zowkower."

Harry sat down and focused fully on the call.

"Yeah, I am," he confirmed. "We have three arrest warrants waiting for his return home."

"Well, I got three women, two in Seattle, one in Vancouver, who have reported he married them under a false identity, perpetuating the long con, that being him muddling their heads with his dubious charms, after which he robbed them of everything he could lay his hands on. When they were cleaned out, or they got fed up, he vanished. Had no clue who this guy was, until the woman in Vancouver reported her missing, deadbeat husband who also happened to steal a bunch of stuff from her, your office's preceding and subsequent inquiries about Zowkower, and us putting two and two together and coming up with grift, larceny, identity theft and bigamy."

Jesus Christ.

So that was what Willie had been up to.

"I'm going to need to punt you to my investigator, Sanford," Harry told her. "I'm in a relationship with Zowkower's ex-wife."

"Interesting," she muttered.

"Lillian kicked him out fifteen years ago," he stated stiffly. "After he read the writing on the wall he wasn't getting back in, she hasn't spoken to him in all that time. And bigamy would be off the table if the man just let her divorce him way back when she initiated those proceedings."

"Didn't mean anything, sheriff. A small town is a small town."

"It is that."

"I'd be keen to talk to this guy," Sanford remarked.

"I would too. We find him, you'll be my first call," Harry replied. "You find him, one of those charges is assault. He put a man in the hospital. So I'd appreciate the same."

"You got it, sheriff. And we're in the know here in Seattle about what all's going down there. Good luck with that."

"Appreciated."

They rang off and Harry went back to what he'd been doing before Dr. Theresa Pfeiffer called—reading the reports on the complaints lodged that morning—when Rus showed at his door.

Harry's stomach twisted.

"It's time," Rus said.

Fuck.

Harry nodded and picked up his phone. He texted Lillian, not telling her what was about to happen, because he didn't want her to spend the next ten minutes fretting.

Then he shut down his desk, got up, went to the door, shrugged on his jacket, and he and Rus left the station.

FORTY-TWO

A Fusion?

Lillian

I heard the dogs get restless, then the door opening, and I knew it was Harry because he'd texted he'd be home soon, because the dogs didn't lose their minds barking and because Harry had a key.

"As you know, I had four units to prepare for their owners today, and I was ambushed by Kimmy. I'm afraid I got in the spirit and bought more than lights and Jawa witches," I told the oven I was sliding a casserole into. "I don't have it in me to cypher something healthy. We're having the last of the alfredo gnocchi casserole, but I made you a salad to go with."

I closed the oven door, turned, and smiled, because not only was Harry standing there, so was Rus.

So much for our quickie while the casserole heated up.

I moved in their direction, saying, "Hey, Rus."

"Heya, Lillian," Rus replied.

I went right to Harry and gave him a lip touch.

When I rolled down off my toes was when I noticed the vibe.

I put my hand to his flat abs. "Is something wrong?"

"Rus has some questions for you, Lilly," Harry said, his voice tight. "About the days before your parents died."

My stomach did an impersonation of a pretzel.

I looked to Rus.

"Is something happening?" I asked.

"We don't know, Lillian," Rus said. "Maybe. It won't take long. Just a few questions."

I nodded and gestured to the kitchen table. "Do you want to sit down?"

Rus moved that way.

Harry took my hand and guided me that way.

Rus was waiting until I took a seat, but I didn't take a seat.

I was freaking out.

I wasn't sure what I was feeling from them, but it seemed... *electric*.

However, I'd been trained by my mother and Ronetta, so I offered Rus, "Can I get you a drink?"

"This really won't take long, so no," Rus declined. "But thank you."

I nodded.

"Sit down, Lill," Harry murmured.

I sat down.

Rus did too.

Harry did as well.

I was at the end of the table, they were on either side of me.

"What do you want to know?" I asked.

"In your mother's journal, she wrote that your father heard someone talking to Gerald Dietrich about his financial situation and setting up to make a fraudulent insurance claim," Rus began.

I nodded.

"Did you hear either of your parents talk about that?" Rus inquired.

I shook my head, trying to calm my heart. It was beating like crazy.

"Nothing?" Rus pressed.

I again shook my head.

Rus switched topics. "You mentioned that Dern was harassing your mom."

This time, I nodded.

"Did you notice him doing that?"

I shook my head.

"Not at all?"

"Dad was really protective," I said in a small voice. "Mom was too. I mean, I did hear them discussing it. But I didn't see anything. I just know Mom was super freaked about it, and Dad was super pissed."

"Did you notice any other sheriff's deputies paying particular attention to your parents or this house?"

"Well, they arrested Mom and Dad, and after they took off, Dern would come around every once in a while to ask if I'd seen them. But other than that...no."

Rus looked to Harry.

"Except the guy he had sitting on our house," I added.

Rus's eyes raced to mine.

"What guy?" he asked.

"Youngish. Dark hair. Beard. I thought it was weird, because he was never in a police car."

If the electric level could ratchet up between these two guys, which I didn't think it could, it did.

Astronomically.

"Do you remember the kind of car he was in?" Rus asked.

"Yeah, I remember everything about all of that," I whispered, and it was safe to say, I was more freaked than I was freaked before, so that put me off-the-charts freaked.

"What kind of car was it, Lillian?" Rus pushed.

"A Ford. Dark blue. I don't know what the model was called. Maybe a Fusion?" I asked like Rus could answer.

"A dark-blue Ford, you're sure?"

I nodded again.

"And you knew he was one of Dern's deputies?" Rus queried.

More nodding. "I saw him at the station when they took me in."

"But when he was watching your house, he was never in a cruiser?"

I shook my head.

"And you thought he was sitting on your house, waiting to catch your parents if they came home?" Rus asked.

"Yes. I also thought he was messing with me, because he was really obvious about it, and sometimes he'd follow me."

Rus instantly looked at Harry, and I knew why.

The vibe coming off him wasn't electric anymore.

It was homicidal.

"Stay cool," Rus said low.

"I'm cool," Harry replied, even though he was *not*.

"What's going on?" I asked again.

Rus returned to me. "Lillian, I'm sorry. I was wrong. This is going to take some time. I need you to come to the station and make an official statement."

Oh God.

"Again, I'll ask, what…is…*going on*?" I demanded.

Rus turned to Harry.

Harry jerked up his chin.

Rus came back to me. "We're working on a theory. Lillian…"

He reached out a hand on the table toward me.

Automatically, I took it.

His fingers closed around and held tight.

I knew this as the warning it was and braced.

"A dark-haired man with a beard in a dark-colored Ford car was seen outside your parents' motel room in Idaho."

My stomach dropped, and my lungs deflated.

"Oh my God," I wheezed.

"We think we have our guy," Rus said. "And if you give me an official statement of all you remember, it might help us nail him when we find him."

I broke Rus's hold as I shot to my feet. "Let's go."

Slowly, Rus stood.

Harry did it a good deal faster and walked to the hall closet to get my jacket.

Rus went to the oven and turned it off.

Then the three of us walked to the station so I could give my official statement.

FORTY-THREE

Peace of Mind

Lillian

When we returned home an hour later, Harry went direct to the oven, pulled out the casserole, but switched the oven on to reheat.

Totally out of character, he completely ignored the dogs when he did this and continued to do so as he tugged off his jacket and went to the hall closet.

"Yours," he grunted once he'd hung his up.

I shrugged mine off and handed it to him.

He dealt with it, walked by me and headed to the fridge, whereupon he pulled out a beer, grabbed the opener from a drawer, popped the cap and took a healthy swallow.

I flipped off my shoes, moved to the couch and got onto it on my knees, settling back on my calves, facing him.

For my part, I was jazzed. Seriously jazzed. Not only because they seemed to be closing in on my parents' killer, but because I got to make an official statement. I got to say something that might be used to nail this guy when they caught him. And that meant something to me.

I couldn't find him. I couldn't try him. I couldn't sentence him.

But I could do that.

And I did.

So, oh yeah.

I was jazzed.

However, Harry was in a mood I'd never experienced from him, and it brought to the fore for the first time since we began just how new we were.

Harry Moran wasn't predictable.

Harry Moran was just a down-to-his-soul good man. He wasn't about guessing games or walking on eggshells or solving relationship mysteries, the solution to which eventually bit you in the ass.

He was Harry.

You got what you saw.

He was not that now.

"What's troubling you?" I asked cautiously and immediately stiffened, preparing for an emotional blow.

When I asked Willie this kind of question, the answer was usually issues with his family, which meant he got defensive, and he'd throw a tantrum, shouting about how I was trying to turn him against his kin (when I wasn't, though I should have been—transference anyone?), and I just *didn't understand*.

With Alex, I got impatience and such things as, "Well, you'd know if you'd move here, wouldn't you?" Which led to secret keeping or twenty questions. It was exhausting.

Stormy was all about the brood. He didn't talk feelings. He had a temper, but he didn't lash out (at least, not to me). He didn't make a scene. He just disappeared into himself.

I was expecting one of these three from Harry, in large part because he *couldn't* talk due to his job, which had to be crazy frustrating.

And my heart was beginning to hurt because I was seeing this might be a problem for us.

But right then, being who he was, *all* he was, Harry proved me wrong.

He answered.

Put it right out there.

Honestly.

And fully.

"I did another death notice today. Ex-wife, two kids. The wife hated her ex. The kids had distanced themselves from their dad. But he was still their dad. They were confused, upset, and facing a life of never knowing if they could have fixed what was broken between them and their father."

"Oh God, Harry," I whispered.

"And this was after I walked to a man in full decomposition because his dead body had been sitting out in his car for over a week. I worked next to this guy for years. I didn't respect him. I didn't even like him. But I never wanted to see him like that."

I closed my eyes as the heaviness of this overwhelmed me.

I opened them when he continued.

"I've also got a man who lost the use of his legs because his neighbor is a felonious asshole, and what, with probably the *slightest fucking hint* of decent police work, would have been an open and shut case, wasn't. That man will live out his entire life in that wheelchair, doing it in a house next to the neighbor who it is very likely fucking *shot him*."

Oh my God.

That was horrible.

Harry kept going.

"Further, I learned the FBI is after your ex-husband because he's been laying to waste women in two different countries in the Pacific Northwest, marrying them, living off them and cleaning them out. If I ever find that asshole, I'll have to wait to put him in one of our prisons for assaulting a man, because first, he'll be spending time in a federal one."

I was stunned. "Willie is doing all that?"

Harry nodded curtly. "Willie is doing all that."

Good Lord.

How had I not seen what a mess he was?

I felt for those women, but thank God he'd never stolen from me.

Then again, back then, I didn't have anything to steal.

Wretchedly, Harry wasn't finished.

"This morning, I had a station full of women charging ex-officers with stalking, harassment, attempted coercive sexual assault and actual sexual assault. Seven women were stopped for alleged traffic violations and a deputy wearing this exact goddamned uniform tried to barter a blowjob for forgiving a ticket. Five of those women took the ticket, which they swear was falsified, so their fines were excessive, but they told him to go fuck himself. However, two women, the younger ones, the easier ones to manipulate and scare, got on their knees for this monster. None of these women came forward to report, because they knew it would go nowhere, and they had to live for years with the fear it might happen again and the injustice it happened at all."

My heart sank, and I swallowed.

Harry kept letting it out.

"That might be the tip of the iceberg. Since that seal has been broken, we're preparing for there to be more."

"Oh, honey," I said softly.

Harry kept going, "The same man who did that to those women is on the run for more than those heinous crimes, and obviously, that isn't spray-painting my house. It tracks that he assisted a local couple in an insurance fraud and subsequent frame job, he crossed state lines to take the lives of your parents, he continued an extortion scheme for a decade and a half, he murdered a man who found out what he'd done, he used department resources to cover it up, and now the man who helped him do it is very dead. And there are three people who have gone into hiding for very good reason. If this guy keeps it up, they're all next."

I pressed my lips together and waited for him to get it all out.

"Which means I have to find him not only so they don't get dead, but so he can pay for all he's done and just simply end the liberty of a man who is an out-and-out menace. And not least of that, to get the woman I have deep feelings for, the woman I sleep beside and wake up next to, answers and justice."

I stayed silent, sensing he wasn't done.

"Now, I learn when you were *nineteen fucking years old…*"

Oh Lord.

He was losing it.

"…he sat on this house and followed you for the purposes of scaring you, warning you, if you knew what he thought your parents knew, or just dicking with you, because that's who this motherfucker is. He knew your folks were gone because he took them from you. He wasn't waiting for their return. Then, after he committed that act, he came back to *my fucking town* and *fucked with you*, my *fucking woman.*"

Totally losing it.

"Baby," I whispered.

"So that, Lillian, all of that is what's troubling me," he concluded.

I didn't know what to do.

He was more than prickly. He wasn't inviting approach.

But he was Harry.

My Harry.

So what if we were new?

He'd had an incredibly shitty day after weeks of shitty days and freaking years of working with hugely shitty people.

I got off the couch and walked to him.

Harry didn't move a muscle when I got close and curled my fingers around either side of his neck.

"I have a new doorbell with a camera," I said softly.

"Lillian—"

I squeezed his neck and talked over him. "I have a thermostat I don't have to remember to turn down. I didn't even have to program it to turn itself down."

A muscle in his cheek jumped.

"I've had dinner at The Lodge, something that is rare, because I can't afford it. Same with the Bon Amie. I've also had my first spa visit," I reminded him.

"Lill," he murmured.

I edged closer to him and got up on my toes. "Those women

came forward today, Harry, because they trust you'll take care of them."

He put his hands to my hips and whispered, "Sweetheart."

"I don't have to tell you that the police don't have to be corrupt for women to hesitate to make those kinds of reports. It's been embedded in our DNA there's a good chance we won't be believed, and if we are, the road to justice will be rocky, if justice is at the end of it at all. They need to know they'll be handled with care. Those women came forward because they knew you'd handle them with care."

That muscle twitched again.

"You were deep in it, it was all around you, so you don't know," I said. "You don't know the sigh of relief that swept through Misted Pines, through this entire county when you were elected sheriff."

He rested his forehead against mine, and he was hoarse when he said, "Baby."

"Mom and Dad wouldn't be dead if you, or a man like you, was sheriff back then, Harry," I whispered. "You doing the job like you do, it keeps people safe every day in ways you'll never know, but it happens."

He closed his eyes like he was in pain.

He opened them when I continued whispering.

"It guts me. Absolutely *guts me* how crappy your day was today. I wish I could do something to make it all go away. But I can't. The only thing I can do is remind you that you do the good work, Harry Moran. People know bad things are going to happen. People here also know they can trust you to knock yourself out to figure it out for them when it does."

His fingers tensed on my hips. "I can handle it. Promise, Lilly. It was knowing he was fucking with you that put me over the edge."

My smile was trembly, but grateful, when I replied, "I sensed that."

"And I want answers for you."

"You're getting them, honey. You know this. Trust the process."

He lifted his head from mine. "Let's not get in the zone of thermostats and expensive dinners. This right here"—he pulled me so my body was flush to his—"is you giving yours back, Lill."

"Good. A relationship doesn't work if it's not balanced."

He took one hand from my hip to cup my jaw, and his brown eyes were so intense, it felt like they were branding me.

"Fuck, eight years ago, I thought I was the unluckiest man alive. Dead wife. The future I thought I had, gone with her. Working the only job I knew would fulfill me, but doing it for a man I had no respect for. And here I am. I do a job that's hard to love, but I still love it. And I had her, I got to make her happy, for a time. And now I have you."

"Now you have me," I asserted firmly.

"Maybe the luckiest man alive," he muttered.

Wow, that felt amazing.

Still.

"No, Harry, you're just a man. A good one. A decent one. A smart one. A strong one. You're the kind of man this world needs more of. Though, I might be the luckiest woman alive, because you're also mine."

"Thank you, Lilly," he whispered.

But I wasn't done.

I started swaying my hips, using my hands on him to encourage him to do the same.

"*Before the day I met you*," I sang.

His eyes flashed, and he groaned, "Lill."

"*Life seemed so unkind*," I continued.

His forehead came back to mine, and he growled, "Fuck, Lillian."

"*You're the key to my peace of mind.*"

I got no further.

With that, he dropped his head, kissed me, and we had our belated quickie while the oven preheated.

He took me to the bedroom, and it was fast, but not desperate. It was scorching, but not reckless. It was supremely satisfying, but not greedy.

It was us.
It was Harry.
It was perfect.

FORTY-FOUR

Pleased As Punch

Lillian

"Up, baby," Harry ordered.

I slid up, sucking the length of his cock as I did so, and swirling the head with my tongue before I let him go.

I was going to move over him. I knew his sounds. I knew I'd gotten him close. And getting him close got me close.

So it was time to take my favorite ride.

"Hold there," Harry said.

This was new.

I stilled and looked up at him, lazed naked in all his glory against the pillows propped up on my headboard, his long legs cocked and wide open.

Then I looked down, because his arm moved, and I watched Harry wrap his hand around his pretty cock.

I was on my knees between his legs, but I still squirmed as I watched him begin to jack himself.

"Oh God, Harry," I breathed, eyes glued to the action.

He slid down in the bed, and so I didn't interrupt any of this goodness, I scuttled out of the way.

Then, his voice thick, he commanded, "Climb on."

He didn't mean his dick.

I might have broken a record crawling up the bed, turning and hitching a leg over his head.

I settled over his face, positioned to see his body.

Harry curved his other hand warmly on my thigh, pulled me down and immediately started eating me.

That was when I rode his face.

He did all the work, between his legs and mine.

There was a fabulous pause in the festivities when I watched him come and felt him do it as he groaned into my pussy.

And then both his hands came to my hips, and he pulsed me down as he ate me out until I climaxed magnificently on his face.

He lapped as I rocked against his tongue while I came down.

Then he pulled me off, set me in bed, kissed my shoulder, and rolled the other way to take his feet and hit the bathroom to clean up.

The dogs followed him.

I settled in by curling up until he got back.

God, that was *hot*.

I grinned to myself.

One thing I'd learned for certain, Harry *did* like control.

And I liked how Harry controlled things.

He was very imaginative.

Harry came back with the dogs bustling around him, and I uncurled so we could do what we always did post-nighttime sex.

Turn the lights off and snuggle in under the covers.

It was Sunday night.

Friday afternoon, Leland Dern had been arrested for criminal stalking and harassment. He was still in Fret County jail because our courts deferred bail hearings until weekdays.

With the gate open to Harry sharing more (though, not all) about his work (and I promised I'd never breathe a word to anyone), he'd begun to share more.

This being, Dern flatly refused further comment on the situation surrounding my parents' murders, denied knowing all Karl Abernathy had gotten up to, and vehemently denied the criminal stalking charges and using his deputies to pursue that behavior.

So that was that.

For now.

He still had to answer for his current charges, and that had MP in an uproar, though, not a bad one. Most folks were in fits of glee to see Dern answering (again) for his shenanigans.

I was one of them.

Harry had elected not to tell Willie's mom just how hot the water was that Willie was in. I'd heard nothing from him since the first call (then again, I'd blocked him, but in looking at my history, no blocked calls had come in either).

And everything else was in a holding pattern as they searched for Karl Abernathy.

They had an APB on him, but so far, no luck.

As for the rest of it, since Harry couldn't be intimately involved in that case because of me, Harry took the weekend off.

We had Jawa witches in the yard, and they surrounded a cauldron that produced smoke from a smoke machine situated inside. The porch was strung with orange lights, the bats hung on the outer wall, with more hanging from the ceiling of the porch. And the porch steps were strewn with a variety of shapes, sizes and faces of white jack-o'-lanterns with orange interiors and lights on timers.

It kicked Halloween's ass.

It was the best decorated house on the block.

So much so, that day, I noticed not only Ronetta, but my neighbors on my other side, Allen and Susan, had been to Kimmy's, and they'd ramped up the Halloween goodness in their decorations.

I was sure this was Kimmy's ploy, but you didn't make a go of a holiday store in a town the size of Misted Pines without deploying some strategy to keep sales going, so more power to her.

We'd spent that day at Jenna and Trey's, watching football and stuffing ourselves with chips and dips and other football fare.

We'd spent that evening like the one before. With dogs lazing around us (on floor and couch), Harry watching football with his feet on the ottoman and my head in his lap while I played a phone game.

It was chill.

It was fun.

Even the cleaning and laundry I did on Saturday was both, because Harry helped. He swung a mean vacuum, and he was really good at folding clothes (specifically T-shirts—so good, I redid my entire T-shirt drawer in the way Harry folded).

Oh, and we popped by his place so he could pack more stuff to bring over, which meant his dad was smiling ear to ear our entire hour-long visit. I thought this was sweet, but I didn't get it or Harry telling him, "I don't want to hear it."

I didn't ask.

I expected dads and sons had secrets, and if he wanted to share his, he would.

I needed to hit some shops to find a cozy-country-cottage-chic dresser for him, but I'd find time to do that during the week.

For now, it was all good.

I knew it wouldn't last. Mondays were Mondays for everybody, and Harry's was probably destined to be less fun than most people experienced.

But he'd had a great weekend. The edginess had leaked out, he was relaxed, quick to smile, same for laughter.

So I felt like I'd done the best work I could to help him face the next day.

"Sleepy?" he asked after he'd collected me under the covers in the dark room.

"Mm," I hummed in affirmative. "You?"

"Yeah, sweetheart."

I cuddled closer, mumbling, "Trust you to make sex hot by taking care of yourself, and me, with no penetration the day after I got back on the pill."

And yeah, we also swung by the pharmacy so I could take care of that, and Harry could ditch the condoms.

His chuckle was soft. "There was penetration this morning."

"Mm," I hummed again.

"And last night. Twice."

"Oh right," I muttered like I forgot (which I did *not*).

"I could delete what we just did from our catalogue."

I pulled my head back. "Don't you dare."

The chuckle from him wasn't soft as he cupped the back of my head and tucked my face in his throat.

"Okay, baby," he murmured, humor still in his tone.

I so freaking *loved that.*

I closed my eyes and gave him a squeeze. "Goodnight, Harry."

He returned the squeeze. "'Night, Lill."

One of the dogs sighed.

And I fell asleep.

"LILLY."

I blinked.

It was dark.

I felt my hair tucked behind my ear, then a finger slid down my jaw.

"Lillian."

I opened my eyes.

I did not see what I expected to see.

Harry waking me for some midnight hanky-panky.

He was standing beside the bed, and the room was in shadow, but from what I could see, it seemed like he was fully clothed.

I got up on a forearm. "What's happening?"

"Callout, Lill," Harry told me. "I've got to go. Be back as soon as I can."

Callout?

My groggy mind wasn't computing.

It finally hit me, my man was the sheriff, and that wasn't a nine to five, Monday through Friday job.

"Okay, honey," I mumbled, then offered, "Do you want me to get up and make you a quick coffee?"

"Got one already in a travel mug. Just go back to sleep."

I settled in to do as told.

He bent over me and kissed my temple.

"Is this dangerous?" I whispered.

"The threat is subdued," he whispered back. "Just routine."

I wasn't all fired up about *the threat is subdued* part, so I focused on the last part.

"Okay, Harry, be safe."

"Will do."

Another kiss on my temple, and he was gone.

I DIDN'T KNOW what routine meant, and I'd be finding that out as soon as Harry got home.

What I knew was, I woke up without Harry. I fed the dogs. I made some coffee. I took a shower.

And I was sitting at the kitchen table at a quarter to eight, when we were usually in line at Aromacobana.

This was when I heard the garage door go up.

The dogs got excited.

I got excited.

And we weren't disappointed.

Harry, in faded jeans, boots, a walnut-colored sweater, over it, a shit-hot forest-green jacket with a yellow-stitched badge at the left breast and yellow shields on the arms just under his shoulders, his lustrous dark-brown hair windswept, walked in the side door.

"Hey," I called.

"Hey, Lill," he replied, bending to give his pups some love.

Totally liked Lill better than Lilly.

"That took a while," I observed. "You want me to make you some breakfast?"

He went right to the coffee machine and put in a pod. "I've got to chat with you, shower and get to the station. Polly can run to the bakery and get a donut for me."

My brows shot up at the donut mention, even if he couldn't see them. He was pouring creamer in a mug he'd placed under the Nespresso spout.

He put the creamer back in the fridge before he came to me.

That was my first full look at his expression, and the first I realized he hadn't given me his normal Harry greeting, which was kissing some part of my face (usually, he went for the lips).

He did that now, choosing my forehead.

Then he yanked a chair close and sat in it, our knees brushing.

Oh boy.

I didn't take this as a good sign.

"I'm wondering if my guy told a fib with all that 'routine' business," I remarked after he sat, and his searching eyes found mine.

"Caught," he whispered.

Oh boy!

"I'm sorry, Lilly." (Okay, maybe I did like Lilly better, even if he was using it while admitting a fib.) "I wanted you to sleep. I also wanted to know all that was going on before I told you."

Great.

"So, what all was going on?" I prompted.

"Willie burned down the stables at my place last night."

I jerked in my seat.

"*What?*" I shouted.

"Unfortunately, my dad caught him after he lit the match. More unfortunately, this for Willie, he tried to get away, Dad took out one of his tires with his shotgun, and Willie lost control of his car and hit a tree. Fortunately, he only has mild whiplash and a sprained wrist. But Dad was able to call 911 and get close to him. Not many people defy the orders of a man holding a shotgun whose barn is burning behind him, and you lit the fire. He didn't try to make a break for it. The deputies showed. Arrested him. Took him to the hospital. Had him looked at. Then checked him out, and he's in the cell next to Dern."

"Oh my God," I breathed.

"I called the FBI in Seattle. They're on their way. They took off several hours ago, so they'll be here soon. I gotta get to the station."

"Willie burned down your stables," I said wanly.

"Dad's fine. Willie's fine," Harry assured. "The stables, though, are toast."

"And your dad had to shoot my ex-husband."

Yep.

Still talking dispassionately.

Harry grabbed both my hands. "He's fine, Lillian. And he didn't shoot Willie, just his tire."

"Oh my God, what a moron," I whispered, stunned, embarrassed and pissed, equal measures of all of those, but those measures were overflowing.

"This is the thing," Harry said after shaking my hands. "He *is* a moron. He's fucked right now. So fucked, he's not going to be unfucked for a very long time. Dad is thrilled. Said it proved he was right to stay there when I fought him on it. He's been crowing about that since I showed in the middle of the night."

My lips parted in shock.

Harry kept speaking.

"And we were going to demolish those stables anyway. Now, the insurance can pay us to haul what remains away, and we'll have extra to build what we wanted to put there. Although my premiums are probably going to go up after all this shit, we still made out good with that."

I blinked.

"So, Willie kind of did us a favor," he finished.

"He did you a favor," I repeated after him.

"More than one. He showed his ass, now I've got it in a cell, and we don't have to worry about his shit anymore."

There was that.

The Nespresso was finishing its blurting, so Harry said, "I gotta get a move on. You okay to skip Aromacobana today?"

I nodded.

He grinned at me, and I saw it then.

Harry was right as rain and pleased as punch.

Seeing this, I started giggling.

Harry started laughing.

"I cannot wait to tell Ronnie about this," I said, still laughing. "Can I tell her?"

"Crime will be on the official blotter. It won't be a secret."

"What a dope." And I was still laughing.

Harry kept grinning at me then he came in for an actual kiss on the lips. It didn't linger (regrettably) because he had stuff to do (understandably).

He pulled away, went to get his coffee and took it into the bathroom with him.

I grabbed my own coffee and took a sip.

Smokey showed and rested his jaw on my thigh.

I stroked his head and told him, "Daddy got a big win last night."

Smokey's mouth opened so he could pant, but it made him look like he was grinning.

"I know, it's awesome," I shared.

Smokey licked the inside of my forearm.

"Totally," I agreed.

He kept me company while I drank coffee and only left me to follow Harry to the door after he came into the room ready to roll and gave me another kiss.

"See you later, sweetheart," he said from the door.

"Later, honey," I replied.

Harry left for work.

I got up and started my day.

FORTY-FIVE

Go to The Mat

Harry

"Every woman he dated. Every friend he had, though there aren't many, or ex-friend who got sick of him. Every blood relative. Every relative by marriage. Every bartender he bought a drink from. Every homeless person he roused. Every tweaker he hassled. Every informant we've got. We've hit them all up, and no one has seen him, they're too scared of him to say they have, or they're covering for him," Rus reported on the latest in trying to find Karl Abernathy. "Wade even went out with Paddy Tremayne to hit up caves and abandoned cabins to see if he's holed up somewhere. Nothing."

They'd also searched unlet rentals and second homes that might be unoccupied.

And they got zilch.

It was Friday, nearly a whole week after Willie pulled his stupid stunt.

During that week, the only shakeup was another woman coming in to report that Abernathy had attempted to coerce fellatio, and mercifully, she was one of the ones who told him to go fuck himself.

Dern had found a way to make bail, and he was back home, waiting for the wheels of justice to grind him through.

They'd hauled in the ex-deputies that helped Dern pull his shit and were treated to attitude, bluster, denials, some fear, and a whole lot of "I was just following orders."

A conversation with their DA, and Harry knew it was unlikely he was going to be able to do much with those fucks, but he was still going to try to get one or several of them to flip so they'd testify against Dern.

Nothing from Cheryl Ballard. Nothing from the Dietrichs.

That said, Cheryl's sister was freaked, and the Dietrichs' son was attempting to hide it, but he was too. The Roy Farrell news shook them (and his death was ruled a homicide, as suspected, there were sedatives in his gut, but he also had two missing teeth and a frac-tured jaw—Harry didn't like the guy, but it was good to know at least he didn't go down without a fight).

The sister had promised to share if she heard anything from Cheryl.

Rus felt the son was going to cave soon.

But for Harry, already it wasn't soon enough.

"If he was smart he'd be in Canada or Mexico," Rus went on. "I didn't know him. So far, he doesn't seem smart to me. But if he's close and hiding, he's really damned good at it."

"He's hunting," Harry said.

Rus's expression was grim when he nodded in agreement.

"Got no more, as much as it fucks me to say," Rus remarked.

As frustration bubbled inside him, Lillian's words came to him. *Trust the process.*

"Lill told me to trust the process," Harry shared.

Rus cocked his head to the side in surprise.

"She's more chill about this than I am, and she's got more riding on it," Harry explained.

"She seems pretty chill on the whole."

Harry's lips tipped up. "My first middle-of-the-night callout, she asked if I wanted her to make me coffee, and when I said no, she went right back to sleep. Got in later than she expected, she offered to make me breakfast."

Now Rus's lips were tipped up. "Damn, brother."

"I know," Harry agreed.

"Happy as fuck for you," Rus said quietly.

It wasn't too long ago, the two of them sat in this same office, sharing Irish whisky, Harry talking about Winnie, one of the first times he ever shared deeply about his loss, Rus listening.

And now there was this.

Rus's eyes went to the credenza, and Harry knew what he was looking at.

The picture of Winnie was still there.

Harry hadn't decided if it would remain. He'd moved on, but she'd always have a place in his heart and his life.

What he did decide was that he was going to task Polly with finding a nice frame and then he was going to frame the picture George took of them on Lillian's front steps after they got the Halloween decorations done last Saturday. And that was going to go on the credenza too.

"Never thought…" Harry didn't finish that.

Harry's phone went as Rus said, "That's just when she hits you, man. When you've given up."

"Seems like," Harry replied, reaching for his phone.

"Well, at least that's what happened to you and me," Rus said, straightening from his chair.

He looked at the line then answered, "Hey, Polly."

"Rita Zowkower is here for you," she snapped.

He knew her tone meant she tried to put Rita off, and Rita was having none of it.

So be it.

This was something else he was anticipating that took longer than he expected to happen.

"Can you bring her in?"

"I don't want to, but I will," Polly said and hung up on him.

"Ma Zow," he told Rus as he put the receiver back in its cradle.

"Want me to stay?" Rus asked.

"Probably best, since this is now personal, and she's a wildcard, a wily one. Got the time?"

Rus answered that by resuming his seat.

Polly stormed in and flung an arm behind her as Rita walked in after her.

"The madame is here," Polly announced.

He should admonish her (not now, later), but he wasn't going to. It was rare to nonexistent when Polly put a foot wrong. If she felt animosity toward Rita, there was a reason.

Anyway, unless Rita was there to report a crime, which she could take her pick of deputies to report it to, Harry knew Rita had wheedled her way to where she was right then, and maybe how she did it, courtesy wasn't called for.

Polly stormed out and Harry and Rus stood.

"How can we help you, Rita?" Harry asked.

Her eyes went to Rus, then she said to Harry, "I'd prefer this be private."

"I prefer it wasn't," Harry returned.

Her lips thinned.

"Have a seat," Harry invited as he took his own.

Rus resumed his again as well.

She came forward and sat.

Harry rested his forearms on the desk. "Now, how can we help?"

She again shot a glance at Rus.

"Rita," Harry called her attention back to him, "I know you know we're busy. If there's something we can do for you, it'd help if you got us started."

"My boy wants to see his wife," she bit off.

Harry refused to rise to the bait.

"I'm not sure he has a legal one of those," Harry noted.

"You know who I'm talking about," she spat.

Harry sat back and linked his hands on his stomach.

He then said, "I understand, as a mother, you want your children to have what they want. As a flight risk, your boy is being held without bail. He's probably not thrilled with his accommodation. I'm afraid I can't dredge up much empathy for him, considering he burned down my stables and grifted tens of thousands of dollars from unsuspecting women, and left three men, whose identities he also stole, in debt they have to untangle themselves from, illegally wed to women they've never met."

Her face a mask of banked fury, Rita said nothing.

Harry continued, "Now, he's in Seattle, which isn't all that close. But it doesn't matter where he is, what he had with Lillian was over years ago. She has no relationship with him. She's not thrilled he woke up my father in the middle of the night while committing arson, but other than that, he does not factor in her life in any way. He can want whatever he wants. She is not going to visit him. She is not going to take a call from him. Except as a memory of a mistake she made she's since rectified, he doesn't exist for her."

Rita remained silent.

"I take it you're coming to me in the hopes I'll intervene for him," Harry guessed.

"You're a fair man," she snapped. "Usually," she added sarcastically. "And I do believe you understand his feelings for her."

Oh yeah, he understood Willie not being able to give up on the thought of being with Lillian, no matter how much time had passed.

Even so.

Harry leaned forward on his forearms again. "Right, and being fair, I'll warn you, not as the sheriff, as Lillian's man, this is one hundred percent *not fucking okay*."

Rus shifted.

Harry didn't break eye contact with Rita.

"Rita, I feel for you. You love your boy. He's in a load of trouble. But do not ever come to me again asking for a favor for that man. You won't get it. Not ever. And absolutely not if it has one fucking thing to do with Lillian. Am I understood?"

She sat rock solid and then she jerked her head in what Harry was going to take as an affirmative.

"You've changed," she accused.

"No, I haven't, Rita. You know me. You do because we're the same. We'll both go to the mat for someone we love. So you know where I'm coming from."

Her eyes flickered on that.

She knew where he was coming from, and the wrath he sensed in her wasn't aimed at Harry.

She was pissed at her son not only for being stupid, but also for getting caught doing it, and further because she knew if he'd stayed in the family fold and did what he was told, he likely wouldn't be where he was.

The same thing happened to her other boy who decided to start a side gig apart from the family by cooking meth.

"He should have come forward," Harry said quietly.

"I've never been able to control that boy," she replied frustratedly.

And with that, Harry knew with certainty what he suspected. The ongoing cons weren't her idea. That was all Willie. He'd gone maverick. And now he was fucked.

Harry sat back again. "No matter his age, a man should listen to the wisdom of his momma."

She opened her mouth, but Polly was there again.

"Harry, Rus…" Polly's eyes darted to Rita, but Harry was already strung tight by the voltage he saw in them.

"Rita, if you'll excuse us," Harry said urgently.

She got up and gave Harry even more to chew on about how he felt about her, knowing who she was, the gang she ran that she'd birthed herself, and still thinking there was some inherent good in her.

She did this by reading the room and not wasting any time in leaving.

Polly slammed the door on her and rushed to the desk.

She didn't make them wait.

"Michelle Dietrich is here."

Harry only took the time to share a glance with Rus.

Then they were both charging toward the door.

FORTY-SIX

Consequences

Harry

H arry had no idea where Special Agents Fatima Bakshi and Joseph Patterson were.

But he was pleased as fuck they swung into his station just over an hour after Harry phoned them about Michelle Dietrich.

The observation room was packed with Harry, Wade, Sean, Karen, several other deputies, along with Cade, Jason and Jesse Bohannan.

Rus was in the interrogation room with Mrs. Dietrich and the two FBI agents.

And Michelle Dietrich looked as if she'd just left her salon after a hairstyle and a makeup touchup.

As far as Harry knew, she did.

"Let's start at the beginning, Mrs. Dietrich," Bakshi began.

"I want protection for me and my husband," Dietrich retorted.

"We can talk about that later, now—" Bakshi tried.

"And immunity," Dietrich cut her off. "Protection and immunity."

Bakshi sat back and looked at Patterson.

Patterson shrugged.

Harry reckoned Bakshi would hand it over to Patterson at this point, her the good cop, Patterson the bull.

That didn't happen.

Bakshi returned her attention to Michelle Dietrich, and she said, "We know about the insurance fraud. We know about Karl Abernathy's subsequent extortion."

Dietrich's eyes grew large, and her face faded of all color but her cosmetics.

Bakshi didn't let up.

"We know Simon Avery overheard your husband talking about committing the felony he eventually committed. Abernathy stole your stuff, but you and your husband sold it to get out of the debt you'd accrued in Misted Pines and to live your life until the insurance payout you fraudulently received gave you breathing room to recoup from bad investments. We know Abernathy was a whole helluva lot more gung-ho than you expected him to be in covering all your bases. So we know you're fucked, Mrs. Dietrich."

Michelle Dietrich sat completely immobile, her eyes still wide. And it didn't take an investigator who did hundreds of these interviews to see they'd nailed every bit of it, and she was into it up to her neck.

"Now, allow me to educate you about what it means when you're fucked in this manner," Bakshi continued. "You don't get to make demands. If you don't make a statement of your own free will, I'll invite you to walk right out of this station and take your chances with Abernathy running amuck and snipping loose ends. Choose. Now. We got shit to do."

Dietrich remained still, her eyes filling with tears, everyone tensed, waiting for her to ask for an attorney, before she burst into sobs.

"We loved Sonny!" she cried.

Harry felt eyes on him, but he didn't take his attention from Dietrich.

"I still can't believe...I can't...I can't..." Her breath hitched three times. "I can't believe Karl did that to him and Avery. *They came to our Christmas parties!*"

Fuck.

They nailed every *bit of it.*

Bakshi, Patterson and Rus didn't move and none of their expressions shifted from mild interest.

"It got out of control!" she shouted. "I told Gerald! *I told him!* And now—" She tossed both hands out to her sides, collapsed back in her chair and said no more.

"Where's your husband?" Bakshi asked.

"He's...our son has some friends with a condo in Aspen. He's there."

"Fuckin' bitch," Jesse groused at learning the Dietrichs were hiding out in a rich person's playground.

Harry tore his eyes off the woman and looked at Wade.

Wade instantly left the room.

"We've been arguing about it, *for weeks*. He was dead set against me coming. I had to leave in the middle of the night," she continued. "He's been calling incessantly, demanding I come back. Well, no. I will not." She sniffed. "I'm tired of running and I'm so damned tired of *hiding*. I haven't been home in *a year!*"

"Did you know about the murders of Simon and Avery?" Bakshi asked.

"He...he"—more breath hitching and tears—"he told us. He said they'd talk." She leaned forward and put her hand on the table. "I swear to you, *I swear*, Ger and I had nothing to do with that. *Nothing*. We...were...*horrified*. We couldn't believe it. And we were so very sorry for their daughter. So, so very sorry for that young woman."

Not sorry enough to ease her pain at not knowing where the fuck they were for sixteen years.

Cade shifted close to Harry.

Harry didn't move but it felt he might break his jaw at how hard he was clenching his teeth, so he forced himself to relax.

"Then he told us, Karl that is, he told us we were implicated," she carried on. "He had to leave the gun with their…um, *remains*. And it was one of the ones he stole from us."

"One of the ones you instructed him to steal from you," Bakshi corrected.

Dietrich looked away.

"And that's when the money demands started?" Bakshi asked.

"Yes," Dietrich answered and looked back at Bakshi. "And they were *never ending*. Sometimes, he'd disappear, a month, two, three, even four, we'd think it was over, then *he'd be back*. You cannot *even* imagine. It was a nightmare."

"Now see," Patterson entered the conversation, "*my* definition of a nightmare is being nineteen, having my parents accused of a crime they didn't commit, they disappear, I don't know where they are for sixteen years, then I hear they've both been shot multiple times, including in the head and buried on the side of a mountain so all I got back of them is bones. *Not* I got my shit fucked by making bad investments and I didn't tighten my belt. Instead, I decided to do something illegal, and as illegal shit has a tendency to do, it spiraled out of control, and I gotta pay for it in a variety of ways over the years. That sounds to me more like consequences."

Dietrich's mouth tightened.

"Let's talk about Dern," Bakshi suggested.

Dietrich turned to the other agent, her face going slack. "Leland?"

"Shit," Jason muttered.

Yeah.

She sounded confused his name was brought up.

"Yes. Leland Dern," Bakshi confirmed. "Did he play a part in all of this?"

"I…" She shook her head. "No. I honestly don't know how Ger found Karl. He never said. He just said he had an idea, because you're right, we were having money troubles, and he was going to work with this man to sort it all out. Then it all got crazy."

"So Leland Dern played no part in it?" Bakshi pushed.

Dietrich's face got hard. "I honestly don't know what so many people's problems are with that poor man. He was a good sheriff."

"Depends on how you define 'good,' considering, after he did time for corrupting his office, he's up for further charges right now for criminally stalking and harassing women in this county," Patterson drawled.

Dietrich rolled her eyes.

The woman actually rolled her eyes.

She then said, "People always like to tear other people down. Especially if they have power. Or money. It's ridiculous. It's pure jealousy. Kicking a man when he's already out? Shameful."

"Karl Abernathy is not only wanted for the murders of Simon and Avery, a man named Clifford Ballard, and Roy Farrell, but also six counts of attempted sexual assault, two of actual sexual assault, all of which he committed while wearing a uniform. Was he a good deputy in your eyes?" Bakshi asked. "I mean, all of that as well as him assisting you and your husband with stealing from an insurance company, that is."

Dietrich just stared at her.

Rus leaned forward, and while doing it, he pushed a pad with a pen on top in her direction.

"If you would," he started politely, "write down in your own words all that happened, starting from the beginning."

Dietrich looked Rus over, her expression turned coy, and she requested, "It'd really help if I had a skinny mocha latte from Aromacobana."

Both agents appeared ready to intervene, but Rus just said, "You get on writing, Mrs. Dietrich, we'll get on that coffee. You want a brownie too?"

"I shouldn't," she said like she was fishing for a compliment about her figure.

"This bitch is a trip," Jace growled.

"We'll get you a brownie as well," Rus murmured then he got up and left her in the room with the agents.

She squinted between them.

Bakshi reached out and tapped the pad. "How about you get started."

She let out a huge sigh and picked up the pen.

Rus stuck his head in. "Get Polly ready to type."

Harry lifted his chin.

Rus disappeared.

"You good?" Cade asked him.

"We're getting there, we only need Abernathy," Harry replied.

Cade clapped him on the shoulder.

Harry turned back to the window to see Dietrich bent over the pad, writing.

He then left observation to find Polly himself and get her ready to type out the statement so that woman could sign it.

FORTY-FIVE MINUTES LATER, they were all back in their places. Harry and his crew in observation, Rus, Patterson and Bakshi with Mrs. Dietrich.

She was signing the statement she just read that Polly had typed out from her handwritten confession.

The empty Aromacobana cup was set aside, the brownie just nibbled on, and she ended her signature with a flourish and put the pen down.

"Oddly, that's very relieving," she declared.

The cops in the room stood.

"Michelle Dietrich, you're under arrest for insurance fraud, accessory after the fact of a double homicide and obstruction of justice," Bakshi announced to Dietrich's face under her expertly applied foundation and blush going white as a sheet. "Please stand so I can handcuff you and take you for processing."

"But...I just helped with your investigation," she protested.

"No, you just confessed to three crimes," Bakshi refuted. "Agents from our fraud division will be discussing with you the part you played in that. Warning, insurance companies tend to like us to go hard with people who steal their money."

"I...this...*that wasn't my intention!*" she yelped. "I was helping."

"She helped," Jess said. "Helped put her own Pilates ass right in the slammer."

"Please stand," Bakshi requested.

"We're the victims here!" she exclaimed, stabbing her chest with a perfectly manicured finger. "He's been demanding money from us for *years*. *Tens of thousands of dollars!*"

"You should be aware that the police in Aspen are moving on apprehending your husband. He'll be extradited from Colorado to Misted Pines," Bakshi went on.

"What?" Dietrich whispered.

"And your son is being picked up for accessory after the fact and obstruction as well," Bakshi finished. "Now please stand."

"My boy had nothing to do with this!" she cried.

"Did he provide you with a safe house after you found you were wanted by the police as a person of interest in a variety of felonies?" Bakshi asked.

"Of course you help your parents when they're in a jam," she sniped.

"You can talk to your attorney and a judge about your concerns. Now please stand," Bakshi requested once more.

"*This is outrageous!*" she shrieked.

That was when Patterson had enough.

She jumped nearly out of her seat when the side of his fist landed on the table in front of her.

"This is justice, Mrs. Dietrich," he clipped. "Now, please stand, or we'll be forced to restrain you in a way you will probably not care for."

For a second, Harry thought she'd give them a show.

She didn't.

Shooting venom from her eyes, she stood.

Bakshi moved in with the cuffs.

Patterson put his fists to his hips and Rus crossed his arms on his chest as they watched.

"Michelle Dietrich, you have the right to remain silent..." Bakshi started and finished the Miranda.

Rus opened the door for her to lead Dietrich out.

"She should probably watch more true crime shows. She'd know to ask for an attorney if she did," Jason drawled.

Fuck, Harry was about to laugh.

Cade got close again. "Two down, one to go."

Harry let out a long breath.

Two down.

One to go.

FORTY-SEVEN

A Kind of War

Lillian

Harry and I were stretched out on the couch, Harry on his back, me down his side tucked between him and the couch.

He was sharing about all the big stuff that had gone down that day.

"Two down, one to go," he finished, after telling me what happened with Michelle Dietrich.

I smiled at him. "I knew you'd do it."

His handsome face got soft. "There's still one to go. And he's the big one."

I leaned in and touched my lips to his, before pulling back and saying, "I have faith in you."

His beautiful mouth quirked. "It isn't actually me investigating."

"I have faith in the team you lead," I amended.

He chuckled.

Enough of this.

Michelle Dietrich might be in a cell for a couple of days, she might be facing years in one.

Oddly, knowing she was lying on what was probably a very uncomfortable cot in a jail thinking about this did wonders for me.

There were all kinds of penance.

I met her when Dad worked for her, even if I didn't really know her. I'd also seen her around town, even though, after it all started, she took pains to avoid me.

Before Mom and Dad disappeared, she thought she was queen.

After they did, she still thought she was queen, she was just quieter about it.

She could no longer convince herself she was queen.

She'd had sixteen years of constant reminders of what she'd been involved in and the tragic consequences of that, and she'd have a lifetime of all of this following her wherever she went so she'd never be queen again.

I knew her son, I went to school with him. He thought he was a little prince. And definitely her husband thought he was king.

They'd never really held those thrones, they'd just convinced themselves they did.

They couldn't do that anymore.

Was that justice?

I didn't know.

In that moment, though, it worked for me.

That moment might fade.

But I was going to ride it while I had it and move the eff on.

"So, I'm going to BBs because they have full-size Snickers and Twix on sale. We're giving those out for Halloween," I announced.

BBs was what everyone called the Box and Save, the big box store, because BBs was easier to say.

"We are?" Harry asked.

"We are," I confirmed, enjoying watching his eyes dancing, especially after the day he'd had. "We're also giving out hot cocoa and hot cider. Two kinds of cider, one for kids, one for adults."

"Ah," Harry replied.

"You will note that there's a kind of war happening on the street."

"I did note that," Harry said.

But of course he would, he didn't miss anything.

"Molly texted today and said everyone is talking about hitting our street with their kids, or even if they don't have kids, because the decorations have gone insane."

It wasn't only me and Harry, Ronetta and George, and Susan and Allen who'd pulled out the stops. Nearly everyone on the block got in on the action.

Kimmy was probably in fits of glee.

But Harry frowned.

"What?" I asked.

"If that's the case, maybe I should station cruisers at each end to close down the street so pedestrians will be safe."

Okay.

I loved this man.

I knew that already, down deep in my heart.

But damn.

I loved this man.

"There may be a lot of kids, and they can get excited, and you never know what kids are going to do, especially when they're excited, so I think that'd be awesome if you could do it," I replied.

"I'll put it out on the bulletin, and we'll get some fliers made up so your neighbors know they'll be blocked in or out, so they need to plan accordingly," he muttered.

Yep.

I seriously *loved this man*.

"Can you rig some speakers so we can play some Halloween noises?" I requested.

"I'll figure it out."

Of course he would.

I gave him another kiss.

It was meant to be a swift one, but Harry leaned into it, rolling me so my back was to the couch, and he was on top.

And Michelle Dietrich, her husband, son, Snickers, Twix, cider and a Halloween décor war slipped my mind.

All I had room for was Harry.

And all he had room for was me.

FORTY-EIGHT

The Natives Are Restless Part II

Lillian

I t happened four days later when I was in the backyard with the dogs.

I had two tennis balls I was throwing. Lucy and Linus were chasing after them and bringing them back.

Smokey wasn't a fetch kind of dog. He was sitting next to me, watching his brother and sister going for it.

I was doing this at the same time looking at the leaves all over the ground and remembering Harry's edict that I was not to rake them. He told me he'd do it on Saturday.

I'd noted he seemed very evolved, what with his stellar clothes-folding and vacuum-pushing abilities, but there were some things Harry had strict gender role rules about.

For instance, even though I'd been raking my own leaves for years, now, he'd let me help him rake them, but if he came home to the leaves being raked, he would not be happy.

We wouldn't fight. Harry wasn't a fighter. He was a discusser.

That said, he didn't have a problem with sharing what didn't make him happy.

364

I could remember maybe two fights my parents got into. Perhaps they hid it from me the other times they did it, but I didn't think so. They just got along. If something was miffing one or the other of them, they'd disappear into their room, discuss it and come out all lovey.

I'd hated fighting with Willie because I knew that proved I hadn't picked the right one. Not that couples shouldn't fight, just that Willie and I did it a lot. He could get mean, he had zero ability to self-reflect, but he was a whiz at deflection, and it always felt icky.

I sometimes wished Stormy would fight with me, so maybe he'd let loose the control he held on the wrath he felt at what Angelica had done to him, and he could start to heal and move on.

But this, with Harry, was what I'd always been looking for.

We didn't agree on everything (case in point, the leaves—I had time, a looser schedule and partially worked from home, his job was crazy, and he needed to relax when he wasn't doing it—pointing out the obvious, I lost that discussion).

It was just…he and I had learned life could bring you to your knees, so you didn't sweat the small stuff. You talked it out and got on with it.

Though, I'd add that Harry was kind of stubborn.

But honestly, if he wanted to rake leaves, if that meant something to him, who was I to argue?

It was on this thought that Smokey shot to his feet on a ferocious bark.

And then he took off like a shot toward the back gate.

Linus was running back to me.

Lucy was grabbing a ball I'd thrown.

At Smokey's actions, they both stopped and watched him.

And then Karl Abernathy burst through the gate after putting his shoulder to it.

He was carrying a gun.

Smokey went right at him, and Linus and Lucy raced that way, barking up a storm.

Abernathy raised the gun toward Smokey, my heart squeezed so hard, I felt the pain, and every ounce of it was in the word I screeched.

"*No!*"

A shot rang out.

"*No!*" I shrieked again just as Smokey leapt and hit Abernathy right in the chest.

He staggered back.

Lucy leaped and chomped on his gun arm.

Linus attacked a leg.

"*Smokey! Lucy! Linus! Come here!*" I screamed, racing to the side door. "*Come! Now! Come now!*"

I got to the door, and to my shock, all three dogs were zipping toward me.

Abernathy seemed to be looking for his gun in the leaves.

Thank God, we had a reprieve.

And thank fuck I didn't rake those damned leaves.

"Come! Come on now! Come!" I encouraged, frantically slapping my leg.

Smokey dashed in first, then Linus, then Lucy.

I slammed the door and locked it, right before I heard the shots and the terrifying thumps hit the door.

I flattened myself against the side wall, staring in shock at the door.

More strikes I knew were bullets, but they didn't go through the door.

Dad had installed that door. I knew why now, since Harry had told me about the break-in I'd never known about in LA.

It was a security door. Like the one in the front (though that one had windows, this one did not), it was reinforced, and there was a knob lock and a deadbolt.

No one could shoulder through that door.

And apparently, it stopped bullets.

"Come on," I pushed out to the dogs as I ran to the side door and into the mudroom off the kitchen, pulling my phone out of my back pocket.

I heard more gunshots, and it seemed now there were different ones.

I got the dogs in the house, locked the side door and then raced to the bathroom, the dogs coming with me as I engaged my phone.

That was when I heard a shotgun blast, somewhat close, but also somewhat far away.

Fuck!

What was happening?

Once the dogs and I were in the bathroom, I closed and locked that door too, hit go on Harry and put the phone to my ear.

I wasn't even sure it rang before I heard a curt, "Lill."

"Karl Abernathy—"

"I know," he said, and I could tell he was running.

Oh my God.

He was probably running to me.

"Where are you?" he bit off.

"Locked in the bathroom."

"Stay there. I'm coming."

He disconnected.

Oh God.

He was coming.

And people were shooting.

And Karl Abernathy was there.

Oh God.

Harry

HARRY BURST through the front door and slammed it shut behind him, shouting, "*Lillian!*"

She and the dogs came out of the bathroom, dashing to him.

She threw her arms around him.

He gave her half a beat to hug him then he set her away, scanning her head to toe as the dogs clamored around them.

"You good?" he asked.

"I'm good. The dogs are okay. It's a miracle. He shot at Smokey, but somehow, he missed," she stated breathlessly.

That fuck shot at his dog.

Harry tamped down the fury that threatened to consume him, something, right along with paralyzing fear, he'd been doing since dispatch called his office to report shots fired and Abernathy was sighted in his own fucking backyard.

"Stay here," he said and ran to the curtains.

He was closing the ones behind the couch when the front door opened.

He whirled.

"It's us, just us," George said as he and Ronetta hurried in.

George shut the door behind him. He had a gun in his hand.

Ronetta hastened to Lillian.

George saw what Harry was doing and ran to lower the kitchen blinds.

Harry returned to Lillian.

"I nicked him," George was saying. "I think I nicked him, Harry. And Allen got him in the back with his shotgun in the alley."

"He down?" Harry asked.

"Man took the hit, got up and kept on running," George told him, finishing with the blinds and joining them.

"Which way did he run?"

"Toward Main."

Fuck!

People.

Lots of fucking people.

"You stay with her. Doors locked. You do not open to anyone but me, Rus, or one of my deputies," Harry ordered.

George nodded.

He turned to Lillian. "I'll be back."

She swallowed and nodded.

But her heart was in her eyes.

His heart, because hers belonged to him, as his did to her.

"I love you too," he said.

No matter all that was happening, her lips curled up in a sweet smile and tears filled those gorgeous green eyes.

Memorizing that expression, Harry sprinted out the front door to the cruiser he'd parked in Lillian's drive.

He got in, started her up, and the radio was going berserk.

"Suspect sighted. Cinema," dispatch said.

"In foot pursuit," Rus's voice panted.

"Fuck, fuck, fuck," Harry chanted, slammed the cruiser in reverse and hightailed out.

He turned on his lights and siren, and on a screech of tires, he tore down the street.

"Alley, behind the cinema," Sean was saying. "Headed east."

Harry turned right at the end of the street, grabbed the mic of his radio and pushed the button.

"Do not shoot," he commanded. "I want him subdued and brought in."

"Copy that," Rus said.

"Copy," Sean said.

"Copy," Wade said.

He had four more copies before he ordered, "Shut down Main. I want our civilians inside with doors locked."

He heard dispatch sending out the call to units to fulfill his order as he swung a left off Main and then another quick left down the back alley.

And there he was, a block and a half ahead.

Karl Abernathy.

Harry could see he was leaking blood at his shoulder, but that's all he took in when Abernathy cut down a side alley and Harry lost sight.

Rus and Sean were in foot pursuit half a block away. Harry raced down the back alley and into the side one just as Abernathy darted out of it.

Harry made the end, he could hear other sirens, and he saw Wade tearing across the street.

He also saw Abernathy doing the same.

Harry threw the cruiser into park, powered down and shot out of it just as Abernathy ducked into Kimmy's shop.

"Shit, shit, shit," he bit out as he sprinted across the road, all traffic had stopped, cruisers were angling, deputies were everywhere.

A gun blast came from Kimmy's shop.

Shit!

Harry raced up the sidewalk, unclipping and unholstering his weapon, just as Abernathy reeled out of Kimmy's shop.

He saw Harry, raised his gun and shot wild.

People screamed.

"*Down!*" Harry yelled, his command mingling with the same one from Rus, Sean and Wade. "*Everyone down!*"

Abernathy had turned to run from Harry, but he stopped dead as Pete, Polly's husband, and the owner of the Double D, came out of the diner, the butt of a shotgun to his shoulder, his eye squinted at the sight, the barrel aimed at Abernathy.

Harry raised his own gun and slowed to a creeping gait, ordering, "Karl, drop your weapon and put your hands behind your head."

Harry could see the wet stains on the back of his dark sweater, many of them, clustered around his left shoulder.

Buckshot.

Allen did get him.

"Lower your weapons!" Rus shouted, causing Harry to stop moving and cast a quick look around.

Pete wasn't the only civilian training a gun on Abernathy.

"*Lower your weapons!*" Rus bellowed.

"He preyed on our women!" Tim, the manager of the tack shop, who was pointing a revolver at Abernathy, shouted.

Abernathy swung around wildly.

Shit!

"Lower your weapons!" Rus repeated.

"He killed Sonny and Av!" Chuck, the owner of the greengrocer, who was pointing a rifle at Abernathy, yelled.

"*You are putting my deputies and my civilians in jeopardy!*" Harry boomed. "*Lower! Your! Weapons! NOW!*"

Weapons lowered.

"Back away from the suspect!" Harry ordered.

Everyone backed away but Harry's crew.

Abernathy turned on Harry.

Harry's adrenaline spiked.

Quick assessment: gunshot wound to the shoulder, probably from George. Mangled gun arm, one of his dogs. Torn leg of his pants, blood visible, another one of his dogs. Further weeping at his side, maybe Kimmy.

Hollowed cheeks, sharpened cheekbones, that slight gut Harry saw in the video from his house was gone. Too busy hunting or not enough money meant he'd done without food, and from the sunken look of his eyes and the dark circles under them, also sleep.

"You're injured and you're surrounded," Harry told him. "Lay down your weapon. Put your hands behind your head. And get on your knees."

Abernathy just stood there, staring hate at Harry, his gun aimed at Harry's chest.

Harry had put on a vest, but he didn't like this one fucking bit.

He'd already shot at Harry, but Harry knew it, he saw it.

The man was already dead, he understood that. He just had to make it happen.

"Lay down your weapon, Karl," Harry commanded. "Do not—"

Harry didn't finish that.

With a primal yell, Abernathy ran toward Harry, raising his gun's aim to Harry's head.

"Don't shoot!" Harry shouted, tilting his eye to the sight of his weapon and lowering his aim to the man's thigh.

His shout was drowned by a blast.

Abernathy's chest exploded in a cloud of crimson, and he collapsed to his back, his gun clattering off to the side.

Harry turned and looked up to see Karen on the roof two buildings down. She had a tactical rifle.

She always got the blue ribbon in their marksmanship competitions.

Christ.

Harry holstered his weapon and raced to Abernathy.

Wade was kicking away Abernathy's gun.

Rus had already gotten to him, and he was on his knees putting pressure on the wound while yelling, "Get an ambulance here!"

Harry dropped to his knees on Abernathy's other side, and he put his hands over Rus's.

He looked to Abernathy's face.

He was staring, glassy-eyed, at the sky. A weak buck of his body, and blood bubbled out of his mouth. He expelled a breath, and it sprayed his skin and once-obsessively trimmed, now scraggly beard with crimson dots.

"Do not fucking die on me," Harry demanded.

How did you get Sonny and Avery out of their motel?

How did you subdue Sonny enough to put bullets in Avery, and him?

Where is his wallet, her purse?

Did Leland tell you to target them?

Why did you take it that far?

Why did you hurt women the way you did?

Where is Cheryl Ballard?

Why did you waste your life?

Why?

Another bubble of blood erupted from Abernathy's mouth.

"Do not fucking die on me," Harry whispered.

The tension leaked out of Abernathy's body, and the light winked out in his eyes.

"Goddamn it," Harry kept whispering.

Rus took his blood-covered hands from under Harry's and checked for a pulse in Abernathy's neck.

Harry looked to Rus.

Rus caught his gaze and shook his head.

Harry surged to his feet and shouted, "*Goddamn it!*"

"Stay back. Back. Stay back," he heard Wade order and felt his deputies milling around them, keeping the perimeter clear.

Another siren was heard and then Harry and Rus were shifting away as the paramedics moved in.

They did what they'd been trained to do, but for naught.

He was gone.

"Goddamn it," Harry whispered once more, fifteen minutes later, as he stood on the sidewalk outside Kimmy's store and watched the paramedics load the sheet-draped body of a monster in the back of their ambulance.

HE HAD a fresh shirt on and was conferring with Patterson and Bakshi in the open hall beside the bullpen when it happened.

A hush came over the bullpen.

He turned toward the front of his station and saw Lillian, with George and Ronetta following, coming in.

Her gaze came right to Harry.

Raul opened the front bench to let her in, and Lillian ran toward Harry.

He turned fully to her and started walking her way.

She hit him like a rocket, so hard, he went back on a foot.

He thought this was a demonstration of her relief it was over.

But she pulled away and patted him down frenziedly, mumbling, "You're good. You're safe. You're good."

"I'm fine, honey," he murmured.

She looked up at him.

He caught her face in his hands and put his to hers.

"It's over, Lilly."

The tears hit her eyes before she planted her face in his chest and circled him with her arms.

He wrapped both of his around her shoulders and held her close.

He looked over her head at George.

George's expression was a study of concern and relief, more the latter than the former.

Much more.

George nodded to him.

Harry nodded back.

FORTY-NINE

Think About It

Harry

I t was dark.

The paperwork was done.

The nightshift was on.

The world was still spinning.

That was when she came.

Harry had already powered down and closed up, and he was pulling on his jacket, ready to head home to Lillian, when Karen appeared in his door.

They'd already had a discussion. She was on paid leave until the shooting was investigated, and until a counselor said she was good, after taking a man's life, to get back to work with a gun on her hip.

She'd been calm when they'd talked, accepting, and she'd handed over her weapon without demur.

Harry tried, but he couldn't read if she had a problem with what she had to do.

She seemed to be...just Karen.

"You'd take a hit so she had answers, Harry," she stated. "I know you."

"Karen—"

"I'll do the downtime. I'll do the counseling. But I can already tell you, I won't lose sleep for taking him out."

Harry regarded her thoroughly.

"It isn't what he did to women," she continued. "It wasn't all the shit he did. I wasn't playing judge and executioner. The reason why you couldn't be involved is the reason why you didn't take that shot. You wanted answers for Lillian, and you'd do anything to get them for her. You wanted him alive. I wasn't about to let you get dead so she'd know all that happened to her parents. In the end, those answers don't matter. What matters is, she knows who took them away, and he's paid. And what matters even more is, you're going home to her right now."

Suddenly, he was reminded of the conversation he'd had with Megan.

"I'm running unopposed," he told her something she knew.

"I know," she confirmed she knew.

"Fresh perspectives after this term, Karen," he stated. "If one of my investigators becomes sheriff, there'll be an opening for an investigator, so I can go back to doing that."

Her eyes widened in shock.

Harry walked the two steps to her and stopped.

"To do this job, you have to make tough decisions every day, carry them through, and be able to live with them," he said. "Rus has had enough stress in his life, he won't run. Think about it."

With that, he cuffed her on the arm.

And then he walked out of his office to get home to Lillian.

FIFTY

The Rundown

Lillian

T here was a lot to go over.
So here's the rundown:

WE'LL START WITH WILLIE.

Harry was right, he was going to see a lot of prison time in a lot
of different prisons.

First, he was tried for so much stuff in Seattle, I lost track of all
the charges (though, I did that because I wasn't really keeping track
in the first place).

Even though Rita got him a high-priced attorney, he was found
guilty.

For all of it.

He was then extradited to Fret County, and the same thing
happened.

After that, he was extradited to Vancouver, and yep, you guessed
it, the same thing happened.

So he'd start in federal prison, and when he was done with his sentence there, he'd do time in a state prison, and after that, he'd head up to Canada.

By the time he finally served all of his sentences, even if he was granted early parole along the way, Willie would be in his fifties.

I thought I should feel badly for him or at least feel something.

I just didn't.

SURPRISING EVERYONE, the Monday after Karl Abernathy was gunned down on Main Street, Albert Tremblay came into the station and confessed to shooting his neighbor, Terence Dinklage.

Harry told me he suspected Tremblay got antsy, knowing there'd been a case audit, and after Sean started asking questions, then the Dietrichs were arrested, and Karl was shot dead, Harry deduced Tremblay saw the writing on the wall, and he was next.

Tremblay had no idea they didn't have enough to pursue.

Time in the pokey before he got bail, and perhaps his attorney sharing his fees, made Tremblay rethink things and he recanted.

It was too late.

They had his confession. They had his gun. They had the ongoing dispute and argument earlier that day, which was witnessed by Dinklage's wife and was reportedly heated. And they had witness after witness testifying about Tremblay's animosity to Dinklage, with two of them sharing Tremblay had stated, "I should just shoot the sumabitch and be done with it."

He was found guilty by a jury of his peers.

His wife sold the house.

And word was, the Dinklages got on with their new neighbors splendidly.

LELAND DERN DIDN'T FARE TOO WELL in the courts either.

After two of his former deputies testified he'd ordered them to harass women (and one woman's ex-husband) who were not accepting his advances, he was found guilty of three counts of criminal stalking, fined fifteen thousand dollars, and he did another three months in prison.

Lamentably, these deputies testified so they could avoid their own charges, and as they were the only two who were Dern's go-tos for this kind of thing, outside Abernathy, those were the only consequences they faced.

Though, both of them moved out of Fret County pretty damned quickly after Dern's trial was over.

When Dern got out, he sold his A-frame and moved to Florida.

With Abernathy dead, we would never know if Dern was involved in what happened to my parents. If he chose them, or if it was just Abernathy thinking that Dad had seen him at the Dietrich's.

I would admit, part of me would like to know.

But I never would.

So I let it go.

THE SITUATION with the Dietrichs became known to citizens of MP as The Infernal Dietrich Folly.

Yes, they vamoosed the second they heard Harry was doing an audit of Dern's files. They'd lived mostly in Seattle for a year, doing it keeping a low profile, and doing it living in the rental of another friend of their son, paying cash so there was no record of where they were staying.

The low profile was a thing for them, after they got their hands slapped by Abernathy proving they weren't omnipotent. They'd genuinely lived in fear of being found out since their insurance scheme took a turn for the very worst, and not just Abernathy maybe blabbing, but my parents being found, or someone like Harry taking an interest and reopening the case.

One could say, Gerald Deitrich Senior was beside himself with fury his wife screwed the pooch so deeply by talking to police without counsel to the point she inadvertently wrote out and signed her own confession, implicating both her husband and son.

At first, she attempted a united front.

But apparently, Gerald kept writing her letters (when they were both incarcerated) and then saying it to her face (after they were bailed out, though they both had to wear ankle monitors seeing as they were definitely a flight risk), telling her what a fool she was and placing their current predicament squarely on her shoulders.

As such, she stopped feeling the unity.

She also got smart and hired her own attorney.

In the end, she gave testimony against her husband in return for a reduced sentence. She was fined a thousand dollars and would serve one year and be on probation for another one.

Gerald pushed it, claiming his innocence to the bitter end, which was probably why he was also fined a thousand dollars and given the maximum of five years.

Though, both his and his wife's behavior during his trial probably didn't help, since it seemed, even while she was testifying, Gerald thought he could snap things at her, and she thought she could snap back. Twice, they got down and dirty into it, to the point the judge told them he'd arrest them for contempt if they didn't stop it.

So, yeah, the deposed king and queen didn't know how to behave like mere mortals.

But they were going to learn.

AND THIS DIDN'T TAKE into account the fact they'd both stand trial for fraud, which Harry shared that theirs was considered a Class C felony and could include restitution, a ten thousand dollar fine and up to fifteen years in prison.

So, yeah.

They were oh-so-totally going to learn.

GERALD JUNIOR PLED OUT. Accessory after the fact was dropped, he pled guilty to obstruction, got a year's probation and a two thousand dollar fine.

He also lost his lobbyist job.

Evidently, helping your parents evade police and knowing they'd committed felonies and keeping silent after knowing they'd inadvertently caused two people's murders was frowned on in that profession.

So he had to leave DC, and last I heard, since it was hard to find a job practicing law when you had a felony conviction, he was in Texas, doing what, I didn't know.

And I didn't care.

GERALD JUNIOR further sided with his mom and threw his dad right under the bus.

Then again, both his parents came from money, she just came from more.

Why they didn't ask their parents to help them way back when was another mystery that would never be solved.

They didn't.

But (understatement of the century) they should have.

I DIDN'T WANT TO, but I attended the trial, and every day, Ronetta was beside me. Some days, Jenna or Molly or Kay or Janie were with us. Harry also showed occasionally, when he had the time.

I went because I wanted the judge and jury to see me, and if that swayed them in any way, I was all for it.

I went because I wanted the Dietrichs to see me.

Sure, Gerald took pains to avoid looking at me.

But Michelle didn't, and she flinched every time she laid eyes on me.

Gerald Junior's face got soft, and he was decent looking (though, I knew he thought he was a lot more), and I suspected he figured for some reason that would move me.

When I just stared him down, he took the route his dad did.

And last, and most importantly, I went to represent my mom and dad.

I didn't know if me being there held any sway over the judge and jury.

I did know that my victim statement—one that was not directed at any of them, I just told everyone how great my parents were, how much they were loved, how much they loved me, how very, very much they loved each other—left few dry eyes in the courtroom. Even the judge seemed to get choked up.

So I did the last thing I could do for them.

And it was done.

IN NOVEMBER, two weeks before Thanksgiving, two hunters in Umatilla County in Oregon called into the police sharing they'd found a body in the woods.

It was the remains of a female, buried in a shallow grave that had since been disturbed by animals.

What couldn't be disturbed was the bullet hole in her skull.

She was identified as Cheryl Ballard.

NOW...

Karl Abernathy.

Not that there was any doubt, considering both the senior Dietrichs pointed the finger at him, along with his subsequent spree, but even so, the motel owner in Idaho was shown a picture of him, and he said he was "relatively certain" it was the same man he saw in his parking lot that night long ago.

Karl's stolen SUV was found in the alley behind my house, and a bottle of sedatives with a few little blue pills left in it was found in that SUV.

And the gun Karl had was absolutely the gun used to kill Cheryl.

However, even if Cheryl Ballard could no longer talk, nor could Clifford Ballard, or Roy Farrell, it was without a doubt he was my parents' killer, along with it seeming pretty obvious he was Ballard's and Farell's.

There were so many things we'd never know.

But I could guess.

Karl told my dad he had me.

Karl told him he and my mom had to go to the side of that mountain to get me.

That was the only reason why they would leave that motel room.

How he managed to convince them of this, and further kill them both, I had no idea, but I suspected Dad went first. He would never stand there no matter what and watch Mom die.

Then again, she wouldn't either.

Again, I'd never know.

After he took their lives, he'd taken anything that could identify them easily, like Dad's wallet and Mom's purse, and tossed them. Those items were probably disintegrating in some landfill.

This didn't upset me, thinking it was me used to lure them out.

It was just them. It was who they were. What they'd do.

If I was in danger, they'd put themselves in danger to free me.

And that was simply that.

IN THE END, Karl Abernathy was a forty-two-year-old man who never married and never had any children.

He hadn't been tall, but he'd been fit, and some might've found him good-looking.

Why he came after me was also anyone's guess. Maybe he had a thing against Harry and heard we were together. Maybe he thought, after all these years, I knew what he did.

Or maybe he knew his time was up, considering Jason and Jesse Bohannan had found the abandoned hunting cabin several counties south he was holed up in, doing this chasing down reports on stolen vehicles, and they were ten minutes behind him as he made his way back to Misted Pines. And because of that, he got it twisted in his mind that my parents were to blame for his predicament, and he wanted to go out doing something to make them pay.

He was very dead, so that was another question that would go unanswered.

This one I didn't mind not knowing.

This one, it was a matter of all's well that ends well.

JUST IN CASE you were wondering…

Kimmy *did* shoot Karl Abernathy when he came into her store.

She said it was clear he wasn't looking for the back door, but instead a hostage, and "There's no hostage taking in a holiday shop!"

She'd become kind of a local celebrity because of this, something I thought she'd like, but she detested it.

"If one more person speaks of it to me, I'm shooting *them*," she told me and Harry (loudly) one morning in Aromacobana.

Considering she'd already discharged her weapon, and she was more than a hint crazy (in a lovable way), no one mentioned it.

At least, not to her.

Even so, Harry took her out to dinner one night at the Double D to have a chat and take her pulse.

Kimmy might be a bit loopy, but she was good to the bone, and Harry learned she wasn't the kind of person who could shake off shooting a man, even if he was a bad man, and what she did, she did to protect other people.

She and Harry had a couple more dinners before she told Harry he was off the hook, and she was good.

Harry still kept an eye on her.

So did I.

As far as we could tell, she told no lies. She was good.

We still did it.

HARRY TOLD me Clifford Ballard's mother came to visit him.

Harry closed that case, certain that Ballard was murdered by Abernathy.

She sat in his office, weeping and thanking him for giving her answers.

"And that's why you do it," I whispered after he was done shar-ing, knowing this already, because he gave the same to me.

"That's why I do it, sweetheart," he replied.

I knew it was more than just that. Much more.

I was simply glad Harry got a win.

And Mrs. Ballard got answers.

MOM AND DAD'S suitcases and the letter Mom wrote me were released by the Idaho police.

I also got their wedding rings and Mom's engagement ring. They were in the grave with them.

Make no mistake, I'd wondered where they were, but I thought Abernathy had taken them.

So I was beside myself they were returned to me.

When they were, they were clean as a whistle, bright and shiny, courtesy of some woman named Lynda.

I sprang for an expensive gold chain that dangled low, close to my heart, and wore them around my neck every day.

I ALSO GOT Mom's journals back, of course, but I didn't read them.

I told Harry enough people were privy to her private thoughts, so for now, I wasn't going to become one of them.

I also told him I'd read them later, for the sole purpose of making sure they weren't too private, and if they weren't, when the time was right, I'd let our kids read them so they'd know how much their grandma loved their grandpa...and me.

JUST TO SAY, Harry and I took a trip to Coeur d'Alene so I could meet that woman named Lynda, and Harry could take her out for a steak dinner.

He'd made arrangements before, and at that dinner was not

only Sergeant Lynda Westwood and her husband, but the husband and wife who had retired from the motel business, and their daughter and son-in-law who took it over.

I'll admit, I cried just a little when the man looked at me and said, "God, you're the perfect combination of those two lovely people."

But after I got over that, it was a nice night.

They'd asked if I wanted to see the room Mom and Dad stayed in, but I declined. We didn't even go to the motel.

Though, I discovered Coeur d'Alene was an insanely gorgeous place, and weirdly, I felt some peace that Mom and Dad rested in such splendor before they came home to me.

That said, I told Harry I never wanted to go back.

I knew he thought it was gorgeous too.

But he agreed.

BY MYSELF, I went through their room and picked a few things I wanted to keep.

Once I'd done that, I let Ronnie and George, Shane and Sherise, and a few of their other friends make their selections.

Then Harry, Ronnie, George and I donated what we could, sold what we could, and got rid of the rest.

Rus and Doc came over, and they and George helped Harry paint the room.

(Painting, by the way, was also "man's work," and that was okay by me, considering, while they did it, I hung in the kitchen with Ronetta, Cin, and Doc's very pregnant wife Nadia, with Maddie, and Doc's son, Ledger, out back, playing with the dogs.)

I left all my stuff in my old room and created a cozy, cottage-y space that was a whole lot more unisex in taupes and soft mushrooms with a fun pouf at the end of the bed and fluffy dried grass instead of flowers in vases on the nightstands.

Harry's dad had been an electrician before he retired, and he installed two droplights covered in wicker shades on either side of the bed. And there were lots of fluffy pillows for lounging (and other).

We did this because Harry found an architect who was going to design the blowout of the back of the house, and he said, if we didn't mind some dust and noise, he could do it while we were still living there.

This thrilled Greg and Josh, and they moved forward with the sale of Harry's place (though Amanda and Caroline had already had the old kitchen gutted before that even started).

The detritus of the burnt down stables were removed, and a large, attractive garage/storage building was going to be put up.

I was excited for them, and for Harry.

Same place. Same people.

But a fresh start.

And he'd always have the home his mom and dad gave him.

GREG WASN'T ONLY AN ELECTRICIAN, but like Harry, he was handy, and he liked to be busy. So when he was in town, he helped me with my properties, and my owners paid him for any electrical work that needed to be done, not to mention installations and repairs.

He liked this so much (along with being close to his boys, his grandchildren, Amanda, and...well, *me*), eventually, he was up in Misted Pines more than he was down in Phoenix.

Though, part of this might have been because Caroline's daughter pitched a fit when Caroline asserted she did have a life outside of unpaid babysitter and daycare duties, and she was going to live it.

This caused ongoing dissension because Caroline was hurt, Greg was angry, and as such, Misted Pines was a more peaceful option.

They got ATVs and a speedboat, and Josh and Amanda and the kids came out all the time, even if the drive was quite a haul.

Though, I noted Josh and Amanda didn't have the same relationship Harry and I did.

I noticed this around the time they got in a huge fight over Josh not wanting the living room changed and Amanda demanding it be changed (I didn't weigh in, but I thought Josh was right, sure it was semi-kinda dated, but it was still attractive and hella comfy).

To let them have at it, Harry and I took the kids to Double D for sundaes (and Harry's adorable niece Eugenie got hot fudge and ice cream all over her face and even in her hair, but what was more adorable was watching Harry dunk a napkin in a glass of water and clean her up).

Greg called when we were about ready to head back, telling us not to because, "The fight is over, and from the sounds of it, they're busy making grandbaby number three for me."

I could hear Greg's laughter over the phone.

I could also see this information made Harry throw up in his mouth a little.

So my laughter joined Greg's.

OH, don't think I missed Greg's ploy.

My dad was a handyman.

And Greg pretty much gave up on retirement in order to horn in to be my handyman.

Honestly, the more I got to know all of them, it was no surprise Harry turned out to be all that was Harry.

No one could replace my dad (or my mom).

But straight up, there was nothing but beauty adding Greg, Caro, Josh, Amanda and the kids to my life.

Yep.

Nothing but beauty.

YES, Harry did close down our street so that everyone who showed (and *so many people* showed, it was amazing!) would be safe as they wandered the Halloween extravaganza, the kids got their candy, and the adults were offered wine, beer, cider or hot cocoa.

We one hundred percent gave out full-size candy bars.

A few weeks later, Harry went with me to Indiana to spend Thanksgiving with my grandparents.

Ronnie helped me find them, and I gave my grandparents pretty little boxes with some of Mom and Dad's ashes mingled inside.

There were tears. A lot of cooking. Wholehearted approval of Harry.

And I learned Harry was a sucker for my gram's pecan pie.

So it was good I had the recipe.

THINGS CHANGED AT OUR HOUSE, and I didn't mean just Mom and Dad's bedroom becoming Harry's and mine.

Primarily, Harry lifted the ban of no human food for the dogs.

So, okay, it wasn't like we fed them rashers of bacon every morning.

But we both knew there was a good possibility Harry would have returned home from work that day to find me dead or dying of gunshot wounds in the backyard if those pups hadn't intervened, which would be a different but no less tragic repeat of something he'd already endured.

And that left one puppy daddy both proud...

And very, *very* grateful.

RONNIE AND I TALKED, and she shared the touching information about where George was at that he shot a man.

"That was about you, darlin', but it was also about Sonny. I think he feels better now, more at peace with the whole thing, because he was there when Sonny wasn't, and he got to look after you."

A chat with Susan gave me much the same thing.

Had I mentioned how much I loved my neighbors?

Well, I loved them.

With my whole soul.

THOUGH I KNEW someone else saved me that day.

My dad.

If he hadn't put in that door, those bullets would have hit me.

So I treasured that moment, as crazy as it sounded.

And that door.

Harry had wanted to switch it out.

I refused.

Since it still would (Harry's words) "stop a tank," he left it.

And Dad left something else behind. Something he was always so good at.

His protection.

WHAT DIDN'T CHANGE WAS that work was work, and Harry's work was *a lot*.

Along with the day-to-day grind, he still had eleven more cases he and his team had to look into.

But those were other stories.

Maybe.

THOUGH LOTS of other stuff changed.

Sherise introduced her man to all of us, and although Ronnie never gave up, they got married and lived their child-free lives saying yes to every adventure that came their way.

Not long later, the love bug hit Shane too.

And Ronnie got her grandbabies.

But just to say, those also came from Harry and me.

HOWEVER, I'm getting ahead of myself.

Let's go back.

And I'll let Harry finish the tale.

OH!

One last thing.
Harry did give boba a try.
We also finished *We Are Lady Parts*.
And just like me, he loved them both.

Epilogue

JUST RIGHT

Harry

Harry closed down his computer, cleared his desk, locked it and got up to go get his coat.

He was pushing his chair under the desk when the lights caught his attention.

Egged on and helped by Lillian, Polly had lined his window with multi-colored Christmas lights.

Harry's lips quirked, and his eyes fell to his credenza.

Winnie was no longer there. She was on the chest at home with Lillian's parents.

But the picture of Harry and Lillian outside her house at Halloween was there. A picture of Harry with Eugenie on his shoulders was also there. Further, there was a picture of Harry with George, their arms around each other's shoulders, George giving a thumbs up for some dad-doing-something-for-no-reason reason. Also added, a picture of Harry and Lillian, Trey and Jenna, Mark and Kay, all sitting around a table covered in glasses of beer and nacho remnants at the Squirrel's Nest. Not to mention, a snap of

Rus and him sitting in that very office and another of Harry with Doc and Ledge out on their pier.

And last, a picture of Lillian with her face in a bunch of sunflowers that Harry had brought home for her randomly one evening.

He left the Christmas lights around his window burning and went to his coat. He put it on, turned out the overhead lights and gave himself another moment to take in how those lights around the window transformed even his office, made it more cheerful, more joyful, more peaceful.

On that thought, he walked home.

When he got there, only his dogs greeted him.

He gave them pets, words of love, and hit the kitchen to toss them some treats.

He then let them out for a bathroom break while he went to the bedroom and changed out of his uniform and into a pair of jeans and a pine-green sweater.

After he got the dogs back in, and gave them more pets, he headed out the front door, made sure it was locked, and walked across the yard, driveway, and Ronnie and George's yard.

He put his thumb to the pad on their door, heard the locks whir, and then he stepped in.

"Harry's here!" Sherise yelled over a hum of chatter and Christmas music. She grabbed his arm, tugged him in farther and exclaimed, "Finally! Mom wouldn't let us break into the sausage roll wreath until you showed."

Shane arrived with a beer and handed it to Harry, with a, "Hey, brother."

Harry took the beer, got a chest bump and back clap from Shane, a kiss on the cheek from Sherise, and then he had Lillian beaming up at him.

"Hey, honey," she greeted, rolling up on her toes to give him a kiss.

"Hey, baby," he murmured, smiling at her as she rolled back.

"Can we eat now?" George boomed. "I've been tortured by these food smells all freaking day."

He hadn't, the man still worked.

But he came home for lunch most days, and thank God he did, or he wouldn't have been home when the dogs were barking, and Lillian was shouting when Karl Abernathy showed next door.

"Yes, George, you can eat," Ronnie sighed, making her way to Harry to give him a cheek kiss too.

She did that and immediately turned and issued orders.

"Shane and Harry are on unpacking ornaments. Sherise and Lillian are on ornament placement on the tree. The old folks get to sit, eat, drink and watch you all work." She clapped her hands twice. "Let's get to it."

"Can we make a plate of food first?" Shane asked.

"Yes, then get to it," Ronnie answered.

Shane headed to the coffee table, which was covered in what was clearly Christmas themed finger foods.

Caroline and his dad moved in, and Harry got a hug from the first, a handshake and a playful slap on the face from the last before they moved to the living room.

Harry followed them.

"I get to do the angel," Sherise declared.

Shane had bent over the food, but he shot straight at that.

"You do not. You did it last year. It's my turn."

"Actually, I did it last year," Lillian put in.

"Then it's still my turn," Shane stated.

"It's Harry's turn," Ronnie decreed. "And no lip. Eat. Unpack ornaments. Or we'll be at this all night."

Harry approached the coffee table and muttered to Shane, "You can put the angel on our tree when we get over there."

"Thanks, man," Shane muttered back.

"I heard that!" Sherise cried.

"Calm, darlin'," Greg said. "You can put the star on our tree when we get to the dessert portion of this extravaganza."

Sherise shot a sunny smile at his dad. "Thanks, Greg. You're the best."

And the extravaganza was: hors d'oeuvres at George and Ronetta's, entrée at Harry and Lillian's, dessert at Caro and Greg's, tree trimming at all of them.

How he didn't have a gut living with Lilly and next to Ronnie, he had no fucking clue.

Harry sidled up to Lillian and said low, "I thought Sherise was bringing her boyfriend this weekend."

Lillian returned in an undertone, "She's decided to spring him on them at Christmas. She thinks Ronnie will be more distracted then."

Harry looked for Ronnie and found she'd ensconced herself in an armchair with her wine, catty corner to where Caroline was on the couch with her wine, and they were relaxed and chatting.

"Probably a good plan," Harry replied.

Lillian's eyes twinkled at him, more cheerful than any Christmas tree.

Then she dug into the sausage roll wreath, shoved her piece into the sauce, then shoved it into her mouth.

Harry did the same.

Ten minutes later, he was ass on the floor beside Shane, unwrapping carefully packed, fragile ornaments.

"We got the case of wine you sent, brother, thanks for that," he told Shane.

"Wanna say it's my largesse, my man," Shane returned. "But I'm gonna be up here a lot this month and I'm not drinking shitty, five-dollar wine when I am."

"You are such a wine snob," Lillian accused as she took an ornament from Shane.

"And?" Shane asked. "It *is* kinda my job," he pointed out.

Lillian rolled her eyes.

Sherise laughed.

Harry handed her an ornament when she was done laughing.

"Oh my goodness!" Caroline cried. "I can already see this is going to be a *beautiful* tree."

"Ronnie doesn't do anything but create beauty," Harry said.

For some reason, once he did, the entire room went silent.

"I'll be...just a second," Ronnie whispered, got up and rushed from the room.

People kept doing what they were doing, just soundlessly.

Harry caught Lillian's eyes.

"Did I say something wrong?" he mouthed.

She came right to him, bent and framed his face with her hands, hers an inch away.

"No, baby, what you said was just right," she whispered.

Then she kissed him, took an ornament from Shane and went back to the tree.

"Mom's not good with compliments. She likes to pretend she's incognito with how awesome she is," Shane murmured an explanation.

Well, shit.

"But with this, Sonny used to say stuff like that," Shane continued murmuring. "He loved Mom. Thought she could do no wrong."

"Shit," Harry muttered it out loud this time.

"No, Harry, like Lilly Bean said, it was just right," Shane assured.

George had given it enough time, so he traced Ronnie's steps.

Harry caught his father's eye, and Greg winked at him.

It was then, it hit Harry that this was their tradition.

Tree trimming at theirs, tree trimming at Lillian's.

And now there was an added tree trimming at his dad and Caroline's.

They'd lost.

And now they'd found.

There was fullness again.

Happiness again.

And more love all around.

He didn't fuck up.

He just pointed it out.

So Harry got back to unpacking.

After he grabbed a stuffing bite.

"OKAY, Mom and Ronnie could *do it up*, but Caroline? What *was that*?" Lillian asked after they came in the side door to clamoring dogs and a bright Christmas tree shining in their front window.

"She never came up for Christmas, spent it with her family, so no clue, except I know I have to run another two miles tomorrow, at least," Harry replied.

"Gingerbread trifle is *soooooo* on my Christmas go-to list every year from now on," she decreed, shrugging off her coat.

Harry took it and hung it in the hall closet, then he did the same with his.

"But I am so stuffed. Aren't I, sweet Lucy? So *stuffed*," she said, and Harry looked her way to see she was rubbing Lucy's head with both hands and Lucy was staring up at her like she understood every word, and each was a morsel of absolute wisdom.

Harry took that moment to sync his phone to their Bluetooth speaker.

He then queued up the song, pushed the ottoman so it was flush to the sofa, moved to the front of the tree, and hit go on his phone.

The first strains of Michael Bublé's "Have Yourself a Merry Little Christmas" came on.

Lillian's eyes shot to him.

Harry held out his hand and asked, "Dance with me?"

It came over her, as it sometimes did, the memories, the love, the loss.

And then there was just the love.

Lillian walked to him, put her hand in his, and he pulled her into his arms.

She rested her other hand on his shoulder and her cheek on his chest.

Bublé crooned.

They swayed.

The Christmas lights twinkled.

The dogs settled with groans and watched.

Eventually, Harry was forced to do some fancier moves, some spins, some twirls, all totally worth it considering Lillian's smiles and giggles, and it was then he understood why Sonny pushed back the furniture as often as he could and danced with his wife.

The song segued into Bublé's "It's Beginning to Look a Lot Like Christmas."

And he and his Lilly kept dancing by the lights of their tree in the living room of a house bought with love, left with love...

And still filled with it.

The End

The tales from Misted Pines will continue...

Afterword

In case you missed it, this book is a study of the goodness of human beings.

Yes, in a time of strife, of such deep divides and staunch divisiveness, I'm pointing out, when the rubber meets the road, the goodness outweighs the bad.

Recent to my writing this afterword, my beautiful cat, my beloved Starla, shared with me that she could no longer cope with the neurological issues we'd been dealing with. She quit eating, drinking and using her litter tray.

It was time to say goodbye.

It was Christmas Eve.

We had to wait for her vet to be back in his clinic on Boxing Day. We took that time to do a lot of cuddling, for her to share hours of purrs, and for her to be home and safe, mostly napping.

And then we went in.

Oddly enough, not long before, I'd seen a TikTok made by a vet answering the question, "Do I need to be there when *it* happens?"

He'd said yes. No matter how hard it was, your pet needs you there. They might be scared, in pain, confused, and you are their touchstone. They need you in that moment, more than any other.

I absolutely did not want to be there, but I forced myself to stroke her and coo to her as Dr. B saw to her.

Standing two feet away were my sister and my ex-husband (still best friend). Tears in their eyes, but stoic while I faced my pain.

Eventually, Dr. B said, "I'm sorry," and my wee furry baby was gone.

Mark said later, "I will never in my life forget the sound of your sob when you were told she'd slipped away."

My first thought was that I hated he had that memory.

My next thought was, I didn't know if I'd have been able to give Starla that in her last moments if Erika and Mark weren't there with me. Further to that, just how much it cost them to be right there.

And my next thought was, people are so, *so* good.

Yes, there are shitty people. Yes, even non-shitty people do shitty things. Yes, shitty things just happen, and it sucks.

But in this book, outside all Ronnie and George gave to Lillian, all they gave to Sonny and Avery, outside Greg, Caroline, Josh and Amanda hightailing it to Misted Pines to be with Harry and Lillian during the memorial, outside the town bearing down on Karl Abernathy because he'd caused such pain and heartbreak, outside Rus looking after Harry's dogs and packing his bag, Maddie sharing her wisdom with Lillian, even Rita Zowkower knowing she had to leave to let Harry do his work, outside all of that what really struck me about this book was this:

Jenna and Janie, Molly and Kay were bustling around a table filled with finger foods, and Trey and Mark were still shoving soft drinks and waters into tubs of ice.

Oh yes.

That was what struck me.

So many people, in so many small but significant ways, make this world a good place to be.

If we get out of our trenches, we'll see the subtle beauty of all that's around us, and how it fortifies us, how it is what truly makes us. If we peek above the fray, we can let those who wish to wallow in it wallow, and we can grasp on to the good parts of life, even if we have to do it while we're fighting the bad.

In these times of strife, in this world of divisiveness, this is what I cling to.

In fiction.

And in fact.

Acknowledgments

I'd like to thank the usual suspects for all they do to make me look good, and my books all they can be.

Kelly Brown
Kimberly Callahan
Marybarb Galeziewski
Tanaka Kangara
Amanda Simpson
Emily Sylvan Kim
Stacey Tardif
Grace Wenk

Newsletter

Would you like advanced notification about Upcoming Releases? Access to exclusive content? Access to exclusive giveaways? The first to see a new cover reveal? Sign up for my newsletter to keep up-to-date with the latest from Kristen Ashley!

Sign up at kristenashley.net

About the Author

Kristen Ashley is the *New York Times* bestselling author of over eighty romance novels including the *Rock Chick, Colorado Mountain, Dream Man, Chaos, Unfinished Heroes, The 'Burg, Magdalene, Fantasyland, The Three, Ghost and Reincarnation, The Rising, Dream Team, Moonlight and Motor Oil, River Rain, Wild West MC, Misted Pines* and *Honey* series along with several standalone novels. She's a hybrid author, publishing titles both independently and traditionally, her books have been translated in fourteen languages and she's sold over five million books.

Kristen's novel, *Law Man*, won the *RT Book Reviews* Reviewer's Choice Award for best Romantic Suspense, her independently published title *Hold On* was nominated for *RT Book Reviews* best Independent Contemporary Romance and her traditionally published title *Breathe* was nominated for best Contemporary Romance. Kristen's titles *Motorcycle Man, The Will*, and *Ride Steady* (which won the Reader's Choice award from *Romance Reviews*) all made the final rounds for Goodreads Choice Awards in the Romance category.

Kristen, born in Gary and raised in Brownsburg, Indiana, is a fourth-generation graduate of Purdue University. Since, she's lived in Denver, the West Country of England, and she now resides in Phoenix. She worked as a charity executive for eighteen years prior to beginning her independent publishing career. She now writes full-time.

Although romance is her genre, the prevailing themes running through all of Kristen's novels are friendship, family and a strong sisterhood. To this end, and as a way to thank her readers for their support, Kristen has created the Rock Chick Nation, a series of programs that are designed to give back to her readers and promote a strong female community.

The mission of the Rock Chick Nation is to live your best life, be true to your true self, recognize your beauty, and take your sister's back whether they're at your side as friends and family or if they're thousands of miles away and you don't know who they are.

The programs of the RC Nation include Rock Chick Rendezvous, weekends Kristen organizes full of parties and get-togethers to bring the sisterhood together, Rock Chick Recharges, evenings Kristen arranges for women who have been nominated to receive a special night, and Rock Chick Rewards, an ongoing program that raises funds for nonprofit women's organizations Kristen's readers nominate. Kristen's Rock Chick Rewards have donated hundreds of thousands of dollars to charity and this number continues to rise.

You can read more about Kristen, her titles and the Rock Chick Nation at KristenAshley.net.

facebook.com/kristenashleybooks

instagram.com/kristenashleybooks

pinterest.com/KristenAshleyBooks

goodreads.com/kristenashleybooks

bookbub.com/authors/kristen-ashley

tiktok.com/@kristenashleybooks

Also by Kristen Ashley

Rock Chick Series:
Rock Chick
Rock Chick Rescue
Rock Chick Redemption
Rock Chick Renegade
Rock Chick Revenge
Rock Chick Reckoning
Rock Chick Regret
Rock Chick Revolution
Rock Chick Reawakening
Rock Chick Reborn
Rock Chick Rematch
Rock Chick Bonus Tracks

Avenging Angels Series
Avenging Angel
Avenging Angels: Back in the Saddle

The 'Burg Series:
For You
At Peace
Golden Trail
Games of the Heart
The Promise
Hold On

The Chaos Series:
Own the Wind
Fire Inside
Ride Steady
Walk Through Fire
A Christmas to Remember
Rough Ride
Wild Like the Wind
Free
Wild Fire
Wild Wind

Also by Kristen Ashley

The Colorado Mountain Series:
The Gamble
Sweet Dreams
Lady Luck
Breathe
Jagged
Kaleidoscope
Bounty

Dream Man Series:
Mystery Man
Wild Man
Law Man
Motorcycle Man
Quiet Man

Dream Team Series:
Dream Maker
Dream Chaser
Dream Bites Cookbook
Dream Spinner
Dream Keeper

The Fantasyland Series:
Wildest Dreams
The Golden Dynasty
Fantastical
Broken Dove
Midnight Soul
Gossamer in the Darkness

Ghosts and Reincarnation Series:
Sommersgate House
Lacybourne Manor
Penmort Castle
Fairytale Come Alive
Lucky Stars

The Honey Series:
The Deep End
The Farthest Edge
The Greatest Risk

Also by Kristen Ashley

The Magdalene Series:
The Will
Soaring
The Time in Between

Mathilda, SuperWitch:
Mathilda's Book of Shadows
Mathilda The Rise of the Dark Lord

Misted Pines Series
The Girl in the Mist
The Girl in the Woods
The Woman by the Lake

Moonlight and Motor Oil Series:
The Hookup
The Slow Burn

The Rising Series:
The Beginning of Everything
The Plan Commences
The Dawn of the End
The Rising

The River Rain Series:
After the Climb
After the Climb Special Edition
Chasing Serenity
Taking the Leap
Making the Match
Fighting the Pull
Sharing the Miracle
Embracing the Change

The Three Series:
Until the Sun Falls from the Sky
With Everything I Am
Wild and Free

The Unfinished Hero Series:
Knight
Creed
Raid
Deacon
Sebring

Also by Kristen Ashley

Wild West MC Series:
Still Standing
Smoke and Steel
Smooth Sailing

Other Titles by Kristen Ashley:
Heaven and Hell
Play It Safe
Three Wishes
Complicated
Loose Ends
Fast Lane
Perfect Together
Too Good To Be True

www.ingramcontent.com/pod-product-compliance
Lightning Source LLC
Chambersburg PA
CBHW022239230425
25633CB00008B/26